SLATE WAS READY TO BE KILLED . . .

Slate felt them behind him. Two on his right, two on his left. As he turned to face them—smiling, rejoicing at their nearness—he wondered how they'd known that he would come here. And where the fifth one was.

One of the four—a tall woman with albino coloring—took a step toward him and stopped. In her hands were matching Dueling daggers. She grinned. "I am Kaleen Brady, Grade 2 Expert Duelist. Are you prepared, Master Slate?"

He nodded, surprised at the traditional courtesy. It took only a moment to focus himself completely. In that moment he felt real—*alive*—again. "Yes, since it must be so."

She lunged. . . .

LEGEND OF THE DUELIST

RUTLEDGE ETHERIDGE

ACE BOOKS, NEW YORK

This book is an Ace original edition,
and has never been previously published.

LEGEND OF THE DUELIST

An Ace Book / published by arrangement with
the author

PRINTING HISTORY
Ace edition/July 1993

All rights reserved.
Copyright © 1993 by Rutledge Etheridge.
Cover art by Royo.
This book may not be reproduced in whole or in part,
by mimeograph or any other means, without permission.
For information address: The Berkley Publishing Group,
200 Madison Avenue, New York, NY 10016.

ISBN: 0-441-47962-6

Ace Books are published by The Berkley Publishing Group,
200 Madison Avenue, New York, NY 10016.
The name "ACE" and the "A" logo
are trademarks belonging to Charter Communications, Inc.

PRINTED IN THE UNITED STATES OF AMERICA

10 9 8 7 6 5 4 3 2 1

LEGEND OF THE DUELIST

PROLOGUE

Of the thousand billion human beings living and dying among the fifteen hundred worlds of the Great Domain, fewer than 30,000 bore the title Duelist.

The name was first applied to a small band of men and women who, in the late twenty-second century, fought alongside Admiral Simon Barrow to pave the way for humankind's expansion into an unknown, waiting galaxy. Simon Barrow and his followers were successful; thus was born the Great Domain.

By the twenty-fourth century the original meaning of the term "Duelist" had been lost in antiquity. The name now represented not a quest but a profession. The powerful Duelist Union provided a loose unity for the men and women of this calling—who arose from all of the diverse peoples and the rich variety of cultures flourishing among the worlds of the Great Domain.

But the work of Admiral Simon Barrow was not entirely forgotten. Many of the legends and the traditions which grew around the first Duelist survived him and assumed a life of their own. Perhaps most important was the credo that Barrow had lived by, and which found new meaning with every generation of Duelists: Go. Reach. Do.

Modern-day Duelists were heroes, rogues, knights-errant, Peacekeepers, villains, entertainers, mercenaries, bounty hunters. In a word, they were individualists.

But above all, they were combat artists—the finest ever produced, or dreamt of, by the human race.

Of the 30,000 men and women following this way of life fewer than one hundred at any one time bore the ultimate rank: Master Duelist.

A.D. 2320

His name was Benjamin Slate. It was his third—and according to the rules, final—day at the remote mining colony known as Dianymede Site 782-A. The last two days had been wasted, searching for an enemy who had chosen to remain unseen. But that morning four Gold Team Duelists came after him, and he'd killed them all. He needed one more for a perfect score. It didn't look good; the transport was nearly ready for boarding.

There were two others waiting with him in what would some-day be a lounge and restaurant. It already bore the name Voyager's Retreat, etched into the stone archway in foot-high script. At present it was a rough-hewn alcove, a dent in 30 million tons of rock wall. Three bolted-in chairs were the only creature comforts available. They were gyro-suspended and padded to the softness of air, warm and smooth as flesh; a sensuous respite, courtesy of the inventive geniuses at ProLab. Each chair offered a pull-down helmet to dampen the jarring thrum-and-shriek of construction machinery. Slate appreciated the seat, and ignored the helmet. It wasn't a bad effort at accommodation—actually quite good, con-sidering that just three days ago the Retreat hadn't been there at all.

The primary irritant was the lack of filter-masks—available in most places by dispenser. The air here glittered with rock dust that rose up in choking clouds each time someone walked past the archway. Just down the corridor he'd passed an enterprising group, no doubt off-duty miners, doing a brisk trade in full-suit rentals. He'd considered it, but the suits were a damned nui-sance. Aside from severely limiting peripheral vision, which was dangerous for his work, they made reading nearly impossible.

Someone had left a book there, one he was familiar with. It was Volume III of Calley's Introduction to her *History of the Worlds*. This was a new edition, which featured an expanded section on the "oddest of the odd," the planet Eusebeus. Thumbing through the tome, lingering on the holo-plates that were new to him, Slate passed the time pleasantly while he kept his senses focused on the entranceway.

Somewhere beyond that stone arch was Grade 2 Expert Duelist Rudolf Kiner, the leader—and only surviving member—of this particular Gold Team. The game was still on, then, until either Slate or Kiner was dead, or until the transport left the ground. Kiner was sure to come after him. Killing Slate would guarantee him a chance for advancement to Grade 1. Kiner was ambitious. He would do everything in his power to kill Slate. Damn him, he'd better. *Whoa!* he thought. *Unwrap. Relax.* He isolated the impatience in his mind and mentally walked away from it, concentrating on the book. Senses drilled by thirty years as a professional monitored all movement and conditions around him.

Calley was a good writer. What she said about Eusebeus was more interesting than being there. He'd visited the planet years ago, decades after the last colonists had given up and moved on. The whole world was dead sand, except for one spot. Now only scientists and tourists visited the world that refused to be terraformed. Nothing—not the atmosphere, not the soil, nothing—did what it was supposed to do on Eusebeus. Someday somebody was going to figure out why, and streak to the top of the theory trade. And good luck. Getting to the top was easy, compared to the ordeal of staying there. At least scientists only butchered one another in the professional sense.

The main attraction on Eusebeus were the plants. In the equatorial zone grew three mountain-sized plants that stirred in the dead air and never stopped humming. They measured over a mile high, three at the base, and nobody yet had explained what they were, how they got to be there, or how they could survive in the arid hell of equatorial Eusebeus. Calley got it just right: "The enigma of Eusebeus, whatever time may reveal it to be, now stands as a thriving monument to the youthful ignorance of humankind."

He stopped reading at the sound of someone approaching the alcove from the corridor. This one was coming in. A quick flex of practiced muscles brought the dagger springing hilt-first up into his palm. He yawned, scratched at his neck, and was ready to throw. An old man walked through the stone archway as though the quarter-gravity were too much for him. Slate finished the yawn and slid the dagger back home. *Damn* Kiner. He looked again at the old man and stood to offer him the chair.

"Thank you, young son." The man settled himself comfortably and looked up at his benefactor. "The Blessed Heir will repay your kindness."

Slate nodded politely and began to move off. Every few minutes while waiting he'd gone out into the corridor to be seen, offering himself as a target, hoping to be attacked. So far it had been a waste of time. Kiner was apparently doing the sensible thing, hiding. There was no time to go and look for him; too bad. It bothered Slate to leave this detail unfinished. But there wouldn't be another transport for fifteen days. If he missed this one, he'd forfeit the next arena. Five more of the Gold Team were already there and waiting. Corpses, although they didn't know it yet. The hell with Kiner.

"You are troubled, young son," the old man called after him. Slate continued walking. The old man raised his voice. "Your hands," he said. "They touch lives, and souls pass through them."

Slate stopped and turned. He was intrigued by the unusual, but accurate, description of his trade. He wondered if the old man recognized him, or if the reference was one of the obscure riddles Priests of the Heir were known for. The name Benjamin Slate was known on most of the fifteen hundred worlds of the Great Domain. But few, if asked to spot the Master Duelist in a crowd, would be able to pick him out. He liked it that way.

In his profession, anonymity was sometimes the only safety. Younger Duelists worked too hard at destroying that sanctuary before they came to need it. Slate cherished the freedom to work only when he wanted to, and considered his average appearance to be a great asset. He was slightly under normal height, medium brown in complexion, slim of build, and not overly muscled. His one remarkable feature were his eyebrows, which were thick, asymmetrical and steel-gray. His paramour, Sweetie, likened them to aging caterpillars locked in mortal combat.

The seated man said, "I am Paragonus Veritas, which is a

flawed expression for Model of Truth. And therefore the name is accurate."

Slate was amused. "Accurate? Does that mean that you're a model of truth, or that you're flawed?"

"Yes," Veritas said. "That is precisely what it means." The priest's voice carried humor, and his smile filled his face. "Your question demonstrates training in the subtleties of discourse, young son. You were raised in a priestly household?"

Slate had been taught, early in life, the power and the effective use of words. Such training was traditional and highly valued in all generations of the Slate family. But from adolescence on, Benjamin Slate had chosen a different, more direct, method of confronting the world. And he'd dedicated his life to the perfection of that choice; he'd become a Duelist. He believed that a priestly calling was useful to those who needed a buffer between themselves and reality. Benjamin Slate felt no such need. "No," he answered. "I was not."

The priest seemed disappointed. The smile left his face. But an instant later he looked bemused, detached, and interested, as before. Slate recognized the facial expression as reflexive; professional, from many decades of practice. How many decades? He suddenly realized, looking at the ancient priest, that he'd never seen a human being this old. The man's skin looked like yellow parchment on which had been etched the tales of ten lives.

As if sensing the question, Veritas said, "I was born on Earth in the year 2090. I am two hundred thirty years old."

Slate believed the priest. He'd seen things more strange than a man who'd outlived a normal life span by eighty years. He accepted the old priest's statement the way he accepted the existence of the plants on Eusebeus; such things simply *are*.

Half an hour remained before the transport would be ready for boarding. He looked forward to stretching out in the cabin, relaxing, perhaps even the rare luxury of a hot bath in transit. Why not? The Duelist Union was paying for the Tour. Slate tried to picture the expression on Colonel Pritcher's face when the bills finally reached him at Barrow Academy. His former mentor would either laugh or explode in rage. The old warrior was unpredictable. That, and consummate skill, had kept him alive through hundreds, perhaps thousands, of battles.

In the meantime, the Master Duelist decided that there were

worse ways to wait than by passing the time with an ancient
Priest of the Heir.

"I've touched many lives, Priest. Not all of them had souls."
Certainly not the four he'd killed that morning. Along with
Kiner, they'd killed the five Blue Team Duelists set against them
at their last testing arena, on Basalt Site 465-F. Nothing wrong
with that; that was the game. But they'd also killed six innocents.
And when Basalt's Peacekeepers had them cornered, they took
more innocents as hostages. Seventy of them, in a Family
compound—men, women, and children. Kiner and his Team
were given the scouter and the money they'd demanded, and
they escaped without interference. But what they'd left behind
was a scene from Dante's Inferno. The holo-images were still
fresh in his mind.

The seventy hostages had been gagged to stifle their screams,
then gutted and thrown into a pit. When the holographers arrived, most of the innocents were still alive and burning from
barrels of acid dumped on them. One poor soul volunteered to
gas the moaning wretches and end their agony; his wife and
child were in that pit. The young man cried the entire time, and
when all of them were safely dead he activated a rock shredder
and walked into it. A number of miners had been close enough
to stop the man. But they'd understood, as Slate had when he
saw the holo, that to interfere would have been an act of ultimate
cruelty.

"There are three souls, young son," the old priest said. "There
is the one that each of us imagines, the one that each of us has,
and finally the one that each of us may someday share." Veritas
assumed another professional facial expression: kindly sincerity.

Slate's reply was interrupted by a grunting sound from behind
him. He spun hard to the right as a circular cleaving blade flew
past within inches of his left arm, and split Paragonus Veritas
from face to groin. In a fraction of a second the Master Duelist
had jumped to his left and crouched low, turning to face the direction from which the attack had come. He spotted his prey immediately. There was no mistaking that shovel-pointed red beard,
and the mole that stood out like a blue beacon in the center of
Kiner's forehead.

In their moment of eye contact Slate saw Kiner's terror; he
was a dead man now, and they both knew it. The big red-haired
Duelist turned and loped away through the stone archway. Slate

exhaled forcefully to lower his center of gravity and launched himself like a missile. He caught the edge of the archway with his outstretched hands and used it to brake, then launched himself again. He caught Kiner in a running dive and the two skidded ten yards through a cluster of people who jumped away so hard a few of them became airborne.

By the time they stopped, Slate had the grip he wanted, and the matter was settled. Kiner's skill and strength were now irrelevant. Slate's grip could not be broken. And he would not release Kiner to regrapple, as he would in an exhibition fight. This wasn't an exhibition. It wasn't even a fight. This was a kill.

Slate pushed his thumb a full inch into the back of the doomed man's neck, then applied pressure against a vertebra. Intrusion Techniques such as this had been developed by Duelists to cause maximum damage and shock, shattering an opponent's ability to resist the attack to come. This particular move was fatal, as often as not. At the least it induced paralysis and crippling pain. But always, it achieved its objective. That was all that mattered now.

Kiner gasped. His torso spasmed and his head snapped backward.

"You've beaten me, Slate. But I'll . . ." Kiner hissed through clenched teeth. Slate was of no mind to hear empty threats or noble last sentiments from a fallen adversary; no respect was due this man. The strained words were choked off with a nerve-pinch that sent a jolt of agony through Kiner. An instant later Slate's knife slid easily up through soft tissue, stopping just short of the brain. The razor-sharp blade sliced down, forward, and out. Kiner's opened neck spewed like a volcano. Slate jumped to his feet and left his prey kicking and gurgling his life away. If this man had a soul, Slate didn't want it staining his fingers.

After a quick look around, the Master Duelist knelt and wiped his hands, and then the knife blade, on Kiner's tunic. He would definitely have that bath aboard the transport. Slate stood and kicked the dying body away. The former prize-fight champion of eleven worlds gave a weak, final scream and relaxed, dead.

A small crowd had gathered. Slate studied the silent faces, his own expression blank. He was looking for a gesture or an expression that would reveal an accomplice. Only five Golds were supposed to be here, but Kiner had had no more regard for Duelist traditions than he'd had for those seventy innocents. Eleven people stood watching Slate, none closer than fifteen feet. Their faces registered shock, fear, disgust, morbid excitement. The usual. Slate turned his back on them and pushed the dagger firmly back into the wrist-sheath. He sat cross-legged on the floor and waited.

A Peacekeeper arrived and spent ten minutes with him. When the proper forms had been signed and witnessed, Slate gave her money for the old priest's funeral. He felt the same rage and remorse he always experienced at the death of an innocent. It was some comfort—not much, but some—that the man was old and had passed a normal number of years alive. But who knew? Maybe Paragonus Veritas had been destined to set a record of some sort. Maybe Slate had interfered with that destiny. There were no answers—or perhaps too many answers—to such questions. If there was any consolation at all, it was that members of the Heir cult looked forward to death. They called it Claiming the Inheritance.

An hour later Slate was aboard the hyperspace transport, bathed and in fresh clothes. He sat back in his small cabin with a worn copy of *Troilus and Criseyde*, a gift from Sweetie, and let his mind begin automatically the familiar gymnastics of reading Chaucer. It had been a good day. Five authorized targets, five registered kills; perfect. He thought briefly of his next stop. It would be the last for him; his second Elimination Tour as a Master of the trade would be complete. Then on to Barrow Academy, for a long-overdue reunion with Colonel and Maggie Pritcher, and for the quadrennial Tournaments.

Maybe Sweetie would change her mind and go there with him. He'd always wanted to show her the best of the Duel Schools. It would be a welcome break in routine, for both of them. And she really should meet Mom and the Colonel before the wedding.

After a few minutes he closed the book and drifted into a contented sleep.

⇥ 2 ⇤

The instant his boot touched the moondust surface, the clock began ticking; he had seventy-two hours Standard to find and kill five Duelists whose identity he did not know. They could run, hide, or attack. It all depended on their willingness to face a Master, measured against their hunger to advance in the trade.

The man behind the desk was small, rude, and arrogant. He stared at Slate for several seconds, then turned away and pointedly ignored him. A young woman, who'd been paid to watch for someone like this newcomer, rose from her chair three desks away and hurried out to the corridor leading to the elevators.

Ben Slate brushed the remaining dust from his suit and counted silently to himself, noting that nearly everyone was watching now. He did his best to hide the smile that threatened to spoil the moment. He'd always considered himself a poor actor, and that, his one weakness as a Duelist. But this was going precisely the way he'd hoped—as if a good script had been written and rehearsed in advance.

The setting was perfect. One hundred desks, ten rows of ten, were bolted to the floor of the cavernous workspace at precise intervals. Meter-high partitions gave a weak illusion of privacy. But those standing had a clear view of the Master Duelist and his quarry. This busy place was the top floor, at ground level, of the omnibuilding that stretched twelve stories down toward the core of the Luna-sized planetoid.

At the count of ten he drew out the 9-kilo Barrow and slammed the weapon hard against the side of the desk. The little man jerked upward and flew straight at the ceiling. At the last moment he jammed his hands ahead of him, narrowly avoiding a concussion. He hung there for a second, an indignant fly, before beginning a slow drift downward. His fellow workers kept a discreet distance and snickered quietly.

A woman standing three paces behind Slate stepped forward to touch his shoulder, thought better of it, and backed away. She laughed nervously at the attention she'd drawn to herself and deflected it by pointing upward. "Maybe next time he'll remember what weighted boots are for." At that moment a loudspeaker voice announced that the generator had been repaired, and half-grav would begin shortly. "Don't believe it, mister," the woman said.

An old bespectacled man said, "Yah. That generator spends more time on its back than she does."

Slate turned and smiled at them both. They were afraid of him, but they didn't dislike him; just right. He holstered the weapon and waited.

The man drifted down from the ceiling and took his seat. His eyes were needle-sharp when he looked up at Slate. Wispy black hair settled slowly around his red cap held in place by a green Clerk's pin.

Slate felt his weight build slowly, then level off. It wasn't much, but it felt good. He said, "Let's try again. How do I get a notice published in your Plan of the Day?"

Of all the roles a Duelist might assume in pursuing his objective—in this case inviting other Duelists to come and try to kill him—the part of swaggering bully was the one he liked least. It was unnatural, cutting across the grain of his self-image. He prided himself on leaving innocents alone, as much as possible; he'd never killed even one. But sometimes a little jostling was helpful. It was precisely what most people expected from a Duelist, and therefore most likely to bring him the attention he wanted. He'd chosen his mark carefully. This arrogant little clerk was the perfect foil: apparently a mid-level manager, probably in production statistics, or supply. Definitely a keypounder—the type who sent memos demanding more and better and faster everything. Slate had no liking for the type. Petty tyrants, most of them, with just enough power to make the lives of those around them miserable. Life was already bad enough for people who signed on to work these god-awful rocks.

The small man held out his hand for the card on which Slate's notice was printed. "Let me see it." He scratched beneath the cap and studied the card at length.

Slate said, "It's written in six languages. Can't you read any of them?" The crowd edged closer, sensing more fun.

The clerk looked up. His eyes softened and then grew sharp again. "I'll have you know, sir," he said indignantly, "that I am a Grade 7, fully trained and competent in—"

He stopped when Slate put his hand back on the holstered Barrow. The man met his eyes calmly and said nothing; a welcome surprise. He relented just enough to allow the little clerk to save face.

"Here." He dropped a coin over the desk. Before it reached the surface it was palmed and pocketed. The clerk looked a little more friendly.

Slate said, "Get it printed in today's issue, and I'll give you another one."

The clerk nodded and stood up. He turned to go, moving with a curious twisting motion of his torso.

"What's going on here? Come here, give me that."

A large bald man pushed forward through the swelling crowd. He was bare-chested, but it took a moment to realize it. From neck to waist he was covered with tattoos. Slate recognized the patterns. This man was one of the old Gaasmund Zealots. He'd always wondered where they went, after their cause had been won. This one had become a bully-boss for a mining company—a logical progression. He towered over Slate by seven inches, and his neck was nearly as wide as his head. He snatched the card from the little man and read aloud.

" 'I will fight. To the death or by referee, all local ordinances observed. Your choice of weapons. Reply to this source.' " The bully-boss eyed Slate up and down. He scanned the rest of the card silently and crumpled it two inches from Slate's face. "You're a Duelist. Oh, my. We're all terribly impressed." His smile became an open-mouthed grimace; a baboon baring its fangs in warning. Every second tooth had been removed and replaced with a ruby. He'd fought at least sixteen times against the Bordelons; one stone for each battle.

He grinned around at the onlookers. "Aren't we impressed?" A few lowered their heads and looked away. Most grinned back nervously, nudging one another. It was obvious that they were all afraid of him; and that they didn't like him.

Slate gave him a cold stare. Inwardly, he was delighted with his luck. "And you, sir, are a genius. From the meager evidence of that card you have deduced that I'm a Duelist. And you did it all by yourself. Amazing." He returned the mocking grin and waited for the attack. He would go easy on the bully-boss, but he'd make it look good; word would spread quickly.

It happened as he hoped it would. The man's eyes telegraphed the blow, a whistling backhand that swept by ineffectively; it was a feint. The follow-up was a straight-hammer fist aimed at Slate's chest. The Master Duelist stepped aside, let the bigger man's momentum carry him forward, and leaped onto his back. "Down!" He punctuated the command by boxing the man's ears. The larger man struggled for a second, then felt Slate's legs close around his midsection. He clawed at the viselike grip and Slate boxed his ears again, exerting quarter-power with his legs.

"Down," Slate said quietly, tightening little by little. "You'll be more comfortable." The breath gushed out of the man, and he dropped compliantly to the floor, arriving on hands and knees. Slate eased off enough to let him breathe.

"Good. You're not going to move, are you?" The bully-boss shook his head vigorously. Slate relaxed his legs. The man was powerful, and could've fought harder. But apparently he wasn't stupid.

It was time to end the scene. The printed notice would satisfy the legal requirement of identifying himself, his profession, and his stated purpose—a public and paid exhibition—for being on the colony. But the real purpose was to entice his quarry—five Gold Team Duelists—to come after him. For that, word-of-mouth was infinitely more effective. That was assured, now.

He stood on the man's back and faced the audience. "Spread the word, friends." His projected voice filled the mass workspace. "The meanest, toughest, and most endearingly modest warrior in the Great Domain is among you. Master Duelist Benjamin Slate, at your service." He spread his hands and made an exaggerated bow. When he straightened, his face had taken on a comic fearsomeness. "I'm half beaksnake, half mountaintooth, and three-quarters mathematician. Bring me your tried, your sure, your fuddled masochists yearning to breathe no more." There was a quick ripple of laughter and applause. The bully-boss glared around him. The laughter ended abruptly.

Slate jumped lightly to the floor. "And now," he said in a softer voice, "if someone will direct me to the visitor's station?"

"Follow me," the tattooed man said, rising and brushing his knees.

The corridor was crowded and noisy. A long line of workers pressed against one wall and extended around a corner to the bank of elevators. The elevators were idle; it was still a few minutes before shift-change.

"Hey, Crow." A tall, thin youth stepped out of the line and stood in their path. He was bald also. Fine blond stubble announced that he'd shaved his head. Hero worship?

"Ho, Marty." They changed direction to go around the young man.

Marty stepped in front of them. "Why won't you call me Hawk? Everyone else does."

"No one does, Marty. Get out of the way."

"Westlake does," he said, lying and wishing it was true. "Westlake says I'm . . ."

Crow ignored the youth and walked around him. Marty turned to Slate. "You're a Duelist, aren't you?" Without waiting for an answer he stuck his hand out. "I'm Marty Partusian." He glanced at Crow's retreating back. "*Some* people call me Hawk. I'm a roustabout, but I'm studying to be a rigger. I'm going to save my money and enroll in a Duel School. I'm twenty-four, and that's a little too old to start training, but I'm strong and fast and it's what I've wanted to be all my life. I know everything about Admiral Simon Barrow, and I never fight without a good reason. Is it true that you're a Master Duelist?" He said it all in one breath.

Slate smiled and shook the offered hand. "I'm Ben Slate."

"That's what they said! I've heard of you. You've got over eight hundred registered kills! You're from Earth, right?"

"I was born there."

"Well, I've never been to Earth, but I have a friend who's been to Mars, and that's in the same system, right? I think it is. Is it true you don't use weapons when you fight death matches? I like swords, but they say it's best to start with daggers and work your way up to the big stuff. Westlake says I should work more on my feet, but you're a professional, so I thought I'd ask you."

That was the second time he'd mentioned that name. "Who is Westlake?"

Crow came back. "Marty, bother someone else." He glared down at the youth, who flushed and walked away.

They were nearing the elevators when Slate said conversationally, "I can remember wanting Duelist training that much." He added, "This Westlake seems to know something about the subject. Who is he?"

"A man," Crow said. "A good man." He looked at Slate, and the Master Duelist saw hatred in his expression. "I'll tell him you're here."

The elevator opened. Slate stepped into the cab, alone. "Level H," said Crow. "Follow the signs." As he walked away he said, "And be ready."

Ready for what? Slate wondered. The respect in Marty's voice and the look in Crow's eyes said this Westlake was someone special. A Duelist? Possibly. But if he'd been here long enough to make friends among the workers, he wasn't with the Gold Team. What, then?

The cab jerked into motion and Slate automatically grabbed the crossbar to hold himself down.

Level H was hot and dry. Steam pipes and cable conduits ran along both walls of a downward-sloping corridor that led finally to the visitor's station. The lobby was thirty feet by fifty with a mix of old and new couches and chairs spread haphazardly throughout. In the background was the hum of humidifiers and the dull rasp of overworked ventilators. Bright lighting made the heat seem even worse than it was. The discomfort was inevitable, given the eco-design of these mines. Heat from the various machinery—particularly the voracious gravity generators—was directed to the center of the planetoid. It made ore extraction easier and radiated naturally outward, reaching a comfort level toward the surface.

Someone had tried decorating the room with potted plants. Most of them were brown and dead.

A few people looked up briefly as Slate entered, and then ignored him. Some were playing cards, some were reading, and some were staring straight ahead at nothing. Slate recognized the look; those were the long-haul spacers.

Sometimes he envied the peace and solitude of their profession. Two days on a colony to unload supplies and fill the holds with ore, and then weeks or months alone in the deep night of space. Every day the same, while the mind was free to roam the great caverns of thought. He chuckled silently. He was thinking to himself the way Sweetie spoke to him.

But he remembered something she'd said. *Suppose the stars were reachable three thousand, or even three hundred, years ago. Would Plato have spoken differently, away from the clustered ways of Athens and instead face-to-face with the Universe? How would Tar Manque have framed her symphonies, seeing the crystal rings of the Bralia Formation glittering with a thousand colors against infinite darkness? Wouldn't you like to know the answers to that, Ben?* Sweetie's eyes glazed over when she said things like that.

He gave her the answer. Great thinkers might be happy in the long solitude of space. Ben Slate was a Duelist, with a Duelist's needs. He'd go berserk. But Sweetie never gave up. She kept sending him the books. He never told her that he'd read most of them years before, in his youth.

In the center of the lobby a hologram projector displayed a group of children playing in a field of snow. They came and went into thin air as they crossed the border of the image field. The presentation was crisp, seamless, and full-sized. The sound was turned off, and no one was watching it.

He passed through the projection to the registration desk and tapped a bell. After a few minutes a young woman with short dark hair came through a door behind the desk. He stared until he caught himself at it. Nudity was out of style this year on most of the major worlds. But in places like this, fashion bowed to utility. Hers was the perfect solution to the stifling heat. And, he thought appreciatively, she was the perfect argument for making the style popular again.

She appeared to be in her early twenties, and radiantly healthy. She was slim, devoid of body hair—one concession to current vogue—and carried herself with a hint of self-consciousness. She knows how beautiful she is, he thought. He found himself contrasting her to the older and more voluptuous Sweetie, back on ProLab. Sweetie, known to the world as Arika An' Nor, had once told him that he would someday come to this.

"You will see me in every woman, Ben, because you recognize in me the deep dreams of the aging warrior." He'd waited for her to laugh, but she didn't. The odd thing was, he hadn't laughed either.

The young woman accepted his money card and handed him

a tied bundle of linens from beneath the desk. "You can have fresh towels every day, and sheets every third day." She kept her eyes averted and spoke matter-of-factly.

He amended his impression. She wasn't self-conscious; she was shy. He said, "You're the first friendly person I've met today." When she finished with his card he took it and added, "Thank you."

She seemed surprised at the simple courtesy. "You're welcome, Mr. Slate." Then she added in a whisper, "There's ice in the supply room. Help yourself."

He smiled at her and nodded. It felt good, the way she was smiling back. Aging warrior, indeed.

The room was typical of small outposts, fifteen feet squared, with a bed, dresser, and night stand all in one unit and bolted to the floor. This one was cleaner than most that Slate had seen in recent months. The walls were a characterless shade of white, but the paint looked fresh. There was a large picture over the bed, giving a space-eye view of the planetoid. At the bottom were the words:

"Site 652-E, Dianymede Mining Company. Two Centuries of Service to Humankind, and Every Day a Privilege."

The picture was touched up with colors that would never be found on this remote hunk of rock.

Slate unpacked his satchel and laid out an assortment of small weapons. He checked them all thoroughly before repacking them and sliding the satchel under the bed. Two items he left on the bed. One was a scanner. He checked the room carefully and found nothing out of the ordinary. He hadn't expected to, but even Senior Duelists were intimidated by a Master; they'd do what they had to do, to win. He clamped the scanner onto the ventilation intake and reset the device to sniff for gases.

The other item was a gift from Sweetie which had caught up with him only a few weeks before. He carefully removed the cloth cover and let his fingers search out the grain of the fine old leather. The volume of Shakespeare's Histories was titled in gold. He opened the book at random and let his eyes sweep across the tiny print.

> Grim visaged war hath smoothed his wrinkled front,
> And now, instead of mounting barbed steeds
> To fright the souls of fearful adversaries,

He capers nimbly in a lady's chamber
To the lascivious pleasing of a lute.

As always he felt sympathy for the villainous hunchback,
Richard III. A misunderstood man, if ever one lived. That "Sun
of York" was no worse than most of the Royal Family members
who'd ruled Old Europe for centuries. History had treated him
poorly, and even the genius of Shakespeare did little to correct
the record. Richard, at least, had never shrunk from a good fight.
His dying wish had been for a horse, so he could continue the
battle. He played the game the way it was supposed to be played.

Not much had changed, really. There was still the game, and
the basic rules never changed. Winners won, losers died. The
arenas were better now, thank the Blessed Saint Barrow. Earth
was old, unlucky, and too damned regulated for a proper test of
fighting skill. So was most of the rest of the Great Domain.

But the colonies were perfect. The Duelists owned the right, in
perpetuity, to test themselves on the mining sites of Dianymede
and Basalt. The companies hated it, having to give out
hazardous-duty pay to their employees every four years, but
they'd never renege on their agreement with the Duelist Union.
To do so would cost them everything.

Dianymede and Basalt were gigatrillion-dollar giants, the un-
disputed leaders of the most powerful industry in the Great Domain. Science had opened the way to human expansion. But the
materials that made it all work came from the mines. Other in-
dustries had long ago developed the technologies that made their
products nearly free to all. The power to drive machinery was
everywhere; hydrogen fusion was child's play. Food and water
were managed as engines of perpetual production. But building
those engines where they did not exist—terraforming—
demanded ever-increasing supplies of essential raw materials.
The ores had to be found. And taken. And transported. And
processed. And sold. A few of the mining companies grew to be
giants. Giants have huge appetites; over the centuries they swallowed up the manufacturing and transportation companies.

Dianymede and Basalt were the biggest; between them they
controlled more wealth than any hundred worlds of the Great
Domain combined. But even so, they could not operate without
the Duelists to do those special jobs that were always necessary.
And they could not stand against thirty thousand Duelists united

against them. Duelists knew how to kill giants; open the right veins, and they'd bleed like anyone else—just longer, before they died.

With the lights off he paced the room, getting the feel of it. Back to door. Four paces, bed. Right and five paces, wall. Left two, wall. Back six paces, door. Simple. The dimensions became a part of him, until he could move at full speed with half-inch precision anywhere in the room, in total darkness. With the lights still out he removed a three-ounce steel ball from his pocket. He held it at arm's length balanced on the back of his left hand, then spun in a full circle to catch it with the back of his right. The ball dropped less than an inch in the spin-time; he was fully adjusted to half-grav. After a few times doing the same thing with his feet, working alternately at knee and then chest-height, he put the ball away. Two hours of snap-drills allowed him to isolate and to test each muscle and reflex against and with each of the others. When his body told him it was satisfied—eleven days in a transport at zero-grav brought doubts to his mind—he stopped.

He stripped and stretched out on the bed. He was tired, and amazed to be tired. That was something he hadn't anticipated when he'd agreed to do this Elimination Tour. The last one had been mandatory, four years before. Every Master Duelist had to make at least one. He'd forgotten how strenuous it had been. Or maybe he *was* getting old, as Sweetie . . . no.

He'd agreed to the Tour because it paid well. Money had never before been a major concern; he had always earned big, and spent big. But now he wanted something bigger. This job would buy a memorable honeymoon and a year's loss-of-services payment to the employers of Arika An' Nor, Sweetie. Fortunately, spectranalysts didn't earn very much. He could never afford to marry an executive, or a welder.

He decided it was restlessness, not fatigue. That felt better. He wondered how the five Golds were taking the news that they had a Master to deal with. They'd been expecting a Team of five Blues, which was the common practice. But the Union always threw in a couple of Masters, to make things interesting. Masters went in alone; five-to-one odds were considered about right. To be fair, the Masters were never told who they'd be facing. The Golds could strike from anywhere, at any time. A miner, a secretary, a cook—anyone who was new on a colony could be a Gold.

He wondered how Batai Watanaba was doing. Batty was the other Master Duelist weeding out the losers before the Tournaments at Barrow. The last he'd heard, she had forty-five registered kills on nine different outposts. She'd been on the job for seven months: A double Tour. Then, if past patterns were followed, she'd take a few days of leisure in the sculpted gardens of Miyoshi Academy, and reissue her challenge to any fool who'd stand against her, one-to-one. That was Batty.

One Tour was enough for Slate. Then there would be rest, relaxation, and Sweetie. For at least a year.

He gave up on sleep and spent another hour pacing the room, going through series after series of hard-drills. It didn't help. At half-grav, it was more like *thinking* about hard-drilling. Like those gourmet meals Sweetie took so much pride in: color, texture, aroma; everything but food.

He crossed the hallway to the public shower compartment. It was empty. He twisted the master valve until cool pellets of water sprayed from all the nozzles and bounced on the tile before settling in a pool. Gradually he increased the temperature of the water until the compartment was filled with steam. The deep heat worked magic. The sweat poured out of him, and he felt renewed.

In nearly thirty years as a Duelist, Ben Slate had never known defeat. That was rare, in that nonlethal bouts accounted for 90 percent of exhibition work and most Duelists found it good business to lose one to a talented amateur now and then; it kept the odds reasonable, and the easy money flowing. Slate had planned to do this a few times, but could never quite go through with it.

The recent business on Site 782-A had increased his total of registered kills to eight hundred seventy. He'd stopped counting nonlethal matches more than ten years ago, when the number streaked past three thousand. He was fifty, and only thought about age when he was tired. He took comfort from Duelists like Wilkington Mosher—who, at seventy or more, was still getting better.

By the time the water was ankle-deep he was soothed and relaxed. He dialed the water down to a fine mist and stretched out on a low table.

The name Westlake came to him. What was another

Duelist—he sounded like one, but not a Gold—doing here? How high was he ranked? Would it be necessary to kill him? He would visit Mr. Westlake, and find out.

The thought was disturbing. Apart from the game and the Tournaments, he avoided fighting other Duelists these days, except in nonlethal exhibitions. Duelists tended to be killed nearly as fast as the Academies churned them out. Slate felt no need to add to the toll unnecessarily.

On many worlds of the Great Domain killing Duelists on sight was not only legal, it was a sport. In some places there was a bounty. Slate accepted that philosophically—and stayed away from those worlds. An Instructor at Barrow Academy had once told him, "That's life among the stars. You get the worst with the best. On some worlds we're royalty. On others we're fertilizer."

Barrow Academy. He smiled, and at last felt his mind relaxing. The water and the memories eased him into sleep.

A noise from the corridor snapped him awake. He slid from the table and moved behind the opening door, ready to spring. A pair of long, nicely tapered legs descended the three steps into the water. There followed other interesting parts he remembered very well, from the girl at the registration desk. The light clicked off.

"Mr. Slate?"

His last serious thought of the night was, *Forgive me, Sweetie.*

⇒3⇐

The man known as Westlake was seven feet nine inches tall, and his Standard weight had been steady for more than thirty years at 502 pounds. His arms, unflexed, were thicker than the waists of most men. His face was a patchwork of color—white, pink, tan—and he was as bald as Earth's moon.

He was moving backward, shifting flat-footed and lightly, arms weaving asynchronous patterns in front of his chest and head. He saw it coming—telegraphed, slow, and poorly timed—and lowered his guard just enough to allow the fist to slip through. It was a powerful blow, and the sharp crack of it echoed through the full-grav gymnasium. His head snapped back and he grunted.

"Shit!" His opponent took two steps backward and dropped his arms.

The giant roared and charged. He lifted the smaller man by the shoulders and shook him like a toy. "Damn it, Crow, *never* do that!"

He released the tattooed man and bent to pick up a towel. Crow backed away and sat with his knees tucked up under his chin.

"Look at this," Westlake said. He pulled the towel from his face and showed Crow the spot of blood.

"I—"

"You backed away, you idiot!" Westlake saw the look of concern on his friend's face and sighed. He said patiently, "It was a good clean shot, Crow. You had me. You got through! Why the hell did you back away?"

It's useless, the giant thought sadly. A clear moment of triumph, given as a gift. And the warrior—one of the bravest men

20

he'd ever known—backed away. He knew why, and it sickened him. This never would have happened during the Gaasmund Wars; Crow had never understood the concept of retreat, in any form. And the people he'd known at Barrow Academy . . . But that was another life.

"Go take a shower." When his friend hesitated he said, ashamed of the words, "I'm fine. You didn't hurt me."

"What about—"

"Do I have to say it again? Don't interfere. You're good, Crow. You're strong, you're fast, and you've proved yourself hundreds of times. But that one could kill you in his sleep. Do you understand me? Stay away from him."

"I—Yes. I understand. Tomorrow?"

"I'll be here."

Crow jumped to his feet and trotted away toward the shower compartment. Inside, the young man was toweling off his freshly shaven scalp. "What did he say?"

"Nothing. Don't do anything."

"That's what I thought he'd say."

"And it's what we're going to do. Understand, Marty?"

"Sure, Crow." He finished dressing and walked out the corridor entrance. He smiled to himself and whistled an old warrior's march. The martial music livened his step and made the thinking easy. After a few minutes he was dogtrotting happily, counting cadence, imagining Crow and Westlake straining to keep up with him. "The name is Hawk!" he called to a young girl as he passed her in the corridor. She ignored him, but in his mind she turned and followed him. The fantasy continued as he stepped into an empty elevator cab. Picturing Westlake there with him, he said, "After today you'll *really* call me Hawk, big man. *Everyone* will call me Hawk."

Back in the gym, Westlake draped a towel over one shoulder and began a slow walk around the perimeter. He'd felt Crow's eyes on the back of his neck. His friend knew what was happening. Or thought he did. It was the pain again. It throbbed from the back of his neck and shot like hot lightning through his arms and down his spine. He remembered the knife. Fifteen years ago, but like yesterday. Cutting slowly, evenly, expertly. First the nose. Then the ears, and eyes. Then the scalp, great bloody clumps of hair and skin peeled back and ripped. And the woman's voice.

"You're dying. Why do you have to die so quickly?"

And the awakening. He shuddered, remembering. The awakening was worse.

He completed one circuit of the gym and stopped in front of a brown canvas hundred-pound bag that hung from six metal chains. The pain flowed, and he waited for it to pass. Next would come the fatigue, and then violent sleep.

A woman's voice called, "Hey, Westlake! Stand aside!"

He didn't turn as the group of joggers passed around him. Three women, two men. Laughing, naked, roughhousing with one another as they ran. One of the women turned and waved, then turned away again. He watched their backs absently. They rounded the corner and passed out of sight.

Turning his attention to the bag, he pushed it away easily and let its bulk swing back against him. Then faster, and higher, until the hard weight was slamming in a rhythm against his flat stomach.

Slate. Benjamin Slate. The eager young face, the quick smile. Those ridiculous eyebrows. Always practicing, always reading. A genius with his hands.

A Master Duelist now.

The blow caught the bag in mid-swing. The chains snapped and sand exploded against the wall.

Slate waved a cheerful hello when he passed the registration desk. The woman—her name was Leonora and she was twenty-three, from Meersopol in the Pacifico Belt—smiled at him. He noted that despite the unchanging heat, she was dressed in a neck-to-toe jumpsuit. Interesting.

He scowled when the elevator opened its doors to Level A; back to business. It was still early, and most of the workers stood near the entrance in the corridor, talking in small groups. A few nodded to Slate as he passed. Inside the workspace only a few of the desks were occupied. He found the little clerk hunched over his keyboard, humming to himself. Slate didn't recognize the tune. But if Dianymede Mining Company had a corporate anthem, he was sure that he was hearing it.

"Remember me?"

The man pursed his lips and continued staring at the screen. Slate sighed. There was no reason to go through the routine again. He rested his hand on the holstered Barrow.

"Don't bother, Mr. Slate," said the little man, not turning his head. There was a sharp edge to his voice. Here and there the desks were beginning to fill. Slate watched from the corner of his eyes, marking them all as faces he had seen there yesterday.

The man tapped a final key with a flourish. "There," he said. A grid of numbers appeared on the computer screen. He glanced at it quickly and referred to a slip of paper on the desk. "So." He switched the machine off and rotated the chair around. He put on a twisted smile and looked up at Slate. "Thank you for the privilege of serving you, sir. In what capacity shall I grovel?"

Slate chuckled. There was more to this clerk than he'd thought. The slip of paper had disappeared from the desk; the little man was quick physically, also. Slate asked, "Did you have my card printed in the Plan of the Day?"

"Of course I did. You paid me, didn't you?" Then he lowered his voice so that only Slate could hear him. "And you owe me more. I don't mind being used, but I expect to be paid for my time."

"That's reasonable," Slate said agreeably. "In fact it's what I want to talk to you about."

This time the smile was real. The man picked up a thick black pen and tapped the desk with it. "What do you have in mind?"

"There's a man here named Westlake. I want to know—"

"If he's a Duelist?"

"Yes. That's right. And—"

"And how did I know you'd be asking about him?"

"I hope your answers are as good as your questions, Mr.— what is your name?"

"Call me Darret. I can help you, Mr. Slate, and it won't cost you. Not directly, that is." A woman approached the desk from Darret's right side. He took a sheaf of papers from her and waited until she'd moved out of hearing range before speaking again. "Here's my idea. I'll take care of setting up your exhibition matches. You transfer a block of money to me. I'll use it for betting on the matches. I keep a quarter of whatever I win. Fair?"

"That's high commission. Why should I pay you an extra ten percent?"

"Because I know this arena better than anyone else. I can set it up with none of the usual problems. And I can give you whatever else you need." He tapped the pen against the computer screen. "Westlake, for instance. Bargain?"

"You've done this before."

Darret shrugged. "My brother was a Duelist. I made him rich before he died."

Slate straightened. "Died? What kind of match did you arrange for him?"

Darret reddened. "My brother was Manner Longley."

The caterpillar eyebrows crept upward. Manner Longley? The Long Man. He knew of that one, although they'd never met. Longley was fast becoming a legend, as one of the best ever to come out of the New Worlds. He'd heard tough people with misted eyes say of The Long Man, "Now *there* is a *Duelist!*"

Manner Longley had made Grade 1 Expert in less than ten years. Other than the legendary Wilkington Mosher, Slate knew of no one who had done that. The word was that The Long Man had earned it the hard way, taking up the dirty jobs on those worlds most Duelists avoided—the worlds where Duelists were hunted like game animals.

He looked at the small man. "What happened?"

"My brother was killed twelve days ago. I was with him." The sharp eyes probed. "You didn't hear about that, eh?"

"No." During the past months he'd been on this Elimination Tour, moving from one isolated outpost to another. On any of the major worlds he'd have heard the news. The death of a Grade 1 Expert was a significant event, to the millions—billions—of folk throughout the worlds who attended matches, bought holos, read the innumerable books written by and about Duelists. And of course, such news would spread fast among the Duelists themselves. There were fewer than six hundred Grade 1 Experts in all of the Great Domain. Of Master Duelists there were fewer than a hundred. He wondered, *Who could have bested The Long Man?*

Slate repeated, "What happened?"

Longley hesitated before answering. He knew about the Tour; he'd been involved in enough of them. And he assumed that the arrival of a Master Duelist meant that the Tour included 652-E. That seemed a remarkable coincidence, considering what had happened to his brother. He suspected that someone—maybe Benjamin Slate—may have believed that Manner Longley was a part of the game, and taken steps to eliminate him early on. "Since you don't know, I'll tell you." *And your reaction will tell me a few things,* he thought. "Manner picked me up here and we headed home. Home is Paulus, out in the New Worlds."

"I've been there."

"Yes, I know. My brother and I saw you fight in King Town. We were just children then."

Slate smiled. "Was it that long ago?"

"Twenty-two years. You had a partner, I remember."

He swallowed hard. "I asked you about your brother."

"My brother, Mr. Slate, brought me the news that our mother had died. We were headed for Bertha Station to connect with a fast transport. Two days out, there was an explosion." He paused, watching Slate carefully. When he spoke again his voice was deeper, more deliberate. "When I came to, I was suited up, in the lifelaunch. My brother was at the viewplate." He stopped and looked at the blank computer screen. After several seconds he recoiled as if he'd seen the face he was describing. He looked up and continued.

"He was smiling, Mr. Slate. The way he did when we were young, when he was about to pull me out of some stupid thing I'd gotten into." He looked at the screen again. The small hands were clenched and trembling.

Slate said, "Take is easy. What happened then?"

"The scouter's hull collapsed. I was protected. My brother was torn to pieces."

"I'm sorry. Your brother was—"

"He wanted me to live, you see. Me, instead of him. If there were any justice in life . . ." There was no point in going on with the rest of the story. Slate wasn't involved; his eyes said it clearly. Reliving the nightmare had brought him nothing. "I didn't intend to tell you all this. I wanted to know if you—"

"I didn't know your brother, Mr. Longley. I wish I had. We called him The Long Man. He was one of the best."

The small man smiled. "Yes. I know about the nickname. Manner liked it, maybe because he was the same size as me."

That was a shock. Slate had envisioned Manner Longley as a very big man. Then it dawned on him: he was. "So you made it back safely?"

He shrugged, and pain flashed across his face. "I suppose you could say so. The hull's collapse damaged the launch. It knocked out the Pathfinder, the radio, the lights, and the Fine Control System. It also broke my back." He laughed. "That's why I walk this way. It's not a lifelong trait, you see. Just a temporary inconvenience."

"You piloted that launch without computers? And with a broken back?" Slate was impressed. "You said you were two days out. But without computers—" He calculated, and gave up. There were too many variables. "It must have taken you weeks to get back."

"Five days. They say I made a pretty good landing, but I don't remember coming in."

He saw the look on Slate's face and grinned. "Don't be so surprised, Mr. Slate. I grew up with Manner Longley. He was a good brother. And a better teacher."

Blessed Saint Barrow, Slate thought. Twelve days ago. A Duelist coming here, just then . . . of course the Golds would try to kill him. They'd arrived just a few days before that. Perhaps, in doing his job here, he would avenge the death of Manner Longley. "Mr. Longley . . ."

"Call me Darret, Mr. Slate."

"My name is Ben. And please accept my condolences for your brother. You are a fit vessel to carry his memory." He extended his hand.

Darret Longley shook the hand with surprising strength. "You wanted to know about Westlake."

"Yes."

"Then our bargain is sealed?"

"I'll transfer the funds through the bursar this afternoon."

"Westlake is the largest man I've ever seen. And he is most certainly a Duelist."

"How can you be sure?"

Longley shrugged. "A Duelist can't hide what he is. In the case of Westlake, it's his arms. I've noticed that Duelists tend to focus speed on one side of the body, and power on the other. In practical terms that doesn't mean much. Any Duelist can kill effectively, from any angle. But the difference is there, and it gets more noticeable as the years go on. I'd say Westlake has been at it for about as long as you have, thirty years or so."

"That's a good observation, Darret. But some of us—"

"Your development is even on both sides. Even if I didn't know it already, that would tell me that you're an empty-hand specialist. My judgment is that Westlake favors the Twoyard sword. Or the war axe. He's fast-left, and strong-right. But that's for comparison only. On either side, he's four times as powerful as the average Duelist. At *least* four times."

"How long has he been here?"

"Over six months. Too long to be a part of the Elimination Tour." Before Slate could reply he went on. "That's why you're asking, Mr. Slate. You were thinking he might be a part of the— what Team are you representing? Blue or Gold?"

"Blue," Slate answered.

"Well, don't worry. Westlake's not with the Gold Team. And whoever the Golds are, I'm sure they've noticed him by now, and have concluded that he's not a Blue. Otherwise they'd have killed him."

"Good enough, Darret. Thanks." The small clerk was correct in his reasoning. Six months ago no one, not even the logistical planners of the Tour, could have known that 652-E would be used as an arena. Site selection was made only a few days before a site was to be used, randomly, from thousands of possibilities. Westlake wasn't here because of the Tour. No reason to bother with him then, Slate thought. But something—a gnawing *something*—told him otherwise.

Longley said, "You expect the Golds to come at you during your exhibition?"

Slate was unaccustomed to answering questions about his business, especially while it was in progress. He liked what he saw in Darret Longley. But it was foolhardy to trust him with more than he needed to know. "Your brother taught you a great deal," Slate said.

Longley understood. "We worked well together. And I won't repeat my question. But I'm entitled to say this much, Ben. You've got a good reputation for protecting innocents. I hope that's justified. There'll be three or four hundred there, I'd estimate."

"The Duelist Union is paying my expenses," Slate said. "That binds me by law to put on the exhibition. You know the rules, Longley."

The clerk reddened. "Sure, I do, Slate. Except it's not law, it's tradition. And *you* know the difference. This exhibition is part of your strategy for flushing out the Golds. That's your right, and I know that, too. But it's also your responsibility to protect the innocents."

"Exactly," Slate said calmly. "It's my responsibility." He

noted with approval that the smaller man had absolutely no fear of him. In fact Longley had balled his fists, and then self-consciously opened them, as he'd spoken. "Unwrap, Darret. Relax. Just set it up the way I design it. That'll protect the spectators as much as possible. Odds are that the Golds will wait for the matches to end."

Longley regained his composure. "When you can be presumed to be tired and off-guard."

"That's how it works, usually."

"Is this Gold Team really that stupid?"

There was no good answer to that question. The Golds would pick the place and time of attack. When they did, he'd end it as quickly as possible. He repeated, "That's how it works, usually."

"All right," Longley said, giving up the point. "You'll need to present your credentials to the Director of Operations. I'll go back later and pick up the permit."

"Thanks."

"And good luck with the D.O."

"What do you mean?"

The clerk waved away the question. "I don't think Westlake will want to play. And there's no way one of the Golds will climb into the ring with you. You'd know you were facing another Duelist immediately."

"And I'd kill him," Slate said, growing irritated with Longley's continued probing. "The Golds know that. What's your point?"

Longley snapped, "Unwrap, Ben!" Then he sat back in his chair, and grinned full-mouthed.

After a moment's anger Slate understood, and grinned back. The man was goading him! Incredible! It had been a long while since he'd been with his own kind; talking with Longley reminded him of that.

"You won't find much of a challenge here."

"No." This was the brother of a Grade 1 Expert; he knew what a Duelist could do. To anyone else, Slate's answer would have been the stock, "You never know. That's what makes it interesting." A lot of income flowed from the old adage that there's one born every minute.

"The bet is that you'll beat all challenges within—?" Longley let the words hang in the air.

"Make it two minutes. That's long enough to build a little suspense, but not long enough to be boring. Choice of weapons, and I'll be unarmed."

Longley nodded. "Good enough. I'll give you an honest accounting."

"I know that," Slate said. "You're a good man, Darret."

The clerk looked around them and said in a quiet voice, "Thanks, Ben. But keep your compliments to yourself. I have to get along with these people. And the best way is to be a surly bastard."

"You've got it down to an art."

Darret Longley scowled through narrowed eyes. He said in a loud voice, "Get away from me, Duelist, before I call a Peacekeeper. I'm an honest man with honest work to do."

Slate took the cue and left, glaring at the few people who looked up.

In the corridor a man blocked his path, grinning widely. "I saw you gig that little weasel yesterday. That was the funniest . . ."

He shouldn't have tried to take Slate's arm. Maybe he'd reflect on that, when he woke up to look for his teeth.

In twenty-eight years as a credentialed Duelist, Slate had met the full spectrum of response that his trade evoked. Everyone, in one way or another, reacted to the presence of a Duelist. Some looked the other way, and pretended not to notice. Many displayed outright hostility; that was usually safe, within recognized bounds. Some saw Duelists as heroes, and others saw them as degenerate criminals. Both groups were wrong. Still others tended to cluster around them, as if something exciting were about to happen; usually they were wrong, also. The most common reaction to a Duelist was one of careful, if somewhat distant, deference. Slate didn't mind any of these. But he hated to be kept waiting.

He was sitting outside the office of Dianymede 652-E's Director of Operations. So far he'd been kept waiting for half an hour. Slate cleared his mind of the gnawing irritation; it served no purpose. He regarded the room and was struck again by the sharp contrast with the grim utility of the mass workspace one level above. The enormous anteroom was breathtaking, by the standards of any major world.

The dry air was cool and freshened with ionized filters. Best

of all was the generated full gravity. After so long without the
opposition of Standard weight, it was a luxury beyond compare.
The couches were deep and plush, lined with what seemed to be
genuine leather. He could only wonder at the cost. Here the sense
of Dianymede's rich and flamboyant past was powerfully recap-
tured.

In the center of the room a marble fountain gurgled, sending
bright bows of multicolored water cascading into a thirty-foot
replica of a grass-banked stream. That in turn flowed into a wa-
terfall, which emptied somewhere out of sight. He could vaguely
remember a similar scene in a theme park, from his early childhood on Earth.

It was a beautiful scene, more pleasant than the personal
memories it evoked. But the appearance of profligate luxury was
just that—appearance. Like everything else Dianymede did, it
had a purpose: to make money. Nothing in this room would be
wasted, because it would all be sold at a huge profit. Decades
ago, Dianymede had developed the technique which was now
standard in the industry.

The largest mining planetoids advanced in stages, from the
core outward. As material was removed, separate crews built
within the space created. Eventually fantastic grottoes, mammoth
conference centers, private rooms, storehouses, hangars, kitch-
ens, and penthouse retreats honeycombed the colony. By the time
a planetoid became useless as a mining center, it had been transformed into a thing of gargantuan luxury and beauty. These were
sold to hotel companies, governments, or to the wealthy families
of the Great Domain.

The E designation on 652-E indicated that it was well advanced toward transition. In another decade or so this would be
an F class. Soon afterward it would be ready for final conversion
and sale.

On one great wall of the anteroom were dozens of holostats
and paintings. Slate recognized reproductions of Monet, Valerie,
C. W. Smithson—and surprisingly, a Quazel. He was impressed;
Quazel starscapes were strictly protected from reproduction. This
original would have to be at least two hundred years old.

Mounted by itself in a prominently lighted alcove was the inevitable portrait of the Four Sisters, the founders of Dianymede
Mining Company. Grace, Alicia, Dominia, and . . . what was the
other? Matilda. He noted that the anteroom had been designed to

draw the observer's eye to that alcove. Any student of history would appreciate the intended message: This is how it all began.

Those had been rough days, at the beginning.

Humankind had barely survived. Fragmented nations. Bristling weapons pointed in every direction. Fear, mistrust, and a few genuinely evil and fanatical national governments. Society was sick, as hemmed-in societies always are. Everywhere, there was animosity and unrest. Everyone had feared The Great War That'll Sure As Hell Kill Everybody. Fortunately, self-interest had prevailed. After a number of false starts humankind stared across a conference table and recognized—itself.

But there had been a deeper, more insidious threat to humankind's future. At the time of man's first tentative probes into space there existed political and social leaders who had no interest in the Universe, who considered space exploration and development a waste of time and money. Their vision—confine humankind on one little planet, don't even *think* of leaving Earth until everything is perfect—would have guaranteed that *any* major war would be The Great War That'll Sure As Hell Kill Everybody. They should have known better. The old farmers even had a saying about it; something about all the eggs in one basket.

The Universe awaited. Infinite. Eternal. The UNIVERSE! But No, said the marching morons. Let's not go there. Slate was appalled at the dimness of that vision. Imagine! All the splendid worlds, the unimaginable diversity of the Great Domain, the epic tales of heroism, exploration, colonization! The great geniuses who led the way!

Not go there? What about the billions upon billions of folk scattered throughout the spiral arm of the Milky Way, for whom the birthplace of ancestors was but a wink in the great night sky? Not *go* there? *Not* go out *there*? What kind of dead, wonderless mind could ever allow such a thing?

Slate shook his head. Thank the Blessed Saint Barrow, there had been some of vision in those days. The writers, the poets, the scientists, the capitalists, the engineers, the pilots, the folk who worked hard and paid taxes, the little kids and brilliant dreamers who read, and thought, and wondered . . . All the folk who'd gazed outward at the stars, and knew—knew from the core of their being—that humankind belonged out there among them.

The vision was organic, elemental; the species needed room to breathe.

The beginning was small, as are all beginnings. Souvenirs from Earth's moon. Orbiting observatories, then laboratories, then construction sites, the groundlings moving further and further out from Earth. But slowly. It was as if a psychological barrier needed to be broken, or an umbilical cord cut. And it happened.

Colonies grew up at the stations and became self-sufficient. Children were born and raised, grew up, got old, and died, never touching the soil of Earth. Mining colonies began breaking up or boring out the asteroids. Pioneers like the Four Sisters, and Marcus Lopez, and Christian-Bey, and Lovitch & Carey, carved empires out of those rocks. Some of the material went to Earth. But more and more, as years passed, the materials were used to build other stations, even more distant from Earth—where more mines were opened, more stations built, more ways of life established. And more, and more.

Earth? That's that little light over there, son. Ask your grandmother why they call it The Big Blue.

To move faster than light was the big problem, the only real obstacle to deep-space exploration. And that barrier, like the last and the biggest in a long chain of dominoes, fell at last. Scientists had long believed that at the Big Bang certain particles had been propelled, even if only for a nanosecond, into a dimension that "walked around" the barrier of lightspeed. That was just a hope, just a clue. It was enough. If such dimensional—or hyperspace—travel was possible, human genius would make it inevitable. And that's the way it turned out.

It was in the year 2094, still remembered as The Great Light Year, that an object—a miniature portrait of Dr. Harry Lyndon's wife encased in a gold heart—was sent from Earth's orbiting Fujiwara Laboratory Complex, directly into the Sun. There was no certainty that the propulsion device would work, or what might happen if it did work. But the scientists were convinced that whatever might happen, the Sun would safely absorb it. Events proved that the scientists were correct. It worked.

Lyndon's Locket Rocket proved the reality of hyperspace, in effect traveling 94 million miles at twice the speed of light.

Less than a decade later, at the dawn of the twenty-second century, the true exploration of space was at last underway. Humankind was taking its first steps away from the local neighborhood—to the stars. And now, a mere two centuries later, there was the Great Domain. Fifteen hundred settled worlds, and counting. All within the one great spiral arm of the Milky Way that had produced Earth.

This spiral arm, and by extension the galaxy, and by extension the Universe, was unimaginably rich.

As a child, Slate had learned in First School that humankind could conceivably go on expanding and multiplying, literally for ever. That word "conceivably" was thrown into the equation to allow for something humankind had never found in space exploration—competition. Most of the planets were barren. Some teemed with life. But nowhere was technologically developed life found. It—they—had to be out there somewhere. Slate could not imagine a Universe with only one truly intelligent species.

Was there anyone out there? That, along with the who-what-why game of "Is there a God/gods?" was one of humankind's oldest questions. And that was as it should be. An infinite Universe, Slate reasoned, by nature imposes infinite questions. But it guarantees no answers; that's the fun of having a mind. Was there anyone out there? No one really knew, yet. In the meantime, humankind would go on about the business of flourishing and expanding—making more room to breathe. And a few would pause to reflect, now and then, and think that sometime, somewhere, there would be—competition. But not yet.

Slate looked into the fountain's bubbling cascade of sparkling mixed colors. He saw the water rise and separate into gleaming droplets, and then fall into the current that flowed out of sight.

He stood up and stretched and grew impatient again.

4

Twenty yards across the great room a door opened. A young man stepped through, reading from a clipboard. "Mr. Slate." He looked around as if waiting for a crowd to produce the right person. Except for the two of them, the room was empty. "You can—"

Slate brushed by him.

". . . You can go in now."

The Director of Operations was seated behind an immense desk carved from a single slab of rock. Slate's first impression was that the Director had been similarly constructed. She was a large woman, with tightly pulled-back, sand-colored hair. He judged her to be a few years younger than himself. Her facial features were smooth, firm, and hinted at a strongly diverse racial heritage. Other things about here were evident to Slate's practiced eye. That she was a highly disciplined person, he saw from the contours of the form-fitting coverall she wore. Hers was a body-type that tended to obesity, but was obviously controlled by both diet and exercise. Her eyes were clear blue and steady as she glanced up, appraising him. She looked away quickly, as if she had seen quite enough in that brief instant of eye contact, and was no longer interested in her visitor. This is an impressive woman, Slate thought, her manner and appearance giving the impression of a strong individual, ready to meet the world on her own terms. Her name—Myra Stanley—was sewn prominently into the uniform fabric.

She was trying hard to pretend that she had forgotten his presence there. Her eyes jerked from object to object on the desk, every few seconds looking up as if deep in thought, but always away from him. Subtlety shouldn't be so strenuous, Slate reflected. He'd seen this type of behavior before, primarily in corporate executives and psychologists. It was a game that asserted authority, as if to say, *This is my office, I'm in command here. You are an interruption. Speak and begone.* It was a waste of time. Slate had no intention of challenging the Director's authority. He merely wanted to be certain that the Director knew just how small that authority was.

He ended the game by taking the seat facing the desk, and at the same time slapping down a packet of papers directly in front of Director Stanley. She started at the sharp sound.

"Please sit down, Mr. Slate," she said, glaring at him. "Thank you for the privilege of serving—"

He pushed the packet closer to her. "These are my credentials, Director." The chair was uncomfortable. It also was carved of rock, and thinly cushioned. "And thank *you*, for seeing me so quickly."

Myra Stanley studied the documents closely for several minutes.

Slate watched her face for reaction, more curious than concerned. He didn't need her approval to do his job. The Tour was sanctioned by the Union, and approved by Dianymede. There was nothing she could do.

She finished reading and looked up coldly. "And how is business, Mr. Slate?"

The woman truly had remarkable control. The odds against any particular site being used were high. Dianymede and Basalt owned 5,290 sites, of which only eighty would be used for the Tour. Lightning had struck, but she hadn't batted an eye. He realized that he liked this woman. But to let her know that would spoil the relationship.

"I asked you a question, Mr. Slate."

"That wasn't a question, Director."

She stared at him for long moments. Finally she said, "I know about your mistreatment of Darret Longley yesterday, Mr. Slate, and your demonstration of brutality an hour ago. I've spoken to that poor man you assaulted. I have advised him to file legal charges against you."

So. That was what this hostility was about. "He won't do that, Director."

"Why? Because you continue to intimidate him?" After several seconds of silence from Slate, the Director sneered. "Of course you have no answer. But I *do*. If civilization means anything, *Duelist* Slate, it means that we can protect decent people from your kind of predatory behavior."

He nearly rose to the bait. As a reader of history, particularly the decades leading up to the formation of the original Duelists, Slate had come to believe that "civilization" inevitably led to a permanently controlled, manipulated, and terrified population. Also inevitably, that degree of control created more, not fewer, victims of "predatory behavior." But he had important business to attend to, so he cut the discussion short.

"Director," Slate said levelly. "That man will not file charges against me for assaulting him. He told you that, didn't he?" A slight flinch in her eyes confirmed that he was right.

"Yes," Myra Stanley said in obvious disgust. "He provoked a Master Duelist, and he's alive to tell about it. He's so damned proud of that, he'd give you his first-born, if you promised to hit him again!"

Slate had judged the man correctly. "Then why waste my time, and yours?"

She took in a deep breath and let it out slowly. "I want you to understand that I am not prepared to accept the same type of behavior from you. You people take great pride in your ability to kill, don't you?" She waved away his response. "I know about Duelists, Mr. Slate. Prize-fighters. Soldiers of Fortune. Aren't those some of your euphemisms? Performers, right? I've even read about you. The so-called experts who determine such things say that you're one of the ten most lethal combat artists in human history. What an accomplishment! Well, I am impressed neither by you, nor by your disgusting trade. You're here legally, and I'm to cooperate with you. Fine, you'll have your exhibition permit. And if this Gold Team kills you first, your Union can still expect to be charged for the time and work involved. Now if there is nothing else, get out."

Slate hid his irritation, but only with great effort. Rarely had he been spoken to, by outsiders, as he had been since arriving at 652-E. He'd heard from others in the trade that anti-Duelist sentiment was growing throughout the Great Domain. No one could say why. Slate guessed that it was merely the normal cycle of trends and fashions and popular opinion. He'd seen little of it, before now. That tattooed bully-boss, Crow, had challenged him directly, *knowing* that he was a Master Duelist. Myra Stanley clearly had no respect for the trade. And Darret Longley . . . but that was different. Longley had been around Duelists enough to know that by and large, they were like other folk. *Except that in practicing our trade, we kill people. But so do others.* No, that was oversimplification, he amended as he watched Myra Stanley, waiting for her to be the one to break the silence between them. Soldiers and Peacekeepers killed professionally. But they were mostly anonymous men and women who went off duty at the end of a shift, and slipped neatly into their anonymous social circles. They weren't thought of as fighters, as killers. At least not *all* of the time. Slate's trade was different. Whatever else they might be *part* of the time—husbands, wives, parents, and dozens of other roles—his compatriots were Duelists, *all* of the time. As his former partner, Brother John, had once remarked, "We're the most watched, and the least known, people in the Great Domain. Thank the Blessed Saint Barrow, that's the truth."

As he usually did, his friend had said a great deal in a few words. Not many people knew—or maybe they knew, but just didn't care—that the original Duelists were criminals, an illegal band of anarchists. What modern crowds cared about was The Performance: Who Kills who, with what, how quick? It had been that way for decades. Today's Duelists were entrepreneurs, absorbed in day-to-day living. To them, also, what mattered was The Performance.

But because of the nature of their craft, because in the arena life-or-death situations flew at them with the rapid-fire percussion of a laser-drum, because nothing but *self* was always-and-instantly responsible for survival, Duelists were never far away from their roots of lawlessness. That was easy enough to understand. Duelists *obeyed* laws, but could never *live* by law; skill, training, and judgment—not law—kept them alive from one professional encounter to the next.

Myra Stanley was looking at him, and he could see the dislike in her eyes. He knew it wasn't personal. How could it be? They'd just met. He should be used to this by now. Still, he admitted to himself, it bothered him. He loved his profession, and the life it had enabled him to live. And he accepted outsiders' animosity as natural, as a product of their fear: It was natural that outsiders would fear him. That was part of the allure, in the early years. But long ago his faith in his abilities had become absolute; he no longer needed anyone to be afraid of him. As a result, he'd found himself more and more open to friendships among non-Duelists. It wasn't something he sought, but it did happen, the prime example being his engagement to Arika, Sweetie, who was as far from being a Duelist as a human being could be. So while Slate still understood why he was feared and disliked, he no longer welcomed it.

"Is there anything else, Mr. Slate?" Myra Stanley asked, tapping her desk. "I have many more important things to do, if your business with me is complete."

"There is one more thing," Slate said, gathering his thoughts again. He was tired, and didn't know why. All of this day he'd been unusually contemplative, his thoughts ranging far from the business at hand. Normally he was more focused. Why not now? *There I go again.*

She was waiting for him to speak. "Yes?" she prompted.

"It concerns the agreement between Dianymede Mining Company and the Duelist Union."

"Go on, Mr. Slate," Myra said impatiently.

"You understand that—"

"That I face disciplinary action if I disclose information relating to your Murder Tour. Yes, yes, that's clear. I can read, Mr. Slate. And I understand contract law very well. Is there anything else?"

"I want to know who transferred in here during the past twenty days."

"A list will be sent to your room."

He stood to leave. She said, "One moment, Mr. Slate. Please." The "please" was out of character. He sat down.

"My given name is Myra. May I offer you something to drink?"

"Cold water, Myra. And call me Ben." He'd seen this type of abrupt, complete transition before: Business is over, let's get friendly. In his experience, most of the trouble with executives began at this point. He was curious.

Myra Stanley drank steaming black coffee while Slate watched her and wondered what form of bureaucratic unpleasantness she had in mind. He drained his glass and refused the offer of a second.

Myra said, "I have a favor to ask." She added quickly, "Your credentials remove you from my authority. But I'd like you to listen."

"Go ahead."

She hesitated, and it piqued his interest. This was a woman accustomed to the surety of command. Whatever she was going to say, it wasn't easy for her.

She began, "These outposts are rough places, especially the A's and B's. By contrast, E's are relatively safe."

He nodded and said, "Myra, I don't have the authority to move the game somewhere else, if that's what you're asking."

"No, it isn't. This is about Leonora D'Meersopol."

"What about her?"

Myra flushed. "It's not my concern who you ... or with whom ... First of all, she's an engineer. An extraordinarily brilliant one. Did you know that?

"Yes." Leonora had mentioned her education, briefly, during the time they'd spent together. That she was an engineer had been only one surprise in a night full of surprises. She had come to him in the shower compartment, apparently interested in companionship and a sexual encounter, both of which had appealed to him strongly at the time. In his bed he had held her naked body in his arms, kissed her forehead and lips as she spoke to him. And yet the night had passed without sex; his strongest desire had been to know more about her. He'd had the—to him—alien feeling that to go further with Leonora at that time would be wrong. This had been a first for Slate, and he was still uneasy about it. There were many more contradictions he'd seen in Leonora; some he could put in words, some he could not. Director Stanley had just mentioned one. Slate had meant to ask Leonora the question, but for some reason had not. Now he asked Myra. "Leonora graduated *cum laude* from two top engineering schools before she was twenty. Why is she handing out towels for a living?"

"She can tell you that, if she wants to. I'm asking you to ... the child has been through hell, Ben."

Slate bristled. "I see. And contact with a Duelist will bring her more of the same."

Myra's eyes hardened to chips of granite. "People do tend to be hurt around Duelists. If Leonora is harmed I'll ..." Her voice wavered but her eyes held tightly to his. "I'll kill you, Ben. Somehow. I'll kill you."

Slate relaxed. He liked this woman a lot. "I believe you, Myra. Goodbye."

• • •

The old chair creaked again and Leonora bit her lip in frustration.

"Throw it away. Dianymede can afford to buy a new one."

She dropped the plastic bottle, spilling oil onto the threadbare carpet. She sopped it up with her sleeve and looked up at the stocky bearded man grinning at her from the doorway.

"What are you doing here? This is a private area."

"I like private areas, Leonora." He took a step into the supply room and stopped. The scaled blue fabric of his tunic caught the dim light and broke it into small patterns of squares and triangles.

"If you want something, Mr. Gower, I'll be right out. You're supposed to ring the bell."

"Call me Dave, remember? I don't want anything that's out there." He took another step and leered. "I thought you might appreciate some company."

"No. Thank you." She got off her knees and brushed sawdust from her uniform. "I have work to do."

"You need help with that chair. I'm good at making things better."

"Please go, Mr. Gower. You're not supposed to be back here." She saw the tiny point-saw on the bench beside her and looked away, ashamed of her thought. "Please go," she repeated.

"You like Duelists, I hear. Lots of people do." His eyes were hard when he smiled. "You like men who deal in death and pain? He's not here now, Leonora. But I am."

She wanted to say, *Yes, he knows how to give pain. That's common enough. But he also knows how to give* no *pain. And that's rare, friend. Rare.* Instead she set her jaw firmly and said, "Mr. Gower, I can have a Peacekeeper here in two minutes."

He laughed, then said harshly, "You think I'm ugly."

"No, Mr. Gower. I don't."

He pulled aside a small bandage on his forehead. "Now you do." Before she could answer, he said, "I'll see you tomorrow, Leonora. You'll like me then." He spun on his heel and stalked out of the room.

Leonora watched him go and breathed a sigh. He wasn't ugly. But she'd never seen a mole like that before. It stood out on his forehead like a blue beacon.

She dropped into the chair and rocked, unmindful of the creaking. She wanted to go Home.

The job with Dianymede had come like the answer to a prayer. The Home's prayer, not hers. She had never wanted to leave. The day she'd made up her mind was overcast. The rain that came was so sudden and fierce that she'd run from the soya field, blinded by the torrent, and slammed a shoulder against the gazebo before she ever saw it. A gentle hand guided her up the three steps. They talked while the rain fell straight down, cascading in sheets off the gabled roof and leaving a dry spot in the center of the platform for them. The cold and the darkness were eerie, and Leonora was thankful that she was not alone.

"I've decided to go, Aunt Elaine."

"You don't have to. You earn enough for them already. The others should work harder. They're lazy." The woman was a hundred and thirty-nine years old. Her animated blue eyes and jaunty voice made her seem twenty years younger.

"They're not lazy. They do what they can. The Home paid for my education. I'm worth more to them if I go."

"Leonora, the modifications you've made to our procedures and equipment have tripled our output this year. Next year we'll do even better. You have paid us back. For everything."

"It's only for three years, Aunt Elaine. Maybe the experience will be good for me. I've never been away from Meersopol."

"Of course you have, child. You weren't born here."

"But I was too young to remember anyplace else. And I feel very strongly that it's important for me to go."

The venom in the old woman's voice shocked her. "There're devils out there, Leonora."

"I'm not afraid, Aunt Elaine."

And she hadn't been afraid, at first. She knew about devils and angels, because the uncles and aunts at Home spoke of them daily, for as far back as Leonora could remember. It was a devil who took her parents, and an angel who brought her Home. Her parents were only words to Leonora, because they were taken too early to leave her their faces and the memory of their touch. And the devils were only words, because there were none of them at Home.

When she went to work for Dianymede the first thing Leonora learned was that devils looked like everyone else. On Site 872-A no one looked like an angel or a devil. But eighty people died when an oxygen generator exploded in a working shaft. Leonora disassembled the remaining generators—140 of them—and found the marks of apathy and neglect. Only devils could allow that. On 712-B she saw a small Oriental woman kill four large men with her hands in the space of a heartbeat. That savage incident still terrified her.

The Director who had been so kind to her explained that they weren't devils; they were people. Leonora believed her. And she was terrified of them all.

The creak of the old chair intruded on her thoughts. She reached for the bottle of oil and cradled it in her hands as she rocked. She hummed a tune that came without thought, and it soothed her.

⇒ 5 ⇐

Every bulletin board on the mining colony carried the notice the next morning.

The Digger's Lounge was the natural choice for the bouts. Slate saw why, the moment he left the elevator and entered the great cavern. "Blessed Saint Barrow. It's . . . perfect."

Darret Longley maneuvered the gravi-chair out of the elevator cab and came up beside him. "Look the place over, Ben, and give me a list of what you need. I'll have a crew of roustabouts set it up in plenty of time."

The Master Duelist was spellbound by the size and the beauty of the place. It was outside, brought inside. After a minute he said, "How did you manage to get workers assigned so quickly?"

"That surprised me too. But all I had to do was ask." The tiny man shook his head. "No money changed hands. No one told me it was impossible . . . It isn't natural." He shrugged. "Maybe somebody with influence here likes you."

43

Or wants a favor, Slate thought. Despite what she felt about Duelists, Myra Stanley was keeping her word. "Any progress on the list?"

Longley handed him a printout. "Nothing obvious. Twenty-nine new workers came in. I ruled out the extremes: too old, too young, physically infirm. That left eighteen. But add to that the number of transients, merchants, and, in one case, an entire family here to visit their daughter. The five Golds could be any of forty-three people. I've listed them all for you. But—"

"It was an idea worth trying."

"No, it wasn't. You were right. Too many to check."

Slate pocketed the paper. "Thanks, Darret."

"I earn my money, Ben."

"How are the bets coming?"

Longley looked around conspiratorially before he answered. It was a joke: there was no one within a hundred yards. " 'Wagering is strictly prohibited,' " he said solemnly. "But when I left, there was a long line of degenerate gamblers at my desk. I'm going back there now and explain company policy to them."

The gravi-chair whined and backed into the elevator cab. The doors slid shut and Slate turned his attention back to the Digger's Lounge. The Reconstruction crews had achieved a marvel. The lounge itself was one small part of a vast artificial grotto, stretching 500 yards from the elevator. High cavern walls swept grandly upward for ninety or more feet, gradually tapering inward until they met to form a domed ceiling. Neatly spaced throughout the entire area, gigantic stalactites reached down to meet massive stalagmites. Braced between the pinnacles were blazing chunks of glowstone.

The natural textures and colorings—blues, grays, and reds—formed sweeping swirls of shadow and light that seemed to chase one another in the subtle, unpredictable flickering of the glowstones.

A sizable chunk of the cavern floor—Slate estimated an acre—was carved into a shallow bowl that would someday be filled with water to form a lake. All around the rim of the crater, and in oases throughout the grotto, were planted great trees and shrubs. Their lush growth was more than decorative, he knew. These were natural oxygen generators that would replenish themselves in the nitrogen-rich loam provided. Slate was stunned with the beauty that had been created here.

On impulse he scaled a 40-foot stalagmite for a better view. Far across the grotto was an area set aside as an outdoor—the illusion was that good—gymnasium. On a large field of what looked like real grass there was a game of soccer going on. He watched as the players wandered in groups between the field and the bar. As one group left the game, another would take its place. The game could go on perpetually, like this. He ached to join the players. But business first.

He climbed down and walked around the perimeter of the crater to the bar. There were ten rows of tables, five tables per row. He selected one that gave him the best view of the area. Only three other tables were occupied. Most of the patrons were at the bar, which was carved of rock. Slate counted thirty people there—young, old, male, female, some elegantly dressed, some naked, some nearly so. No one was in work uniform.

It dawned on him that the place was strangely quiet—not like a lounge at all. The level of conversation was low and subdued. A few people glanced at him quickly, and then looked away. They'd heard about the Tour, as he'd expected. This was common enough to be inevitable. The Director's protective instincts—militant in the case of Leonora—had led her to disclose the confidential information. It was another example of the best intentions leading to the worst results. Even though it was clearly explained in the documentation, Myra Stanley had not understood—few ever did—that the secrecy was for humanitarian purposes; the disclosure attracted more spectators to the exhibitions than it discouraged. Duelist traditions were there for a reason.

Still, he would do what he could to protect the innocents.

He ordered ice water from a waiter and sketched the area quickly, paying special attention to exits and blind spots. After that he drew a small circle that corresponded to an area thirty yards away. He wrote "Put mat here, 20' X 20', 4' elev.," and underlined the words. He shaded in aisles leading from the mat to the exits and wrote "9' width. Leave open. NO SPECTATORS HERE." When he was satisfied with the arrangement he tucked the pad and pen away and looked up toward the bar. Where was the waiter?

He saw her immediately, carrying a tray which held a large pitcher and a single glass. But his eyes were drawn to a doorway fifty yards beyond the waiter. A silhouette was framed in bright light from behind. The man's shoulders were broader than the doorway; to pass through it, he'd have to turn sidewards. But that was not his intention. He stood peering into the relative darkness, his face obscured by the effect of backlighting. But the giant could see Ben Slate clearly. The moment he did, he stiffened perceptibly, turned, and disappeared from sight.

The waiter arrived. "You're the Duelist, is that it?"

"I'm Ben Slate," he said absently. Who *was* the giant? A Duelist, Longley said; definitely. Slate had known only one of that size, dead now for more than fifteen years.

The waiter had been speaking to him. He glanced up at her and nodded. "Yes, that's fine."

"They said you're not very friendly," the woman huffed, and set the pitcher down in front of him.

"What?" He caught the glass as it tipped from the tray.

"I just told you I'll pay for the drinking water, Mister Duelist. To me that's a lot of money. I didn't expect much of a thank-you, but—"

"Wait."

The woman stopped and turned to face him. She was old. Her face bore the permanently etched lines of filter masks that had been obsolete for more than fifty years.

"Thank you for the water," Slate said. "But please don't pay for it. Send the bill to my room, and add something for yourself."

The woman nodded and turned to go.

"Can you sit down for a moment?"

"I'd like to know who says I can't." She took the chair opposite him.

Slate could see the wariness in her eyes. "When you retire," he said, "you should go to Arkana."

She cocked her head sideways like a confused pup. "That's stupid, you'll pardon me. There are no miners on Arkana. That world has to import dirt, it's so bad."

Slate said, "That's the point. Arkana is so poor in minerals, they invite miners to retire there. Everything is provided, and it's all free."

"I never heard about that. Why?"

"Because when the miners finally die, the government gets mineral rights to the body."

She looked at him skeptically, and then her face split into a wide grin. "And they'd make a fortune on this old carcass!"

He laughed with her, and it felt good. Her name was Noreen and she would work there for another year until her pension fund was full. Three husbands, "all bad, but fun," had been a lifelong drain on savings accounts.

He asked her about the giant, Westlake.

She cocked her head again, thinking. "He's quiet, that's it. But then he's no trouble like some of the quiet ones." She drank from his glass and made a face. "Recyke. If the bill says new-made, don't pay it. They say you can't tell the difference, but I say the kidneys leave a trace. Extra molecules. Real small ones, but they taste like piss."

He grimaced and pushed the glass toward her. "It's yours. What about Westlake?"

"I've seen a few of them go up to him when they think he's drunk. I mean the ones who'd feel smart about carving into a man that big and then telling about it. But he just looks at them." She shrugged and finished the water. "I think he won't challenge you, if that's it. He's too quiet in himself, I judge." And then she laughed. "It would be a good meeting, though."

Slate stood up. "Thank you, Noreen. Will you be watching tonight?"

"Yessir. That's why I made to pay for the water. I judge I'll win all of that back, and more. I bet hard on you." She shook his hand and said in a sympathetic tone. "Don't worry, Ben. You'll find them."

"Yes, I will." Everyone knew about the Golds. There were no secrets on a world this small. But he'd misunderstood her.

Noreen said, "You won't find many, but a few will bet against you." She laughed. "I know that's why you talked to me, to see if a little of my money wants your company."

"You're a smart woman, Noreen."

"I'm old," she said, "and still alive. That's the best you can get from being smart."

He took the elevator back up to the top floor. He could feel the cab passing out of the field produced by the gravity generators. Their effect was priceless, but the machines were prohibitively expensive; in a lifetime he would never earn enough to buy one. He wondered at the kind of wealth that would someday buy this entire colony, after the changeover was completed. Slate neither desired nor resented great wealth. All that he had ever really wanted, he had. Of the hundreds of billions of people in the Great Domain, only thirty thousand or so were Duelists. And of those, he was among the very elite. He could not imagine himself as anything other than a Duelist.

From the moment he had first seen the naked face of the world, his destiny was sealed.

He was eight years old when he'd watched his parents torn apart by a mob on Earth. It was the first of the famine years, and hunger was a faceless terror that no one remembered. Against stern warnings from his father, Slate's mother walked into the park to address the rioting hordes. She was a city supervisor and they were her responsibility; her mind could not be changed.

His father fought to protect her but he'd never had a chance of saving either of them. Slate remembered that gentle man's features twisted in outrage and defiance, his space-black face spattered with blood and tears. He could not fight, he had never learned to destroy a human body. Asher Slate was a physician, devoted to saving lives.

He remembered his mother's screams. Her perfect white skin, unblemished in sixty years of life, was a savage mass of blood. His father looked once at him—it was love, agony, and goodbye—and ran to her side. The boy could do nothing. The woman and the man were lynched, and the mob cheered and looked for more blood.

Benjamin picked up an iron bar someone had dropped, and he learned to kill. He struck out madly, blindly, running from one target to another, escaping each time because he was small enough and fast enough to become invisible to the mob. After the crowd went away he ran home and hid for two days, without food or water, in his bedroom. He was not afraid of the mob anymore. He drew pictures of his parents until his uncle came and took him away.

Uncle Card was a bachelor who accepted the boy as his own. He was a restless, jovial man who had never found the deep contentment of his older brother. But he had great humor and he had the Slate eyebrows; Benjamin loved him and wherever they traveled together, they were home.

Cardelius Levi Slate was a trader in rare books and art. His business allowed them to escape the seven years of famine suffered by Earth and dozens of other worlds. But to Benjamin it seemed that they never traveled far enough away from Earth to escape the memories of that day. He relived it a thousand times. Each time he came closer to saving his parents from the grisly torture that killed them. Each time he failed.

He found no release until he was eleven years old and was set upon by a pack of older children during a trip to Basille. He was badly beaten, and afterward his uncle stared at him thoughtfully while the boy recounted with dry-eyed precision each moment of the fight. When the tale was told the boy beamed happily at his uncle and said, "I know what I did wrong. Now I can win."

It became the passion that loosed his soul and ruled his life.

One day when he was thirteen his uncle said it, and Benjamin saw his future: The books and the art were his constant and good friends. But the fighting was his lover, and therefore his master. Only in the fluid drama and the instant, final judgment of combat did the boy know magic, and freedom, and life.

Benjamin envisioned the knowledge of personal combat as a large, stingy ogre. Each day he attacked the ogre with his mind and his body; sometimes the ogre backed up a little, and Benjamin took something from him. The next day, he'd take more.

He read. He analyzed. He devoured. He practiced until he could no longer stand, and then he worked harder. He read biographies of Admiral Simon Barrow, Hector Horatio Hernandez, Wilkington Mosher, and dozens of others. He studied the holos of Duelists in action, and he marveled at the superhuman skill. And then he began to see it; the patterns, the techniques. It was not superhuman; it was possible. When it was necessary he used what he learned. And he was never beaten twice in the same way.

On his seventeenth birthday he achieved his life's ambition. After three days of competition among thousands of hopefuls from every part of the Great Domain, he won acceptance into the premier Duel School. Barrow Academy. It was the happiest day of his life. After six years of intense study and practice Benjamin considered himself tough, fearless, and skilled. On his first day at Barrow Academy he learned that he knew nothing. Nothing at all.

The elevator stopped and Slate stepped away from old ghosts and back into business. He walked past the line of people that stretched from the corridor to Darret Longley's desk. The tiny man took the folded sketch of the Digger's Lounge from Slate and put it in a drawer without looking at it. "I'm busy, Duelist. Next time you want to see me, you wait in line." He turned away and an unctuous smile spread across his face as he looked up at a beautiful young woman. "Whatever you want, the answer is yes."

When Slate entered his room Leonora was sitting in the only chair, half asleep and still holding the small bottle of oil. She jerked awake and said, "I hope you don't mind, Ben. I didn't want to be alone."

He sat on the bed and rubbed his eyes. "I'm glad you're here, Leonora. I want to talk with you."

She reached for his hand and squeezed it gently. "About what?"

"Everything. Nothing. You decide."

"All right." She smiled and began to speak. Her words were soft and rhythmic. He followed them and remembered again what it was to be terrified, defenseless, and alone. Leonora was childlike, naive. But he saw a youthful strength in her; she was a lion cub, now only playing with life. So very easy to be with . . .

He closed his eyes and the ache in him ebbed away, like fog drifting from his mind. But then it formed a cloud just beyond the reach of his senses. It took shape around the woman and he stared until his mind recoiled; it couldn't be. But there it was. As clear and startling as the stars themselves. Leonora D'Meersopol was . . . "What?"

"Ben."

"What!"

"Am I boring you?"

He jerked his eyes open. "Oh. No, I . . . My mind was wandering." He didn't remember lying down. "I'm sorry, Leonora. I need to sleep."

"I can help."

As she touched his temples lightly he relaxed, wondering what that silly dream had been about.

Slate pulled off his robe and leaped onto the elevated mat. The crowd roared its approval and he roared back at them until the din was overpowering. He clawed the air and stamped the mat, and the crowd went wild when it realized what he was miming—a cornered mountaintooth, the beast that symbolized ultimate defiance and unrelenting savagery. Genetically engineered from Earth stock—with an ancestry that included Kodiak bear and Bengal tiger—the mountaintooth lived wild and usually unmolested on dozens of worlds. It was a beast stalked only by hunters who valued glory over life itself.

This pantomime had been the trademark of his former partner, whose uncanny mimicry never failed to bring a crowd to its feet. Even now, fifteen years after his partner's death, a few old-timers stood and grinned with that special catch-in-the-throat excitement that always greeted the legendary Brother John. The Master Duelist smiled at the few who remembered, warmed by their shared memory. Those who'd seen his friend in action, even once, could never forget.

But most of them here had never seen any Duelist in action, except on holo. They expected something exceptional from this Master of the art, and he was ready to deliver. He wore the standard gray loincloth and he was sweating comfortably from the light warm-up and the intense heat of the lights. He held out his hands, palms downward, and the crowd responded. Within a minute the grotto was quiet again.

His first opponent was a tall and solidly built young man who glared at him from across the mat. A thin scar that ran from cheekbone to forehead on the left side—purposely left unretouched—was a clue to the man's self-image. A quick glance told the rest of the story. Calluses on the knuckles and knife-edge of his right hand indicated that he'd worked a little, probably four or five years, at personal combat—and was poorly taught. His upper body was tightly muscled, and his legs bulged at the thighs and calves: development geared to looks, rather than quickness and utility. He probably held an amateur ranking of some degree, and undoubtedly considered himself an expert. Perhaps he was, among other amateurs—but he was light-years away from Duelist level.

The challenge then would be to make the bout interesting for the spectators. Slate smiled across the mat and raised his hands in mock supplication. His opponent spit and the crowd roared its approval.

The Digger's Lounge was arranged exactly as Slate wanted it; Darret Longley had done his work well. The mat was twenty feet squared and raised enough to offer a clear view from any of the six hundred seats. From his vantage point Slate could monitor all nearby entrances, and would see any sudden burst of activity among the watchers; they were his alarm system. The aisles were kept clear by stanchioned ropes and five Peacekeepers who patrolled and acted as couriers for last-minute bets between sections.

The Master Duelist scanned the crowd, wondering which faces belonged to his prey. He estimated the odds at about even that they would strike at him here. If not, the attack would most likely be from ambush as he returned to his room. If they were the least bit careless, he'd know where they were before he left the arena. In any event he hoped that none of the Golds was someone he'd known personally, because he thought of them as already dead. They had to strike soon; less than a full day remained before the time limit expired.

Above the expectant chatter and impatient shouts from the audience Slate heard a high-pitched whine. He turned to see Darret Longley maneuver his gravi-chair into a front-row position two yards from the mat. The brother of the deceased Long Man snarled at a woman who protested that he blocked her view. He cut the power to the chair, and it lowered slowly onto the floor. Slate didn't hear his whispered reply to the woman, but he saw her blush furiously and look away.

He studied his opponent again while he waited for the bout to begin. The man was terrified, but was masking it well. He looked into the man's fear and understood it. It was true, he thought; the eyes are the window to the soul. And the moment of truth brings honesty to the eyes. The man was not frightened of him. His was the fear most common in brave men: the fear of being humiliated.

As the sounds of anticipation swelled up again, a young woman stepped to the center of the mat. She was dark and long-limbed and dressed in a frivolous garment that did nothing to conceal her body.

She nodded at Slate and his opponent and waited with professional poise while the crowd quieted. Her voice carried well in the cavernous grotto. "Good evening! And welcome! Dianymede Mining is pleased to welcome Master Duelist Benjamin Slate, of Earth. There are five bouts scheduled at present, and I am informed that other challenges will be accepted as events progress. Unless, of course, Mr. Slate is unable to continue." She smiled pointedly at Slate, as if issuing a challenge herself.

He smiled back, impressed. This woman had clearly attended Duelist matches before; her tone was exactly right. He offered her an exaggerated bow and then straightened, flexing his arms. His answer carried to the crowd.

"I will continue until *you* are satisfied, little one!" The crowd laughed and hooted.

"You'll never outlast *her*, Duelist!" a male voice shouted. "We've all tried, believe me!" More comments erupted from the spectators as they edged closer to the frenzy they'd come for.

"There is an announcement before we begin," the woman continued. Slate could see her pleasure at being a part of the spectacle. "Our Director of Operations reminds you that wagering is prohibited. And she adds that no one will be excused from reporting to work as scheduled. Anyone reporting late will be fined a full shift's pay." The crowd jeered, and Slate chuckled. Some things, such as human nature, were beyond control; even for a Dianymede executive.

"Bet on me, and you'll win back the wages!" the opponent shouted. His boldness brought laughter and applause. Slate looked at him with new interest. It took courage and self-control to risk laughter from a crowd, which might at any moment pronounce a death sentence on a person's self-esteem. This man was conquering his fear. Slate respected him for that. He caught the man's eyes and smiled quickly. *I understand, friend. Don't worry.*

The woman continued, pointing to Slate in the loincloth. "For those of you too blind to see, Mr. Slate is unarmed." Her sly reference brought more laughter. Slate threw her a kiss. The woman grinned and went on. "The first challenger tonight is Borst Kagill of Titan who, his friends tell me, is a psychopath."

"Psychopathologist!" Kagill protested, red-faced.

"We'll see." The young woman laughed. "Our psycho is fighting with double sticks, and abbreviated body armor. Once the bout begins, he is free to do as he pleases, but Mr. Slate is not permitted to strike a crippling or a lethal blow. Are you ready?" Both men nodded.

"Yes!" "Go to it!" "Chop him, Borst!"

"Then, BEGIN!" The woman stepped from the mat, and the bout was on.

Kagill rushed straight across the mat, both sticks raised to strike. Before he'd moved two paces, Slate arrived at a solution which would have disarmed and rendered him defenseless. But as quickly as it came, the solution was discarded; this was a show, not a fight. Instead he merely walked out to meet the charge, arms at his side, letting Kagill close the distance.

Slate judged precisely what his opponent's effective striking range would be. And he saw that the man's swing began much too early. And so as Kagill brought his right arm around in a powerful sweep, the Master Duelist did nothing. The weighted stick flashed past his eyes, missing by two inches.

He reflexively prepared a quick series of punches that would have dropped his opponent like an ox. Again, he overcame the embedded training. This time he allowed the heavier man to crash into him. He grunted and bounced backward in a controlled roll that ended at the edge of the mat. He sat up, feigning grogginess.

The crowd roared its surprise and approval. "Borst!" "Borst!" "FINISH HIM!"

Slate glanced quickly at Darret Longley. The tiny man was grinning like an ape. It was difficult not to grin back.

Kagill was more wary now. He circled carefully while Slate got to his feet. The Master Duelist was disappointed. He understood the young man's astonishment, and his desire to retain the advantage he believed he had gained. But it was a typical amateur's mistake; a Duelist, always prepared for a trap, would have moved in immediately to finish the job.

Slate affected anger and charged. Kagill set his feet to face the charge squarely. He crouched low, bringing both sticks up to chest level. Again, Slate was disappointed. Standing in that way, Kagill was off balance and vulnerable to any force meeting him head-on. Another mistake. Slate jumped high, flying feet-first, aiming his heels at a point one inch over Kagill's head. All his opponent had to do was to move fractionally down or aside, and he'd miss cleanly. But Kagill froze in position. The impact was light, and Slate twisted in midair and fell as if he'd hit a mountain. Kagill took a step backward, visibly amazed to be conscious and standing.

The crowd reacted with mixed laughter and catcalls. They all knew it was a show, but the illusion had been broken a bit too obviously. Still, Slate didn't dare apply any real pressure. Kagill's eyes revealed what was going on in his mind; his confidence and will had dissolved. He understood how easily Slate was controlling him, and he was terror-stricken.

Slate judged the elapsed time to be one minute eight seconds. It was time to end the match—before this man hurt himself.

He charged Kagill again, and at the last instant dropped to the mat and rolled. He passed well under the futilely swung sticks and slammed into Kagill just below the knees. The young man left the mat and fell forward heavily, landing flat on his stomach. Immediately Slate was up and kneeling on his back. Kagill strained forward with all of his strength, but was powerless to stop the relentless, almost casual pull on his wrists. They were forced upward and behind his back, then twisted just enough to force him to release the sticks. Kagill grunted out his effort, kicking the air in a vain attempt to gain traction from the mat, then went limp.

Slate said loudly, "Enough?"

"Yes," Kagill grated from between clenched teeth.

It had been just enough of a contest to please the crowd. They cheered as Slate stood and offered his opponent a hand up. Kagill climbed to his feet and clasped Slate's shoulder.

"I saw what you were doing," he whispered. He was visibly shaken, but unhurt. "I would never have believed—" Slate took his arm and raised it high. Kagill's eyes widened in pleasure when he realized that some of the applause was for him. He

basked in the shared glory and said from deep in his throat,
"Thank you, friend."

Slate smiled at him. "Any time, friend." This man wasn't a
fighter in any real sense. But he'd been a good sport about it.

The next challenger insisted that Slate be armed also. She was
polished and aggressive, and he allowed her to knock the blunted
dagger from his hand before he ended it by forcing her epee up
against her throat and pinning her in that position. He timed the
finish for one minute fifty seconds exactly. It was a dramatic moment which satisfied both the challenger and the crowd.

His bouts were alternated with match-ups between amateurs.
It was a novel arrangement, and he approved; no doubt many old
disputes were settled, and new ones inaugurated in this way.
Some of the bouts were hysterically funny, and most of them
spilled more blood than his own carefully controlled efforts.

The last scheduled match nearly caused Slate to lose his tem-
per and drop the stage persona. His opponents were a man and
a woman, two huge and particularly uninhibited twins, who delighted the crowd by repeatedly thrusting the spears they wielded
at his manhood. At the end of the first minute he'd had enough.
He snapped the spears in two and threw the twins off the mat,
none too gently.

Slate was pleased with the way the show was going. There
were no real challenges, as Darret Longley had predicted. But
he'd put on a good display, working with what was available. It
didn't surprise him that no further challenges came from the
crowd. They were quiet now, anticipating the main event: a
deadly earnest attack from this Gold Team—real Duelists, with
genuinely murderous intent—they'd heard about.

The young woman came back to the center of the mat and motioned for Slate to join her. Darret Longley tossed him his robe.
As he put it on he noted that Longley had slipped a weighted
throw-dart into the pocket. He was earning his money. The small
clerk left to scout the corridors that Slate planned to follow back
to his room. He'd return if he saw anything that aroused his sus-
picion.

"Five matches," the woman's voice rang out, "FIVE VICTO-
RIES!" Slate knew from the mixed cheers and catcalls who had
bet with, or against, him.

"I regret to say," she announced, "that there have been no further challenges offered to Mr. Slate." And then she added in a

stage whisper, "At least, none that I care to make public." He returned her wink, and the crowd roared.

Slate raised his arms to acknowledge the applause and made the ceremonial walk around the perimeter of the mat. Then he jumped lightly down and began what for him was a tradition; he went to the crowd. Part of it was to invite the attack he hoped for, and he was ready. But it was more. After twenty-eight years of Dueling, this part of his profession was always fresh and new.

He worked the front rows, taking his time, and then the aisles. The banter, the good cheer, the slaps on the back and the offered hands to shake, affected him as it always had. Master Duelist Benjamin Slate felt good, alive, and proud of his profession.

As he neared the end of the circuit a young woman was pushed out in front of him. He remembered seeing her briefly once before, when he'd first met Darret Longley. She looked uncertainly at the jeering faces behind her and then faced Slate, the embarrassment plain on her face.

"Go ahead, Babs! Kiss him!" someone yelled. The crowd took up the chant. "Yeah, kiss him!" "Lay one on him!" "No! *You* lay on him!" "And then on me!"

The woman blushed. She was dressed in a billowy white sleeveless dress that nearly reached the floor. Slate wanted to laugh; who wears formal attire to a Duelist exhibition? But he smiled reassuringly at her as the crowd urged the girl on. She looked undecided for a moment and then reached for Slate. He bent to take her in his arms, and her head exploded.

He dropped to the floor and rolled between seats into the crowd. In a quick glance back he saw the crumpling body of the girl jerk twice as two red dots appeared on the front of her dress. His internal clock was running; one second had elapsed. The attack was underway; and again, the Golds were cheating.

Clanging chairs and the screaming crowd raised a deafening wall of sound. Slate stayed down and feet trampled over him. He folded inward and brought his hands up to protect his head, knowing that it would be suicide to stand and look for the enemy. He'd learned about mobs many years ago, on Earth.

The crowd was in full flight now, and Slate used it to advantage; anyone not moving would be the enemy. But they were all running, away from him. This was no good. They *had* to come at him before the crowd was gone; if they fled the arena to set up another ambush, the advantage would be theirs again. He

jumped upward and to his right, raising his head above the flee-
ing crowd. "Here! I'm here!" In half a second he was down
again, losing himself in the tangle of legs and turned-over chairs.
The crowd cursed and jostled, unsure of which way to escape.

His internal clock measured: Eleven seconds had elapsed since
the girl's head had exploded, killed by her own Team. That left
four.

Suddenly the crowd was clear of him, the cover they provided
gone. Slate was up instantly, crouched and ready to move in any
direction. He spun around at the click behind him. A man was
kneeling twenty paces away, the rifle at his shoulder leveled directly at Slate's midsection. He jumped to his left and the rifle
fired. A sharp sting burned along his right side.

He flattened himself, pulling a metal chair close and holding
it as a shield. It was a reflex; the chair would do no good against
a rifle. He expected to die, but the emotion that overwhelmed
him was rage. Duelists *never* used firing weapons in competition.
He saw the one aimed at him and had no doubt that three others
had him in their sights. There was only one thing to do: Stand
up, and accept it. A Master Duelist would not die cowering on
his belly.

He rose from the floor and mentally prepared himself for the
shocks that would rip his body to pieces. Facing the one rifleman
he could see, he said, "You expect to win advancement with a *rifle*? With your face covered like a common coward? Put it down,
Duelist. Face me honestly and—"

"I am *not* a coward!" The rifleman stood from his kneeling
position and tore off the dark headcap. The harsh lights reflected
dimly from his freshly shaved scalp. He lowered the rifle
slightly, keeping its muzzle pointed directly at Slate's chest.

"Marty," Slate said. "What are you doing? You're not a
Gold."

"Call me Hawk, Mr. Slate. You came here to kill Westlake. I
won't let you. From now on everyone—"

"Who else is here?" He took a half-step forward, watching
Marty's eyes.

"I'm enough. Westlake said Crow couldn't beat you. But I
will."

"Who was that woman you killed?"

"I don't know. Just a girl who works in Supply. That wasn't
my—"

"Did Westlake tell you to murder her?" He'd closed the distance to fifteen paces, moving steadily, six inches at a time.

"That was an accident. Innocents get killed. Duelists have to live with that."

"You're not a Duelist, Mart—Hawk. I am. Put the rifle down and I'll tell you about Duelists."

"I know enough. Westlake used to be one."

"I don't know him, Hawk. I didn't come here to kill him." Eight paces. He stopped.

"Yes you did. We know who you are." His right shoulder tightened.

"Hawk, don't do this."

"Westlake is a good—" His eyes widened.

"Marty, don't!" Slate dropped low and brought his arm around in a tight arc. The heavy dart flashed through twenty feet of space and lodged six inches deep in the center of Marty's chest. He teetered backward at the impact and lost his footing as the rifle barked and an angry bee tore away a piece of Slate's ear. Marty wobbled, staring open-mouthed for a second, then collapsed.

The young man lay on his back, still trying to raise the rifle. Slate removed it gently from his grasp and bent to examine the wound. He said, "Don't try to get up, Hawk. I'll get help."

"Westlake," Marty whispered. "He's a good man. Don't—" He fainted. Slate took his hand. From behind him came the sound of a Peacekeeper klaxon. He turned and shouted for a medico.

A middle-aged woman appeared beside him and bent over Marty. "Any poison on that weapon?"

"No." Blood was seeping from the corner of Marty's mouth.

She shrugged. "Doesn't really matter. His heart's cut clean through."

"Can't you—"

She turned to face him. "We'll try. But this isn't ProLab, and what the hell do *you* care? Now get out of the way."

He stood aside as two Peacekeepers helped the medico slide Marty onto a stretcher. The young man moaned and opened his eyes. "I'm not hurt bad." To Slate he said, "She doesn't know about us Duelists, Mr. Slate." He began to cry, and looked straight up. He said softly, "Oh, no." Then Martin Partusian closed his eyes and whispered, "Goodbye, Marty."

Slate touched his hand, unable to tell from whose fingers came the coldness. "Goodbye, Marty." He watched as they loaded the boy onto the sled and headed for the entrance. They stopped just short of the door and the medico yelled back at him, "He's dead, Mister Duelist. Don't forget to claim credit."

⇢ 7 ⇠

He barely heard the rumbling motor grinding from across the otherwise silent grotto. The heavy-transport sled was visible first as a broad plume of dust rising above the stalagmites as it raced around the lake crater. It came to a stop—oddly switching on its klaxon as it braked—ten yards from him. A team of nine Peacekeepers jumped to the ground and spread out in formation, weapons held at the ready. The klaxon was silenced.

Myra Stanley stepped out of the cab and around to the far side. When she came into view again Darret Longley was behind her in his gravi-chair. "So," she said. "You survived."

The comment struck him as funny. He looked back at the door the medico sled had passed through, and said nothing. Darret Longley drove the chair once around him. "You're all right, Ben," he pronounced.

"I'm wonderful."

Myra spotted the headless woman forty yards away, lying in a pool of blood. She trembled slightly and gulped air, but made no comment. She gestured to two of the Peacekeepers and nodded toward the corpse. They pulled a body bag from the sled, showing sickened faces as they approached the remains of the young woman.

"I'm surprised to see you here," Slate said. He was more surprised at her facial expression. It gave away nothing of the loathing and disgust he sensed from her.

"It's my job. You're finished, then?"

Darret Longley said, "Not yet. The Gold Team is still—"

"The hell with the Golds," Slate said. . . . *an accident . . . just a girl who worked in Supply . . . She doesn't understand about us duelists.* Wrong. The medico understood about Duelists. She un-

61

derstood perfectly. "And the hell with me." He turned away from them and walked out the same door Marty had passed through.

Longley stared after him for a minute and began following.

Myra caught the chair and slowed it with a hand on the backrest. She said quietly, "Let him go. We'll rerun the tapes of the past ten minutes. I want to see what happened."

"We know what happened. You heard the radio as well as I did. I'm going after him. Now."

She looked down at him, surprised. "But you said—"

He shook his head, still putting the incredible thought together. "I've heard it a hundred times over the years, and I never believed it. But apparently it's true, Myra. Ben Slate has never killed an innocent. Not directly. Until now."

"What are you getting at?"

"Something else I've heard about him. Sometimes he goes a little nuts. Right now he's hurt. Badly. I think he doesn't give a damn if he lives or dies. And I'm sick of this charade. Now, let go." He revved the chair, breaking her grip.

During the long walk back to his room he passed every intersection and byway that might hold an ambush. He wandered for an hour, praying—and wishing there were a god to hear him—that the Gold Team would attack. *Now.* He wanted them. Not because they were Golds—because they were Duelists. They deserved to die. And however remote the possibility, they might win. But they didn't come. The hell with them.

He showered, put on a clean tunic, and threw everything else in the satchel. At the registration desk he dropped the key in front of an old man who took it and ignored him. He was glad Leonora wasn't there—had she been, when he walked past before? He couldn't remember.

At the door he was startled by a sudden cacophony of voices behind him. A woman's voice bellowed, "Murderer!"

He crouched and spun, ready for this. There was a brief moment of disorientation, then he stood, embarrassed and relieved that no one was watching him. The holo projector again.

In the center of the lobby an idealized spacecraft banked and flew at a black dragon that breathed fire and raked mammoth claws at its tormentor. The spacecraft bored in, guns blazing blue light, and the dragon shrieked. A close-up of the pilot showed a proud, fearless, determined face. She set her features in a heroic pose and cried, "This is for Omega 7. Die, alien!" Snickers and catcalls cheered her on as she closed in on the dragon. The old man was pounding the desk as Slate walked out.

He hated them for their fantasy, and cursed himself for having lived in it for so many years. It was all lies. Fiction and fantasy—what adrenalin demanded, the mind created. Holo-epics. Duelist sagas. Dreams, of the primeval mind. The irresist-ible yearning for—something—that yanked infant humankind from its cradle and hurled it blind and reeling out into the Uni-verse. To satisfy the dreams. For what? So there could be more people, more epics, more Duelists. So Benjamin Slate could en-danger four hundred people who'd paid to see him. So a boy like Marty could kill an innocent young girl as a part of his own fan-tasy. And die like a dog, his heart cut clean through.

And Westlake. Slate knew who he was, now: a retired Duelist gone mad with the game. How long had he been running? The arrival of a Master Duelist—he'd seen it as an attempt to murder him. It was easy enough to understand. After a few years in the trade, the mind never moved away from the "ready" position. They always came—real or fantasy, they came. It wasn't all para-noia. A former Duelist was an old lion: once to be feared, but now without claws or teeth—ripe for taking as a trophy. The young toughs would challenge him and harrass him until finally he would have to fight. And then he would have to kill again. And again, and again, until someone bested him. Or until he al-lowed himself to be killed—which was nearly impossible. It wasn't the fear of death; it was the training.

Duelist training went all the way to the core. It bypassed the mind and the emotions and even the physical limitations that governed all other activities. It was said, apocryphally, that Ad-miral Simon Barrow had killed three men after his heart had been torn from his body. In fact he'd killed only one, the man who held the knife, by locking his arms around him as he rolled to the edge and plummeted eleven hundred feet from Simon's Mount. The legend that surrounded the founder of the Duelists grew to include all men and women who earned the Medallion. Few saw any good reason to explode the myth.

But it was absolutely true that Duelist training went deep enough to require a monumental effort of will even to allow a simple punch to slip in through practiced hands. For that reason, younger Duelists were notoriously bad at exhibition work. But

for any Duelist to allow death to slip in through those hands—
nearly impossible.

That knowledge tormented Slate as he walked the corridors
and hoped to meet the Gold Team. He was ready for them to
come and kill him. The torment was, there was no way in the
Universe he could allow them to do it.

"I said, what do you want, Mr. Slate?"

The woman's voice reached him as through a dream. He
blinked his eyes twice and realized that he was standing in front
of her desk. He didn't remember coming this way. Wherever this
way was.

"What's in that room?" The desk was in a corridor, just outside a stone archway. From his vantage point he could see forty
feet into the room, which ended at a glassite-paneled wall. Beyond the wall was the barren landscape of 652-E. In the distance
were tall silos, which held the ores extracted from the shafts beneath. Beneath the glare of criss-crossing floodlights suited
workers moved on diagonal paths to and from the tops of the
towers. From here the guy-lines were invisible; the workers
seemed to be flying, slowly.

"That's the departure lounge, Mr. Slate. It's empty. The next
shuttle's not for another two hours." She was polite and deferen-
tial, but her tone said clearly that he was making her uncomfortable.

"I'm early, then," he said, deciding. "Put me on it." The
shuttle would be to Bertha Station. He'd take the first transport
available there, wherever it was going. He searched his pock-
ets and handed her the money card.

She stood, refusing to take it. "Just get on when the door
opens, Mr. Slate." She gathered up a load of paperwork and
walked away.When she'd gone fifteen paces she called over her
shoulder, "And may God forgive us both, but I hope it crashes
and burns," then ran the rest of the way to an intersecting corridor, and disappeared.

He stepped into the departure lounge and threw the satchel.
Forty feet away it bounced harmlessly off the glassite and
dropped to the floor. He felt them behind him. Four. Two on his
right, two on his left. As he turned to face them—smiling, rejoicing at their nearness—he wondered how they'd known that he
would come here. And where the fifth Gold was.

He'd never seen any of them before. One of the four—a tall woman with white hair and albino coloring—took a step toward him and stopped. In her hands were matched Dueling daggers. She grinned, shaking her head in the direction the ticket-seller had fled. "She didn't mean that about the shuttle."

"Or about God?"

She shrugged. "I am Kaleen Brady, Grade 2 Expert Duelist from Bellenauer Academy. Are you prepared, Master Slate?"

He nodded, surprised at the traditional courtesy. It took only a moment to shut out everything, and focus himself completely. In that moment he felt real—*alive*—again. "Yes, Expert Brady. Since it must be so."

She crouched and lunged, and he all but ignored her. He knew she wouldn't face him singly, or be the one to reach him first. He was right. Brady dropped to the floor as the real attack came from his left side, a thrown star-disk that reflected a spark of light as it spun toward his throat. Slate jerked his torso backward and snatched the weapon from the air as it drew even with his chest. He continued the arcing motion and wheeled around to launch it back. As expected, the Duelist who'd thrown it had jumped aside. He was a stocky man who bent low and charged Slate at waist level. The Master Duelist dropped to the floor and met the attack on his back, driving the shuriken he'd pretended to throw deep into the man's throat. Momentum carried the dying man past him, and Slate threw his legs back over his shoulders and hand-sprung to his feet. Ready.

Two were in front of him. He turned his head aside and back, bird-quick, just long enough to see a man behind him. Four yards out, left empty, right small-axe, no belt, standard boots. He focused on the two in front as they separated to three yards apart. They worked well together. Brady on his left feinted toward him and withdrew as the Duelist to his right—a slim man wielding a razor-stick—edged a foot closer. Their strategy was to keep him looking from one to the other.

Brady raised her left arm as if to throw the dagger, and made a mistake fatal to the man behind Slate. Her eyes lost focus for a fraction of a second and told him where the third Duelist was. He stepped backward, apparently about to blunder into axe-range, extending with his right leg. But instead of completing the step, the leg drove upward and behind as Slate bent forward, away from the man, and pushed up from the floor. His extended right foot deflected the haft of the axe from its downward arc. In the same motion he spun and speared a finger deep into each eye of his assailant. Now he leapt past the man, pulling him violently around and curling his fingers downward until he had a secure grip inside the man's skull.

As Slate's feet touched down he whirled, swinging the man outward in a full circle, and released him to fly at Brady, who had nearly reached them. The shrieking man caught her full in the chest and drove her backward to the floor.

Slate turned to his right, ready for the Duelist with the razor-stick. But the man had dropped the weapon and now stood still with his hands extended, fingers spread open.

"You have a better chance with the stick," Slate said, breathing easily and lightly. He was still moving into his personal power-band, not yet fully warmed up.

"I have no chance at all," the Duelist answered quietly. "With your permission, Master Slate, I'll pick up my brother and go."

"You're quitting the arena?" Slate asked, incredulous.

"He'll die if I don't get him help."

"You'll both die if you don't answer my question."

The agony in the man's eyes was unmistakable. "I resign, sir. I will surrender my credentials. Now may we go?" The choice was between saving his honor, and saving his brother.

Slate saw no reason for the young Duelist to lose either. "Go," he said. "You're formally excused. Your resignation isn't required."

The man rushed to his brother, who had fallen unconscious. He tore off his tunic and used it to stop the bleeding.

Slate turned to Brady. "And you?"

She helped the man load his brother onto his shoulder, then bent to pick up the daggers. "To the death, Master Slate. I told you, I'm from Bellenauer. And—"

The voice came from the archway. "And Bellenauer Belles go on forever. Is that the saying, Kaleen?"

He stood framed in the doorway, red-bearded and stocky, holding a nine-kilo Barrow leveled at Slate. The blue mole at the center of his forehead stood out like a beacon.

"That's right, Rudolf," Brady said, smiling. "Forever."

"Kiner." Slate half-whispered. "The fifth Gold? You can't be. You're—" It was like awakening *into* a dream.

The bearded man smiled, savoring this moment he had waited

for. "Dead, Slate. I was. You sliced me up very nicely. Want to know what it's like, Slate? To die?" His finger tightened around the Barrow's trigger.

"No, Rudolf," Brady said. "I want him."

"He'll kill you too, Kaleen." He was grinning when he said it.

"No doubt." There was genuine amusement in her voice. "But you know what to do about that."

"Can we leave, Mr. Kiner? Russel needs help."

Kiner's eyes never wavered from Slate. "Sure, Calvin. Take him to the medicos. They'll give him new eyes. Routine stuff." He stepped away from the archway and the younger man carried his brother past him. The bearded Duelist stepped backward to block the doorway again. He said to Brady, "Didn't I hear Cal offer to resign?"

"Yes."

"I thought so." His hand was a blur as he swung the Barrow to point down the hallway. "Deserters." He fired twice and the weapon crackled as it released two focused beams. Within half a second it was over, and the Barrow was centered again on Slate's chest.

Brady stepped past Kiner and looked. "Down and burning, both of them. They won't be back."

"They couldn't anyway," Kiner said. "They never met Alti—"

"Rudolf!"

"What's the harm, Kaleen? Slate's a dead man. Permanently."

During the past few seconds, Slate had reached the astounding conclusion that he was awake. That made it worse. "You were dead, now you're alive," he said, trying to identify, at least, the things that were wrong with reality. "And when I killed you, there were already five Golds here. Is there another one?"

Kiner sneered at him. "There was. He met with an unfortunate accident, though. So they needed me to lead the Gold Team."

Slate's mind raced. "Manner Longley?"

"No," Brady said. "We thought he was part of the Blue Team of Duelists we expected to find here. Hector"—she indicated the dead man with the shuriken in his throat—"planted a bomb on his scouter." She shrugged. "As it turned out, that wasn't necessary."

Kiner said, "The fifth Gold was Walter Marshall." Slate had met him. A Candidate Master, considered unbeatable by the odds-makers. "He was touring one of the abandoned shafts.

Never came back." He shrugged, holding the Barrow dead-on Slate's chest. "It was a genuine accident. Happened two days before I got here."

"You arrived ahead of me. How—"

Brady said impatiently, "Enough, Master Slate. Rudy is going to kill you. But I want a chance at you first. Will you oblige me?"

"Certainly." He'd watched her move, and knew that she was superbly skilled—and hiding that fact. Still, he was confident that he could prolong the fight for a few minutes before he'd have to kill her. There was nothing obvious to be gained by delaying Kiner's trigger-finger. But it defied all logic—and training—to let the opportunity pass unseized.

"You're a fool, Kaleen," Kiner said. "But go ahead. Over there." He indicated the far side of the room. "And if he maneuvers you within twenty feet of me, I'll burn you both."

"Understood."

They crossed the room together. Once in place, Brady took a stance that brought one dagger up in front of her chest. The other she held at thigh-level, angled upward with the laser-honed tip pointed directly at Slate's throat. Another feint, he realized, becoming annoyed. The position was pseudo-Oriental, a pose more than a technique. It was packed with flaws that any Novice could overcome.

The Master Duelist sat down cross-legged and put his hands on his knees.

"What the hell are you doing?" Brady said angrily.

"When you're ready, come to me," Slate answered. "In the meantime—"

"Quiet!" Kiner said hoarsely. His head was cocked sidewards, one eye—and the Barrow—still on Slate. "Someone's out there."

"Rudy, who cares?" Brady said, exasperated. "This is a legal fight."

"You have friends here, Slate?" Kiner asked. He was straining to hear into the hallway.

"No," Slate said. "It could be the shuttle crew. The ship takes off in less than two hours. Let them pass, Kiner. Brady's right. This is no one's business but ours."

Kiner leered at him. "Wouldn't you like to kill one more innocent before you—Slate!"

The Master Duelist was on his feet, hands rigid and ready. "Whoever it is, let them pass. I won't move until they're clear."

"Your word as a Duelist?"

"Yes."

Kiner nodded. "I believe you. But before I decide, let's see who—" He bent slightly to peer around the doorway. "Ah." He turned to face Slate. "It's that little cripple. I don't like him, Slate."

"Tell him I said to go. He's no threat."

"You won't move?"

"You have my word."

Kiner stepped out into the hallway, swinging the Barrow to point at Darret Longley. Slate could hear him now, the chair whining faintly.

"Turn around and leave, little man," Kiner called out. He raised the Barrow. "Show me how fast that thing can move."

The war axe flashed from behind him, split Kiner from mid-back to skull, and carried him out of sight before Slate's eyes registered the movement. A giant walked from the direction of the axe, looked briefly in at Slate, and was past the doorway in an instant.

By the time Slate was outside the departure lounge the giant had pulled the heavy axe from Kiner's back. He looked briefly at Slate and said, "I'll deal with you next, Sapper." A massive hand pulled Kiner's head back while the axe came down once, decapitating him cleanly at the shoulder. The severed head was tossed aside.

Slate was sure now that he'd gone mad. The giant had called him Sapper, his nickname from Barrow Academy. He'd won it by stunning an Instructor with an electroshock weapon commonly called the sapper. The incident had brought him the kind of attention no first-year student wants, and a lot of pain. No one had ever called him that again after graduation. Except for his partner. This man was Brother John's size. And the easy way he handled the war axe ... But this wasn't him. Brother John was dead. *And so was Kiner.* But the face. Not the same. Brother John was big-eared, jut-jawed, and his nose ...

The giant straightened and glared down at Slate. "You shouldn't have killed that boy, Sapper."

Slate continued staring, reaching to understand.

Longley confirmed his thought. "This is Westlake, Ben. I told you about him."

Slate faced the giant. "Marty thought I was here to kill you."

"He believed I needed defending. He was wrong. But you shouldn't have killed him. You'd never have done that when I knew you."

"Mr. Westlake—"

The giant raised the axe and snapped angrily, "Kill me if you can. But by the Blessed Saint Barrow, *call me by my name*!"

"Your name—" He felt the strength ebb from his legs. There was no agreement between what he saw and what he knew to be so. The only thing to do was to believe, to believe *hard*, that his friend now stood before him. Once he allowed that possibility to slip through his mental guard, he was ready to die before letting it go again. "Brother John. *You are Brother John!*"

He clapped his hands like a child, laughing so hard it hurt, and danced on the stone floor. "You're alive! Damn you! You're *alive*!"

Confusion spread across the giant's face. He lowered the axe slowly. "You didn't know who I was? You didn't—"

Slate launched himself across the six feet between them. The giant raised the axe—then, deciding, he threw the weapon aside and caught Slate easily, nearly breaking his back in the embrace.

"You . . . you were . . . I thought you were killed! On . . . what was it . . . Lancaster! That was fifteen years ago! You were *killed*!" Slate pounded his back, the tears running freely.

Slate's mind reeled, and he was a young and frightened plebe again at Barrow Academy. If he'd ever been able to call anyone brother, this was the man. Everyone knew him as Brother John.

"What happened, Brother John! Your face, and your voice . . . By the Blessed Saint Barrow, why didn't you let me know you were alive? You rat-cursed freak of nature, why—" All the grief Slate had known at the news of this man's death welled up in him again. He punched the giant square in the face and dropped to the floor, prepared to attack again. Brother John stood motionless and plainly amused, not the least injured or disturbed. Slate was insulted; it had been a powerful punch.

"What . . . why didn't . . . damn it, Brother John, what the hell?"

"Hey, Sapper. You know I'd have contacted you if I could. Look. I recognized you that first day. And I thought that you'd seen me, and recognized me. It was all I could do keep from shouting out your name."

"Why didn't you?"

"Those eyebrows still jump!" He laughed. Then he dropped his gaze. "I—I thought you were here to kill me," he said quietly.

"It seems a lot of people did. But *why*?"

He went on. "I was glad they'd sent you. I felt good about that. Kind of an honor, you understand?" He raised his head and his eyes drilled into Slate's. "But then I thought, maybe—" His voice trailed off to silence.

Slate saw sadness, a bottomless pit.

The giant put his hand on Slate's shoulder. "Let's go sit in a lounge. Still only drinking water?"

"When I can afford it."

Brother John turned to go, then stopped and looked back toward the doorway. "Wait. Are any of that Gold Team still alive?"

"Not so it matters," Slate said. "Kiner cheated. Gold forfeits." He noted that his friend had unconsciously reestablished their partnership. It felt good. He turned to Darret Longley, who was watching them without expression. "Will you come with us?"

"I have work to finish, Ben. I'll find you two later."

They turned and walked side by side down the long corridor.

Kaleen Brady heard them go, thanking whatever powers there were that Slate didn't consider her death necessary any longer. With Kiner dead, it would have been suicide—permanent suicide—to face the Master Duelist. Only Kiner could take her to . . . what did he call them? Alti F'ir. She hadn't believed him at first. Who would? But he'd shown her what his transmuted body could do. That thing he'd done with the knife . . .

She listened until she heard the giant and the Master Duelist turn the corner, then stepped out into the hallway. The little man sat, regarding her calmly. When she moved to go around him, he maneuvered the gravi-chair to block her path.

"You're Longley, aren't you?"

"That's right. You and your friends killed my brother."

"It happens, Mr. Longley. He knew that. He was a Duelist."

"My brother wasn't a Duelist," the tiny man said, springing from the chair. "I am." He stretched, flexing his hands. "And Walter Marshall didn't meet with an accident. He met with me."

"Oh my God."

She was even better with the knives than Slate had suspected. Grade 1 Expert Duelist Manner Longley prolonged the fight until he was satisfied that Kaleen Brady had found as much pain in dying as had his twin, Darret.

8

"The stories were true. I was killed on Lancaster. But there was more to it than what you must've heard."

"Obviously."

The Digger's Lounge was back to normal. Slate counted twenty people at the rock-carved bar, and another eleven sharing three tables that had been pushed together. The platform and the seats were gone. Across the grotto the perpetual soccer game was going strong. Curses and cheers echoed through the vast open space.

Brother John caught the direction of Slate's gaze. "You used to play, Sapper. You were almost adequate. Want to join the game?"

"Maybe later."

A waiter brought another round. Water—certified to be fresh-made—for Slate, beer for Brother John.

"It's quiet in here," Slate said. Sitting with this man in a public place had always been a noise-choked and unpredictable experience.

Brother John nodded. "I prefer it this way."

It was difficult to match this unfamiliar face with the memories that filled him. Slate's old friend had charged like a wild man through five years of training at Barrow Academy. By the final year even some of the Instructors were afraid of the giant.

He remembered the things that set his massive friend apart from anyone he had ever known. It wasn't his great size; Brother John's physical stature hid more than it revealed about the man within. Brother John was exuberant in battle, giving the impression of recklessness. But like so much about him, that was an illusion—one he carefully cultivated. In truth the giant was a masterful actor, his movements and demeanor always precisely calculated. He lived and fought with raw courage and intelligence, and an almost inhuman discipline. The awesome brute power was real enough; but Brother John had learned to hide his true skills behind it.

Slate had seen him fight Instructor Bortis Major, who taught advanced pike and sword, six weeks before graduation. It was scheduled as a training exhibition to scare the hell out of first-year students. But it was clear from the start of the match that Bortis Major had something else in mind. He was going to humiliate Brother John, teach this enthusiastic upstart a lesson in humility.

Brother John played his role well, staying on the defensive. Bortis Major was lightning-quick with the seven-foot pike, thrusting and stabbing, whirling, slashing and dancing over the hard-packed dirt, always forcing Brother John back, back. But then Bortis turned vicious, and attacked in earnest. Brother John fended him off for a while, and then allowed himself to be driven to the edge of the circle painted on the ground. He stepped out of the circle, and bowed to his opponent. The audience cheered wildly. That should have been the end of it.

But Bortis was furious that he had not been able to strike Brother John during the exercise. In violation of every rule Duelists live by, Bortis slammed the butt of his pike into the bowed head of Brother John. From five rows back in the crowd Slate heard the blow like a distant clap of thunder. Brother John took a half-step backward—the blow would have felled most men—and smiled at Bortis. Slate and other senior students ran to the ring. Brother John held up his hand to keep them back.

Blood was streaming from under his brown and shaggy hair onto his face. He appeared not to notice. "I believe, Instructor Major, that the bout is ended."

"In that case, you are a cowardly puppy!" snapped Bortis. "I have just challenged you, you young fool. Do you have the courage to fight? A real fight?"

Brother John nodded his head, never taking his eyes off Bortis.

"Since it must be so." It was the ritualistic acceptance of a death match between Duelists. Everyone knew what now must happen.

Bortis lunged immediately, aiming the razor-tip of the pike at

Brother John's midsection. Brother John parried just in time. Or so it seemed. He reeled backward, apparently off balance, and roared as he tried to bring his pike up to meet the inevitable blow that would follow. It was a devastating sweep from the blunt end of the weapon that caught Brother John squarely in the face. Blood spurted, and Brother John collapsed to his knees, his own pike dangling loosely from his hand. Bortis charged, and it cost him his life.

As Bortis lunged to disembowel Brother John, his pike was swept away by a massive left hand. Slate barely caught the next move, and he knew that Bortis Major never saw it. But suddenly Bortis was rising upwards, screaming, his chest neatly impaled on Brother John's pike. Up, up rose Bortis, until his feet were dangling a yard off the ground. Brother John roared again, shaking the pike and Bortis as if he were shaking a toy. He climbed slowly to his feet, the pike and the impaled Bortis held aloft. Then he reared back and whipped the pike forward. Bortis flew off the pike and landed twenty feet away, crumpled in a pile, blood pooling on the ground beneath him.

Incredibly, he was still alive. Brother John calmly dropped his pike and walked over to him. He reached down and took a handful of Bortis's hair, lifting his head a few inches off the ground.

"I believe, Instructor Major, that the bout is ended," he growled. And he snapped his hand back, tearing the head of Bortis Major from his body. He tossed it into the dirt and spit on it. That final action became one of the giant's trademarks; he removed the heads of those who challenged him.

It was said, later, that Brother John had saved himself with a lucky blow. Brother John agreed. But Slate knew better. The death match had been carefully controlled by Brother John, from beginning to end. And Slate knew that even the display of rage and brute strength at the finish of the match had been meticulously crafted to present the desired message:

I am Brother John. Do not challenge me.

Slate finished his water and looked at his old friend. What had happened? They had traveled together for twelve years after graduation, fighting on half the worlds of the Great Domain. They became brothers, in the truest sense. Then on the first day of the Domain-Standard year 2305, Brother John announced that he'd signed on to fight for the Gaasmund Movement. It was a noble cause, one they both believed in. But Slate wanted nothing to do with organized warfare. For him, single combat was the only way for a Duelist to fight. Or to live.

They argued and eventually parted company, still as brothers. One year, Brother John had said. One year later he would resign and find his brother.

The news of Brother John's death shattered Slate; half of him was dead. He didn't fight for nearly a year, taking on menial jobs on world after world. The Duelist's Union issued an ultimatum. Duelists may not be inactive for more than one year, and retain credentials and license. His choice was clear. Fight, or resign. He could not resign.

For the next three years he fought like a demon, everywhere he could get a match: anyone, anywhere, any time. He accepted death matches from Duelists senior to himself. And killed 190 members of his profession; the frenzy would not die. As a result he earned Grade 1 Expert rank in near-record time.

Then, on orders from the Commandant of Barrow Academy, he returned to his school. Eventually the company of friends, those who also had loved Brother John, cut into his rage. He stayed and taught unarmed combat for five years.

They were good years. He traveled often, mastered new styles and techniques as they were developing in the field, and returned to pass them on to students and other faculty.

At the end of his contract he became restless and moved on, believing his grief was finally buried. He yearned for the life he had loved, the free life of a Duelist: to travel as he pleased, when he pleased. To visit the great museums and libraries of the Great Domain and to see the things that could not be, but were. And to see a thousand and more worlds, every one the same and every one unique. There was always opportunity to earn a living.

There were aspects of the life that Slate despised, chief among them the death of innocents. Brother John had not mentioned Marty since their encounter outside the departure lounge. Perhaps his old friend had satisfied himself that Ben Slate was still Ben Slate. But what about Brother John? Was *he* still the same man beneath this new face? No, Slate decided. He couldn't be. But it made no difference.

"I said, do you want another?"

"No. Thanks." Slate cleared his mind. "So. What happened on Lancaster?"

"I won't be able to tell you all of it, Sapper. There are things that were done to my mind that I don't understand. Whole chunks of my life are a blank, beginning with Lancaster. That was fifteen years ago, objectively speaking. But to me it was only two years ago. Do you understand?"

"Of course not. They said you were dead, and you say they were right. And Rudy Kiner—"

"I'll get to that." He swallowed the beer and signaled for another. "I remember being killed on Lancaster, but it wasn't from the battle." He paused, closed his eyes for a moment. "There were three of us left on the field. Everyone else was dead, or close to it. Do you remember Ravi?"

"Not immediately. Who was he?"

"She. Ravi DeKampura."

Slate thought for a moment. "Yes! Blessed Saint Barrow, I haven't thought of her in years." Ravi had been a student at the Academy, three years behind Brother John and Slate. He remembered her as a promising student, a beautiful and headstrong young girl from Atlantis. Slate also recalled that Ravi and Brother John had been lovers.

"She was there on Lancaster with you?"

"Yes," Brother John said. Slate heard the bitterness in his voice. "She was one of the three left standing. We had won, Sapper. The Bordelons were finally defeated, at Lancaster."

"I remember. The Gaasmund Movement was respectable from that day on. But the ideals didn't last long, did they?"

" 'Nobility is the first casualty of victory.' Do you remember who said that?"

"It sounds familiar."

"Commandant Pritcher. Barrow Academy. Lecture 974, 'After War.' First quarter, 2290."

Slate laughed. "What time of the day?"

"Some things I remember so well," Brother John said. "Others—" He shrugged and signaled for the waiter. "Three more," he told her.

"Nothing, thanks," Slate said.

"Ravi is the one who killed me," Brother John said.

"What? But how? Why?"

Brother John laughed. "You're a Duelist to the core, Sapper. The first thing you want to know is, how? How did that little

woman kill the ferocious Brother John?" His laugh turned bitter.
"What technique did she use? Is that what you want to know?"

"Sorry." But he did want to know. How could Ravi have overcome Brother John? How could anyone?

"It's a fair question. And it's one of the things I remember
with crystal clarity." The waiter brought the beers, and Brother
John gulped them down. "Again," he said.

"It was an epic battle, Sapper. Epic! Both sides agreed to that
one final battle, and the Peacekeepers were circling to blast the
first side caught cheating. No firing weapons, no vehicles." He
smiled, remembering. Javelins, then spears—and then the real
test. "Ravi was magnificent! She used a broadsword at the end,
when the fighting was close. Blessed Saint Barrow, she must
have killed thirty of them! I finished with one group and when
I turned around she was down, bleeding from the head. I ripped
the tunic from a dead Bordelon soldier and started mopping her
face with it, to see the wound. She said my name and reached for
me, and . . ." His voice was barely audible.

"You don't have to tell me, Brother."

"Yes I do! You asked, didn't you? How did she do it, isn't that
what you want to know?" He was shouting now, his voice shaking. Several people in the lounge looked over at the two. Slate
could read the fear in their eyes. A few began edging away.

"Brother John, it doesn't . . ."

"Sorry, Sapper. You know how I felt about Ravi." He fought
for control, and won. He grinned. "Best bedmate I ever had,
friend. That girl could ride me into the ground. And she did, I
guess!" He laughed and pounded the stone table with a meaty
fist. The empty glasses bounced and danced. The eleven people
got up from the tables and left.

Brother John spit the words out quickly, as if he couldn't wait
for them to be gone. "So, I was holding her. All of a sudden my
belly split open. It hurt, Sapper. It really hurt. I stepped back, and
Ravi had a bloody knife in her hand. I should have killed her.
And I could have, even with my guts hanging out like that. But
I didn't want to. I just wanted to stop her bleeding, and hold her
some more. Can you understand that?"

Slate nodded. Yes, he could understand that.

"Well, I can't." The giant sighed. "I reached for her. I wanted
to know what was wrong. Then there was someone on my back.
I swung before I looked. It was Crow, and he was trying to pull

me to safety. Luckily I only brushed him. He was alive, but out. That's got to be what saved him from Ravi. Anyway, there had to have been some kind of drug on that knife. I passed out."

"You died, you said?"

"Not yet. I opened my eyes, and there was Ravi, sitting on my chest. She still had the knife. I tried to move. This time I was going to kill her. But I couldn't. I was numb, from the neck down. Just as if I didn't have a body anymore."

"Brother John, this is too . . ."

"Let me finish," he said quietly. "This is the first time I've said these things, but I've seen them happening a thousand times."

"Sure."

"I still wanted to know what was wrong, but I couldn't speak. I didn't have to ask. Ravi wanted to tell me. She put the edge of the knife under my nose and pushed. I felt that, all right. She said she'd been waiting for me to wake up, so she could say goodbye properly. And she kept sawing that knife back and forth. I could feel it scrape bone.

"She said something about a new army and that I was unacceptable, the way I was. I couldn't understand what she was talking about. But I remember the words. She said she was honoring me by killing me personally. She told me that my death would unite us forever. And she kept going with that knife. Saint Barrow, it hurt!" He remembered. Slowly, steadily, expertly, she had butchered him. "And all the while she was so casual, talking, just as if we were having a meal together and she was carving up a steak."

The pain from the knife was gone. But not from the words: *You're dying. Why do you have to die so quickly?*

Brother John saw the pain in Slate's eyes. *Should I tell him all of it?* "Then she told me that her new army would soon take the whole Great Domain. 'I'm a General,' she said. 'You didn't know I was a General, did you, lover?' Then she put the knife back to my throat, and began slicing down to my belly. She said, 'I'll tell them how you died. They'll like that.' She threw the knife away. Then she kissed me. I think that's when I died, Sapper."

Slate couldn't speak. He snatched a tumbler of coffee from a passing waiter and gulped it down, choking on the scalding liquid. "I've heard enough. That's enough, damn it, enough!"

"I'm sorry. I couldn't stop, once I got started."

Brother John pushed back from the table. He'd forgotten how people—living people—reacted. "Look, Sapper, maybe we can talk later. I've got to go back to work."

Slate nodded. "I'll sign the check." He stood and walked to the bar, not looking back.

Brother John lifted an empty glass and studied the chaotic patterns of reflected light. When he'd returned to life he was empty and screaming like an infant. And then the systematic torture, that went on for weeks. The glass shattered and dug deeply into his palm. He watched impassively as the red stain spread over the table. He was not concerned; already the bleeding had stopped. Within ten minutes there would be no sign of the cut.

He looked up and watched Slate pass through the exit. *Beasts*, he thought. *Alti F'ir. And Ravi. They'll come for me again, Sapper. If we're together they'll have you too. They'll like that.*

"Her name was Barbara Ann Canterbury, Mr. Slate. Babs, for short. I spoke to her family this morning. They don't want anything from you. But they asked me to pass the word on to them, if you're killed before you leave here." Myra Stanley pushed the envelopes back across the desk at him. In them were letters that he'd hoped might mean something. He'd spent half the night writing them, and found that there wasn't much to say. Myra had refused to give him the addresses. "As for Martin Partusian, he had no family of record."

"Then there's nothing I can do." He pocketed the envelopes and stood.

"No." She watched him until he reached the door. She'd decided in advance how to handle the interview he'd requested. But now, having seen his eyes, she wasn't so sure. Maybe Manner Longley had been right about him. "Ben," she said quietly. "Wait."

Half an hour later he set down an empty glass. "Twins, eh?"

"Identical. Manner was back here for three days after the explosion before he told me who he really was. I'd never have known."

"I can't help wondering why he told you at all," Slate said. "He didn't need your help."

"He was concerned that his father would be looking for him and Darret. He asked me to route all inquiries to him. His father . . . the mother had just died, you know."

"So that part of his story was true."

"It was all true, except for the name change and the broken back. He told me what he had in mind, and I agreed to keep quiet about it. As long as he could guarantee that no one else would be injured."

Slate nodded. "I see. But isn't there an inconsistency? When I first came to you—"

"That was about a game that I consider legalized murder. Manner Longley had a legitimate and honorable reason to act. I have little regard for your profession. But I respect principles, Ben, no matter who holds them." She offered her hand across the desk. "And I think I may have been wrong about you. Truce?"

He stood and took the offered hand. "Thank you, Myra. I appreciate that."

"Goodbye, Ben."

A thought occurred to him. "Will you come to my room tonight?"

She glared at him. "You presume too much, Mr. Slate!"

"Myra—" His uncle had taught him that all of the Slate men had an infallible 'roguish but innocent' look; it was done with the eyebrows. "I want to make it a proper goodbye, to a few people. I'd be pleased if you could be among them."

She looked at him suspiciously. "My social life is quite adequate already, Mr. . . ." And then she laughed. "Sure, Ben. I'll be there. Thank you."

That evening four of them met in Slate's room. It was apparent from the first half hour that his matchmaking instincts were on target. Sweetie would be proud, he thought. He was disappointed that Manner Longley couldn't be found; Leonora had a "perfect" friend for him. But he understood the Long Man's absence. He'd avenged his brother's murder, and would now be mourning privately.

It had seemed only natural that Brother John and Myra would gravitate toward one another. The one complemented and added to the energy and physical presence of the other. The Director of Operations had loosed her hair, put on a semiformal gown, and—to Slate's amazement—was stunningly beautiful.

As he watched Brother John he saw in his friend something he had never seen before: shyness. But because she liked him, Myra Stanley put the giant at ease with only a few words. His eager-to-please grin became a permanent fixture as he fawned over her like a small boy who'd just discovered what hormones were about.

Leonora was dressed casually in a white one-piece jumpsuit, and was fascinated with the both of them. As a child might she giggled and nudged Slate every time Myra and Brother John seemed lost in each other's eyes, or when the giant leaped to his feet to refill Myra's wineglass.

Myra had agreed to have the room set at full gravity. Even so, the housing supervisor had refused adamantly, citing his over-strained budget, until the proper degree of threat and the correct bribe amount had been delivered.

They talked long into the night, mostly about homes, and childhoods, and old friends. And then Slate had an inspiration.

"Brother John. Do the dance."

"What?" It took a moment. "Forget it, Sapper!"

Slate told Myra and Leonora about the two performances Brother John had given at Barrow Academy. "It's artistry in motion," Slate said, grinning. "You couldn't believe that a man that size . . ."

"Forget it!"

But he was lost. Leonora asked quietly, and then Myra began. Within her good-natured pleading was a tacit promise of future rewards for a good performance. Brother John took the floor like a mad bull.

Slate opened his satchel and dug out a harmonica. Leonora and Myra laughed and clapped time as the giant warrior stepped and wheeled about the room. The agility was still there, Slate noted, as Brother John sprung across the room and snatched up a chair to be his imaginary partner.

Myra joined him. Slate was amazed at how quickly she mastered the basic movements. Within a minute she was matching Brother John in the raw power and controlled abandon that made up the dance. Sometimes together, sometimes on opposite sides of the room, the two moved and spun in perfect symmetry.

And then the movements changed; this was what Slate remembered. What was taking place now was as primitive as the soul of humankind. Myra and Brother John were moving in rhythms that came from the deepest recesses of the psyche. Slate felt the cry of the beast lurking just beyond the small lighted space of civilization.

Leonora grabbed up the satchel and began pounding out a rhythm that soared and plummeted, growing in intensity. At first the patterns she wove with her hands corresponded exactly to the movements of Brother John and Myra. Each movement of the dancers was remarked, embellished upon, and anticipated by the skill of the drummer.

But then she was gazing into space, oblivious to everything around her. Slate stopped playing and stared. Leonora was lost in her own rhythm: beautiful, intricate, beguiling—and wrong. It was not the rhythm of the dancers. It was not the dark stalking of the beast just beyond the fire's glow. This was—alien.

As if snapping awake from a dream, Leonora suddenly jerked her head around at Slate. Her eyes were glazed, and then instantly cleared again. She smiled at him and returned her attention to the dancers, her fingers once again following and anticipating the dance. Again, she was perfect. No, thought Slate. Not perfect. A perfect *imitation*. It was as if Leonora were reaching down into the depths of her psyche and finding—not the deep rhythms that the other three had shared—but instead only the ability to *imitate*.

Leonora's drumming rushed to a crescendo that pulled Slate out of his sudden insight. He picked up the harmonica for the last few bars and ended on a high, plaintive F.

Brother John and Myra froze in mid-movement, and it was over.

They sat quietly for several minutes afterwards. Slate turned the harmonica absently in his hands, his mind transported to a world he had never seen, a world that had ended millennia before his birth. And he understood, again, why primitive man had made music and danced against the flickering fires of night.

One among them, however, had experienced something beyond the human. Or was it his imagination? He had noticed it twice—no, three times—now. That first night they'd met, he had held her, naked, in his arms; and something—what?—kept him from letting nature have its way, even though she'd been willing, and beautiful. Then the next day in his room, she had soothed him to sleep with her voice, and in his mind's eye he had seen her become—what? There were no words for the image. Now, this. The music and the rhythms that came so naturally to himself, Brother John, and Myra, seemed contrived, artificial, in Leonora. How was that possible? The only word that seemed to fit—but couldn't possibly make any sense—was *alien*. He searched Leonora's face. Her—difference—had come, had spoken briefly, and was gone. Whatever it was, Leonora had no awareness of it. Somehow he was sure of that.

The silence was more eloquent than applause. "Thank you, my friends," Brother John said solemnly. "Thank you." Myra wrapped herself in his arms.

Leonora kissed Slate on the cheek. "I haven't had friends since I left Meersopol."

"Now you have three," Slate said.

"But you're leaving."

Slate nodded. "Tomorrow." Leonora turned away and said nothing.

Brother John said, "So am I."

The three of them looked at the giant. Myra said, "Why?"

He looked back at her and averted his eyes.

Slate was overjoyed at the abrupt announcement. He'd asked his friend repeatedly to join him again. Brother John had agreed only to consider it. And he'd refused outright to speak about Kiner's, or his, apparent return to life. One thing about the giant had not changed: He couldn't be pressured; when he was ready, he would answer. And now it seemed there would be a time for that.

Slate answered Myra's question, choosing his words carefully. "It's known now who he is and what he was." There was no need to explain anything else.

Brother John smiled at him gratefully. "That's right." His mind raced. Was any of this right? Fifteen years ago they had taken his life and made him into a monster. He was not fit to live as a man. But now he remembered what it was to be *alive* . . . He wanted to go with Slate. But when they found him again . . . He'd tell Sapper the truth, and let him decide. Tomorrow.

There was a timid knock on the door, and a messenger passed an envelope through before the door was fully open. "It's marked urgent, Mr. Slate." He left immediately.

"Good news?" Brother John asked dryly.

"From Barrow," Slate said, reading the to/from box. "Transmitted twenty minutes ago by warpsignal." He scanned it quickly and passed it to Brother John without comment. It read:

Dest. Master Duelist Benjamin Slate Dianymede Site 652-E
Orig.   John C. Pritcher   Commandant, Barrow Acad-

emy (In Situ) [BCST 2X: 14:23:16 Domain Zulu : 05/29/20
Standard : **NOREPNEC**]
Ms 1   Ben—Am assuming you won't have heard the
news yet, out where you are. Miyoshi, Lochmann, and
Kin'Te Academies were attacked and destroyed within the
past six hours. No indication yet of who, how, or why. No
apparent survivors.
Ms 2   Have issued a Domain-wide call (I chair the Un-
ion this year) to Duelists. My Peacekeeper friends in the Pa-
cifico Belt have already dispatched half their ships, will
arrive in three days. Others to follow. The game and the
Tournaments are herewith suspended until further notice.
Come home, son.
END

Myra read over the shoulder of the seated giant. She said to
Slate, "Tell me your reply, Ben. I'll leave now and send it personally."

"No reply is necessary," Slate said. "The Colonel knows I'll
be there. When is the next shuttle to Bertha Station?"

"Tomorrow, at 1125 hours."

"Nothing before then?"

"Nothing as fast as the shuttle. And it won't be here until
1050. I'm sorry."

"Thanks." He looked at Brother John, eyebrows raised and
asking.

The giant said, "No reply is necessary."

Myra stood up. "We'll be saying good night now." She
reached for Brother John's hand. "Come with me, you dancing
maniac."

Leonora stood. "I should go. I'll see you again, Ben. I'm very
sure of that."

"Stay for a while," Slate said. "Please. The past two days—"
She kissed him. "I know."

She sat in his lap and pulled his arms around her. She told him
again about Home. It sounded like a wonderful place. When she
was ready to leave they rose from the chair and he kissed her
forehead and said goodbye. After the door closed behind her,
Slate prepared for bed, a frown on his face.

Something within Leonora, something stirred by Brother

John's eerie dance, was ... wrong. Unmatched to the human rhythms of the others. Myra said she'd been through hell. But it was more than trauma, he was sure. This was an elemental "difference" that set her apart from ... the thought was a cruel one, abrupt and meaningless: Leonora D'Meersopol was not a human being. But there was no time to find the correct thought.

Brother John was waiting in the departure lounge when Slate stepped out of the elevator. The tunic he wore was the deep crimson of a Grade 2 Expert and the leggings were thick leather that were tucked into wide black boots. Leather armlets reached from mid-forearm to shoulder, and then flared out to form rounded wings. To each wrist was strapped a small iron buckler engraved with the crossed pike-and-sword: the family crest of Admiral Simon Barrow, founder of Duelists.

Across the expanse of his chest were the ribbons and medals he'd won in the Gaasmund campaigns he'd fought prior to Lancaster. Around his neck hung the Duelist Medallion bearing the Roman numerals CCC: Three hundred registered kills in personal combat.

Slate crossed to Brother John and the men clasped arms.

"It still fits, Sapper."

Slate said, "Perfectly."

The two sat in silence and watched the shuttle come to the loading door. The lighting was better than it had been the day before, and the activity was more frantic. No doubt an ore freighter was due. The landing field was a flat seven acres that ended at a sharp line of low, pitted hillocks. Beyond that were the silos. Suited workers seemed to be flying in slow motion diagonally from the ground to the tops of the silos.

"I was hoping you'd be here," Slate said at last. "I went to your room." It had been a strange morning. He had looked for Leonora, Brother John, Manner Longley, and Myra; none of them could be found.

"I came close to changing my mind," Brother John said. "But ... hell, I shouldn't even be wearing the uniform. My credentials expired fourteen years ago."

"You'll get your skills back," Slate said, grinning. "I'll put a sharp edge on you again. You can retest." And he added silently, *That uniform is your soul, my friend. You, more than anyone I've ever known.*

"Thanks, Sapper. But that's not the problem." It had been a difficult night, after leaving Myra. Pacing the corridors, thinking. In the end it came down to one thing: He wanted to be alive again. He would tell Slate the truth, all of it. And then his friend would either accept him or kill him; either would do. But there was one terrifying possibility. He might reject him.

"Brother John," Slate said. "Tell me the rest of it when you're ready. We'll do what we have to do. As always."

"Ben! Oh! And Brother John!"

Myra ran out from the elevator. Both men rose and took a step toward her.

She looked at Brother John in the uniform, and Slate sensed his friend's mixture of self-consciousness and pride.

Brother John extended his hand. She pushed it away and hugged him. "You look . . . wonderful!"

"You're shaking, Myra," Brother John said. "What's wrong?"

"They've taken Leonora," she said, looking at Slate.

"Who? When? Where is she?"

"I don't know."

A voice called, "Boarding! Shuttle's ready!"

"Myra," Brother John said, "how could anyone have taken Leonora anywhere? This is the only shuttle leaving today. They must still be here."

Myra shook her head. "They took a private scouter. A man and two women were logged as leaving at 0642 hours. Damn all Peacekeepers! They just wrote it down, and no one knew until an hour ago! Morons!"

"A scouter can't get far in this time," Slate said. "You'll find them."

Brother John nodded. "What have you got that's fast?"

"We don't have anything that's fast enough. We located them on radar. A ship came out of hyperdrive, picked them up, and disappeared again. They could be anywhere by now."

"The ship came out right *near* them? How . . ."

"Who *cares* how they did it? She's gone, that's what matters!"

Slate said, "Maybe they left something in the scouter."

"No. The scouter went with the ship."

"Boarding!" the voice called. "Last call!"

"What are you going to do, Ben?"

Slate sighed. "You were right, Myra. That ship could be anywhere by now."

Brother John felt his friend's anguish and finished for him: "Myra, three Academies were attacked. We've got to go."

"So you'll go help your Duelist friends, and the hell with poor Leonora," Myra said angrily. "Code of honor, is that it? Duelists for Duelists?"

Slate said, "Myra, three Academies are gone. Don't you understand?"

"I understand loyalty, but what about Leonora? She's a child! Defenseless!"

"You don't understand," Brother John said. "There are twenty-one Duel Schools. Four of them occupy entire planets. Miyoshi, Lochmann, Kin'Te—"

"Only Barrow is left now," Slate said.

"I didn't know," Myra said. "And I'm sorry. But you can't help your compatriots who died in those attacks, and the rest can get along without you two for a while longer. Leonora needs you *now*! Don't you *care*?" She looked from one to the other, and saw the resolve in their eyes. "Then go on you two, your shuttle is waiting!" She spun on her heel and strode to the elevator.

"Goodbye, Myra," Slate said to her back. He turned and walked to the loading door. "Nothing's simple anymore, Brother John." He passed through the door into the shuttle.

"More to come, Sapper," Brother John said quietly. He watched the elevator doors slide shut and turned to follow Slate. "You haven't met Alti F'ir yet."

⇒ 10 ⇐

"How does it feel?"

"Fine, Sapper." Brother John was sweating, holding shut a coil-spring cylinder that measured the force exerted on it. "How am I doing?"

Slate read the gauge. "Fifteen minutes, ten seconds . . . mark. You're supposed to hold it at two hundred fifty pounds exactly, but the needle has wavered seven percent in the last two minutes. Not very good, Brother John."

"Blessed Saint Barrow! Was it this hard the first time around?"

"You were younger then," Slate said. "You're halfway there, you can do it. Remember it's not strength, it's balance of force. The tendency is to push too hard. Keep it steady. Your effort will change as you get tired, but the result has to remain the same."

"Theory be damned." He grunted. "If you want it diagrammed out, I'm ready. Basic, Quanta, New Set, you name it. But this is . . . when's the last time you did this?"

"At least twice a week." He didn't add that he used the hundred-pound setting. "And more often with the legs."

"You would," Brother John said, disgusted.

They were still two days from Bertha Station. Barrow Academy was six days in hyperdrive beyond that. Waiting was difficult.

There was still no explanation of what had happened to the three Academies. They were lifeless cinders now, too hot to approach closely. Forty-eight thousand people, Duelists, their families, and students, were dead. Barrow had been untouched, so far. During the last warpsignal conversation Slate had had with staff there, he'd been asked the whereabouts of Master Duelist Batai Watanaba. All attempts to contact her had failed.

Miyoshi Academy—known among veterans as The Jewel—had been her school, and frequent home. It was an exceptionally beautiful world, mostly ocean, with a belt of habitable islands that stretched around the planet near the equator. No terraforming had been required, or performed. The islands basked in a climate that was nearer to ideal than humankind could ever have devised.

Slate had attended three graduation ceremonies there, and visited informally twenty or more times. Miyoshi's parade ground, Iyaesu Ginza on Purity Island, had never failed to affect him deeply with its simple, overwhelming perfection. It was the true heart of Miyoshi Academy, and Batai Watanaba was its breathing embodiment.

Batai Watanaba was the only human being Slate had ever known who truly frightened him. He liked Batty; two exhibition tours together had established a sort of friendship. Never close, but comfortable. He'd never understood why she affected him as she did. The crowds loved her. When the matches were over they would stand and chant "Bah-Tai! Bah-Tai!" until she came out once more with the katana and bowed to them formally. And five thousand shrieking, stomping spectators would come to absolute silence and return the bow, holding it until she released them.

She was somewhere around Slate's age, he knew, but she never would say exactly how old she was. She looked nineteen.

He'd seen her fight to the death twice. She was brilliant, inhumanly fast, and absolutely without hesitation or fear; every inch the Master Duelist.

Each of the death matches he'd seen had pitted her against established Duelists, both Candidate Masters. He knew that Batty had not issued the challenges. And each time, there was something utterly odd about the atmosphere.

She exuded confidence. But it was more than that. She had a certainty—a complete, absolute certainty—that her opponent was about to die. Batty left no room for doubt. It was not the swaggering bravado of the amateur, or even the experience-bought confidence of the professional. This was a sure, total, unquestionable certainty—as if the match were already over, and the witnesses were merely viewing a holo to examine the techniques used. Her opponent was about to die. Period.

And each time, it was so. Swift. Savage. Brutal. Perfect. Her opponent died—killed by the first blow, and hacked to pieces before hitting the ground.

There had always been rumors that Batty believed combat to have a mystical dimension. He knew that many people held such a belief, and that it was often automatically ascribed to Orientals. Slate's only interest in mysticism was that it made for fascinating legends. He suspected that Batty used her Oriental heritage the way Brother John had developed and used the persona of a wild man: to create an intimidating illusion. But whichever it was—dark magic, or genius honed against decades of work—the bond between Batai Watanaba and her ancient katana was more than any mortal could overcome.

That didn't explain his fear, though.

There was about Batai Watanaba herself something truly frightening. It was not the prospect of dying at her hand that unnerved him. It was the thought of being killed by something absolutely incomprehensible. More accurately, he thought, it was the thought of dying in ignorance, before he understood what that 'something' was.

Batai Watanaba was missing, and her world was dead—along with 48,000 people, only about a quarter of them Duelists.

The deaths troubled his sleep and dogged his days. Slate saw death as the one constant factor of life, affirmed by every aspect of human experience, from great literature to the cold realities of science. Heroes and villains were never so alive as at the moment of death; every nanosecond trillions of particles winked out of existence. And so it was with real people—nothing could be done to stop the process. All that could be done was to slow it down a little, to make death just a little more selective. Duelists expected early death; few survived long enough to retire, and fewer still died naturally. But the others had every right to expect a long and self-determined life. That was the purpose—and perhaps the only reason—for civilization.

Brother John helped to make the waiting endurable. Their workouts together occupied eight hours of every day in transit. He relearned his craft quickly; it was not long before Slate could barely contain the giant's power and turn back his relentless attacks. In the evenings Slate read while Brother John continued to work. Sometimes they talked for hours, and sometimes no words passed.

Always Brother John wanted to say the things that filled his mind and told him that he was insane, and a monster. But the images brought with them no words, and always it was next time; next time he would tell his brother.

The day they transferred to the FTL liner at Bertha Station, Brother John went berserk.

The cabin they were assigned was ten feet by eight and too low for Brother John to stand without bending. It was typical of the newer liners, with cabin space limited by the new Chatterly-Wang Mark II engines. No passenger complained. At the old rate the trip would have occupied twenty days; at normal-space speeds, the distance to Barrow's Teli-Centauri System was measured in tens of light-millennia.

It was a child's terrified cry that pierced Slate's dream and brought him up straining against the sleep-straps. Brother John had ripped through his own straps like wet paper and slammed hard against the ceiling. And then the giant was twitching out a grotesque dance, running in free-fall and spinning out of control in the air of the cabin. His eyes were closed and his mouth was red and working silently. Sheets of sweat flew off him.

Slate unbuckled himself and tied a strap to his ankles to serve as an anchor. He caught the back of the giant's tunic and squatted to pull him down. Brother John screamed and raked at Slate's face, too fast and too strong to handle. Slate chopped him twice at the back of the neck and the big man jerked and was still.

His first sensation on waking was one of weight on his chest—gravity; the ship was rotating now. He opened his eyes to find himself strapped to Slate's bunk, with the Master Duelist sitting on him.

"Sapper, we never were good enough friends for this."

"You remember what happened?" Slate had bandaged the broken nose and the pulpy mouth, cleaned the blood from the ceiling, and vacuumed it from the air. Brother John's face was wrapped like a mummy. There were slits in the cloth for mouth and eyes.

"I don't have to remember. I know what happened. Loosen my hands, will you?"

Slate released the straps. The material would not hold the giant if he wanted to free himself.

"This would be a good time to tell me about it," Slate said.

"I never was good with words, Sapper."

"Try."

"All right. Let me show you something first." He raised his arms and began to unwrap the bandages. "No, don't stop me. This will help me explain." He held the bundled cloth over his face and then took it away.

"Blessed Saint Barrow!" Slate said, not believing it. Dried blood was the only sign of recent injury. "Brother John, your face was—bad."

"It doesn't matter how bad it was, Sapper. I had a half-grain of alchemite go off in my face a year ago on Titan. It pulverized my jaw, took my eyes, crushed my trachea. Half an hour later I was good as new. Or," he said, and Slate heard the bitterness return, "as good as I am now."

"That's . . ." Slate went silent, and stared.

"Freakish?" Brother John snapped. "Monstrous?" Slate felt him tense.

"Amazing," he said quietly. "I've never seen anything like it. How?"

Brother John studied his friend's face. The eyebrows were up, the eyes were wide and questioning. But there was no disgust. No rejection.

He turned his face away because the tears were coming, and even an immortal monster has his pride.

After the butchering on Lancaster he had come awake in hell. He was blind and deaf and only knew he was screaming because he felt the bones shaking in his throat.

He was strapped to a table, and when a hand jerked free, he touched his face. It was gone. He found empty sockets and patches of something cold and wet, and warm bone. The pain started then, and it was like spiked insects digging tunnels through his flesh. The agony began at his feet and crawled upward. When the pain was something he could see without eyes he fainted. Each time he came awake the bugs had come higher. There was no way to judge time, except that the times when he gasped and fell into the dark tunnel were the best. He saw Slate there, and cursed him for being only an image.

When the bugs reached his head it was worse because he could smell the rotted flesh and the excrement that was himself. And when he could hear again, he stopped screaming. He knew when they were coming after that. There would be the high-pitched whining, and the thumping along the floor. Like hunks of meat, dropping. He learned to find the dark tunnel and to fly to it when he heard them. But they would not let him stay there for long; the air smelled sweet when they called him back.

When he had eyes again he saw Ravi's face, and he knew he had gone mad. Her voice said, "I want you. I will teach you what we are, now." When he opened his eyes again she was gone, but he heard her calling him even in the dark tunnel.

He never saw them. Sometimes they left him in the dark tunnel and when he tried to come out the air was thicker and sweeter and he could not leave. Each time he returned he knew that they had opened his brain again, and changed him.

He came back to panic. And then to dizzying sickness. And then to no pain at all. And then to love.

"Love?" Slate had moved to Brother John's bunk, and now he stood bolt upright and nearly left the deck. "Love?"

"That's right, Sapper. After the last time I didn't hate them. I didn't care that they were ripping me to pieces. I *loved* the damned things!"

Brother John had washed the dried blood away. He sat on Slate's bunk, resting his arms on his knees. "They rebuilt me, is what it came down to. Like a laboratory animal. The same as Kiner, I suppose. They tore away everything that Ravi left and replaced it with—this." He held up his arms and looked down at his body. "Everything's the same, even the old scars. Except for the face and scalp. Ravi carved those up pretty good. And you know about the way I mend now. I don't need as much sleep as I used to. And as long as my brain stays attached to the rest of me, I don't think I can die. Again."

"But," Slate said, "you expected me to kill you when you first recognized me."

"I thought someone found out I was alive. It would have been a mercy killing, the way I am now. I'd have come back. But then everyone would be finally sure that Brother John was dead."

"But why? Why did you want that?"

"Because of what I've become. I have nightmares, like you saw. I hear voices sometimes. Whole years of my life are gone, as if I'd never lived them. I can't hold a job for long because eventually I forget what name I'm living under, and who the people are around me. I don't want anyone seeing what I am and saying, 'Look at that; it used to be a Duelist named Brother John.'"

"You *are* Brother John," Slate said.

"And—" Brother John lowered his eyes and stared at his hands. "They're coming back for me again, Sapper. I know they are."

Slate nodded. "That's why you hesitated to come. To protect me."

"They'd take you too. They'd like that. When they were cutting me up, sometimes I could feel what they were feeling. Do you know what it was? Joy! It made them so damned *happy*, what they were putting me through!"

"And they tinkered with your brain until you loved them for it." Slate was sickened.

"I got over that quick enough. Now more than anything I've ever wanted, I want to kill them. And Ravi."

"If they come for you, Brother John, I'll be right next to you. The way it should have been all along."

The two men locked eyes, and new iron was forged into the bond that had never truly been broken.

Slate said after a time, "Kiner will come back again, then."

"If they find all the pieces in time."

"*Who?* Who are they?"

"They call themselves Alti F'ir. I've never seen them, but Ravi told me a little about them. She told me they're God."

"You don't believe—"

"Of course not. I know what they are. They're aliens."

It was the answer Slate expected; there could be no other answer. Still it was a shock, to hear the word—*aliens*—and to know that it was true. Humankind had ventured into space more than two centuries ago, and had found itself alone in that infinite arena. Not anymore. Now there was competition.

Slate said, "You've never told this to anyone."

Brother John laughed. "I'm a mad giant with a hashed-up face who screams in his sleep and forgets his name. Who'd believe me?"

Slate shrugged. "Just me, I suppose."

When Leonora woke up, the light struck her eyes like a physical blow. She squeezed them shut again and covered her face with her hands. Even through that protection the stark glare was unbearable. The air was cool and dry, and she was lying on something soft. The only sound was her breathing. She took her hands away because the silence frightened her, and it would help if she could see. As if responding to her will, the painful brightness dimmed gradually.

She opened her eyes again, a little at a time, until she could see without squinting. She sat up. The first thing she looked for was a door. There was none.

The room was huge and open and she was lying on a thick carpet that covered the entire floor. The pattern was one she had seen before: onion-domes and minarets, alternating in purple and gold. All four walls were covered with textured gold paper that gave light in even sheets. It looked like the lobby of a grand hotel.

There were seven highly polished wood tables along one wall, each with a thick golden area rug in front of it. On each table was a meter-high statue of some exotic or mythical creature. She recognized the griffin and the gargoyle and the centaur and the manaclid. There was another with three sets of wings and bright red disks—eyes?—that covered its head. Another had four faces, each different, each looking in a different direction. The seventh looked like a man with a serpent's face. She turned away; they were all hideous.

Plants lined another wall, all potted and each distinct from the others. A fern arched over to the carpet, a slim-trunked tree rose

against the ceiling. One was bushy and yellow and dotted with
raised purple circles that looked like open sores.

There were paintings on the walls of pastoral scenes, of deep-
space panoramas, of birds, of strange landscapes. There were
portraits of people, depicted in period costumes she identified as
belonging to Earth history.

She could see no source of light; it seemed to come from everywhere at once, leaving no shadows.

Frightened, she stood up to move next to a wall. Only then did
she realize that she was naked. Somehow it felt wrong, here. She
dropped back down on the carpet and covered herself as much as
possible with her arms. Where were the ones who'd taken her?
She'd come awake to their voices, a man and a woman. The two
were shouting and cursing, using what sounded like a name,
"Robby Slegian," several times, and then they were screaming.
She'd never seen their faces. Dry heat had washed over her in
waves, there was a terrible noise, and then she was asleep again.

Now she was cold, and the fear was a colder thing in her
stomach.

"Child."

Leonora jumped. An image filled her mind; it was a picture,
moving and bright, and she understood it. But it was not an image she could describe to anyone. It was a code, as if prepared
parts of her mind were waiting to be tapped. She wanted to run,
to hide under a table. But she knew her legs would not lift her.

"Where are you?" Leonora was frightened, but strangely
calm. "Who are you?"

"Father."

The mental picture-code stung, deep in her mind. She shuddered. "My parents are dead!" The tears came and she didn't
care. She wanted to go Home.

"We live, child. We have lived from the beginning."

"Who are you? Why won't you show yourself?"

"We are your creator, child. We are with you, as ever."

"Where?" She was near panic. The images—memories? There
was no word for them—hovered like clouds within and around
her. They formed into a corridor, leading to one object in the
room.

"Know us, child. And know yourself."

It moved, and her heart stopped.

• • •

Barrow Academy was one of the most difficult places to live in the Great Domain. It was not a matter of location, or planetary conditions; it was a matter of earning the right to be there.

The planet known as Barrow Academy circled Teli-Centauri at a distance of one astronomical unit. Teli-Centauri was a class C sun, very similar to Earth's Sol. From one A.U. out, having a mass of 1.04 Earth, Barrow Academy could have been a virtual double of Earth. It was not.

Barrow Academy was twice a rogue. Two billion years before humankind came to it, the planet was struck by a behemoth meteor. Knocked on it axis and bumped out of its orbit, it crept sunward in a slowly decaying orbit around Teli-Centauri. A scant 300,000 years later its slow meander toward oblivion was interrupted. The planet was struck again. The impact sent it back to its original orbit, where it stabilized.

Geological evidence told the story clearly. Scientists said that the odds against these two impacts, the latter coming at precisely the right time and with precisely the right mass and angular momentum, were—astronomical. But they added that in an infinite Universe all that is even remotely possible is inevitable.

Nearly 2 billion trips around Teli-Centauri began the life cycle all over again. The wanderer produced green plants pumping out oxygen, vast oceans teeming with protozoan life, Earth-standard gravity, a 23.874-hour rotational periodicity, north and south magnetic poles about where a visitor would expect them to be, high snow-capped mountains, low sand-blown deserts, forests, lakes, blue skies, white clouds. It was not like Earth at all.

The difference was in the people who lived there. Barrow Academy had one, and only one, purpose: to change young men and women into the finest combat artists ever known by humankind—the Duelists.

The selection process had been the same since Admiral Simon Barrow founded the modest school that later occupied a world and gave the Great Domain many of its finest, and worst, citizens: A certain man or woman is the ablest athlete in his city, perhaps on his world. His reflexes are blindingly fast, with hand-eye coordination that borders on impossible. He can run ten miles at a slow heart rate. He probably has spent many years in advanced martial arts training. He can live for weeks at a time in the wilderness, returning well-fed, clear of eye, and sound of spirit. He discovers that fear is a springboard, not a barrier. He respects those weaker and slower than himself; and that is everyone he knows. He wants, more than he wants life itself, to become a Duelist.

If he perseveres, he will one day receive an invitation to compete at the annual Domain-wide tryouts on Landfall. The goal: to be accepted as a student at one of the twenty-one Duel Schools. If courage and determination and skill and endurance and luck are all working together at that three-day event, he or she may be asked to attend Barrow Academy. That is the ultimate prize to be won on Landfall.

He will enter the Academy along with 800 other hopefuls. Within a year, half of those will be gone. At the end of five years he will stand alongside one hundred fellow graduates. Never more, often fewer. He will be wearing the wrist-bucklers of Admiral Simon Barrow, as a Grade 13 Novice. A miracle will have occurred. That clumsy, slow, uncoordinated, defenseless piece of human awkwardness will have become a Duelist.

Slate thought of that young student as the transport circled for final approach to the old SugarRay Base on the North continent. That student was him. It was Brother John, and the treacherous Ravi. From other schools it was Batai Watanaba, The Long Man, Bortis Major, the charismatic Wilkington Mosher, and others. They all shared a heritage which had formally begun one hundred fifty-two years ago, in the year 2168; exactly one century, to the day, before the birth of Brother John. The heritage was a rich and varied one: from a band of criminal anarchists called together by Simon Barrow, through a brief period of heroic acclaim by the worlds of the young Great Domain, through times of being regarded as physical freaks and degenerate killers, to today's image of Duelist-as-media-performer. Public image was a delicate thing, always in flux.

Slate was thinking, as the transport made its final turn before landing, that yet another turning point had been reached. Everything was about to change. Everything. The one thing humankind had not found in its expansion into the Universe—competition— had come hunting. Duelists were its first prey. Fair enough. An answer was being readied.

If he was right about Colonel Pritcher's intentions, Duelists were about to go to war en masse. That had happened only once before. Then, there had been fewer than five hundred men and women following Admiral Barrow and his successor, Horatio

Hector Hernandez. Now, there were more than 30,000 who would answer Colonel Pritcher's call. Then, they'd fought against other men and women, who came against them with ships and weapons they understood, using tactics that Barrow could anticipate, plan for, and defeat. Now the enemy was completely unknown. What assumptions could be made about them? Only that they possessed unknown ships and weapons. They'd butchered Brother John, and apparently been entertained by his agony. And now they'd destroyed entire worlds. And slaughtered every man, woman, and child on those worlds.

Little had been said of this during the trip to Barrow Academy. Slate was outraged, and burning with professional curiosity, about the worldwide destruction. So was Brother John. But seeing either of them, no outsider would detect their feelings. Duelist training taught that if emotion served no purpose in a fight—such as terrorizing the enemy—it was to be avoided. Conversely, if emotion did serve a purpose—such as terrorizing the enemy— it was to be faked. True emotion was always a distraction in the buildup to a fight. For this and other reasons, the techniques of theater were indispensable to warriors who faced the enemy directly. Seated next to Slate in the transport was the finest practitioner of theater-art he had ever known.

The ship touched down on the east side of the base, the Leonard Complex, and Slate and Brother John took a groundbus over to the Robinson side. The driver was a retired Duelist, an old woman whom Slate vaguely remembered. She was courteous, nodding politely as the two men boarded. She had no new information to offer; for the moment, all was quiet.

The day was hot and clear, the sun standing alone in a cloudless sky. The old bus clattered along the gravel road, kicking up a tail of dust. Slate watched the familiar landscape as they passed field after field. Most were vacant; some held groups of Duelists, training. There were no students or Novices here. These would be Journeymen, Grades 10 up to 5, working to hone their deadly skills, to learn and to share new techniques acquired in the field. Apparently these warriors believed that the tournaments would begin in two weeks, as originally scheduled. That was understandable. Duelists were trained to anticipate combat as quick, deadly, and final. Slate hoped that the principle would hold true this time.

Other than his participation in the elimination tour, Benjamin

Slate had not planned to be in competition this year; there was no higher Grade for him to win.

The bus pulled to a stop in front of a single brick home. It was a house Slate had visited many times as an Instructor, and a few times as a student. Sometimes it was for disciplinary purposes, where he was flown up from the South continent to be ripped apart and threatened with expulsion. At other times it was to witness another student's ordeal, let-that-be-a-lesson-to-you-Ben. A couple of times for dinner. And once—he was twenty—for his birthday.

Out on the neat, square green lawn an old woman knelt over a patch of newly opened roses. Slate tossed his satchel through the bus window and dove after it. He hit the road headfirst with open palms, did a forward handspring, and came up running.

Taking the old woman around the waist, he lifted her up gently and wrapped his arms around her. "Mom!" he cried, "I'm home!"

"The Colonel won't believe this. He just won't," Maggie Pritcher said for the tenth time, pushing another plate of food at Brother John. "Why didn't you tell us? Are you sure you don't want me to call him home?"

"Mom," Brother John said between mouthfuls, "how many times during the last thirty years at the Academy has General—excuse me, Colonel Pritcher—missed a minute's work?"

John Claremont Pritcher had retired from the Pacifico Belt United Peacekeeper Force as its first and only five-star General. As Commandant of Barrow Academy, he officially still held that rank and title. But to everyone who mattered in his life, he was Colonel—the battlefield commission he'd won seventy years ago, in his home sector.

Maggie pondered Brother John's question. "This would be the first. I suppose you're right. But Brother John! He'll want to see you! He thought you were dead." Seeing the cloud cross his face, she quickly changed the subject.

"And Ben! You're a Master now! The Colonel was so proud . . . well, I'll let him tell you about that. How long ago did you win the Master's Belt? Let's see, I remember . . ."

"It was right around the time the Duelist Museum was robbed of all those uniforms and belts and medallions," Brother John said, shoveling soup. "Just coincidence, of course."

"I have an alibi," Slate said, warming to the familiar banter. This was vintage Brother John. "I was on Aqualine, fighting for my life. There were witnesses."

"Poor ones, after that week," Maggie said. "I hear most of the smart money was against you in the final eliminations."

"Mutually exclusive," Slate said. "Smart is never against me." There had been seventy-three Candidates for one Master's Belt that final night on Aqualine. Fifteen survived. Slate won.

"And so modest," Brother John said. He stood up. "Mom, where is the . . ."

Slate raised his hands in mock horror. "He's still hungry. Hide the dog!"

"Same as always. Down the hall. Second door on your left." She smiled after him. "Oh, it's good to see you two again. Together." She looked at Slate seriously. "What happened to him, Ben?"

He told her everything, unable to explain any of it, while she listened without interruption. Her facial expressions commented eloquently. Brother John rejoined them after a few minutes and sat silently as Slate continued. It would never have occurred to him to ask his friend to keep anything from this woman.

Margaret DurNow Pritcher nee Barrow was a direct descendent of Admiral Simon Barrow, "first and foremost" among the Duelists. Her family had lived here for six generations, since the world once known as Havilon was donated by a grateful trade-confederation of worlds to the Duelist's Union. The planet was renamed, and the old Barrow Academy on Molvar was moved to its new home. Over the decades, three other Academies had made similar transitions, each occupying an entire planet of its own.

As a young woman Maggie had won entry to the Academy, competing in the same way as other hopefuls. In her fifth and final year she'd lost a leg and an arm while instructing a class of middies on rock scaling. The fall had broken her body, but not her spirit. After a year of rehabilitation and clonic surgery, primitive in those days, she'd returned to complete the course. After that she'd gone to war, just as the Pacifico Belt was becoming a major battlefield.

Again, disaster. Her troop transport was struck by a meteor while grouping with others after a major victory. Maggie was found in a lifelaunch three months later, on the verge of starvation. She'd eaten her uniform, boots, and five leather-bound editions of *History of the Worlds* someone had stored in the launch. Recycled body fluids had barely preserved her life.

The man who rescued her was a young Major who defied orders, going off course to pick up a drifting lifelaunch that emitted no signs of life. He was courtmartialed down to Lieutenant. Five months later he was field-promoted. Five months after that, Grade 12 Novice Duelist Margaret DurNow Barrow took as her groom, Colonel John Claremont Pritcher.

"She looked so beautiful in that lifelaunch," he would often say. "It was love at first sight."

"No," was Maggie's standard reply, "he married me because we have similar tastes in literature."

After their honeymoon Maggie resigned from the Duelists against the Colonel's wishes and devoted herself to a life she truly loved, much to her own astonishment. She had always envisioned for herself a life in combat, then combat instruction, and then Academy administration. That was the expected career path of a Barrow. But she broke tradition and worked fulltime as partner in the career her husband had chosen before they'd met. That decision estranged her from some of the Barrow clan. She was patient with them, knowing that eventually they would realize that times, and people, need to progress beyond old patterns.

Five years after their marriage, the war in the Pacifico Belt ended. The Colonel competed for entry to the Academy and became its oldest student, "just to get a little respect from this woman." Five years later he graduated, and returned to his "regular job."

For the next thirty years the Colonel continued his career, rising to command the entire Pacifico Belt United Peacekeeper Force. Upon retirement he was offered, and accepted, the post of Commandant, Barrow Academy. The Pritchers had been at Barrow for the past thirty years.

Their seventy years of marriage produced no children, except for the nearly 3,000 students who graduated during their tenure at Barrow. They called Maggie, "Mom." And they called the Colonel—Colonel. Sir.

He walked into the house at precisely 1815. Maggie set the kitchen clock back a minute when he hit the front door. "It's always been accurate before," she lamented.

"Hot day, Maggie," he called out, ignoring the two men standing in his living room. He removed his coat and smoothed it out, draping it over a hanger. A damp washcloth was folded over the back of a wooden chair. He reached for it without looking and used it to wipe dust from his face, hands, and shoes. He refolded and replaced the cloth and pushed back the few remaining strands of white hair on his head. Turning to his wife, he snapped to attention. "Handsome enough?"

"Same as always," she said. "Sorry."

"Frieda tells me she drove two prospective students over from Robinson. She said they'd never make it here, no sense wasting our time. They haven't come around bothering you, have they? One walking mountain, and one miniature—"

"Hello, Colonel." He stood at Student's Rest until Brother John nearly convulsed him by whispering, "Your *shoes*, Sapper. They're *disgusting*!"

Colonel Pritcher looked Slate up and down. "Well, I don't know, son. You look kind of stringy to me. And old too, I think. Not too bright, either. Ever been in a fight?" He stepped back and threw a left hook at Slate's nose. Slate leaned away and the fist whisked by, glancing off Brother John's upper arm.

"Agh!" The giant crumpled to the floor. He rolled and grimaced, clutching his shoulder.

"Well, your friend here has promise," the Colonel said. "At least he knows when he's met a good left hand."

Slate wrapped the old man in a bear hug.

"So. At last we found them. Or they found us. Good. I was hoping I'd live to see it." He looked at Brother John. "But I'm sorry for what they did to you, son."

"I understand what you mean, Colonel," the giant said. "And thanks. But you don't seem—"

"Surprised? About you, yes. But not about . . . what did you call them?"

"Alti F'ir. It's not exactly a word, but—" He shrugged.

"I see." He turned to his wife. "Maggie, where's that report I wrote a few days ago? The one about Ed—"

"Under the tablecloth," she said. "I assumed you'd be wanting it."

"Ah." He retrieved the folded paper and opened it. "This is

not for public release, or discussion with anyone, until I authorize it. Clear?"

"Yes, sir," both men said.

"Good. I'll skip the parts you already know. Here it is." He read from the report. "Date . . . Time . . . I told you that . . . Ah. 'Captain Edgar Joyce of the Beta Epsilon United Peacekeeper Force detected an unusual heat source from the direction of Miyoshi Academy while patrolling that sector. He was approximately seven A.U. from the planet at that time. Captain Joyce increased speed to maximum and broadcast a standard communication detailing his activities. Fifteen hours later he was close enough to obtain holo-images. He began transmitting them at approximately twelve thousand kilometers from the planet.' " He looked up at his former students. "I'll spare you the description of what the holos recorded." Maggie moved to stand behind him and put a hand on each of his shoulders.

" 'Captain Joyce detected ships in formation leaving the area of Miyoshi Academy. Ed Joyce was a pilot of forty years' experience. I knew him, and there is neither a finer pilot nor a more reliable observer in my memory.' " The Colonel cleared his throat and continued. " 'The following statement was broadcast on audio-only while Captain Joyce was apparently in pursuit:

" 'They've turned back toward us. There are three of them. Our instrument readings are identical and constant on all three contacts. The data matches nothing in the computer memories. I'm recording for future analysis, but the only explanation that occurs to me at present is that these ships are not of human origin. We should be within visual range in just under three minutes. I don't remember when I've been as excited as I am now. That's not the proper thing to say, as I watch The Jewel burning. But this is—' "

Colonel Pritcher raised his head. "That was all. Eight hours after Captain Joyce broadcast his final set of images and audio, another unit arrived at Miyoshi. There were no signs of the ships the Captain had reported. Captain Joyce and his Lieutenant are presumed dead."

The Colonel drank from his glass of iced tea and said firmly, "I believe Ed Joyce was correct. And Brother John's story supports his conclusion. We've finally encountered another species capable of interstellar flight. And we've seen evidence of their intentions toward us." He paused, scanning the document again. "At the end of the report I stated the obvious, and the Duelist Union has affirmed it as a unanimous resolution. We're at war."

Brother John finished his coffee and set the mug down. "Good. Sapper and I can use the help."

⇒12⇐

On that bright morning at Barrow Academy they were expecting 600 ships. Thousands arrived, and more were coming in by the hour.

From every corner of the Great Domain the call was answered. Something new, exciting, and dangerous was happening among humankind. Three worlds had been obliterated—no planet had ever been entirely destroyed before—and a war with aliens—that secret could not be kept—was on.

Singly, in pairs, by three or fives or tens, they came. The larger ships took up concentric orbits, glittering like rings of diamond dust in a silver sky. Smaller vessels dotted every available landing field on both continents, and patches of forest were scorched to accommodate the spillover. Hundreds of shuttles streaked skyward into the mad traffic, taking up personnel and bringing others down to Barrow. It was exhilarating, frantic activity. It was a taste of things to come. And Slate thought for the hundredth time—it was insane; it could cost them the war.

"We have to get these ships *out* of here." He glared out from Colonel Pritcher's South Office window, watching the shuttles drop down to deposit more and more Duelists onto Hernandez Field. The square mile of parade ground had already become a campaign camp, with hundreds of bivouac tents flown to Barrow and set up to quarter the arriving warriors. Everywhere men and women were mingling on the field, shaking hands, pounding backs. He longed to be down there with them.

"I know, son," The Colonel said from his desk behind Slate. "You've said it ten times already, and you're right. All the eggs in one basket, that's the expression, isn't it?" He put down a

108

stack of reports and rubbed his eyes beneath the reading spectacles.

"Exactly," said Slate, turning to face the older man. "We don't know how Miyoshi and the others were destroyed. But if Barrow is hit the same way, right now, the war could be over before it begins. There must be two thousand ships out there."

"The count so far is eight hundred fifteen orbiters, and two thousand thirty-nine small craft. The total is two thousand eight hundred fifty-four." He pushed back from the desk and looked up at Slate. "I agree, they shouldn't be here any longer than necessary. Not only are they all vulnerable to a single attack, but they're useless like this. I'll assume you remember my lecture about the Maginot Line."

"Sure. The most elaborate defense line the Earth had ever seen, all in one place. The enemy just walked around it."

"Good boy, you were paying attention. We'll disperse as soon as we have some semblance of organization. In the meantime I've given the order that newly arriving orbiters are to take up station around Montaigne, and are not to approach Barrow until given specific clearance. There are seventeen headed out now, and at least half of the orbiters circling us will be en route there within the hour. But the small craft, we have to allow down. They need to replenish."

"Good." Montaigne was the next world out from Teli-Centauri, presently 1.3 A.U. from Barrow. Slate, looking out at the field again, hoped it was far enough.

"You've made some valid and professional observations, son. The Union chose wisely."

Slate glanced away from the window to see the old man looking at him thoughtfully. "What are you talking about?"

"We conferenced this morning by warpsignal. You've been selected as Commander of the Fleet. Admiral, actually."

"What?" Slate swiveled around to face his mentor. "That's not funny, Colonel, and if you're seri . . . no, you're not serious."

"I'm serious, Admiral. Very." He was.

"But that's insane! I'm not a spacer. I've never commanded troops in battle. I've never—"

"We know your record. The matter was discussed at length, and you were chosen. I should add that because of our friendship, I abstained from the vote. But I agree with the result."

"You should have voted against me. I won't take the job."

"Are you refuting the judgment of the Duelist Union?"

"You're damned right I am."

Colonel Pritcher frowned. "That's a serious matter, son. Particularly now."

Slate stared, unsure of how to react. Colonel Pritcher had a highly developed and sometimes perverse sense of humor. Except about business. But this was absurd. Impossible. "I don't understand this."

The Colonel pulled off his glasses and wiped his eyes. He said tiredly, "You'd understand if you were thinking instead of arguing. You're a Master Duelist. As it happens, you're the Master Duelist that I know and respect more than any other. But more importantly, you're the only one here, yet."

"Colonel, you're talking about thousands of ships. I don't know anything about organized warfare. I've attended lectures here and read a few books, but that's all."

"Then you know that organization of any kind concerns itself strongly with symbolism. The other Duelists will rally around you. And the rest of humankind will follow behind the Duelists. We hope. Remember, the worlds are mostly concerned with their own defense. What we've got here is a small part of one percent of the ships and people who'll be engaged in this war. We need more, if this fleet we're putting together is to do anyone much good. So we've got to produce a central rallying point that will draw from all of the worlds. Clear?"

"Yes, sir."

"As to your first point, your command extends only to the six hundred warships that will be the core of the fleet. The others will be support, and will be coordinated by a desk-specialist. That's me, until I can delegate the job to someone else. For now I'm the best choice. And so are you. Clear?"

"I'm a symbol?"

"Of course. That's part of the title you bear. Your behavior as a Master has always been consistent with that role, and so we've never had to issue you specific instructions. Until now."

"But I volunteered to fight, Colonel. Not to stand around and pose."

"You volunteered to fill any position the Union assigns you, until this conflict is decided." The old warrior's face hardened, and Slate felt himself transported back thirty years to his student days. This wasn't a give-and-take discussion; these were orders.

"I see. But, sir—"

"I know you, and I knew how you'd react to this. That's why I'm telling you, not asking you. Don't force me to go further, Master Slate."

He took a deep breath and let it out slowly. "Yes, sir." He'd been foolish to argue. The friendship between him and Colonel Pritcher was deep and of long duration; over the years it had become more father-son than teacher-student. But the old man had massive responsibilities, and no maneuvering room for finesse. He'd strip Slate of his Master's credentials without hesitation or regret, if forced to demonstrate his authority. Either way, he'd use the Master Duelist as a symbol. "I apologize, Colonel. I'll serve as instructed. To the best of my ability."

"Good. Now I'll tell you the rest of it." Colonel Pritcher allowed himself the smile he'd been holding back. "You won't be burdened for long, son. Wilkington Mosher is on his way here, right now."

Slate felt the relief flow through him. "Wilky will take command."

"The Union hasn't said so yet, formally. But it will. He'll be here in ten days. In the meantime make yourself visible, and get ready for a training exercise. Brother John will be assisting you in ordnance."

"Yes, sir." The giant, at least, would be more than a symbol. Brother John had a talent for weapons—from war axe to the most sophisticated particle-based systems. Within a week, at most, he'd be teaching the engineers how to squeeze more power out of whatever new technology they put on the warships.

As the big picture formed in Slate's mind, he saw that the Union had arrived at the best possible solution. During these first days, a symbol—a Master Duelist, any nearby one, would do—was needed. After that, a real Commander; and there was no one more qualified than Mosher.

Grade 1 Expert Duelist Wilkington Mosher was both a renowned Duelist and a reserve general in the Peacekeeper force of his native Ynesiez System. Slate had read all of Mosher's books, including the three historical surveys of battle strategy and tactics. While demonstrating a deep respect for tradition, Mosher was capable of breathtaking insights. The battlesims he designed for study were daring, innovative, and brilliant. In Slate's mind he was the ideal warrior: a chess grandmaster who delighted in getting his hands dirty.

The only negatives in his assessment of Mosher were the man's flamboyant posturing and his love of the limelight. But even those had value, now. Mosher's was one of the few faces recognized on all fifteen hundred worlds of the Great Domain. Devotees of the profession worshipped him. Duelists were divided; they either loved or hated him. But all respected him. And his School had been Lochmann, one of the three worlds obliterated. So nothing of the needed symbolism would be lost in the transition. It all fit perfectly.

Slate said, "You haven't lost your edge, Colonel. You had me ready to run."

The old man shrugged. "It's what I do, son. Organize a little, scare the hell out of people, and keep the windows clean. Other than that, my work pretty much does itself."

"Not anymore." Slate turned again to the window. Only a small percentage of arriving ships carried Duelists. The majority comprised various Peacekeeper units, commercial ships hastily thrown into the fray, and private vessels. Even Russel Xavier IX, Regis Vitam of the eremitic Xavier Cluster, had sent his entire Personal Guard—40 orbiters and 109 small craft.

It was the closest the Great Domain had ever come to unity. There were aliens and there was a war. No one wanted to be left out.

The ships were beautiful out there, and Slate made his first command decision. "I'm going out to inspect the fleet, Colonel. Any objections?"

"That's your duty, son. Or should I say Admiral?"

"It's been 'son' for thirty years, sir. No title means more to me than that one."

"Then 'son' it is. Admiral."

The 600 warships were the newest and best available, miraculously assembled during the past eleven days by the sixty-three shipyards of Dianymede and the forty-seven owned by Basalt. It was a tribute to the capabilities of the two great mining companies—and to the motivating power of the Duelist Union.

The four warships Slate toured were like nothing he'd ever seen. From stem to stern they bristled with new equipment. It was discomfiting, not knowing what 90 percent of it was. But he soon learned an age-old technique dear to new commanders: to scowl and say grudgingly to the technicians, "Good work. Now clean it"—and to cut short all discussions that seemed likely to go into more detail.

Each of the warships was equipped with two Chatterly-Wang Mark III propulsion units. They were the newest and fastest engines in the Great Domain, having been perfected at ProLab only months before.

The Mark III's could be run in parallel, which made downtime unlikely. Or they could be yoked in series to boost the ship to the unheard-of normal-space speed of .987 Light. In hyperdrive mode only one unit was necessary, once the initial boost from normal-space had been achieved. And the mode-change could be accomplished in only fifteen minutes. Old barriers had been broken by the geniuses at ProLab; humankind could now cross 300 light-years in five hours. Which meant that in 500 hours, the entire Great Domain—30,000 light-years—could be crossed. It was a humbling thought. What had once required nearly half a year of constant hyperdrive could now be accomplished in less than a month. With stops along the way, and plenty of time for sightseeing. The Great Domain did not seem so vast as it once had. Or as safe.

Brother John was ecstatic over the armaments. He called Slate over the comm-net every few minutes.

"Blessed Saint Barrow, Sapper, you've *got* to see this! We can punch the eye out of a beaksnake at ten thousand miles! And the spread ratios! We can blanket a Luna-sized rock with enough firepower to roast it. All in one shot! And—"

or:

"You've *never* seen anything like this, Sapper! *Nothing* can get through this shield! They just fired everything they *had* at us. Point blank range! Nothing! The GeeBees won't be able to—"

The enemy now had a name, if not a face: Galactic Bloodmaggots. GeeBees, for short. Courtesy of Brother John.

Colonel Pritcher found himself drowning in the complexities and unrelenting pressures of organizing and coordinating so vast an effort. It wasn't the numbers involved; it was the people. So far, more than eleven hundred worlds had sent or promised ships and personnel. Each world's representatives expected their own protocols to be recognized, they all insisted on dealing with him personally, and each group required delicate and distinct handling. He had no direct authority over them until they formally signed on, and so was without the power he'd spent a lifetime acquiring and using. The old warrior soon found his short supply of diplomacy exhausted.

He was beginning to feel each of the one hundred six years of his life as an anchor dragging him under. Maggie tossed him a lifeline, volunteering to act as his adjutant. She dealt with the more headstrong volunteers, and sent them all to work either satisfied or humbled. She was a Barrow, and could use her heritage equally well as a velvet glove, or a spiked club.

Between the two of them they kept a round-the-clock schedule. They assigned commands and subcommands down to the level of the individual ship. They scheduled training exercises and large-scale battlesims. They received and assigned new personnel and equipment. They set up communications and supply lines, support and spare parts, a personnel pool . . . it seemed that every time they delegated one area of responsibility, two new ones arrived to take its place.

Neither of them mentioned it to the other—there was no need—but they hadn't been this happy since their first hectic months after assuming command at Barrow.

Temporary or not, Slate did not like being the Command Admiral. He had lived his life facing opponents one or three or five at a time, relying on his body and mind to work in ways he had practiced all of his life. Those were his terms with life, and he had always won. He ached to stand across the mat from the High Slug or the Grandmaggot of the GeeBees, and settle the war that way. There too, he knew, he would win.

But there was no choice. The best news he'd heard in quite a while was that Wilkington Mosher had commandeered a Super-Fleet transport, and would arrive four days ahead of schedule. Three more days to go.

Brother John was thriving on the activity. "Think of it this way, Sapper," he'd said when Slate explained his mood. "You don't know what you're doing, but that's never been a problem

to you before, has it? So why not keep the job? I seem to be immortal now, so I'll take over after you grow old and die. Now,
I've talked to Mom, and she's designing you a nice new uniform
so you can pose beside me and the other real leaders of this war,
and who will ever know the difference? Ah, sir."

It was good to have the old Brother John back. Sometimes.

As soon as the warships were ready, Slate took them out for
a series of fleet exercises. He divided the 600 ships into three
flotillas of 200 each, and left half of each flotilla to watch for
hostile action from the GeeBees. The others he set against one
another in a round-robin game of war. The experience brightened his mood considerably. He found that he had a natural talent for organized tactics, relying heavily on the written works
of Wilkington Mosher. Flotilla One was led by his flagship
Miyoshi, and it emerged victorious against all challengers. By
the end of the second day he found himself reluctant to return
to Barrow Academy. But it was time to get ready for Mosher's
arrival.

Colonel Pritcher had lost patience, and was no longer willing
to wait for an enemy attack. At first it had seemed likely that
Barrow—the last of the four Academy worlds—would be the
GeeBees' next target. But as time passed he came to believe that
the armaments amassed on Barrow had removed it, at least for
now, from the aliens' target list. Very well. The new priority was
to find the aliens, and take the fight to them. Maggie and Colonel
Pritcher went to work on the problem.

Slate was amazed at what had been done in the two days he'd
been in space. Memorial Hall on the South continent had been
transformed into a mammoth maze of cubicles, each containing
a warpsignal, a printer, a bank of intraplanet phones, a computer
screen displaying updated force availability, and an exasperated
worker. He walked past dozens of the identical cubicles and saw
that each of them was busy. After an hour he had a good sam-
pling of the activity there, and found himself caught up in the excitement. From every world in the Great Domain signals were
flashing in, offering enlistment, money, landing and base sites,
and equipment. These were all valuable. But they were not what
Slate ached to hear.

There were also the predictable nuisance calls: offers of discounted insurance coverage, media teams demanding interviews, reports of neighbors' sons or daughters who were fit to serve but too lazy to enlist, offers of "dead aliens" to be delivered into their hands, for varying amounts of money.

Some calls could not be classified right away as either valuable or nuisance. These were reports of alien sightings, kidnappings, mutilations, or "possessed" people. Slate was gratified to see that the cubicle workers were paying special attention to these reports, on orders from the Pritchers. He believed that the latter two categories were especially promising. Everyone who was known to have had contact with the aliens was profoundly changed by the contact. Ravi and Kiner became butchers. Like the GeeBees themselves. Brother John was a victim, and Slate believed this was because he'd been rejected, or "improperly" altered by them. Or perhaps he'd been too strong within himself to join them. There weren't many known examples yet, but there was a pattern. So mutilations, "possessed" people: These should be the red arrows that would point him—or rather, Mosher, he thought, with some regret—and his forces directly at the enemy.

These calls required the attention of a special team. Maggie had set it up, enlisting local Peacekeeper units in every sector of the Great Domain to conduct first-response investigations. For follow-ups she'd assigned 400 miscellaneous ships. These were hyperdrive-capable, and staffed by 2,000 people of appropriate background from the multitudes at or near Barrow Academy. It was assumed that nearly all of these investigations and follow-ups would lead to nothing. But they needed only one to be genuine.

On his last evening of command, Slate sat alone in Colonel Pritcher's South Office. He was rereading the status reports from each of the 600 warships. They had done well in the brief exercise, and none required significant repair. The enthusiasm of the crews had been exhilarating; he admitted to himself that he'd enjoyed being their leader—symbolic or not. The flight of ships massed against the infinite black tapestry of space was a ballet of mind-wrenching beauty. He'd miss that special view that only a commander could experience.

The door to the Colonel's office opened and a man stooped to enter.

"Admiral Slate?"

He looked up, startled. The man's smile was wide and easy, and said that he was accustomed to this reaction to his presence; he'd have to be. This was the tallest, blackest man Slate had ever seen. Brother John stood seven feet nine inches, from heel to scalp. This man was much thinner, but nearly two feet taller.

He realized that he was staring, and forced a smile. "I'm Ben Slate."

"Admiral Slate, I have spoken just now with Commandant Pritcher. He has informed me that you are the individual with whom I must speak."

"Please come in. And sit down."

"Thank you, Admiral." He pulled a couch from across the room to the desk and sat, stretching his legs. "I am Dr. Jimbalalu Bey, Admiral. And I am pleased to meet you."

It wasn't necessary to stand to shake the man's offered hand. His long arm reached easily across the desk.

Slate said, "You're a doctor?"

"I am. Specifically, I am a diagnostic neurologist. But I am well qualified in other fields."

"I see." It hit him suddenly, why he'd stared. This was precisely the image an eight-year-old Benjamin Slate had locked away forever in his memory. The wide, easy smile. The man who always seemed bigger, more impressive than anyone else. The dark face, the bright, intelligent eyes: Dr. Asher Slate, his father.

The impression was disorienting, and required an effort of will to dislodge. "What do you want to speak with me about?"

"Commanding Admiral of the United Defense—" he began.

"Please, Dr. Bey. Call me Ben."

"Thank you, Mr., ah, Ben," he said. "And in that case, please address me as Jimbalalu." He pronounced it, as before, with that impossible *nnnggockk*! sound. It began between the first two syllables, and echoed for the rest of the name.

Slate tried it. "I'm afraid not, Doctor," he said. "Will 'Jim' do?"

"Nicely, Ben. Nicely." That wide, easy smile was back.

"What is this about?"

"First, your friend Mr., ah, Brother John."

"Go on." Slate was instantly defensive.

"I met with him for most of this morning. He is a fascinating man."

"I know that, Dr. Bey. Did you examine him?"

"Extensively. He told me of his ordeal. I have never heard its like, and I solemnly hope that I never shall again."

"Whose idea was the examination?"

"Why, his, of course. How could it be otherwise?"

Slate shrugged. He was relieved and amazed that his friend had finally agreed to be seen by a doctor. "What are your conclusions? Is he really—"

"Immortal? He was also reluctant to use the word."

"And?"

"He may be precisely that, Ben. In the sense that he heals quickly, and is not aging. But I believe that he is still susceptible to death in the form of massive trauma."

"Such as decapitation," Slate thought aloud. He remembered Brother John's final touch in the killing of Rudolf Kiner. That time, it was more than tradition.

"That is rather vulgar, Ben. But yes. Decapitation would end his life."

"Unless Alti F'ir ... the GeeBees, found him again."

"I would give much to learn their secrets."

"The only thing I want to know from them, is where they are."

"Of course."

"Then Brother John's general health is satisfactory?"

"It is excellent, excepting only questions which for now are unanswerable. And your own?"

"Adequate," Slate said. "My mind has been working harder than my body lately. That's not the natural order of things."

"Ah, the demands of leadership. Please remember to give your body the release it needs. That is most important. Especially to one of your background, Ben. A thoroughbred is not meant for the stables."

"That's a kind thing to say, Jim. I'll accept it as medical orders."

"Which brings me to the other purpose of my visit, Ben. I have volunteered to be a part of your United Defense Force."

"Excellent! I'm delighted, Doctor."

"But they want me to lead a hospital ship!"

"Of course. That would be the natural place for your talents,

Jim." A thought struck Slate. He phrased it delicately. "Would you prefer not to be, ah, spaceborne?"

"Ben, a *hospital* ship! Do I not make myself clear? A hospital ship remains away from the scene of action, does it not?"

"Naturally," Slate said. "In as safe an area as possible."

Anger filled his voice. "Ben, I am Bantu, which contains many groups. My mother was Swazi, my father Zulu. Do you know of us?"

Slate had read of them. Earth, southern Africa. Swaziland. Warriors. He understood.

"Dr. Bey . . . Jim," Slate said, "you are asking for a combat assignment. Am I correct?"

"No, Commanding Admiral. I *demand* a combat billet. It is my heritage. It is my right!"

"Jim," Slate said quietly. "What is your age? Are you trained as a warrior?" This was a good and honorable man. But was he a man for combat?

"I am a scientist, Ben. But first and foremost, I am a healer. I do not dema . . . ask, to kill what are called GeeBees. Although I will, if there is opportunity. My request is to be in a combat unit, alongside my brother and sister warriors. I will heal them, when I can."

"Perhaps—"

Dr. Bey held up his hand. "You asked about my age. I am ninety-six years old. I am in perfect health. Would you care to compete against me in a footrace?"

"No more than you would care to compete against Brother John in a cow-eating contest."

"Precisely," Dr. Bey said, slapping his long legs. "In each case, physical endowment would name the victor. Is it settled then?"

Slate had already made the decision. "Perhaps you would agree to be assigned with me, on my ship?"

"A combat ship?"

"Oh yes, Jim," Slate assured him. "Definitely that. But you understand, my position expires tomorrow. I can't guarantee anyone's billet after the new commander takes over."

"That is sufficient. Thank you, Admiral." He turned and left the office, stooping again to pass through the doorway.

The moment Dr. Bey was gone, Slate picked up the direct line to Colonel Pritcher's temporary quarters. There was just enough time to have the orders formally issued. Knowing the old man, it was a good bet that the orders had been cut before the tall physician entered the office. But with any luck he'd wake his mentor from a sound sleep. A symbolic gesture, Slate thought, from the departing Admiral of the Fleet.

=13=

In the center of a cavernous gold-walled room two Duelists faced one another from a distance of eight feet. One was a tall, heavy man, clad in a gray loincloth and carrying matched daggers. He circled warily, holding one dagger extended out from his left side and the other close to his chest, the needle-sharp point ten inches out from the strong jut of his chin. Two small cuts seeped blood from his forehead and a long gash extended from his right shoulder down across his chest. Courses of dark stain and sweat ran down his stomach and legs.

He trod with heavy, labored steps, struggling for breath as he moved to keep his opponent to his left side.

The other Duelist was a slim woman of average height whose loincloth and halter were a brilliant crimson. Her daggers were identical to the man's and she held them loosely in front of her, flipping her wrists so that the points were sometimes up, sometimes down. Each hand operated independently and at random, the movements at times obscured by the cascade of straight black hair that flew around her body when she shook her head. The woman's startling violet eyes held a look of amusement. She was laughing, moving easily and lightly as her opponent edged cautiously back.

"I am disappointed, Jerzeel," she taunted, moving closer to the man. A flashing arm added a third cut to his forehead. The blood flowed and blinded his left eye. "You are a Grade 3 Expert," the woman said, sneering. "Will you allow your death to be so simple a matter?"

The man snarled and lashed out with his left hand. The woman rocked back slightly and the blade scratched her neck. "Excellent!" she said, laughing. She danced back a step and the man hesitated. "Charge me, fool!" the woman challenged. "Are all Duelists such pathetic cowards now?"

"Jerzeel Berryman is not a coward," the Duelist said with dignity. He reached quickly to wipe the blood from his eye. The woman feinted toward him and he stepped backward, returning his hand to the ready position before he could clear the eye. He spit on the floor in front of her. "You kept me locked in a coffin for three days without food or water. If I had my strength, you'd be dead by now."

"Poor Jerzeel. Here, I will make it easy for you." She threw one of the daggers down, and it clattered along the cold marble floor. "Now what excuse do you have?"

She charged the man, dagger extended straight out from her belly. He stepped back again and crouched low to meet the charge. The woman's foot slipped in a puddle of blood and sweat. She stumbled forward and down, and the man was ready. He brought up his left arm in a straight-elbowed arc and buried the blade in her chest. The woman gasped and sagged. The man jerked the blade free and stabbed her again before letting her fall to the floor. He kicked her body over and snatched the dagger from her hand as he bent to examine the wounds. Blood gushed from two gaping holes that led straight into her heart.

He gulped air and moved like a man at the outer reaches of exhaustion. Climbing stiffly to his feet, he walked ten feet across the marble floor. When the woman stopped breathing, he threw the daggers away. He sat and lowered his head and assumed a lotus position. After a few minutes his breathing was slow and regular, and he was asleep.

The blade came down like a scythe and opened up the back of his neck. A foot caught him flush in the face and burst his nose. His arms flailed and the foot came back again, catching him in the chest and throwing him on his back.

"You lose, Jerzeel," the woman said. She sat on his chest and severed the nerve passages to his arms and legs with quick, deft strokes. The man's eyes widened in pain and astonishment.

The woman laughed and tore off the crimson halter. She wiped the dried blood away. Jerzeel stared in disbelief. Between her breasts, where he had twice stabbed her, the skin was unmarked, clear and smooth.

She held the dagger beneath the man's smashed nose and began cutting away his upper lip. His eyes teared over in agony.

"You are honored, Jerzeel, as many before you have been," she said calmly. "But you were a poor lover, despite your enthusiasm." She laughed. "Beg me, Jerzeel. Perhaps I will have you raised to eternal life." The knife continued its work and the man screamed until she cut his vocal cords.

"There is no greater destiny for a mortal," the woman said, smiling, "than to serve the Queen of Heaven. And now you will give me pleasure, at last." Then Ravi sang to herself softly as she methodically butchered the breathing man.

The image disappeared from the center of the room and Leonora stared at the empty golden walls beyond. Her heart was a jagged stone inside her.

"She is our creation, child, as you are," said the image in her mind. "You will go to her, and learn."

Leonora did not answer. Her words would be understood, but not the revulsion and hatred she felt. Never. She walked from the room, ashamed of the hot tears that spilled down her cheeks. The aunts and uncles at Home were wrong. God was nothing like what they'd taught her.

"No offense intended, Ben, but this is swill," Manner Longley said. "I'll just have coffee, if you please."

They were in *Miyoshi's* galley with a midnight meal of something called smorst, which the chef had guaranteed with his life to be harmless. After a while Slate learned to ignore the pungent flavor, and became accustomed to the purple gel that slid from every forkful.

He filled Longley's cup from the server. The relaxed, confident warrior across from him was a startling contrast to the quick-eyed, fidgety man he remembered as Darret Longley. And yet it was the same man; the ruse had been brilliantly effected. "So, you took your brother's place after he was killed."

The Long Man shrugged. "Better if I'd replaced him *before* he was killed."

"I understand the feeling," Slate said. He'd had the same thought, when he'd heard of Brother John's death on Lancaster. "But we don't have much control over who lives and who dies, do we?"

"That's an odd thing to say."

"For a Duelist, I suppose it is." He thought about his parents, and about Babs and Marty. "Our profession is exactly about deciding who lives and who dies. Usually it's simple. Us, or another Duelist. But in the broader arena, we have no control at all." He speared another hunk of smorst and watched the gel slip back to the plate. "Historically, killing is a grand-scale enterprise. The trend of humankind has always been toward larger, more efficient, easier ways to kill its own. Duelists are more personal in their work—that's what makes us unique.

"When Master Hernandez retired and went into politics, his farewell speech ended this way: 'Many have questioned the continued existence of our profession, following the success of Admiral Barrow's original purpose. Some argue that we glorify death. Others counter that we bring death back to a scale where the ugliness can be seen again. I agree with both camps. And I say that both services are indispensable to humankind.' "

Longley was quiet for a moment. "Politics!" he said, and grimaced. "I hope that's not the secret to winning the Master's Belt. Because personally, I think politics is irrelevant, when someone's trying to kill you."

"I disagree. Politics is usually *why* someone is trying to kill you. You've been in enough small wars to know that." Except for the present situation, Slate still believed that Duelists had no business in organized conflicts. He'd said so to Brother John, before his friend had enlisted in the Gaasmund cause. But he'd questioned those words, and his decision, thousands of times since. "Also," he added, "politics is the physical side of philosophy. It's a process humankind has to go through, to reach a common consensus on truth and wisdom."

"Exactly what I was going to say," Longley deadpanned.

Slate became self-conscious. He rarely exposed his thoughts that way, except to Sweetie, or the Pritchers. Or Brother John, now that they were together again. It was the fatigue, he thought. "Did that sound pompous?"

"No. I've read a few of the books about you. The art, the literature. They mean as much to you as your Belt."

"To tell you the truth, I don't see much of a difference. The things that fascinate me, I go after. And I'll tell you something else, Manner. They're connected somehow." He shrugged. "Maybe when I've learned enough about any of them, I'll understand how they fit together." He finished the last of the smorst and pushed the plate away. "But what interests you? Aside from the obvious."

"Ships. Combat. Winning."

"That's what I meant by 'the obvious,' " Slate said.

Manner Longley, he'd recently learned, was a degreed aeronautics engineer. And he'd amassed a considerable reputation as a combat commander, working the 'little' wars that were always being waged, somewhere. Upon arriving aboard *Miyoshi* for one last tour, Slate had been greeted by its newly appointed Captain—Grade 1 Expert Duelist Manner Longley.

Slate said, "I'm sorry I couldn't say goodbye to you on that mining colony, Manner. I wanted to tell you—"

Longley raised his hand. "Thanks, Ben. Darret was a good man. Now if you don't mind, we'll talk about something else."

"Certainly."

The two spoke long into the morning. Longley shrugged away most of the questions about his phenomenal rise to Grade 1 Expert status. But he was openly excited about meeting Wilkington Mosher. He recounted in detail the dozens of holos he'd watched of Mosher in action, particularly the death matches fought with daggers. "He's a genius with a knife, Ben. There's no good defense against that technique he's perfected."

"I've seen it," Slate said. "And you're right about his ability. But there *is* a defense."

The Long Man's eyes reflected his excitement. "Show me! Now!"

"No." Slate shook his head firmly. "I won't show you. And *that's* the secret to winning the Master's Belt."

Grade 1 Expert Duelist Wilkington Mosher arrived at Hernandez Field with the sunrise. A troop of media representatives was set up to record the event.

The scouter came in from the east, at first hidden in the glare of Teli-Centauri. The ship dropped gradually as it approached the field, then made a low parabolic dive straight toward the holographers. At perigee a bank of laser-lights blinked on from the forward turret, simulating an attack. The crowd laughed at the surprise and cheered as the ship pulled sharply up and away. A siren wailed from the scouter and a bank of multicolored lights flashed from the after end.

Slate watched the spectacle with mixed feelings. It was brazen, but effective; just what Mosher's billions of enthusiasts would expect to see on the holos. And, he reminded himself, even Shakespeare had drawn attention to his touring actors with gaudy parades and vulgar street shows.

At the top of the ship's arc a small dot separated from the craft. The scouter flew on, streaking from sight back into the brilliance of the sun. The dot grew larger as it approached the ground, and a murmur passed through the crowd as they understood what it was. The murmur became wild cheering when the parachute opened with an audible pop.

Wilkington Mosher touched down lightly in the center of a white-graveled circle, in which a mosaic of colored pebbles replicated the family crest of Admiral Simon Barrow. Amid the applause there were scattered expressions of anger from the crowd.

Brother John spit on the grass. "That's going too far, damn it." When he saw his friend's face he put his hand on Slate's shoulder. "Easy, Sapper. If you do what we're both thinking, you'll be stuck with your job forever." He waited a moment for his words to sink in. "What bothers me is all that hair. Look at it. It's not even messed up."

Mosher's shock of long-cut white hair was perfectly preserved. His jumpsuit was silvered foil, trimmed and belted with the royal blue color of his rank. Around his neck hung the golden Duelist Medallion with the numerals MCD: fourteen hundred registered kills.

Mosher walked from the circle, nodding to those cheering and ignoring those, mostly Barrow graduates, who voiced their offense at his choice of landing sites. His trademark smile, broad and white, was fixedly in place. A group of reporters surrounded him and he stopped, shaking hands and telling them all about the dire alien threat to humankind and the humility with which he was prepared to accept the grave responsibility of command.

Slate and Brother John returned to Colonel Pritcher's office and waited until the voting was over.

Two hours later they entered the auditorium and received a smile and a thumbs-up sign from Colonel Pritcher. As the two took seats Slate felt the weight lift, with some reluctance, from his shoulders. He'd done what he could. The fleet was as ready as he could make it in six days. Now it was time for a more knowledgeable and experienced hand to guide the United Defense Force. He was no longer as sure about Mosher as he'd once been; but he believed that the wisdom of the Duelist Union outweighed his own.

There was a cheerful applause in the auditorium when the announcement was made. A gray-haired woman, a retired Duelist whom Slate had seen often in news-holos, rose from her chair and announced that by unanimous vote Wilkington Mosher was designated the new Commanding Admiral of the United Defense Force.

She waited until the cheering died down, and said, "But he hasn't signed the papers yet. Can we convince him?" Seven hundred men and women stood and called him out.

Mosher strode from the wings and jumped easily onto the yard-high stage. He stood at the dais and waited until the applause subsided before filling the hall with his rich baritone.

"Duelists, and honored guests. I thank you for the honor and the privilege you have offered me. Since arriving here on Barrow Academy this morning I have spoken to many individuals who have been involved in the nascent stages of our defense against the invader." He paused and let his gaze sweep over their faces. "And I have been shocked at what I have discovered. I cannot accept your appointment."

He waited until the murmuring stopped, then looked out at the audience until he found the man around whom his plan was centered. "I cannot accept your appointment," he repeated, staring pointedly at Slate, "until I am able to gauge for myself the harm that has been done by entrusting the defense of humankind to a rank amateur."

Slate stiffened and met Mosher's steady gaze. He put a restraining hand on Brother John's leg as the giant moved to stand.

"I say this with no affront intended to Mr. Slate," Mosher continued. "I am confident that Slate has done his best. But—" he lowered his voice—"must I explain to so distinguished a group of *shipboard* combat veterans here, that a leader without direct experience is worthless? Dangerous? The surest way to defeat?" He sighed. "No. I will not insult you by belaboring what you all have observed for yourselves. I know this is so, because you think as I do. You share my concerns. We are as one. One *weapon*!" Mosher's practiced voice had risen measure by measure, reaching out to every corner of the room. If these warriors were responsive he would forge them, here and now, into a single entity: to act as a unit, to think and to feel as a unit. This was their first tentative assignment: to abandon Slate, and to rally to him. Only then would they be his.

Mosher carefully watched his audience's reaction before he spoke. He didn't expect them to bend to his will, yet. If they did, well and good. But the primary objective here was to plant the seeds for the remainder of his plan, which would bring him the absolute confidence and obedience of the UDF. He did not know, or care, what enemy awaited them. He knew that he was Wilkington Augustus Mosher—unbeaten and unbeatable—and that was enough. The war was his to win. He was convinced that this war was the greatest event in human history. All of history yet to be written would be measured from it: Before the War, and After the War. That is how time itself would be reckoned. Of more practical importance: This War would unify forever the diverse worlds of the Great Domain. And his place atop that union? Time would tell.

Some in attendance were nodding in agreement at the remarks he'd made. A few, like the giant seated next to Slate— *that* was Brother John? Grotesque!—were clearly angry. Most wore noncommittal, professional expressions. From decades of confronting and winning crowds, Mosher sensed that he should not push too hard now; these Duelists respected Slate too much. He knew what he needed to do next: step back from the attack on Slate, let the tension ease down, and then strike—hard— once more.

"Therefore," Mosher went on, lowering his pitch to a soft conspiratorial whisper that still filled the room, "let me speak for all of us here. Slate has done what he could. Perhaps he was supremely vain to have sought the leadership position he now claims." He flashed his wide, white, trademark smile. "But who in our profession is not touched by vanity? Why, I myself, me personally . . ." He winked and raised his hands to include them in his joke, and was rewarded with scattered laughter. Then at the correct moment, he turned serious again. "No. No, I don't blame Slate. Rather, I am dismayed that those responsible for humankind's safety have placed him in a position for which he has no qualifications whatever." His quiet and reasonable tone had reached many in the audience. Heads turned to look thoughtfully toward the man they believed had appointed Slate to head the UDF.

Colonel Pritcher rose from his chair at the head table and picked up his notebook. Without a word or a glance back, he walked from the auditorium. Two more at the table and fifteen from the audience followed him through the double doors.

Slate remained seated. He had expected criticism, even good-natured ridicule, from the more experienced Mosher. But he'd expected this in a private meeting, during which they could both speak freely without concern for protocol. That was a mistake, he saw now. He had known from Mosher's books that the flamboyant Duelist believed in straightforward, immediate engagement during the opening stages of battle. And that was precisely what they were witnessing now. He should have anticipated this. Mosher was asserting his own expertise by denigrating that of his predecessor—a time-honored and effective method of establishing control.

Slate was prepared to accept the role of adversary to Mosher, if the result was to be an effective restructuring of the UDF. But he was also bound by Duelist tradition; he could accept personal insult to a point, and no further.

Mosher continued. "Mr. Slate has divided the six hundred ships into three flotillas. That will change, but is useful for the moment. I propose a fleet-wide battlesim. I will command one of these groups against the two remaining flotillas, which will be commanded by Mr. Slate. In that way I can assess the overall condition of the fleet. I propose that the exercise begin within the hour." He locked eyes with Slate. "Will you agree to this, Mr. Slate?"

Brother John answered immediately. "We accept." His face was flushed and his scalp was twitching. "And it's Master Duelist Slate to you, Mosher."

Mosher replied mockingly, "Oh? Can Master Duelist Slate speak for himself, former Duelist Brother John?" He leaned forward as if addressing the man privately. "If what I hear is true, I don't understand your loyalty toward him. Perhaps you'll set the record straight. Is it true that Slate *refused* to fight alongside you in the Gassmund wars? That he considered war beneath his dignity? And so when you needed him he wasn't there? Maybe he could have saved you from that third-rate Duelist who carved—"

The giant leapt to his feet. Slate pulled at his arm, to no effect. Brother John turned and faced his friend calmly. "I'm just making myself comfortable, Sapper." He stretched and yawned, then nodded toward Mosher, who'd taken a step backward at the forceful reaction. "He wants to know if you can speak for yourself." He stage-whispered, "Too bad you weren't with me, though. You could have helped me save face." The audience groaned at the atrocious pun. Brother John bowed proudly to them, turned and made a hand-gesture at Mosher, then took his seat.

As the room quieted, the Master Duelist stood. "I'll take *Miyoshi* and Flotilla One," he said evenly. "Flotilla Two will divide itself and remain free of the exercise and prepared for an enemy attack. Flotilla Three is yours, Mosher. There will be a fifty-hour limit to the exercise. After that you can either take command of the fleet or go back home with your tail between your legs."

Mosher flushed and left the dais. They exited the hall through opposite doors.

An hour later Slate stepped aboard his flagship and sent Mosher the challenge: Begin now. Find us. Destroy the *Miyoshi*.

Immediately after that signal, *Miyoshi* and the ships of Flotilla One established a signal-silence and departed at maximum normal-space speed. They would be given a four-hour lead. The rules agreed upon were the Domain-wide standard for Peacekeeper battlesims: Neither side was permitted to enter hyperspace, where detection was not possible. Shields were not to be activated. All weapons were set to produce a low-level burst of radiation which would mimic the travel and spread of a focused beam. Three seconds of continual exposure, or ten 'hits,' would be considered a kill.

Longley had also studied Mosher's books. He said to Slate, "We have to gain a quick advantage while Mosher is organizing. Otherwise he'll cut us to pieces."

"Any ideas?"

"Yep."

Instead of running and hiding as anticipated, Longley had them spread the 200 ships of Flotilla One into a net-formation that stretched perpendicular to Mosher's point of departure.

Five hours into the battlesim, half of Mosher's force met and destroyed one Flotilla One ship. That triggered the ship's emergency beacon and told Slate where they were. The net closed around the stricken vessel and its attackers. Using the element of surprise and superior numbers, they disabled or destroyed one hundred of Mosher's ships. The total cost to Flotilla One was nineteen ships.

The hunted then became the hunter. Believing—rightly, as events proved—that Mosher would split his remaining hundred ships into smaller units, Slate did likewise. The 181 ships of Flotilla One became 6 units of 30, with *Miyoshi* staying at the center of one group.

It became a seek-and-destroy war of attrition. After his initial blunder Mosher lived up to his reputation. Slate recorded and studied the formations Mosher devised as the units skirmished. They were simple, elegant, and ingenious. And the patterns were never repeated; each time, Slate lost more ships than Mosher did.

At the end of the fifty hours Mosher had eighteen ships surviving. Slate had only three; but one of them was the flagship *Miyoshi*.

They met in the wardroom of *Miyoshi* to critique the exercise. Mosher ignored Slate's offered handshake. "Congratulations, Slate. According to the rules you imposed, you won."

"That was a brilliant performance, Expert Mosher," Slate said. "You know the expression, 'saved by the bell.' In another six hours you'd have had us."

Brother John grudgingly nodded his agreement. "You're almost as good as you think you are, Mosher."

"I've read your texts," Longley said. "You transcended yourself in those final skirmishes. I still don't understand how you knew which of our assaults were traps. And I'd like to ask you about one of the—"

Mosher turned away from him. "Will you get on with the critique, Slate? I have important matters to deal with." He took a seat at the wardroom table and ignored the others.

Slate exchanged a glance with Longley and Brother John while they sat down. It was expected by the three of them that Mosher would take command immediately; if he'd needed to prove anything, he'd done so. They therefore expected the critique to come from Mosher. When it was clear that this was not going to happen, Slate opened the notebook he'd used to record the skirmishes. He found the page on which he had written his observations.

"We cannot assume that this exercise was representative of a battle with the GeeBees," Slate began. "First, we knew where Flotilla Three would be coming from. Second, we knew how many ships the enemy had. Third, we knew what type of armaments and training and experience they—"

Mosher slapped a hand down on the table. "No, Slate. *You* knew the level of training and experience of my group. *You* knew they were stupid enough to take the bait you offered on the first day. I never authorized those morons to attack that ship. They're more incompetent than I could possibly have known."

The Long Man bristled. "You were in command, Expert Mosher. And you'd already assumed that we were all incompetent. Including Admiral Slate. I understand you made an issue of that very point recently."

Mosher reddened. "And I still say that, Longley. But Slate knew which group was the most useless. And he deliberately assigned them to me."

"Want a rematch, Mosher?" Brother John said. "This time you pick the ships you want, and we'll fight from unarmed scouters."

"Enough!" Slate said. His heart sank. Mosher had lost only on a technicality; after a bad start, he'd won every engagement. But it was clear that he could not accept even the appearance of defeat. In his own mind, Mosher had been humiliated. To command, he would need to regain the respect he believed he had lost. And Slate knew what Mosher would do—had to do—to regain that respect. He saw it in Mosher's eyes.

Mosher stood. "Expert Longley, Brother John." He looked at each one in turn. "Your comments to me are based on a misunderstanding of the situation. I therefore take no offense."

He looked at Slate. "But you, sir, have deliberately conspired to humiliate me, and to discredit my ability to command the United Defense Force. That is an assault not only against my honor, but also against the faith humankind must have in me as a leader. Under these circumstances I cannot forgive the insult. By law you have four days to submit your apology to me through the Union. If you do not, I demand that we meet for a settlement. To the death."

Longley and Brother John sat quietly. Once the challenge had been issued they could take no part in the exchange. But no law or tradition prevented them from displaying their revulsion at

Mosher's transparent gambit. The Long Man clenched his small fists, and the scalp of Brother John was flushed red and twitching.

"There is no reason for this, Expert Mosher," Slate said. "It's clear what you're after. You want respect and command. I am prepared to offer you both, as your due." This was more difficult than Slate had imagined. He had committed no offense, and had endured insults to himself and to Brother John. By every right he should accept Mosher's challenge, kill him, and be done with it. But he was prepared to bend, to keep Mosher alive; his knowledge was needed. For now. "There is no reason," he repeated, pushing each word out, "for me to—for one of us to kill the other."

Mosher sneered. "You dare to *offer* me respect and command? *You?* Offer *me*? Slate, you have *nothing* to *offer* me!"

"Wilky," Slate warned, "don't go too far."

But Mosher had committed himself. He was determined to *take* the UDF from Slate. Just as he would *take*, when the time was right, his place atop a unified Great Domain. Who was this man to stand in his way? Mosher would not be condescended to; he would not be *offered* the respect and the command that were his by right. He said in genuine anger, "How dare you! And how *dare* you presume to lead the defense of humankind! Once, Slate, *once* in your *life*, you had the opportunity to defend innocent people. What did you do? You *ran*! You left your mother and your father to die! Yes, you were eight years old! But you showed your character, Slate. And you repeated it when you deserted Brother John. These people need a leader. Not a running dog of a coward!"

Slate was beyond rage. He felt cold and numb, refusing to succumb to the images he believed Mosher was evoking to break him down. And he refused to attack now, as Mosher clearly hoped he would. A death challenge was a formal process. Loss of control at this point would disgrace him. Even Brother John and Longley would have to condemn him for an act of weakness.

He met Mosher's eyes and the two understood one another perfectly. Mosher had four days to withdraw his challenge; he would not. He'd use the time to gather support among the troops of the UDF. Again, he'd asserted control by challenging Slate— this time ensuring that the outcome would be final. One would die, and the other would command. Slate had no doubt about who was best qualified to command the UDF; but he would not be a sacrificial lamb to appease the immeasurable vanity of Wilkington Mosher.

He stood and said formally, "Since it must be so."

14

Ravi DeKampura climbed the marble steps leading from the deep pool of steaming water. Wisps of rose-scent rose from her body in the cool chamber air as three attendants rushed forward with thick white towels. While the men dried her, Ravi glared at the woman who stood quietly ten feet away.

Leonora fought to control the trembling in her legs. She knew why Ravi had summoned her to her chamber. It was not to witness again the spectacle of the Queen of Heaven at her bath. It was to stand amid the bubbling fountains of clear, sweet water while the thirst consumed her.

For two days she had been encased in a narrow glassite-paneled box that Ravi kept suspended above her bed. Three hours into their first meeting Ravi had accused her of offense, and ordered the confinement as a lesson in humility.

There had been no food or water; only the continual mockery by Ravi and her constant supply of bedmates. The aim, Leonora knew, had been to weaken her, to force her to depend on Ravi even for the small amount of air that entered the box. But Leonora found that her determination to resist was stronger than her body's needs. And she would never again be shocked by the things people did with and to one another.

Ravi wrapped her hair in one of the towels and dismissed the attendants. The two women were alone in the chamber. There was silence for several minutes. Finally Ravi said, "You have learned to wait for permission to speak. I have taught you obedience." She nodded in satisfaction. "That is good. Your offense is forgiven." Ravi walked to a table and selected a robe of purple and scarlet. She threw it to Leonora. "Cover yourself, whore. Your filth is offensive."

Leonora slipped the robe on and belted it tightly. She willed herself to ignore the gurgling sound of the water as it splashed in the marble fountains. "I'm leaving today, Ravi. Father expects me to bring your reply."

"You may leave only because I wish it," Ravi said. "I have ordered your ship prepared for immediate departure. Now go."

"Father expects—"

"Do not speak to me of those hideous creatures!" Ravi snapped.

"Then that is your reply," Leonora said. She turned to go.

"Wait."

Leonora stopped and turned.

Ravi smiled. "We are so alike, child. I have shown you that you have strength. You have learned discipline and obedience. Stay with me and I will teach you more. Come to me now. Accept the water. I can give it to you."

Leonora shuddered. She knew what Ravi meant by 'water': Transmutation. She'd become like this monster. Like the thousands of others Father had made immortal. Had Ravi been taught the procedure? For the sake of humankind, she prayed that Ravi was lying again. For herself, it didn't matter. "I don't want anything you have. Father expects me today. I'm going to my ship. Stop me or kill me, if you dare." She turned and walked out of the chamber, praying that her fear would not be seen. As she passed through the doorway she heard Ravi.

"My reply is this, Leonora. I will consider what Father has said. Do you hear me? Tell Father . . ." The voice faded as Leonora pushed the door shut behind her. She walked alone down the long corridor, weak and aching for water.

She would tell Father of Ravi's last words. And she would add that Ravi was a liar; she would never obey. But Father would not be moved.

As her ship departed the tiny moon called Aurora, Leonora looked down on the armada clustered together on the bleak silver-gray plateau. *How beautiful they are,* she thought, as she did each time she saw them. *Incredible, that these ships have crossed galaxies.* More incredible, her mind told her, was how familiar, how close they were to human dreams. And for good reason.

She turned her head away, knowing that soon everything

would be ready, and that billions of innocent human beings were going to die.

"And suppose you're killed, son." The Colonel's four days of tight-lipped anger—he'd refused all direct communication with Slate—had given way to concern. "Mosher is a Grade 1 Expert. He's been at it longer than you, and he's about the best I've ever seen. The man has more than fourteen hundred registered kills. Two of them were Masters."

Slate clapped the old warrior on the shoulder. "You don't think I'd provoke a Novice, do you?" He felt wonderfully light-hearted; this was a familiar situation, his life pitted against the skill of another Duelist. At this moment there were no GeeBees, no Ravi, no fleet to command. For a short time he was Master Duelist Benjamin Slate, and nothing more.

"You didn't provoke anyone, son. It's clear what Mosher is doing. Looking at it dispassionately, it's not a bad way to do things. But in this case it wasn't necessary." Colonel Pritcher bent to pick up a pebble from the grass. "I know, I know. You told him that."

He held the pebble for a moment and threw it outside the painted circle. "Did you know that I fought alongside his mother, in the Pacifico Belt? I knew his father, too. He was a priest of some sort. Extraordinary people, both of them. I always liked the boy. There was real substance to him, despite his cheap theatrics. But—" He thought for a moment. "I don't know. He's changed. He's become a caricature of his own public image."

He took Slate by the shoulders and spoke with a gravity the younger man had not heard since the destruction of the three Academy worlds. "I know you, son. I know what you've been thinking. Now listen to me, and listen hard. You are more important to the Great Domain than Mosher is. I know you don't believe that. But you believe me, and you know that my responsibilities extend far beyond our friendship. If you can win this fight, win it. Clear?"

Colonel Pritcher knew him well. The question had plagued Slate during three days of fleet exercises, and during the past night, as *Miyoshi* returned to orbit around Barrow. He had never before considered that winning could be wrong. But in killing Mosher, was he robbing humankind of a needed resource? He'd taken the question both to Brother John, and to Manner Longley. Their replies had been identical: "Kill the bastard."

On the final night in space he'd sat down to write out an apology, telling himself that it was the noble thing to do; the war was more important than the honor of one Duelist. But it was impossible to put even a single word on paper. In the end it had come down to this: The better Duelist would survive. And that could well be Wilkington Mosher.

Once the decision was reached, he slept soundly.

"I have no intention of losing, Colonel," Slate said. "But if I'm killed, Mosher commands. Watch him carefully. You'll know very quickly whether or not you need to replace him."

Grade 1 Expert Duelist Wilkington Mosher stepped out of his scouter as soon as it touched down on Hernandez Field. By tradition personal matters on Barrow Academy were settled in view of students, faculty, staff, and any Duelists on-planet. With the number who'd arrived to join the United Defense Force, there were more than ten thousand witnesses to what was about to take place. They filled the bleachers and the trees; those standing formed a solid wall of humanity that encircled a sixty-foot white ring painted on the grass. Inside that line was the twenty-foot ring in which the combat would take place.

Mosher led a man and a woman through the crowd to the outer circle where Brother John and the Colonel were standing with Slate.

"Good day to you, Master Slate," Mosher said pleasantly, extending his hand. Slate took it.

"And to you, Expert Mosher." It was as he'd expected; there was no pretense of offended dignity, no show of anger. This was professional. Business.

"Commandant Pritcher," the woman standing beside Mosher said. "May I present myself. I am Grade 5 Journeyman Duelist Eleesa Baur. My husband is Grade 6 Journeyman Duelist Muhamed Kenyata. We are standing as Seconds to Expert Mosher."

The Colonel nodded. "I'm pleased to see you again, Eleesa. Muhamed. And I'm delighted to hear of your marriage. You know Brother John, of course."

"By reputation," Kenyata said. "We were here many years after his graduation."

"A kind way of expressing it," Brother John replied dryly. He added formally, "I am standing as Second to Master Duelist Slate."

"I see," Baur said. She turned to Colonel Pritcher. "Commandant, Expert Mosher has authorized me to make a statement on his behalf." She pulled a card from her tunic. " 'In view of Master Duelist Benjamin Slate's value to the Great Domain in this time of crisis, his impending death is regrettable. Therefore if Master Duelist Slate wishes to remove the cause of this present match, I will accept from him a verbal acknowledgement of error. This must be formally witnessed by all in attendance here today, and documented for Union archives.' "

"I will confer . . ." Brother John began.

"I reject the *offer*," Slate said pointedly. Mosher raised an eyebrow at the reference to his diatribe of four days previous.

To Slate, the ploy was transparent. But it made sense. Mosher had been unable to gather the widespread sympathy he expected. His accusations against Slate had met with a firm rebuff from the thousands who knew the Master Duelist well. Still, he wanted to kill Slate; his plan to establish control over the UDF demanded it. But the act would further alienate many whose support he would need. With this tactic he could claim that he had given their friend a chance to live, with honor.

Mosher said quietly, "I want you to know that I bear you no personal malice, Slate. Privately, I will always honor you as a fallen hero in our cause."

"I'm not the heroic type," Slate replied. He leaned close and said in a tight whisper, "Besides, you're an ass. So I'm going to kill you."

Anger flashed on Mosher's face. He turned to Colonel Pritcher. "Let's get on with it."

"Very well," the Colonel said. "Are you ready, Duelists?"

"Ready, Commandant," they both replied at once.

"To your positions," he said.

From twelve feet they faced one another. Slate pulled off his robe and handed it to Brother John.

Mosher tossed his robe to Baur and looked at Slate. "Your choice of weapons, Slate."

"Single daggers," Slate said, taking one from Brother John. Mosher was a specialist with sword, yawara sticks, and dagger.

Most of Slate's death matches were fought empty-handed, as Mosher well knew.

Slate read Mosher's surprised expression, then saw it disappear; the strategy had scored its first point. Mosher's skill and techniques with the dagger were considered supreme, expressing the highest possible degree of synthesis between human and weapon. Slate had rarely used the dagger formally, and therefore his technique with it was not widely known. Again, as in the Flotilla exercise, he was counting on surprise.

Mosher understood the ploy, and it didn't matter; he intended to win.

"Duelists," the Colonel and Baur called together, "Begin!"

Immediately Mosher dove to his left and rolled. A split second later he stood, as perfectly balanced and still as a sculpture, hands extended in a classic fighting stance. They were empty. The dagger blade was securely clutched beneath his left foot, its razor edge held lightly against the ground. His toes gripped just under the guardplate, with the handle of the weapon extending out from his curled-over toes.

It was a difficult and devastating technique, requiring years to master. Mosher had perfected it, had killed with it hundreds of times.

From this position Mosher effectively had three arms, the longest one clutching a razor-edged dagger. Both of his hands were now free to grapple, punch, chop, spear, defend. And his left foot would be a flashing scythe, striking lightning-quick and severing the flesh it found. If he could take Slate's hands, the dagger would disembowel him in a tenth of a second. Or if Slate dropped his guard it would take his eyes or slice his throat. And be gone before he felt it.

Slate had told Longley the truth; there *was* a defense. Mosher's technique had one subtle flaw. He moved immediately to take advantage. Circling left, he moved to stay on his opponent's right side. In theory, Mosher's left foot, gripping the dagger, would become a poor platform from which to launch a kick with his right. And it would impede, just a fraction, his ability to push off from his left. It was only a theory because it had never been tested in the one arena that mattered—combat.

Slate feinted, darting in low and pulling back. Mosher took a half-step to his left, pivoted, and nearly ended the match. His left foot came whistling down heel-first from over Slate's head, slicing close enough to remove a few hairs as he jerked his head away. Slate backed out of range, inviting Mosher to follow him to certain death. He did not.

Mosher's move had been brilliant, and perfectly executed. And fast enough that the Master Duelist never saw it, until it was nearly too late. Slate grinned and nodded his head in acknowledgement; Mosher was *good*.

Slate continued circling to stay on his opponent's right side. Mosher began a kick with his right foot. Slate knew it was a feint; it wasn't. Instead of dropping the kick and moving in as expected, Mosher extended and changed the motion, pile-driving rock-hard toes into Slate's stomach. Air exploded from his lungs and Mosher's fist flew at his face. He brought his right arm up just in time to stop the straight-hammer blow. The dagger flew from his grasp.

Slate felt his opponent's weight shift. Mosher's left foot was about to leave the ground with its deadly cargo, before his right was down again. It was a killing move. It was Mosher's first mistake.

Only because Mosher's foot was still in contact with Slate's stomach for that brief instant was he able to sense the weight shift. As Mosher left the ground Slate dropped like a stone and rolled under him. He caught him on the rise and used the heel of his palm to poleaxe Mosher's left leg. Direct hit, to the side of his knee. Slate held the contact long enough to deliver all the energy from the blow into a square inch of flesh. Mosher's knee snapped.

The Master Duelist rolled away and snatched up his dagger from where it lay. He jumped to his feet. Mosher was sitting on the ground, his dagger now clutched in his right hand, watching him. There was no sign of pain on his face; the man was in perfect control.

A nonlethal bout would have ended at this point. A death match could have only one ending.

Slate stayed where he was. He wanted Mosher standing, making the broken leg a handicap.

"No, I didn't think you'd come to me." Mosher stood up, dragging his left leg. They circled. Both of Mosher's hands streaked for Slate's face, the dagger-hand changing course at the last instant and slashing downward. Slate dodged and moved right. There was no chance yet to get close. Mosher was too fast.

Slate stayed to Mosher's left, keeping the lamed leg between them. He lunged twice, each time pulling back and dropping low, forcing Mosher to put weight on the leg. It was only a matter of time now, and they both knew it. Mosher would have to attack before his leg collapsed. Slate watched his opponent's eyes and recognized the moment of decision.

"STOP!" The Colonel's voice echoed over the field. "Stop! Ben! Wilky! Stop!" It took several shouts to break the combatants' concentration. Finally, confused, Slate stepped well back from Mosher. What was this? A death match was *never* interrupted!

He kept his eyes on Mosher. But he too had moved away, hobbling back several yards. His face was suffused with rage. "General Pritcher, how *dare* you interfere . . ."

"Quiet, Mosher! Or I'll finish you myself."

Slate watched as Manner Longley stepped toward the combat circle. When had he arrived? And why wasn't he aboard *Miyoshi*? The Long Man halted abruptly at a quiet word from Colonel Pritcher.

"Colonel, what is it?" Slate called.

"Sapper! We found them!" It was Brother John.

"What? Who?" He trotted over to the three. "Found who?"

"Galactic Bloodmaggots!" Brother John said impatiently. "GeeBees! We found them! Come on, Admiral! Let's go kill them!"

Slate looked uncertainly at Colonel Pritcher.

"You never turned over command, son," he said. "It looks like you're stuck with it for a while longer."

The alarm had risen from Paulus, one of the New Worlds, 1,650 light-years from Barrow Academy. With the new Mark III's the transit would take twenty-six hours.

The first call from Paulus had come in six days before, to Memorial Hall on Barrow's South continent. There was nothing to distinguish it from the hundreds of reports coming in from every point in the Great Domain. Odd lights had been seen for several consecutive nights near the moon Barnabus. The caller reported unusual behavior in the shuttleport where he worked—a group of strangers accosting passersby and demanding surrender. It seemed like a routine false alarm. But like all of the reports, it had to be checked.

The Peacekeepers on Paulus were contacted from Barrow. The Major who took the call was concerned about the war, yes, his brother was now a recon-pilot for the UDF, but he hadn't seen any aliens, and what would they be doing on the moon? Of course there were lights. Barnabus was a busy place nowadays; two or three ships a month landed there. Did Barrow Academy think the Paulicians lived in the Stone Age? And there were always people in shuttleports who acted peculiar. But he promised to look into it, as soon as a scouter was available to make the trip.

The call and the response were logged and forgotten.

Six days later the scouter arrived at Barnabus and flew over what looked like, and couldn't possibly be, a city on the barren moon. The scouter became a furnace, pilots screaming into the radio as they were incinerated. The Major reported the incident to Barrow Academy and begged them to send the fleet.

Flotillas One and Two streaked toward Paulus at maximum speed. Flotilla Three had departed the previous night for the Minerver System, its new home base. Under the command of the big Apache, Commodore Manuel Briones, it was already within twenty hours of Paulus when the alarm sounded. Briones would arrive there six hours before Slate's group.

"They should be coming out of hyperdrive in a few minutes, Ben," Longley said. "Shall I establish contact beforehand?"

"No," Slate said. "We'll stick to the plan. Briones will initiate communications, as soon as there's something to report."

Twenty hours of transit, waiting to engage an enemy they had never seen, affected everyone. Slate cursed himself for not having bowed out of the fight with Mosher. He named Longley to command Flotilla One, and spent the time studying tactics. The Long Man was quiet, but visibly worried about his home world. Brother John was asleep.

"Dr. Bey must have put something in his food," Slate said, looking up from his notes. He nodded toward the sprawled figure who snored on the chart table. "He looks like a great white whale." Brother John was as Slate remembered him from their early days together: boisterous, constantly making terrible jokes, and beneath the façade calm and deadly efficient. He'd spent most of the transit in the Duelist stations, checking weapons, exchanging insults, and establishing chains of communication and command.

"You should have seen him and Bey," Longley said, chuckling. "Arguing about who was going to have the first 'GeeBee hide' to nail to his wall."

"Who won the argument?"

"They agreed that Dr. Bey can have the pelt, but Brother John gets the rest of the carcass. If it's edible."

"I think I'm going to be sick."

"Brother John has big plans, Ben. GeeBee Steaks. GeeBee Stew. He plans to go into business when the war is over."

"We'd better hope it's a long war," Slate said. "I don't think the Great Domain is ready yet for Brother John's Tasty Bloodmaggots."

"*Galactic* Bloodmaggots, Sapper," Brother John called out, eyes still closed. "Imported. Better than domestic. That's what'll sell."

He sat up and stretched. "Any word yet?"

"Nothing," Manner answered. "They're scheduled to reenter normal-space any time now." The only sign of his mood was the rhythmic opening and clenching of his small hands.

"Any change in plans I should know about?"

"No change," Slate said. "Half of Briones' ships will come out of hyperdrive at six hundred thousand miles from Paulus. The other half will be out of the System proper, staying in the net-formation. If anything moves they should detect it immediately."

"And when we arrive?"

"Then we see about setting you up in the restaurant business."

⇒15⇐

The words had been abstract ideas, before. Aliens. Contact. War. They were things to prepare for, things that existed out *there* somewhere, unseen—not complete. Not real.

Until now.

Slate stared at the images on the radar screen, unaware that he was not breathing. When his heart hammered against his chest he drew in a deep breath and exhaled slowly. They were there; beings from another part of the Universe. Aliens. Contact. Finally.

They were only images on a screen. But they proved something that had only been dreamt of. From the days of humankind's club-thumping ancestors no one could gaze up into the starry blackness without *the* question pressing against the edge of consciousness. *Is anyone there?*

Ptolemy, Copernicus, Galileo, Hawkings, Geraint, O'Shaunnessey: They told of *how* to look. And then *where* to look. And *what* was there to see. But that was not their purpose. All of them—and all of humankind since—were looking to find the answer. IS ANYONE THERE?

At last there was an answer: Yes. The new question was, *Who is it?*

Fourteen of them streaked toward *Miyoshi*'s position in the net-formation.

Manner Longley spoke calmly into the ship-to-ship Battle Control circuit. "This is *Miyoshi*. We have on screen fourteen GeeBee craft. I say again, we have fourteen enemy craft on screen. We will intercept and engage. Teams Twenty-six through Fifty home in on *Miyoshi*'s beacon. All others close the net and remain on station. Team leaders acknowledge."

The lights above the console went individually from red to green.

"All Team leaders have acknowledged, Commodore."

"Very well."

Hours before, Commodore Briones had signaled in, requesting permission to approach the moon Barnabus.

"What do you see, Manny?"

"Nothing, Ben. I want to get closer."

"Hold station until we arrive," Slate ordered. "Keep your ships dispersed in net-formation. If the GeeBees try to break out, engage your weapons. If they get past you, pursue. I'll contact you as soon as we're in normal-space near your position. Do you copy?"

"Understood, Admiral." The disappointment was clear in his voice.

Hours later they winked out of hyperdrive and formed an outer perimeter for Flotilla Three.

Slate keyed the comm-net. "Go in, Manny. Flush them out."

"Yes, sir!" was the jubilant response from the big Apache.

Half an hour later forty-two GeeBee ships erupted skyward from Barnabus as Briones closed in with one hundred ships of Flotilla Three.

"They went right past our forward positions," Briones reported. "We never got close enough to hold them visually. My ships opened fire at nine hundred miles, Admiral. There were plenty of direct hits, but no visible effect on the GeeBees."

"Any damage to our ships?"

"None, sir. The GeeBees seemed too busy running to return fire. They're taking evasive maneuvers. The forty-two ships split into three groups of fourteen and are presently headed out of the System. We did accomplish one objective, though. I can confirm that these are the type of ships Ed Joyce recorded at Miyoshi Academy. The readings we've got on them are identical to those he broadcast."

"Good. I'll pass the word on the comm-net."

"That'll help morale, sir. It'll be better when we catch the bastards, though."

"Agreed. You're in pursuit?" Slate winced. He'd asked a stupid question. Of *course* Briones was going after them.

"Lucky guess, Admiral. We expect to pass our own pickets in

three hours. I estimate another four hours to the perimeter you've established."

"Good, Manny. You've got one hundred ships on picket, correct?"

"Correct. The other half of the Flotilla is with me."

Slate asked himself what Mosher would do in this situation. The answer came immediately. "Leave the pickets in place, just in case there are more GeeBee craft down there. Split your hundred ships, and go after two of the GeeBee groups. I'll take the third."

"You've been studying, Ben," Briones came back.

"Watch for them to turn on you. And *keep* firing on them. We want them kept busy taking evasive action. If their ships are anything like ours, that will deny them the free run they need to go into hyperdrive."

"That was clear from your briefing, sir. I understand."

"This is all new to me, Manny," Slate said. "If I repeat myself it's for my benefit, not yours."

"For my benefit too. This is new for all of us. And Ben?"

"Yes?"

"Let me offer you some advice. Relax. Unwrap! You've got top-rate commanders, and so far you're doing a good job. As for me, I'm having the time of my life."

"Thanks, Manny."

"Flotilla Three out."

Seven hours later they had them on screen. Longley maneuvered *Miyoshi* directly into the path of the alien ships.

Brother John was staring intently at the display. He said quietly, with enormous satisfaction, "They're coming right at us."

"Hold position," Longley said to the helmsman. "Gunner, commence firing at nine hundred miles. Full spread, full power."

"Standing by," the gunner called out from his console. "Six thousand . . . four thousand . . . two thous . . . *Firing!*"

The lights dimmed fractionally while the 50-gigawatt guns lashed out at the oncoming ships.

"Direct hits on bogies three and five, Commodore," the gunner cried out. "No effect."

"Keep firing until we're out of range," Longley said. "Helmsman, come about. Put us on station ten thousand miles ahead of them. Radar, any change?"

"None, sir," the young operator called out. "Fourteen bogies holding steady on course and speed."

"Helm, increase speed to .5 Light."

"Aye, sir."

Longley turned to Slate. "My intention is to jump ahead, Admiral, putting us directly in their path. I want some point-blank shots at them. Team Twenty-eight is close enough now to provide long-distance harassment fire."

"Good," Slate said. "I suggest you have some of your other Teams jump further ahead, in case they get by us."

"Agreed." Longley signaled the orders.

"Can they take point-blank fire?" Brother John wondered aloud.

"We'll know in about three minutes," Longley said. "It will take us that long to build speed and get around them."

"If our firepower doesn't destroy their ships—" Slate began.

"Ram them." Brother John said.

"Negative!" Slate turned to face his friend. "For all we know these forty-two could be a small fraction of their force. We can't afford heroics until we know how many they are, and how to kill them."

"Sorry, sir," Brother John said.

Longley nodded approvingly at Slate. "You're learning, Ben."

"What do you mean?"

"You had the same impulse as Brother John. But you're thinking like a commander now."

Slate considered the idea for a second; it was possible. He said to Longley, "If they survive point-blank fire we'll give chase and continue the harassment. We're scoring direct hits, and soon other Teams will be in position. Maybe we're weakening them. We want to follow them and keep pumping fire into them for as long as we can."

"In position, Commodore," the helmsman called out. "Range nine thousand, closing fast. Collision course."

"Dead slow," Longley said quietly. "Gunner, commence firing at six hundred. Let's see what they're made of."

The enemy closed while the gunner called out the range. "Eight thousand. Five thousand. Three thousand. One ... *Firing!*" The lights dimmed.

"Steady ... steady ..." The Long Man intoned behind the helmsman. His small hand lay on the shoulder of the young operator. *Miyoshi* held steady, pouring out lethal energy at the four-teen GeeBee ships.

"Past us," Brother John said quietly. He adjusted the scale of the radar screen. "Wait . . . By the Blessed Saint . . . Sapper! We *got* one!"

Slate jumped from the chair and peered around the giant's shoulder at the screen.

"Helm, come about," the Long Man said quickly. "Go back to .5 Light. Intercept at twenty thousand. Gunner, same procedure." He stepped over to the screen.

"Thirteen," Slate said. "Only thirteen now. We got one."

"No debris," Longley said. "Those are big ships, Ben. If we killed one we should be seeing radar return on the debris."

"Not if the ship is in little enough pieces," Brother John said.

"True," Slate said. "But I agree with Commodore Longley. If we finally cracked one open, it wasn't by much. Those ships have sustained constant fire for over seven hours now. Our weapons aren't exactly overwhelming them. I can't picture one of them suddenly bursting into a billion little pieces."

"Maybe we got lucky," Brother John said. "Maybe we hit just the right spot." He straightened up from the screen. "But you're right, of course. Stress coefficients don't accumulate and diffuse that rapidly. Unless we're dealing with a totally homogeneous construction—" The giant turned to see Longley staring at him. He shrugged. "Just thinking out loud," he said, then added more quietly, "Wishful thinking."

An overhead speaker clicked on. "Commodore," a woman's voice said, "This is Radio. We've got a signal from Commodore Briones. He's lost the group he was chasing."

Longley keyed the ship's intercom. "Acknowledge the message, Brenda." He turned to Slate. "Ben?"

"Have him continue the search. Keep his fifty ships together and stay in contact with us."

Longley relayed the order.

"Commodore!" The voice of the radar operator boomed through the compartment. "We have a GeeBee ship! Close aboard! Right *next* to us!"

"Shield *up*," Longley ordered instantly. "Dead stop."

Manner Longley turned and ran at full speed, nimbly ducking through constricted hatchways, as Brother John and Slate labored to follow him down a narrow corridor, then outboard two levels to the observation port.

On arriving, Longley keyed the intercom. "Helm, rotate ship to bring the observation port in line with that vessel."

"Aye aye, sir."

The wall-mounted speaker crackled. "Commodore, this is Radar. The other thirteen bogies have stopped, sir. They're holding steady at twenty thousand miles."

"Understood. Pass the word for all local Teams to stop on station and raise shields. Advise me immediately if the GeeBees move."

"Aye, sir."

The motion of *Miyoshi* was undetectable to them. But slowly, as a sun lights a bleak horizon, the alien ship rose against the dark of space.

It was a city of gold.

It hovered only half a mile from *Miyoshi*. Slate stared, speechless. The alien ship was breathtakingly beautiful. The shape of the craft was flat, squared off on four sides like a platform, two hundred or more yards on a side. Motionless and silent against the blackness of space, it looked for all the world like an ancient walled city. A city of gold.

"Manner," Slate said. "We have our shield up, correct?"

"Yes, Ben."

"Does the shield distort? Image, color?"

"No, sir. What we're seeing is what's out there."

"By all that's holy," Brother John said.

The ship was nearly twice as high as it was wide. Rising up from the base of the golden craft were towers and spires. These would be the communications and control centers, Slate decided. They looked like buildings reaching above city walls. Throughout the sides and the towers of the vessel were geometric patterns of multicolored panels. There were blues, greens, reds, some like pale quartz. Sensors, Slate thought. Or windows, like their own observation port. Or weapons.

The three stood quietly, awe-struck and transfixed by the dazzling beauty of the ship.

Longley stepped back to the intercom. "Radio, any signal from that ship?"

"None, sir."

"Broadcast a standard ID request," Longley said. "Try all bands."

"Aye aye, sir."

Brother John said, "It's them, Sapper. I've never seen one of their ships, that I can remember. But that's Alti F'ir. GeeBees." The giant clutched Slate's shoulder, hard. His hand was shaking. "Ravi's not with them," he said firmly. "I'd know if she was."

Slate said nothing. He put his own hand over the giant's and stared out the port at the eerie spectacle that hovered half a mile away.

"Commodore Longley?" It was the radio operator. There was an edge of panic in her voice.

"Go ahead."

"We have a signal from Commodore Briones, sir. It's the emergency beacon."

Brother John and Slate turned from the port at the radio operator's last statement. Longley glanced over his shoulder at them. After a second he keyed the mike again. "Did you acknowledge?"

"Yes, sir. I've got no response. From him, or from any of the fifty ships that were with him."

"And the rest of his flotilla?"

"I'm monitoring their transmissions to each other. They've all received the emergency signal."

"What actions are they taking?"

"The ships on picket duty are remaining on station. They report no activity. The other fifty ships have turned back from chasing the GeeBees and are following the beacon."

"Damn," Longley muttered. "They should've continued their pursuit."

"Sir?"

"Nothing, Brenda. I'm on my way."

"Yes, sir."

Slate said from behind him, "Manner. The GeeBee ship is gone."

Longley turned to see an empty observation port. He keyed the intercom again and verified what they suspected. All fourteen enemy ships had disappeared from the screens.

"This is where Briones' emergency signal originated, Ben," Manner Longley said, tapping a thick pen against a small circle he'd drawn on the navigation chart. It was empty space, well out from the New Worlds sector. "We have good triangulation from the pickets and Briones' other ships."

"How long will it take us to reach that point?"

"We're eight minutes from enabling the Mark III's. Once we're in hyperdrive the transit will take seven minutes. Total, fifteen. We'll be the first to arrive."

"Good. We'll go in with the Teams that are with us. All others are to stay away until they hear from us."

"Agreed."

The fifteen minutes seemed to take forever.

"Contacts!" the radar operator cried out the moment they winked out of hyperdrive. "Hundreds of them, sir."

"Shield *up*. Analyze the closest ones first," Manner Longley called out. "Coordinate information with the rest of our Teams. I want a report in ten seconds. Helm, keep hyperdrive enabled. Do *not* shift to normal-space drive until I give the word. Gunner, prepare to fire at closest contacts on my order, the instant the shield is dropped. Brother John, pass those orders on to all ships."

Longley's orders were acknowledged.

Eight seconds later the radar operator said, "Admiral Longley, all reports concur. What we're seeing is large debris. Those are our ships, sir. Pieces of Flotilla Three."

Ravi was furious, straining to remain calm and still. She stared at the screen until the last of the images disappeared. "Good. We will not be found now."

She stood and motioned for the technician to take her place. She left the cubicle, ducking her head to pass through one of the archways that divided the compartment into tiny sections. The ship's Captain was standing at attention, waiting for her to approach.

"You!" Ravi slapped the Captain across the face. "I trusted you with command of my Legion. Your incompetence nearly cost us everything!"

The Captain faced the larger woman with outward calm. "We accomplished our purpose, Ravi." She was seething inside. Unconsciously she moved her hand, seeking the haft of her sword. Her shoulders tightened, readying the blow that would remove the head from the Queen of Heaven. The weapon was not there. And it was not time to kill Ravi. But soon.

The Captain smiled at her lover. "Our Legion has proven itself in battle. We destroyed all but one of the enemy's ships. The humans are impotent. They pose no threat to us at all."

"Be careful how you speak, whore," Ravi snapped. "You are human. And so you will remain, if ever again you allow such a blunder."

The Captain bowed formally, firmly in control of her rage. "I apologize, Commander. I make no excuse. But I was not aware that those other ships could approach us as quickly as they did." She touched Ravi's arm lightly. "Please forgive me, Ravi. You know how unhappy I become at the thought of displeasing you."

"They nearly caught us!" Ravi said angrily. "They meant to kill us this time!"

"But we were not killed, Commander. We live. We will always live."

"Yes. Always," Ravi said, mollified. "Very well. You are forgiven. In truth I myself did not know they could come so quickly. Apparently they have given us inferior ships. But now we know. The next time, we will be prepared. The next time we will kill those hideous *things*!"

Even her iron control could not keep the shock from the face of Master Duelist Batai Watanaba. "You will fire on *Father*?"

⇥16⇤

The voice echoed in Slate's mind like a foghorn through dense mist.

"Did you hear me, sir?"

The Long Man answered. "We heard you." He exchanged a glance with Slate and turned to the helmsman. "Shift propulsion to normal-space. Take us to the center of the debris."

Slate said, "Brother John, pass the word to reestablish two-ship Teams. Twenty-six through Thirty will follow our lead. Thirty-one through Fifty will idle at present position, prepared to enter hyperdrive in case we run into trouble. If we do, they are *not* to render assistance. They are to return to base immediately."

"Right." Brother John relayed the orders, then said, "Sapper?"

"Yes?"

"I recommend that five Teams be assigned to search for survivors."

"Agreed. But use eight Teams, not five. Have them sweep the area between here and the System-edge until we recall them."

The orders were relayed. They stood in silence, stunned by the loss of the big Apache and fifty of his ships. *I'm having the time of my life,* he'd said. The long minutes passed, revealing nothing on their screens except normal space-borne objects and the occasional fragmented remains of their sister ships.

"Sir, there's a magnetic field in our path that—" the gunner began.

At that moment the radar operator cried out, "Contact! Ship, sir!"

"Half slow, Helm," Longley said. "Shield *up*. Is that the same source you picked up, Gunner?"

"Yes, sir. Range is eleven thousand six hundred, closing slowly."

"Why didn't you see it sooner?" Brother John demanded.

"It wasn't *there*, sir! I swear to you . . ."

"Gunner, lock him in and wait for my order," Longley said quietly. "If he shoots through our shield, your guns will be enabled. Fire at will."

"Aye aye, sir."

"Admiral," the radar operator said, "That's not a GeeBee ship. Return characteristics indicate that it's one of ours."

"Dead slow," Longley directed. "Range?"

"Seven thousand nine, sir. He appears to be drifting. No heat signature."

"Close him, Helm. Slowly. Give us ten minutes to reach him. Do not approach closer than two thousand."

Eight minutes passed. At 3,000 miles from the ship the radio operator's voice sounded.

"We're picking up a weak transmission, sir. Emergency frequency, from that ship."

"Patch it to us," Longley said.

The speaker crackled. ". . . I say again, this is the United Defense Force vessel *Kin'Te*, Commodore Briones commanding. I am . . ." The voice faded out.

"Put me on the same frequency," Longley said into the intercom. He picked up a handset. "This is Longley. Can you hear me, Manny?"

"He won't hear you, Commodore," the radio operator reported. "What we're picking up is a recording."

"Is that confirmed?"

"Yes, sir. The message is repeating itself. The modulations read exactly the same every time."

"Amplify," Longley said. "Send it through."

The voice came through, weak and cut by static. ". . . vessel *Kin'Te*, Commodore Briones commanding. I am disabled. They're boarding us right now. The Control Center holo is on to record . . ." A burst of static drowned out the voice. Six seconds later it came back with ". . . I say again, this is—"

"Radio!" Longley shouted into the intercom. "We didn't get it all."

"That was all of it, Commodore. Do you want it again?"

"Negative. Thanks, Brenda."

"Sir," the radar operator said, "That ship is emitting something I don't recognize. It's not on my scales."

"Check with the other Teams," Longley said. "Maybe they've got a better reading."

"Sir, my equipment is fine. I don't know why I didn't pick up the contact sooner, but—"

"Do it," Brother John said. "Now."

"Aye, sir." He toggled the special frequency. ". . . that's odd."

"What did you say?"

"No contact, sir. My gear *is* down."

Longley hit the intercom again. "Radio, contact the other ships. Ask them if they're reading anything unusual." He turned to the helmsman. "At my signal engage full speed."

"Commodore," the speaker-voice came back four seconds later. "I can't contact anyone. Everything's out, sir. Radio *and* warpsignal."

"Very well. Helm—" A huge hand clamped down on Longley's shoulder.

"No," Brother John said. "First let me get to a scouter. Please, Manner."

"What are you doing?" Slate asked.

"They *boarded*, Sapper!" Brother John said. He released Longley and turned for the hatchway. "I'll be spaceborne in five minutes," he called over his shoulder.

"Brother John," Slate called. "Stop."

He turned around. "Sapper," he growled, "I'm going. Don't try to stop me. *Please* don't force me—"

"I'm pulling rank, old friend," Slate said, walking to him. "I'm driving." To Longley he said, "The moment we're launched, take *Miyoshi* out of here. Have the other ships follow you as soon as you can contact them. And don't come back until we've got the scouter away from *Kin'Te*. Wait for our signal."

"Ben—"

"Don't argue, Commanding Admiral. Clear?"

"Yes, sir."

Kin'te hung suspended from nothing, lifeless and tumbling slowly. Its sleek silver form was a tiny needle that shone dimly against the infinite diamond-studded fabric of space. Slate aligned the scouter to match the larger vessel's roll and piloted around to the hangar entrance. "I don't see any exterior damage," he said.

The giant was silent beside him.

The hangar door was open to space. As they touched down, Slate tried the scouter's remote. The outer door slid shut smoothly. Immediately, bottled air began pressurizing the small compartment. Within a minute a green console-light flickered on and then glowed steadily.

"Good seal," Slate said. "And look at this. The gravity generator is still engaged." The dial registered .93 Standard. "That means there's still power to—"

"Let's go, Sapper." Brother John pushed open the scouter's door and stepped out. Slate held his breath, reaching for the suits behind the pilot's seat. But another glance at the console told him that the air was pure. He pulled two 9 kilo Barrows from their cases and followed after his friend.

Once they were through the inner airlock door and into the passageway, the signs of struggle were evident. Bulkheads were scorched raw, here and there showing the tracks of metal that had melted and run like micro-scaled rivers. Power panels hung loosely, blackened and still smoking.

Further into the ship they began seeing the more personal signs of the battle. Splotches of blood formed grotesque patterns on bulkheads and decks. Ten feet ahead of Slate, Brother John picked up an object and dropped it into a disposal chute.

"What was that?"

"Someone's boot," the giant said grimly. "The foot was still in it."

The Control Center was more of the same. Brother John strode to the center of the compartment and began overturning equipment, ripping bolts out of the deck.

"Brother John—" Slate shouted above the sound of sheet metal tearing.

"Help me," the giant said tightly. He wrenched the radar console loose and tossed it aside. "I'm looking for bodies."

It dawned on Slate for the first time that except for the one foot, they'd found no remains of the Duelists and technicians. But he understood in the same moment that Brother John wasn't looking for human remains.

"Could they be that small?" he asked. The giant was peering into every corner and cavity.

"I never saw them, Sapper. That means they were shorter than the table I was strapped to." He sighed, straightening. "I can't believe it! Manny's crew didn't get even one. They should have killed at least *one* GeeBee!"

Slate nodded agreement. "It looks like all of our people have been taken."

"That means we'll see them again." Brother John wiped a hand across his perspiring scalp. "But not as they were."

"Blessed Saint Barrow."

The giant's eyes swept past Slate to a spot several feet behind him. He said, "We won't be seeing that one again." He walked past the Master Duelist and shoved aside a power panel cover that had fallen from the bulkhead. Beneath it was the severed head of a man. He turned the head gently over to expose the face. "Know him?

"His name was Morales," Slate said, searching his memory. "He was Briones' radio technician." He turned away and went to a box mounted near the command chair.

"What are you doing?"

"Briones' transmission said he'd switched on the Control Center holo. Here it is." He removed a spool of optic tape from the back of the machine.

"Take the whole unit, Sapper," Brother John said, pulling it from its mounts. "It may be a while before we're picked up. There's no projector aboard the scouter."

"Right."

They carried the holo unit back to the hangar deck and spent another hour searching *Kin'Te*. In the starboard engine room they found a small black box strapped to a conduit that carried power to the voracious Mark III. When Slate approached the box, Brother John restrained him and checked a power panel above the engine controls.

"I thought so. There's still power moving through that line. I think it's a good idea to leave now, Sapper. Very quickly."

"What is that thing?"

"That's the guts of a warpsignal unit. If I'm right, this explains the ether disturbances. And why we didn't detect *Kin'Te* before we did."

"Can it do that?"

Brother John shrugged. "I'm guessing. That's a lot of amperage interacting with whatever's in there. But no one knows what's in those black boxes except ProLab."

"And our Galactic Bloodmaggot friends," Slate said.

"Apparently."

"Could it explode?"

"Do you want to wait here and find out?"

The recorded holo image was of poor quality, but there was no missing the expression of awe-struck rapture on the face of the big Apache. "I have never imagined anything as beautiful. If I didn't know better, I'd swear that thing came straight from heaven. I'm going to take a portable holo-unit back with me to the observation port. We've got to get that thing on spool. Unbelievable!"

Slate empathized. The eerie ships were beyond description.

The small image flickered against the rear bulkhead of the scouter's pilot compartment as Slate and Brother John watched. Briones continued. "It's been out there for about six minutes now. We'd lost the fourteen we were after, Ben. They went off our screens all at once, without a trace. You ordered us to continue the search." Briones shook his head. "Then this one appeared beside us. It came out of hyperdrive half a mile from us. I wonder if that's the closest—"

Briones turned at the sound of shouting, coming from outside the image-field. He jumped from view as the voices grew louder, competing for his attention. It was impossible to understand what was being said. The image showed Briones' empty command chair for several minutes before something jarred the unit and repositioned it.

The view was now focused on the starboard side of the hatchway leading from Control to the main passageway. No one was in sight. The noise from the corridor was chaotic and loud, completely unintelligible. There was no visible movement for fifteen seconds.

Then the deck beyond the hatchway began to ripple. It rose up and moved fluidly down the corridor, peaked like an ocean wave. The image went dead.

"What—"

"Give me a second, Sapper. Just a second." The giant took his hand from the projector and gulped air. His scalp was flushed red, and twitching.

"We can wait, Brother John."

He shook his head. "I'm ready." He hit the switch and the holo image appeared again against the bulkhead.

It came to the hatchway and raised its forward end to meet the edge of the threshold. It moved—flowed—smoothly over the nine-inch obstacle and stopped just inside the Control Center.

"A rug," Slate whispered, blinking to clear his eyes. "It looks like a rug."

Brother John forced himself to look at it. After several seconds he said, "A doormat, Sapper. It looks like a damned *doormat*." His breathing was labored. "I ... I remember thinking that, once. I thought it was funny and I wanted to laugh, but—"

"Slowly, Brother John. Don't force it."

"It's gone," the giant said. "What I was thinking ... it's gone."

"Whatever it is, you'll remember."

"I think I'd better."

Slate stared at the holo image, unable to believe that he was looking at a living, intelligent creature. Lying still as it was now, directly in front of the hatchway, it looked exactly like a thick, golden area rug. Or a doormat.

He gauged its size to be seven inches high, three feet wide, and six feet long. The rug illusion disappeared the moment it began moving in place. Its top was a mass of appendages. Some were rounded at the tip, some sharp, and some blunted. Looking at them, Slate thought of a thousand spindly crabs lying on their backs, legs up in the air, rotting in the sun. He nearly retched.

"It only lasts for a while," Brother John said quietly. "They don't stay ugly for long."

Slate looked at his friend. After they'd opened his brain for the final time, he remembered, Brother John had loved them. For a while. He turned back to the projected image.

The appendages began rippling like flowing waves. *Kin'Te's* Control Center was absolutely quiet now. Whatever had been going on outside, was over. Then a man's voice was heard.

"Father!"

The speaker stepped into the holo's image-field, hands together and head bowed. Morales. "Welcome, Father," he said, extending his hands. "I—"

From ten feet away one of the appendages snapped out. It wrapped around Morales' neck and retracted before anything registered in the minds of Slate and Brother John. Morales blinked, once. Then he trembled slightly and his severed head tumbled sidewards to the deck, impacting and rolling away as his body crumpled.

Brother John switched off the projector again. "Morales was New Army."

"What?"

"That's what Ravi was talking about while she was butchering me on Lancaster. She said she was a general, in a 'new army,' remember? This was one of her troops."

"Aboard *Kin'Te*?"

"You heard what he said, and you saw the way it killed him. We've been infiltrated, obviously. I'd like to know why he was executed."

"Decapitated," Slate said. "Turn it back on. Maybe we'll see why."

The image came back as Morales' body fell to the deck in a position that left only his lower legs visible in the image-field. The creature had not moved from its position, but began backing slowly over the threshold again as a stream of blood flowed toward it. Most of the red stain disappeared through minute expansion cracks in the deck. When the flow dissipated to nothing at the hatchway, the creature stopped again.

As they watched, two thick appendages emerged from its underside and snaked toward Morales. Each wrapped itself around an ankle, and the creature began moving away. Within a few seconds it, and Morales' body, were gone.

The holo continued, showing nothing except the still image of that one small section of the Control Center. There was no sound.

Brother John reached for the switch. "No," Slate said. "Let's be sure there's nothing else."

The image persisted for twelve more minutes before Brother John said, "Briones never came back to Control. He must've made that last recording from the radio compartment."

Slate turned to answer and a flicker of movement caught his eye. "Stop. Run that back again."

The scene was repeated in slowed form. Even so, it was hard to catch. A face appeared from out of view at the hatchway, peered in for half a second, and was gone.

Slate sat bolt upright. "Again. Stop on the face."

The image returned and was frozen.

"Blessed Saint Barrow," Brother John muttered. "It's her, Sapper. Your friend from the mining colony. Now we know where she disappeared. They took her and made her one of them."

Slate nodded. "New Army. But I don't think she was kidnapped. There were things about her—" He let the sentence die as he stared at her face.

Leonora D'Meersopol was still beautiful. But she no longer looked like the warm, frightened young woman he remembered. He recalled something else. The dream he'd had that second night with Leonora. Maybe it wasn't a dream. There was something fundamentally wrong about Leonora that could be felt, but not described. He'd been sure that she hadn't been aware of it. But now it was plain enough; she'd been one of them all along. The beast within her—the alien that had controlled Kiner, and Ravi—had matured.

Given the chance, Leonora would do to him what Ravi had done to Brother John.

=17=

They flew at top speed—a crawl, by warship standards—for three days before they passed from the field that had stymied all communications. During the flight Brother John sequestered himself in the cargo hold of the scouter with the holo tape. He ran it continually, using the image of the alien to jolt his damaged memory. Slowly, piece by scattered piece, it was coming back.

After they'd opened up his brain for the final time he understood what they were telling him. Not with words, because they had no words and needed none. They were part of one another. As fingers are parts of the hand, and the hand is a part of the body—and the body merely an extension of the mind. So it was with Alti F'ir, which was three minds. They spoke to him in images that played out across his mind in poetic rhythms and stark, impossible colors. When they'd shown him who they were, he loved them. And he called them Father.

Brother John switched off the holo and put his cupped hands over his closed eyes. He assembled the tale as he'd first seen it, and watched it again.

It was only primordial gases and flowing rock, still too restive and hot to form a solid surface, when golden city-ships first streaked above the chaos that would come to be Earth. Finding nothing that was interesting, or new, the ships departed. Alti F'ir was millions of years old then, and did not know that it was decaying.

There was within Alti F'ir's memory no time or place of origin; only the eternal ships were home. Memory was a long chain of places and visitations reaching back into time, older than the

163

Alti F'ir individuals. There were millions of them, and tens of thousands of the ships; the Universe was infinite, and so Alti F'ir replicated itself to fill the emptiness. Alti F'ir met itself everywhere, and found nothing greater than itself.

Alti F'ir saw only one great thing that was alive—itself. And that one great thing it saw replicated, created, by—itself.

Alti F'ir saw no evidence that it did not create the stars, and all of the creeping and crawling things that moved upon the cold rocks.

Alti F'ir saw no evidence of another source for creation. All that was mind was Alti F'ir—created by Alti F'ir.

Individuals died, and more were created; the mind lived on, and grew. When the individuals were too many for the mind, the mind divided. There were three, each with its millions of individuals. When the individuals again became too many, the minds could not further divide. And they could not unite.

As the individuals wore away with time they were not replaced; the divided mind was too weak to create life again. And although it had no concept of death that related to itself, the entity that was now three, Alti F'ir, was indeed dying.

When Alti F'ir at last recognized its state of decay, the three minds went in search of the lost memories: the memories of how to unite, and how to create life. Without these memories Alti F'ir would end—as would the Universe itself, which Alti F'ir knew it had created.

The mind which most strongly retained the memory of itself as creator happened upon the Earth again and found there beings which it surely had created, but could not remember. The mind waited there, coming to know the beings, coming to love them as a father must, and waiting for its memory—the power to unite, and the power to create life—to manifest within the beings.

And after tens of thousands of trips around the world's star, that memory took form among the beings and walked as a man.

The mind summoned the others. They came, weaker with the passage of time, and saw. Alti F'ir believed this being was its own memory.

But the being it saw was lost to it. Two of the minds departed to continue the search. The one remained, and waited in hundreds of places for the being to return again. As millennia passed, the mind grew still weaker as more individuals ceased to exist and could not be replaced. The mind watched humankind probe the secrets of matter and energy, and it began to understand these things again. It gained back the skill to extend life. But not its own; its ending was sure.

Because it knew the humans as Father Creator, the Alti F'ir mind gave as much as it could of those things that the being had promised, in its name: a way to the heavens, and the gift of eternal life. The humans would inherit the Universe.

And as these gifts were taken, the Alti F'ir mind learned a new thing which the humans already knew—and called evil.

He was hollow-eyed and gaunt when he pushed the curtain aside and reentered the pilot compartment. Slate looked at him and spoke quickly into the warpsignal handset. "Understood, Manner. We'll be waiting." He cut the engine thrust to dead-slow and slid the handset into its bracket.

"They're sending *Troubador* and *Ulysses*," Slate said. "Team Thirty. Manner's taking the rest of the fleet back to Barrow at full speed."

"Trouble?"

"He didn't say so, but it must be. I have to assume that he didn't want the conversation to be monitored. Are you all right?"

"How long do we wait?"

"Three hours."

"So Team Thirty is a hundred eighty light-years away," he said approvingly. "Longley's a good commander, Sapper. He took the fleet to a safe area." The sweat was forming on his face and floating away in sheets.

Slate said, "Sit down, Brother John. You look like you've seen—"

"Don't say it." He pulled himself into the co-pilot's chair. Despite the zero-gravity, the movement looked heavy. He squeezed his face with the palms of his hands until his cheeks held color again. "Give me a minute. Then switch on the voice recorder. I want to say this only once."

Slate located a blank cassette and touched the button on its side. He set it down between them. "Whenever you're ready."

After a minute Brother John said, "This is how it was told to me, fifteen years ago."

"By Ravi?"

"No. After Ravi. By Alti F'ir. And don't speak again until I'm finished."

"I understand."

"No, Sapper. You don't." Brother John took a long breath and began. "Alti F'ir doesn't know where it's from. But it's been out there, alone, forever. The ships—"

Manner Longley said into the warpsignal, "How many now, Colonel?"

The old man's voice came back. "Sixty-three that we know about. They're jamming the frequencies as fast as they find them, so we're not getting complete information. Are you sure they're all right?"

"They'll be seven hours behind us. We waited as long as we could."

"I know that, Manner."

"What's the word from ProLab?"

"They promise to have a solution by tomorrow."

"Tomorrow! Colonel, at this rate—"

"Sorry to cut you off, Manner, but we've got to keep this short. And I *know* what every minute of delay means. What's your ETA?"

"Nine hours eleven minutes, sir. Have you got the technicians standing by?"

"Affirmative. The moment we have the information, they're ready to start work. Just have your crews ready—" Static blared, ending the reception.

"Jammed," Longley said. He threw down the handset in disgust.

"Shall I try another one, Admiral?"

"No, Brenda. There's nothing we can do until we get there. And I'm not the Admiral. Ben Slate is."

"Yes, sir."

"Then they're deteriorating," Slate said. "They've gone mad."

"That's one of two possibilities," Brother John said, nodding. He'd eaten the rations from six SurviPaks during the past two hours, and swallowed most of the potable water aboard the scouter. His face had returned to its normal patchwork of tan and white. "The other is that Ravi and her New Army have taken off on their own."

"I don't see any reason to believe that."

"It's a matter of knowing the players, Sapper. And I remember some of them, now. I know what Ravi did to me, so I know what she's capable of. But I had it wrong before. What I went through with Alti F'ir was different."

"They were putting you back together," Slate said. "I understand that. But they'd already transmuted Ravi. They *made* her that way. And Kiner—"

"Kiner proves my point," the giant said. "Other than physically, he was exactly the same before transmutation, as after. The process just gave him the confidence to be more of what he already was. I think it was the same with Ravi."

"What about Leonora? And that GeeBee—Alti F'ir—on *Kin'Te*?"

Brother John sighed. "I don't know, Sapper. I don't understand that at all. That's why I'm calling it a possibility."

"You still feel something for Alti F'ir. That holo brought it back."

"Yes, I do. I admit it. Maybe it's something they caused me to feel, and maybe it isn't. But I do know what those gold ships have done. Three worlds, and fifty of our fleet. So I'll do whatever I can to stop them, and it won't matter who's driving them. I hope you'll believe me about that, Sapper. Admiral." He smiled, for the first time in three days.

"I do, Brother John." But he noted that his friend had said 'stop them'; not 'kill them.'

They got the news the moment they boarded *Troubador*. The enemy had struck, hard. Eighteen hours before—while Longley and the fleet waited for the call to pick up Slate and Brother John—the golden city-ships had reappeared. Hundreds of them. And without warning they'd begun to murder on a scale never witnessed by humankind. From Landfall to Far Horizon the worlds of the Great Domain perished. Sixty-three worlds, gone. No survivors. Eleven of those worlds had been host to the smaller Duel Schools. Now there were six, including the only one to occupy an entire planet—Barrow Academy.

The enemy was jamming all registered warpsignal frequencies. Only a few, the ones most rarely used, were left. Slate understood now why Manner Longley's message had been so brief—to give the enemy no time to pinpoint and jam the transmission. Communication was in chaos. Most of the Great Domain did not know that tens of billions of human beings had been slaughtered. Soon they would all know, as word was passed piecemeal on secure channels. That would take days to accomplish; and for that reason, might be a task never completed.

Sixty-three worlds, gone. It was assumed that the death toll had risen since *Troubador* had received its last report, three hours before, while the rest of the fleet headed for Barrow.

They winked into hyperdrive the instant the Mark III's were ready. As they settled into their cramped quarters Dr. Bey knocked once and entered the cabin.

"You have heard?" he said to Slate.

"Yes, Jim." Somehow he was not surprised to see the physician aboard *Troubador*.

"Then I will be brief, and leave you to rest." He examined both Duelists and pronounced them fit. "I am giving you a sedative," Dr. Bey announced. "You will need to be refreshed when we reach Barrow."

Neither argued; there was nothing they could do until they returned to the fleets. And nothing they could do then, if ProLab hadn't found a way through the enemy's defense.

Slate swallowed the dram of thick liquid and washed it down with a cup of cold water. He was asleep within minutes.

It was as if the nightmare were there already, waiting for him to arrive. It began with a scream, a defiant wail of anger. Far ahead of him a diaphanous curtain was ripped aside by a figure moving too fast to see. Beyond the veil was his mother. She was bound and submerged in a glassite tank of clear water. Facing him, drowning. He ran to her, calling her name. But the distance only increased. *Help me! I gave you life. Why won't you help me?* The tank dissolved and another appeared. It was Arika An' Nor, Sweetie. She was immobile, as if made of stone—as if mocking the love-name he'd given her, his ebony statue of Venus. Suddenly she had eyes, and they opened, wide and pleading. Her eyes were condemning. *I loved you. Why won't you help me?* He pounded on the glassite, calling her name, watching her die. And then he was alone in gray nothingness.

A golden ship floated out of the mist. He found himself aboard, plodding through bloody hunks of flesh. Leonora stood against a bank of computers, staring at him.

She wept as he approached. He opened his mouth to curse her but his throat would give no sound.

Kill me, Ben. Like you killed Marty. She lowered her eyes. He tried to ask her, Why? WHY? His hand streaked to her throat of its own accord and someone said, "Ben! Ben!"

Smelling salts. The face of Dr. Bey hovered above him. He pushed the hand away and sat up slowly. "I'm awake." The dream slipped away and was gone.

"Is he all right?" Brother John asked.

"I'm fine," Slate answered, straining to center his mind. *She's gone. You're here. Do your job.*

Dr. Bey peered into Slate's eyes for a moment, seemed satisfied, and nodded. He handed him a towel. "You are soaked with perspiration, Ben. Unfortunately the showers are without water. We have been deployed rather long."

"How long before we get there?"

"Another three hours, Sapper. You woke me up."

"They were mild sedatives," Dr. Bey said. "In case we find the enemy enroute."

"What is the situation now?"

"We don't know," Brother John said. "I called the Control Center while we were waiting for Dr. Bey to arrive. They're not using the warpsignal at all, for obvious reasons. But I wouldn't count on good news when we get there."

It was a catastrophe. The old warrior looked as if he'd aged thirty years in the time they'd been gone. "They were killing us, son," he said to Slate ten minutes after they'd entered the Colonel's South Office. "Slaughter is what it was. The known total as of this moment is one hundred fifty-two worlds. Demolished. Gone. All in the past twenty-five hours. All of the Duel Schools, except Barrow and Bellenauer." Tears rolled down his cheeks. "Billions of people, son. Scores of billions. They're all dead. We couldn't protect them." He looked away.

"Colonel," Brother John said gently. He put his hand on the old man's shoulder.

"I'm all right, son," he said. He looked up at Brother John and touched hands with the giant. "You've always been my second son, you know. All those years I thought you were dead. And then you came back. I couldn't tell you how much ..." He covered his face. His body shook as he wept silently.

Brother John walked to the window. He locked his hands behind his back and stared silently out at the empty fields of Barrow Academy. Small drops of water fell to the tops of his boots.

Slate said, "Why have they broken off the attack?"

The Colonel took off his reading spectacles and rubbed his eyes. "We got the first reports of this six hours ago. About an hour after Longley brought the fleet in. The reports were jammed almost as soon as they began. But we got enough to put together a fuzzy picture. All of the GeeBee ships, from every point of attack, are headed out. We don't know why." He took a long drink of tea and made an effort to stop shaking.

Slate sat next to his mentor, his friend, wishing he could reach inside him and switch off the anguish that filled the old man. More than a tenth of the human race was gone, brutally murdered in just a few hours. The fabric of the Universe was torn. And it was all . . . pointless. Insane.

Why were the GeeBees invading? Slate found only one answer; they believed it was their right. They believed that they owned humankind. The GeeBees believed they were God. The New Army believed they were the Army of God. Perhaps, as Brother John believed, they'd gone beyond their holy commission. It didn't matter. The GeeBees had created them, and launched them like demons at the unprotected throat of humankind.

Benjamin Slate had never known what to believe of God. He had never looked deeply into the question. Perhaps there were no answers. Perhaps there were too many. But he knew what the ultimate sacrilege—the ultimate evil—was: to claim the mandate of God and to do murder. He knew that much of God. And he knew that God was not a race of malignant aliens—who changed people into ageless beings of monstrous evil. And destroyed one tenth of humanity in a few hours of hell.

The Colonel straightened. His eyes were wet and hollow. Slate could see the fight raging in him. *Hold on,* he thought. *Hold on. The same fight rages in me.*

"The GeeBee Ships—" the Colonel continued. Brother John came back from the window. "They all seemed to stop at once, wherever they were. They all began heading in one direction." He cleared his throat. "If you chart the direction taken by all the groups of GeeBee ships, the course lines come together. I'll show you." He went to the huge *Atlas of the Heavens* and began flipping through the pages.

"Here," he said. It was an artist's rendering of the spiral arm of the Milky Way Galaxy. The Great Domain was outlined within it. The entire habitation of humanity occupied a minute fraction of one spiral arm, of one galaxy tucked among billions of galaxies. It was a picture to inspire humility.

"They're headed about here," the Colonel said. "This is where all of their course lines converge." There was nothing there. His finger touched a point of open space in the vast emptiness between arms of the galaxy. "We're closer by two days to that point than most of the GeeBee ships are right now, assuming their top speed is about what ours is. It's the ideal place to meet them. The moment we've got effective weapons, we've got to send out the ships. All of them."

"I think I agree with you, Colonel," Brother John said. "But I have to ask. Suppose there are more of them than we know about? Or suppose those ships outflank us and come back?"

"Then all the ships we have, no matter where they are, won't make a bit of difference," the Colonel said bitterly. "They can attack anywhere, and be back in hyperspace before we get there. And if they hit us with that much firepower again, there won't be a soul left alive to throw a rock at them." He turned to Slate. "You're the Commanding Admiral, son. It's your call."

There were two possibilities. They could let the enemy run, and hope they wouldn't be back again. And humankind would never be free of that fear. If they did return, it would be at a time and place of the enemy's choosing. That had just occurred, and 10 percent of the human race had been butchered.

Or the UDF could go after them, putting all of its strength into the effort. If the UDF won, it would be over. If they lost—it would be over.

A memory—only months ago? Impossible—came to Slate. A bout he'd fought on 652-E, against a young man from Titan. He'd backed away, and the man had stopped. A mistake, Slate remembered thinking; a Duelist would have moved in to finish the job, always prepared for a trap.

He said to Colonel Pritcher, "We go, sir. And I want you with me. Clear?"

The old warrior grinned at him. "You bet your . . . Yes, Admiral. Son."

⇥18⇤

Five hours later Slate was awakened from a fitful sleep and summoned to the South Office. The call from ProLab had come in.

"They asked for me, specifically?" he said to Colonel Pritcher as he stepped through the door. Maggie and Brother John were already there, sitting together on the couch that had been a chair for Dr. Bey.

Colonel Pritcher motioned him to a seat and spoke into the desk intercom. "Put it through, Frieda."

A holo-image appeared in an empty space across the room.

"Sweetie!" The image was so clear, Slate had to restrain the impulse to reach out. The scale was set to full presentation, giving a life-sized image of Arika sitting behind her desk, which, as usual, was neatly arranged with small stacks of reports and boxed tapes. A framed picture sat on one corner of the desk. Even at this oblique angle, he recognized it. It was the one of them together at ProLab's C'est Magnifique, the restaurant in which he had proposed marriage. The magic of that evening filled him again. Arika was wearing the same high-cut blue dress she'd worn that night; highly inappropriate for work, but just right for now. The message was personal and unmistakable. He said her name again, and she smiled back at him across the light-years. "You look wonderful, Ben."

"I'm beginning to feel that way." Her eyes showed the fatigue of nonstop work, but the light in them was dazzling. She was petite, darkly complected, and her hair was a pool of liquid black that poured over her left shoulder and down between her breasts. Her hands were folded demurely in front of her on the teak desk, the left overlapping the right. He looked at them and wished they

172

were alone, so he could reply to the mixed message she was sending him.

He smiled self-consciously and made the introductions.

"Please call me Colonel, Arika."

"And call me Maggie. You're more beautiful than your picture, Arika."

"Thank you. But of course I *am* a picture."

"It was a joke," Brother John said.

"Yes, of course. Hello, Brother John. It's a pleasure to meet you, after so many of Ben's stories. I'll come immediately to the point. My team has been working on the data transmitted by Captain Joyce. We have a solution."

Slate felt the Colonel's hand grasp his shoulder tightly.

Arika continued. "The information is being relayed directly to your ships' databanks at this moment. That should take only a few more seconds. I understand that your technicians are prepared to begin work immediately?"

"Yes," the Colonel said.

"Good. My explanation to you will be brief. We've analyzed the spectrum surrounding those ships. Captain Joyce was correct in that it matches nothing we've encountered before. Fortunately, the GeeBee ships had their shields raised at the time he was recording."

"Arika—" Maggie said.

"I understand, Maggie. Please be assured my long-windedness will not delay your ships' progress." She looked to her right, to a point outside the image-field. "The data has all been transferred. But it's important that I mention a few of the basics."

"Of course, dear."

"A team working with us was able to generate a model which produced the same electromagnetic spectrum as had the shields of the GeeBee ships. The principle involved is that if two objects produce identical fields, the objects themselves are functionally identical. The field my colleagues generated was identical to those of the GeeBee shields, to within thirty decimal places. Rather than examine the field minutely, my team opted to determine how our generated model would react to the types of weapons you deploy. That, it turned out, was the correct path to follow." Slate could guess whose inspiration that had been.

She continued. "In simple terms, the energy sent against their shields was absorbed at the point of impact and diffused along the entire shield. That diffusion produced a momentarily unstable frequency, which varied with the intensity of incoming energy. And that instability is the key. We can use it to get through the shield." She paused for a moment and watched them react.

"Your weapons will be modified to generate a series of disharmonics that will shatter the shields at the very instant they react to your firepower. That is to say, the shields will evaporate precisely *because* they react to your firepower. The result is that your weapons will now penetrate.

"There is an additional item to discuss," Arika went on. She smiled with obvious pride. "We're also sending you new detection technology. Even while they're in hyperdrive, you'll now be able to detect the GeeBee ships, and yours. You, however, will still need to be in normal-space while you scan for them."

"That's astounding," the Colonel said. "We can do this with the equipment we now have?"

"Yes, Colonel." She turned to him. "This development represents a fundamental shift in the way we have thought of distance. Shall I give you a point-by-point conversion—" The image flickered, and was gone.

Frieda's voice came through the desk intercom speaker: "They may be jamming again, Colonel. The signal's dead."

Brother John was halfway out the door when he stopped to look back at Slate.

"Sapper?"

The Master Duelist kept his eyes on the empty space where the image had been, willing it to return. She'd been wearing it. For the first time. The ring had belonged to his mother, and to his grandmother, before that. It was one of his few tangible memories from childhood. Arika knew its history, and its meaning to him. It was why she'd made the call personally, and why she'd prolonged it: a private message, meant only for him. She'd always refused even to try it on, until they were formally married. Her wearing it now meant that she loved him, and that there would be no marriage. Arika was telling him that she believed one or both of them would be dead before the wedding.

Frieda was only half right, he knew with a certainty that left him empty. The signal wasn't jammed; it was dead. Sweetie was drowning. *She's gone, too. You're here. Do your job.*

He said to Brother John, "Let's go, old friend."

● ● ●

From a detached corner of his mind Slate noted the heightened animation and edged laughter of Manner Longley and the five Duelists who clustered around him at the wardroom table.

He had seen this phenomenon, been a part of it, hundreds of times before. The writer Eurnace called it fatalistic excitement; the warrior mind preparing for battle. The warrior mind—it was an odd thing, Slate thought, feeling himself an observer more than a participant this time. Centuries of relative peace among humankind had made it odd, by making it rare. Among the spreading billions of the Great Domain, the warrior mind was common only among the Duelists. It was to be found elsewhere: often on the new colonies and outposts, here and there in the Peacekeeper units. But it was the norm, the currency of life, only among the 30,000 men and women who adopted the warrior mind and code as their profession—the Duelists.

Billions of people were dead. The mind could not grasp the enormity of such a thing. The mind grieved, because it was human to grieve. But the warrior mind—it stood above the human part to listen for the opening shot; and rushed ahead to stand ready in the blocks. War. The warrior mind. Each impossible without the other. It was the age-old paradox, cast in a new metaphor: Which came first—the chicken, or the egg; the war, or the warrior mind?

Watching his fellow Duelists, he felt light-years away from them. She was—No. He would not allow the thought to cripple him. If there was a God, if Benjamin Ronald Slate had been born for a purpose, the time of its fulfillment was at hand. He could not allow himself the indulgence of personal grief.

Manner Longley said, "Ben, did you hear me?"

"What?"

"Hyperdrive in thirty seconds."

"Go ahead, Manner. I promised Mosher I'd see him. It may as well be now."

The six Duelists filed out through the door. A second later it opened again.

"Come in, Wilky."

Wilkington Mosher entered, walking with the assistance of a stout wooden cane. He looked like a different man; from all reports, he was. The flamboyant Duelist had refused a clonic replacement for his shattered knee. In place of the gaudy silver-foil uniform he'd customarily worn, he was dressed in a severe black robe that hung loosely from his muscular frame. His white hair was pulled back from his neck and secured with a black cord that draped to his shoulder, then extended upward again to form a coiled wrapping for his new beard.

"Thank you for seeing me, Admiral," he said quietly. "And thank you for allowing me to accompany your fleet."

"The decision was left to Colonel Pritcher, Wilky. He believes you'll change your mind, and help us."

"I'll help," Mosher said. "But not in a way that will satisfy him."

"Why did you ask to see me?"

"I used you badly, to establish myself with the UDF. I apologize for that."

"That's not necessary. But please, sit down."

Mosher slid into the seat and put his cane on the table between them.

Slate said, "I've thought about our confrontation." He told Mosher how he'd first met the Long Man. "I didn't know who he was at the time, but I used him to draw attention to myself. Do you understand what I'm saying?"

"Yes. The difference is, you didn't challenge him to a death match."

"No. The difference is that you chose someone whom you knew could fight back. In that sense, you acted more honorably than I did."

"Thank you, Admi—Ben. My other purpose in coming here is to convince you to abandon this fight."

Slate shifted uncomfortably in the seat. "Wilky, I agreed to see you because I respect you. I always have, from the time I was a child. In fact, I idolized you. Along with Admiral Barrow, Master Hernandez, and—"

"And I respect *you*, Ben. More importantly, I understand you. I know what you want of me. And I tell you honestly, you won't have it." His expression relaxed. "Since we're being candid, I'll admit that becoming an idol, and then staying that way, was my primary motivation in life. But I was wrong. Horribly, wastefully, wrong. The beating you gave me at Barrow Academy began the process which led me to that understanding."

And Brother John completed it, Slate thought. Everyone he'd spoken to about Mosher said that the taped description of Alti F'ir had had a profound and immediate effect on Mosher. "It pushed him over the edge," Manner Longley said. Maggie Pritcher described him as "Mystical. Scary." Brother John said that he hadn't, and wouldn't, discuss the tape with Mosher.

"Colonel Pritcher told me you're a priest, now."

"I am. Actually I always was, in terms of education. My father was a Priest of the Heir. I was trained from early childhood to follow him into the calling. But as you know, at the age of majority I was distracted. For fifty-five years." His voice had a note of humor, and a smile filled his face. Slate remembered seeing that smile once before, but the memory was indistinct.

"You think it's wrong to fight the GeeBees, because you believe they're God."

"What I'm telling you is that it's *futile* to fight Alti F'ir. You can't win this war."

"I see," Slate said angrily. "We should let them murder a hundred billion people, and retreat peacefully. Or is it that the quicker the GeeBees win, the fewer human lives will be lost in the war? Is that why you won't help us, Mosher? For humanitarian reasons?"

"You can't goad me, Ben. I know what you're trying to do, and I know the game better than you do."

"Then *use* what you know! *Help* us!"

"That's exactly what I'm doing. I'm warning you not to fly into Armageddon. Do you know what I'm talking about?"

Slate sighed. "I've read the legends. The final battle for humankind. Good against evil, the final death match." A sudden thought struck him. "If that's what you believe, Wilky, tell me this. Who's good, and who's evil, in this war?" 'Good' was prophesied to be the victor at Armageddon. No one could describe the GeeBees as good; not after what they'd done.

Mosher smiled patiently. "Ben, don't try to fit God into your narrow understanding. You've got to stretch your mind, reach out with it! Strengthen it, the way you've trained your body."

Slate stayed on the attack. "You don't have an answer, do you? The GeeBees killed a hundred billion people, Mosher. Is that good? Or evil? Answer me!"

Mosher remained unruffled. "God has never refrained from killing, when killing was necessary. If you've read the legends, as you call them, you know that. And you know that what you're doing is futile. And yes, wrong. When my ancient namesake left Egypt for the Promised Land—"

"Wilky!" He'd half left his seat. Mosher never flinched. It was supposed to be a ruse, but Mosher was making him genuinely angry. Slate sat down and composed his thoughts. "I know what you're talking about. Moses, the Canaanites. He slaughtered them because God told him to. I don't believe that, and I don't believe what you're saying now. But if you're right, then God deserves to lose this battle. And I'm going to make sure that happens. With your help, or without it."

Mosher reddened. The Colonel's advice was beginning to work: *Make him babble. Then make him see how crazy he sounds. We need him, son. Get him mad, and get him on our side.*

"Ben, you're being incredibly dense. Don't you see it? It's just as it was written. For twenty-three hundred years there's been a written record of what's going on right now. The spread and increase of humanity, the corruption and evil, the wars. And finally, the Heavenly Host that will descend from the clouds. Space! Do you see? It's Alti F'ir, and the New Army. And"—his eyes narrowed in triumph, as if he were delivering the final thrust in a death match—"the Cities of Gold!"

Slate didn't respond. He'd heard the speculation about those ships. Describe them to anyone, and they would seem instantly familiar. *Humanity's collective unconscious. Universal symbolism. The GeeBees know our legends, and use them against us. It's God.* The Great Domain was bursting with theorists, secular and religious, competing for media time. Slate had his own theory: What the chatter didn't take into account was that the GeeBee ships were built to travel across distances that were centuries in the future for humankind. Their odd design and appearance served practical functions, which were not yet understood. To attribute more to them than that, based on some murky historical coincidence, was stupid. And a waste of time. Whatever the GeeBees were, they were murderers. And they were going to die.

Mosher plunged ahead, mistaking Slate's silence for partial acceptance of the truth. "You see it, don't you? Those ships have been seen for thousands of years. Read the Bible, the Book of Revelation. It describes a city-ship down to the last detail, *landing* on Earth. For too long we have refused to see the truth, Ben. We can't refuse now. *You* can't refuse. It will mean the total annihilation of humankind." Mosher's face was flushed and contorted with fanaticism. He paused and caught his breath. "So you see, you can't beat them," he said more calmly. "You'll die if you attempt it. Because it's already recorded that they'll win. It's done, Ben. Finished. Don't throw away your life and the lives of your friends in a war you can't possibly win."

Slate stared at him. Mosher's eyes were almost luminous; he believed what he was saying, with absolute resolve. Longley and Maggie were right about him. "Wilky," he said gently. "Do you hear yourself? This is—" He hesitated, not sure how to proceed. He wished Dr. Bey were in the room.

"You're not a fool, Ben. You believe me. Half of you does, and the other half is terrified that it's true. But you needn't be afraid. It will all work out for the best." He smiled. "You'll see."

Slate looked away from what remained of a great warrior. No Duelist could ever believe what Mosher was saying. Duelists lived a life that inflicted instant, final judgment—they understood that the future was a result of decisions and actions taken in the present. No fight was over before it began.

The last vestiges of anger had passed. Now there was only compassion. This combat genius wouldn't help them, because he couldn't; he'd gone mad.

Mosher said, "Ben, turn the fleet around. Go home. What's coming, you can't change. And when it arrives, you won't want to."

Slate stood. "Expert Mosher, I'm sorry it's come to this. But I'm ordering you confined to your bunk until this is over. You'll be watched at all times."

"I respect your authority, Ben. I'll do as you order. But—"

"Goodbye, Wilky." He turned and exited the wardroom, headed for the Control Center.

⇺19⇻

"Come here, whore. I want you to see this."

Leonora was shoved roughly forward. She stumbled, recovering her balance three feet from the message screen.

"There," Ravi said, pointing. "Our agent on ProLab reports that your Ben Slate and five hundred fifty ships have completed weapons retrofit and departed Barrow. They will undoubtedly be waiting for us. Are you afraid, Leonora?"

"No."

"You are a liar."

"You know that's not true. I'm not afraid to die. After what I've just seen, I pray for death."

"I hear your prayer. And I sentence you to live. Or I may change my mind again."

"I don't care, Ravi. Why did you call me here?"

"Because," she said, taunting, "I believe you do care, and I believe you are afraid. I enjoy watching your face as death comes closer, and . . ."

"I'm tired, Ravi. And you're boring me. May I return to my quarters?"

"Ten days from now we will arrive at the wormhole. Once we enter, we are safe."

"I see. You want my assurance that you're right about that."

Ravi shrugged. "You are an engineer. You have studied such phenomena."

"The quantanomaly, as it's properly called, will take you away from the Milky Way. I don't know how to determine exactly where you will end up."

"Father can make the calculations necessary to—"

"Then ask Father."

Ravi laughed. "Perhaps I will. Father would be happy to help me." Her expression became serious. "But as long as my Legion enters together, it makes no difference where the wormhole takes us, does it? When we reenter it will return us to our point of departure instantly. And anyone entering the hole after we have passed through would arrive somewhere entirely different. That is correct, is it not?"

Leonora said tiredly, "Yes, Ravi. That's the way it works." She wished she could lie to this creature. But Father's training was too strong.

"Excellent!" Ravi looked again at the screen. "My Legion is nearly assembled. We are entering hyperdrive shortly. When next we return to normal-space, we will be within one hour of escape."

"You're afraid to stay and fight. I'm not surprised."

"You cannot disturb my mood, you pathetic child. We will return when I decide. And our victory will be final. I have plenty of time, Leonora. I am like the stars themselves. I will go on forever."

At maximum speed the UDF would arrive at the course-convergence point in eight days. With luck, they'd be waiting there when the GeeBees and the New Army arrived. Slate settled into a routine of studying everything available from *Miyoshi's* library and data files that dealt with tactics. He made a list of all combat veterans aboard, excluding Mosher, and set a schedule to interview each of them. At precise ten-hour intervals he left his cabin to patrol the Control Center.

On his fourth check—two days out from Barrow—they found them. The screens lit up the moment they dropped down to normal-space.

Manner Longley whistled. "If I'm reading this right, Ben, they're three A.U. out from us. In hyperspace."

"You're reading it correctly, Commodore," the technician said. "Their speed is eight percent below our maximum."

"Your Arika is a genius," Longley said, grinning.

"Yes," Slate said. There were two groups of fourteen GeeBee ships, one well ahead of the other. "Can you get a course on them?"

"Still headed toward the convergence point, sir," the technician said. "Do you want the numbers?"

"No," Slate said. "Let's get moving."

This time, Slate stayed and sat down in the command chair. Twenty minutes later they were at maximum drive. He noticed that it was unusually quiet in the Control Center. The electric excitement that he'd been avoiding for two days was gone, and in its place was the quiet determination of professional warriors. All of them wore the mask that discipline demands of fighting forces. Manner Longley and Brother John were cloistered with the weapons technicians, checking and rechecking the new weapons settings.

Dr. Bey made frequent trips to the Control Center on the pretext of verifying everyone's health. Like the rest of them, he wanted to be there when the action began.

Maggie and Colonel Pritcher walked together from station to station, observing and passing on words of encouragement to the young technicians. Each of them had retired from personal combat decades before, but for this final battle they wore Duelist uniforms. They had earned the right.

After watching his friends for an hour or more Slate stepped down from the chair and left the Control Center. *Make yourself visible,* his mentor had said. *That's part of your duty.* The Duelist teams were resting as well as they could in the cramped quarters available. All had recently lost family or friends. Many had no home world to go back to. But morale was high among the warriors. Vengeance was near; they were on the offensive.

The ordnance rooms were bristling with pent-up energy. The weapons components were polished to a high sheen, indicating the fervor and readiness of the men and women who serviced and operated them. They were aching for battle.

At the end of the tour he checked the emergency vehicles. There seemed little need for them. At normal-space speeds the journey back to the Domain's most remote outpost would be measured in thousands of years. But he inspected them anyway, because battle was a matter of discipline and preparation. Nothing could be overlooked. It came as no surprise to find that Manner Longley's crew had already seen to this detail. The four armored scouters were ready in quick-release airlocks. The fifteen lifelaunches were stacked securely, packed with food and water.

The tour, he knew, was for his own benefit, a way to satisfy the restlessness. *Miyoshi* and its crew were ready. And he knew that those going out to fight were the lucky ones. Each warrior carried a tiny portion of his fate. No matter how small, each had a part to play, something to say about the future. *The warrior mind. Here, now, it owns the future.* The rest of humankind could only wait to see which side returned from battle.

Wilkington Mosher had been in hell for seven days. He turned over in his bunk, biting his lips and pulling the coarse blanket up over his face. He was soaked with sweat and trembling. "I'm sorry," he murmured in the darkness. "Sorry."

The bunk curtain was drawn open and a young Duelist peered in. "Expert Mosher." She waited and tried again. "Expert Mosher, are you all right?"

Mosher jerked the blanket down and blinked in the harsh light. The Duelist drew a quick breath and backed away. His eyes were starkly bright, seeming ready to leap from the dark circles around them. Blood dripped from his mouth. "I'm sorry," he said, reaching out for her. The Duelist took his hand. It was burning.

"I'll get Dr. Bey," she said, turning and rushing from the berthing compartment.

When she'd gone, Mosher sat upright and pushed the blanket away. "I'm sorry," he said. "But today is the reason I was born."

At top speed *Miyoshi* and the UDF reached the convergence point exactly 192 hours from the time they'd left Barrow Academy. The point was actually a broad area, an estimate based on course projections. On arrival the 550 ships spread out in net-formation in a flat plane covering 4 million square miles of space. The 219 city-ships were only two hours away.

There was no guarantee that the enemy would come out of hyperdrive at the convergence point. If not, they would chase them, firing every time they entered normal-space. Eventually the city-ships would either turn to fight, or outrun them. It was not a comforting thought. If the enemy escaped, no person would ever again look into the night sky without wondering, *Where are they? When will they be back?* It all depended now on the enemy's intentions: Fight, or flight.

It was fight. The golden city-ships came out of hyperspace 20,000 miles from *Miyoshi*. Moving fractionally below the speed of light, the net closed within seconds. The UDF ships braked to dead-slow at a distance of fourteen hundred miles from the enemy and opened fire on Longley's order.

Unexpectedly, the GeeBee ships broke formation and charged directly at the UDF lines. Within the first five minutes the battle deteriorated into a dogfight.

It was impossible for the UDF ships to form up. Worse, they could not fire without risk of hitting their own ships. "Gunner!" Longley called above the rush of activity. "Cut your range to ten miles. Tight focus." The word was passed to all ships to cut range. The battle was so close and quick that the radar screens were useless. The moment a blip flashed on-screen, it was gone again.

"All ships, automatic fire," Longley called into the Battle Control circuit. The fleet's weapons systems were instantly set to locate, identify, and fire at a target without manual input. Things were moving too fast, too close, for human senses to follow.

"All ships, random turns," Longley ordered. "Don't stay on any one heading longer than five seconds."

Over his shoulder he called to Brother John, "Go to the observation port and establish a comm link. I'm blind in here." It was a ship commander's nightmare. He could not see the enemy, and could not control his weapons.

"Right." Brother John ran for the hatchway.

"Manner, I'm going with him," Slate said. He was useless here; the niceties of large-scale tactical maneuvering had no place in a fight like this. Perhaps he could be of some value at the port.

"Thanks, Ben."

The view from the observation port looked like an entertainment holo gone mad. Ships streaked through a strobe effect created by the firing of guns. Long tracer-blades of light stabbed into the darkness. Great golden cities flashed and glowed in the illumination of hundreds of weapons firing. One of them charged directly at *Miyoshi*, passing less than a hundred yards below. It was past them before Slate realized that he'd tried to jump away.

"Blessed Saint Barrow!" Brother John roared, watching the mammoth gold ship disappear under *Miyoshi*.

"What? What did you say?"

"Sorry, Manner," Brother John called toward the two-way speaker. "One of their ships nearly rammed us. Nothing to worry about."

"I'm looking for areas of enemy concentration," Longley replied. "That's where I want to take *Miyoshi*."

"There doesn't seem to be one," the giant said. "They're all over, mixing with our ships."

"Ben, can you see what effect our fire is having?"

"Very little," Slate said. "We seem to be scoring a lot of hits, but I don't see any damage."

Brother John grabbed his arm.

"Wait," Slate called into the speaker. An instant later he said, "We've damaged one, Manner. The entire upper section is splitting ... there it goes. Gone. Out of view and burning." He turned to share the moment with his friend. Brother John was staring out the port. For once, Slate could not read the expression on his face; perhaps because it was a new face. Then his expression changed to one Slate had seen often: Rage.

He raised his arm and pointed at the port. "Sapper, they just got one of ours. It's ... oh, Blessed Saint Barrow, another one! Damn it, they got another one! Those murdering—" Two sleek silver craft tumbled, jetting crazily with escaping plumes of ignited oxygen.

"Ben," Longley said over the speaker, "I'm passing the word to all ships to regroup. We'll move out and see if we can form up."

"Agreed," Slate said.

It was no good. They moved out and regrouped, and the city-ships were in among them again like angry hornets. Slate saw another enemy ship burn and explode. And he saw three more UDF ships die.

They pulled back and regrouped again, with the same result. Two more golden-city ships perished. And eight more UDF ships died. It became a pattern: Regroup. Meet the swarm. Kill as many as possible. Regroup.

It went on, a chaotic and deadly ballet, hour after hour.

There was no way to know how many of the enemy remained. It was impossible to count them as they streaked across the radar screens. But radio checks presented a dismaying picture of the UDF ships. After seven hours of battle only 191 remained of the original 550.

Slate felt helpless, watching the carnage through the viewport. He could not cross the mat and grapple with the enemy. He could not pit his strength and skill against lights and mammoth hulks of gold that flashed and were gone in a heartbeat. He could only watch as his forces killed, and were killed.

The pattern continued. Regroup. Fire into the enemy as they swarmed. Fight and dodge and kill, and wait for the blast that would end their lives. Regroup. Begin again.

Longley tried reversing the tactic, sending the UDF ships in different directions, hoping to break up the enemy. He tried it only once. Ten city-ships swarmed around two of the UDF, killing both in a one-sided slaughter.

After nine hours of battle the UDF was down to eighty-one ships. Four hundred sixty-nine ships—17,000 crew and technicians, along with 8,000 Duelists—were dead.

A messenger brought a printed radio dispatch to Slate. One of the UDF ships had managed to slip away to a distance sufficient to count the GeeBee craft. His heart sank when he read the number. Ninety-six. The enemy was killing them by a margin of nearly four to one. Retreat was impossible. Fifteen minutes of idling time to set the Mark III's for hyperspace was suicide. Longley had penned at the bottom of the note, "Any ideas?"

"Mosher," Brother John said from over his shoulder.

"Exactly," said Slate. "But he can't help us. He's insane."

"Maybe. But he's definitely standing ten feet behind you. I think you should turn around. Very slowly, old friend."

⇛20⇐

"Brother John is right, Ben. Slowly is correct."

Mosher was standing inside the hatchway holding a 9-kilo Barrow leveled at Slate's chest. He looked like hell. Dried blood had stained the black robe in streaks that gave the impression of exotic jungle camouflage. His hair was matted with sweat, and the eyes a biographer had once described as 'Roman-keen and deadly blue' were now puffed and red, seeping with clear fluid.

His trademark smile was jarringly out of place.

As Mosher held the weapon, Brother John took two steps away from Slate and regarded him sadly. "I tried to warn you, Sapper. We both did. You refused to see the truth. I'm sorry." He said to Mosher, "We've got to move fast. Have you taken care of Longley yet?"

Slate paled. "Brother John . . . no, I won't believe you're a traitor."

"I'm not. I will not betray Father. Why are you so slow to understand?" He turned from Slate and extended his hand to Mosher. "Welcome, brother."

The blast from the Barrow singed the giant's ear. His head snapped back and he glared at Mosher. "What are you *doing*?"

"Traitor!" Mosher said vehemently. "You'd abandon us for those . . . creatures?" He wiped a sleeve quickly over his eyes and adjusted the aim of the weapon. "The head, Brother John. This will kill you permanently."

Slate jumped between the two, holding his hands out protectively. "Wilky, stop! Don't you see what he was doing?" Mosher held his aim steady—two feet above Slate's head.

"I'm glad *you* do, Sapper," Brother John said.

"I'm not slow to understand," Slate said dryly.

Mosher stared for a moment with wet eyes. Then he nodded and bent over to place the Barrow on the deck. "I brought it to ensure that you'd listen, Ben. Then when he . . . I think we understand one another now."

"I think so," Slate said. But his first reaction had been genuine. For a moment he'd doubted his brother. "Wilky, do you know the situation?" He thanked whatever gods might hear him that Mohser's madness had passed.

"Yes. There is a way. Come with me." He turned and ran down the passageway as quickly as his crippled leg would allow. They passed through the narrow corridors and hatchways leading down to *Miyoshi's* hangars. Mosher jumped for the open deck hatch and slid down the ladder into the compartment. Brother John and Slate landed just behind him, clanging against the steel deck plates.

Mosher snatched the intercom handset from its bracket. "Admiral Longley."

"Wilky! They're looking for you. Where are you?"

"Manner, listen to me. I'm with Admiral Slate and Brother John. We're taking three of the armored scouters out. Pass the word to all ships to launch them immediately. Is that clear?"

"Negative, Mosher. Let me talk to Ben."

Mosher turned to face Slate and explained hastily. "Each ship has four scouters. Launching them will effectively quintuple our numbers. Get them out right away, Ben. It's all we have." He was holding the handset keyed as they spoke, allowing Longley to hear them.

Longley cut in. "Wilky, those scouters carry 15-kilo Barrows. They won't have any effect against the GeeBee ships. You'll be targets, nothing more."

"Correct," Mosher said. "Scouters are fast and maneuverable, ideal for this type of action. The idea is to harass them, to disperse their fire. That will give the warships more time to concentrate fire."

Slate snatched the handset, overwhelmed at the simplicity of the idea. It was so obvious. Now. "Do it, Manner. Everything as he says." He turned around at a noise behind him. Brother John was across the compartment, climbing into one of the armored craft. "We're launching immediately. Pass the word to all ships to get those scouters out."

"Yes, sir." There was a second's pause. "Ben, I'm coming down there."

He'd anticipated that. "Admiral Longley, you're ordered to remain in command of *Miyoshi* and the fleet. I'm sorry, Manner. I know you'd rather be out with us. But we need you where you are." He softened his tone. "I'm pulling rank on you, my friend."

"Yes, sir," came the reply. "Good luck, and . . . wait." The intercom clicked off. Three seconds later it came back.

"Ben, Maggie and Colonel Pritcher want to take that fourth scouter."

He hesitated only for a moment. "Yes." From behind him he heard Mosher sealing himself in a scouter. "Maintain radio contact, Manner. And good luck." He reached to replace the handset.

"Ben—" Longley's voice stopped him.

"Yes?" Behind him the two scouters were whining to life.

"If you don't get back, I want you to know—" The handset clicked off.

"Thanks, Manner. But I'm coming back."

"I want you to know that I'll go and see Arika. I know she's alive, and I'll tell her about this. If you don't beat me to it."

Slate raised the transmitter to speak and then lowered it again. After a moment he found his voice. "Thank you. Brother."

A window popped open behind him. "Let's go, Sapper! What's a dogfight without fleas?" Cables attached to the bottom of the two craft were pulling them forward into launch position.

Slate replaced the handset and climbed aboard the scouter nearest him. Someone had stenciled a name in red letters on the control console. Nancy. He hoped Nancy had a little influence with another lady—Luck.

There was a slight jolt as he activated the cable. In seconds the three scouters were side by side, ready. The inner airlock door slid shut and locked into position. The cables released and snaked away, their metallic grinding lost in the rush of air escaping into the vacuum of space. The air-bleed stopped abruptly. Slate checked the console light. Green. Good seal. He looked across at the two Duelists. The giant grinned and raised a fist, thumb pointed upwards. Mosher repeated the gesture.

Slate brought his hand down, hitting the toggle to activate the quick-release. The outer door jerked open and locked against cushioned steel dampers. Escaping air propelled the scouters out into infinite blackness.

Once clear of *Miyoshi*, Slate applied half-throttle. The engines flared to life, giving him instant control. As he steadied the craft he caught sight of Brother John's scouter ahead and above him, streaking away toward a golden ship. He smiled. The giant was in full control already, taking the fight to the enemy. The image lingered for half a second, and was gone. Mosher was nowhere in sight.

The silver hulk of *Miyoshi* disappeared behind him. He drew in a deep breath and let it out slowly. Free. At last, the open arena.

As the seconds passed, Slate found himself relaxing, letting the tension flow out of him. For too long now he had lived, fought, in a way that was unnatural to him. This was better. This was the way a Duelist should fight. Here he was in control. Here he could see the enemy, the distant and the nearby golden city-ships that flashed in the lights of battle. He smiled as the familiar thrill of individual combat returned. And with it came the sobering confidence of the consummate professional. This was a death match. Like the hundreds of others he'd fought—and won. The scouter was effectively unarmed; no matter. His preference was always to fight empty-handed. It was a lesson learned and taken to heart early in training. YOU are the weapon. YOU are the death of your enemy.

He pulled the scouter into a tight downward bank and rolled until he was directly in the path of the nearest GeeBee ship, fifty miles distant. The seat slammed against his back as he pushed the throttle to full open. He sighted in the Barrow and depressed the firing button. There was a satisfying hum from below. After two seconds he released the button and jerked back on the control stick. The golden ship flashed under him. It felt so good, he laughed out loud.

He could not damage the colossal ships, but he could force them to pay attention. He could dive and swing around and fire. Again. And then again. He could drive them mad. What had Brother John said? Fleas. Yes. He could drive the enemy to a frenzy, scratching at the flea. *Soon there'll be a swarm of us. And then the warships—avenging birds of prey—will form up and kill all of you.*

It was good, being a Duelist again.

He knew he was fatigued, pushed beyond any sane limits of endurance. All of them left alive, were. And he understood that

his mind was fighting to keep itself focused on the job at hand—
and so it was lying to him, creating this illusion that painted ugliness with bright and glowing colors. He approved. *Lie to me,*
he thought gratefully. *Keep me in the game.*

The panorama was suddenly, stunningly, beautiful. The enemy
ships were eerie, strangely splendid, great walled cities of gold.
The UDF ships were sleek and silver, gleaming needles piercing
through the black fabric of space. *She* would agree, he thought,
wherever she was. She would be sickened at the human cost,
but—

"Ben!" He jumped half out of the seat, the straps holding him
down. He snatched the handset from its bracket.

"Go ahead, Manner." He reached below the pilot seat for the
headset. Checking to see that it was tuned to the command channel, he pulled it on, freeing his hands for flight.

Longley's voice came through clearly. "All of the scouters
have launched. There was nearly a riot, we had so many volunteers."

"I'm not surprised," Slate said, watching the battle unfold
against the limitless Universe. "This is the best, Manner. Next
time you can come out and play."

"I'll hold you to that. Anything to report? Other than how
much fun you're having?"

"Negative. It'll take a while to know what effect we're having." He spotted another enemy ship moving in his direction and
careened over to head directly for it. "What is your status?"

"We're down to sixty-seven ships, Ben." Slate's heart sank.
"Whatever you can do, this is the time. I'll check back with you.
Good luck."

"And to you, Manner." Suddenly the illusion was gone. His
friends were dying. It was not lights and pageantry out there; it
was death. He sideslid into the path of the golden ship and
opened up with the Barrow. The ship never wavered. Damn! He
wished that this time, this time when it counted for so much, he
was not empty-handed. He pulled up and watched helplessly as
the mammoth ship passed under the scouter. It didn't even bother
to swat him.

Wilkington Mosher sang softly to himself, a happy song he'd
learned early in childhood. "When the faithful . . ." He spotted
two more scouters flying toward a city-ship and yawed his craft,

waving hello at his comrades. ". . . it's the twilight of their la-
bors, the dawn of their joy . . ." Longley said they were all out
now. A good man. They were all good, the Duelists and
". . . forever safe and home . . ." *Not for Wilkington Augustus
Mosher.* There was another of Father's ships. Gold was so beautiful. So good. ". . . that passeth understanding . . ." *I war against
God. I am damned.* But seven days in hell hadn't been so bad.
Not for Wilkington Augustus Mosher. ". . . shall ever see His
face . . ." *Let's see what an eternity there is like.*

He hit a switch and pressurized oxygen dumped to a cut-open
exhaust line, incinerating him instantly.

The battle fell into a pattern. Charge, fire, pull away. There
was no lack of targets. With every burst of fire from the larger
ships, the deep blackness revealed the enemy. Slate dove and
twisted and banked, flying into the face of the beasts. But his efforts were met with the greatest insult a fighting Duelist can receive. He was ignored.

Every few minutes he saw other scouters swarming like fleas
over the dogs of war, fighting the same fight that consumed him.
They too, were ignored.

One by one sleek silver needles exploded and burned, tumbling out into the void between spiral arms. Fury mounted like
a living thing inside him, burning his flesh and choking off his
breath. There was nothing he could do. The only moments of relief were the fiery spectacles of golden cities erupting in death.

"Ben," the voice came softly through the headset. "Ben, can
you read me?" He switched the radio to transmit on the side-
channel.

"Yes, Mom." He wondered if they were in one of the scouters
he'd seen. No matter. They'd be out there somewhere, giving it
everything they had. Colonel Pritcher was a Tournament-grade
scouter pilot.

"There's a lot we want to say to you," her voice said. "But . . .
Brother John, are you monitoring?"

"Yes," Brother John's voice came on. "I'm here. How is your
hunting trip?"

"We want to say goodbye," she said. "To both our sons."

"What?" Slate shouted. "Are you hit? Where are you?" He
craned his neck, looking in every direction. It was a reflex,

useless. Even if they were in sight, one scouter could not be distinguished from another.

"We're not hit." There was silence for a moment. "The Colonel is dead."

"He's not!" It was Brother John's voice. "Blessed Saint Barrow, what are you talking about?"

"His heart stopped, Brother John. Fifteen minutes ago. I couldn't save him."

Slate cut in and said slowly, "All right, Mom. Return to *Miyoshi*. Admiral Longley needs all the help you can give him."

"No, Ben. I'm not going back."

"Maggie, that's a direct order," he said, more harshly than he'd meant to.

"You can't give me orders, Ben. I was born a Barrow. And I'm dying a Pritcher. Either way, I outrank you."

"Mom, you're not going to die. Now listen to me."

"*You* listen," she said. "There's something you don't know about me." Slate couldn't believe what he was hearing; Maggie was laughing. She continued, "I never learned to pilot a scouter. Not these new ones. The Colonel always—" Her sobbing was quiet, as if she'd pulled the mike away from her mouth.

"Mom, turn the beacon on," Slate said, his eyes sweeping constantly across the scouter's instrument panel and viewplates. "Hit the red switch just below the fuel gauge." The battle continued outside the viewplates, the ships of both sides moving in random, chaotic patterns. The only thing predictible was that the patterns ended in death. Slate's mind reeled from the force of a sudden thought. *It was happening again.* He was eight years old, the last time. Now, again, his mother and father were dying; and there was nothing he could do to save them. Again. All around him a deadly mob, this time in spacecraft, moved and killed, and moved again. *There was nothing he could do.* "Mom," he said weakly into the transmitter, "please hit the red—"

Maggie Pritcher's voice came clear and strong through Slate's speaker. "And Brother John, there's something I promised not to tell you. But I'm breaking that promise. There's a woman. Myra Stanley. She said she knew you on some mining colony. She's called us several times in the past few weeks. She loves you, and I couldn't talk her out of it. You go and see that woman as soon as this is over. I want your promise on that."

Brother John's voice was quiet. "I promise. I've never forgotten Myra." He switched on his own beacon.

Slate understood immediately and headed away, to avoid duplicating search areas.

"Good," Maggie continued. "And when you two get back to Barrow, open the safe behind the portrait of Grandfather Simon. His diaries go to you. Everything else, we've left to your children. Don't leave it unclaimed, either of you. Goodbye, sons. We love you." The radio clicked off.

Brother John's voice came over the radio. "Sapper, I'll search the area within fifty miles of me. You—" The transmission cut out.

She'd toggled the all-frequency transmitter. Her voice was low and calm. "Is this the beacon? I think so. Don't worry, they'll find us. One last ride, Colonel. Too bad there's no moon. Here, give me your hand. I do believe one of us is shaking. Good, keep a steady course. We met this way, isn't it wonderful? It was a good partnership. You're still the most—" The crash was a shriek of metal, ending in thunder. Slate saw them then, ninety miles away and falling from a city of gold, flaming like a new star.

A second later the heavens were black again.

The next voice came through thousands of tiny bells that nested like insects in his ears.

"Sapper."

"Yes, Brother John." Space ahead was empty. Slate shook his head. There was the enemy. He headed for them.

"I'm switching back to the command channel."

"Yes."

"There's nothing to say, Sapper. Do you understand?" His voice grew lower as he spoke. "They're gone. Let's get on with it."

"I know, Brother Jo . . . Brother. I know." He took a deep breath and pushed it out until he was empty. It helped. Twice more, and his mind cleared. Slate said in his best command voice, "Listen to me. I know you, and I know what you're thinking." *Blessed Saint Barrow, I sound like the Colonel. He was so proud, she said. I brought him here. I've killed them all.*

"What am I thinking?"

"You wanted to ram them once before, Brother John. We may

have to do just that. But until I determine that it's necessary, you will *not*. Clear?"

"Yes," Brother John said. "I was about to say the same to you. We may be hurting the GeeBees. The only thing to do is to go on."

"Agreed." Slate suspected that his friend's words were only to prevent him from doing what the giant had already decided to do—ram. The fleas were having no effect, and they both knew it. Even ramming was probably useless. But it was not time yet to find out. And not Brother John. He'd been cheated of fifteen years of life. A good woman waited to give a portion of it back to him. But Longley was wrong; Arika was gone. Life owed Slate nothing.

He switched the radio back to monitor the command channel. There was only silence, as expected. The Duelists commanding the scouters would keep the channel clear for its intended purpose.

He fought back the impulse to check in with Manner Longley, to satisfy himself that *Miyoshi* hadn't been destroyed. Part of him didn't want to know. If *Miyoshi* were gone like the Pritchers . . . And if Manner were still alive and fighting, he would have no time for conversation. And there was nothing he could do for him now, from where he was. But . . . the argument went on inside him.

The wall of gold came from the left side, sudden, mammoth, filling half of the viewplate. Reflexively Slate jerked hard on the control stick and pushed the throttle to full speed. He was thrown backward and wrenched to the left as the scouter tried to stand on its tail and twist away. The golden wall filled the entire viewplate. He stared, transfixed. The plating looked like individual bricks. He ripped the straps away and jumped behind the seat. Where was the suit? Should have put it on before . . .

The impact ripped away the tail of the scouter and sent the craft spinning end over end until it slammed like a wind-borne flea against the speeding tower of gold. He thought, as the darkness came, that it should have sounded more like thunder.

"Sapper! Sapper!"

He opened his eyes, disoriented. There was no light.

"I'm on the way. Hold on."

"Brother John." The headset was pushed down against the

back of his neck. He moved it up slowly, wincing. His left arm was pinned beneath his back. It was impossible to roll to his side and free it. Eventually he worked the mouthpiece back into place. "Brother John."

"Your armor held. The scouter's armor held. But it may not hold for long. Can you get to your suit?"

"I don't think I can move." He tried. "Did I just scream?"

"Don't think about that. I'm going to land next to you. Do you understand? I'm coming down to get you."

Land? Down? "Where am I?"

"You're on the deck. You're on the deck of the ship you rammed. You stopped it. It's not moving. You *survived*, you idiot! I told you not to ram. Why don't you ever . . . never mind. I'm in my suit, I'll hook a towline to your scouter. Just stand by. I'm on my way."

The aborigines of Earth's Australia called it Dreamtime, he remembered, marveling that his mind was suddenly so clear. It was almost pleasant. But it hurt like hell. Still, it was funny. A Master Duelist, squashed like a bug.

"Good, keep laughing. Anything to stay awake. I'll be down there in five minutes."

Dreamtime was over. "No!" The sudden movement sent pain flowing like hot oil through his veins. *The nerves are intact,* he thought. *Good. And bad.* Aloud, he said, careful to lie absolutely still, "You will *not* come down."

"Sapper, I'm four minutes out. Keep awake, and stand by."

"You can't help me. Do you understand? You can't help me. Get away from here. Bring *Miyoshi* to this ship. Destroy it. That's a direct . . . My word as a Duelist. You can't help. Don't land."

"You're an idiot. I'll be there in three and a half minutes."

"No!" Tears welled in his eyes from the pain of moving. "Bring *Miyoshi* back here before the GeeBees repair the damage. That's an order." He managed a weak laugh. "Let me go out as a hero." It was funny because it meant absolutely nothing. The Ancient Greeks were right. Comedy and tragedy were the same thing.

"There must be a chance—" The giant's voice faded.

"I swear to you on the soul of Asher Slate, Brother John. You can't help. Please go. Bring *Miyoshi* here and finish this ship. Please."

"Sapper. I . . . goodbye. I love you. I . . . goodbye, Brother."

"I know, Brother. I always knew. Goodbye." He relaxed and felt it all flow away from him. It was peaceful. Rivers of peace. *Miyoshi* was coming. The death of a Master Duelist would not be accomplished cheaply.

There was a trembling. Searing pain jarred him awake and he gritted his teeth against it. He pushed it into a corner of his mind and mentally walked away from it, as they'd taught him. Soon he felt himself pulled away in a current of fatigue. Delicious, warm fatigue. More trembling, but it didn't hurt. The scouter seemed to be shaking apart. But he knew the trembling was only in him.

There was a tunnel into light. He gazed up into it, astonished to see that the old stories were true. Peace like a river. A tunnel into light. There was a face. Only a shape, a dark outline lost in the light, but familiar, smiling. Kind. Loving face. But pain! Why pain?

The tunnel ended at the face. Something cool and soft touched his cheek.

"Ben?"

⇒21⇐

He had come for her at last, but he was near death. For three days she stayed near his bed while delirium wracked his body. Only once did he open his eyes—one glorious moment that added hope to the ordeal of waiting. His glazed eyes may not have seen her. But he had smiled fleetingly when she spoke his name. That was enough. He would know that he was not alone in the fire that consumed him.

She dipped the cloth rag into the bucket and sopped up the last few drops of water. It would be enough to cool cracked lips, but only for a moment. She opened the cloth and draped it over his forehead.

She didn't turn around at the opening of the heavy metal door behind her. "Is he dead yet?"

"No." She bunched up the cloth and wiped his face. "I must have more water."

"You'll get more tomorrow. It's your own problem that you're wasting it. I understand he was your lover. If you want a better man, I'm interested."

"The infection is burning him alive."

"Good. I'm delighted that his death isn't an easy one."

"Help him!" She admonished herself immediately for the show of anger. It only amused them. She said quietly, "If he dies, you have nothing to bargain with."

"The Army of God doesn't bargain. We've offered mercy to this pagan. Personally, I'll be glad when he's dead. But it isn't us that's killing him."

"You injected him with the bacteria," she said levelly. "His body is strong enough to destroy it. But the dehydration . . ."

The door slammed shut behind her. She lifted up the cloth

from his forehead. It was dry and hot. "Stay with me," she whispered. "Stay with me, my love."

The desert sand of Eusebeus baked the skin of his back. The sun was worse. It beat against his chest, pushing him deeper into the sand with every heartbeat. What was the name of that sun? He couldn't remember. It should be Hephaestus. Or Vulcan. Then he remembered. Lea. Stupid name for an inferno that burned a man to death.

The first drops of rain on his forehead stung like falling icicles. He opened his mouth to capture the life that suddenly fell in torrents. Every pore of his skin drank deeply in the swell of water. The coolness trickled down his throat and washed through him in wave after ecstatic wave. He raised his head, begging the sky for more.

"Ben?"

The sand made a statue, and the water gave it color and life.

"Ben, drink slowly. Too much is dangerous."

Eusebeus disappeared. He blinked the dryness from his eyes. It *was* her face. Clear, this time. The words formed in his throat, but he couldn't hear them above her warm laughter.

"I have told you a hundred times, Ben. It was Aphrodite who came down from Olympus. Venus was a Roman deity."

"My ebony statue of Venus," he repeated, "come down from Olympus to the valiant warrior." He smiled, loving her. "Haven't I ever explained? Aphrodite was wanton. Your only need is me, Sweetie."

"Yes, Ben-bug. That is true."

They embraced in silence while he marveled at the joy, the strength of her. He stroked her hair and face and tried to hold her closer, and still closer. She pulled away gently.

"No." He half-rose to catch her. "Stay where you are."

"You are still weak, Ben. You must—"

He grinned. "I'm not *that* weak. Come back here."

Arika backed away, holding his hands, laughing with him. "You must remain lying down. I am tempted to take advantage of you. But not now."

"Sweetie, I love you. I want you."

"Yes." She smiled. "But now is not the time."

He protested, "This is exactly—"

The voice came from behind his head. "Hello, Ben."

Arika laughed at his expression. "I believe you remember Leonora D'Meersopol."

"Wha—" As he craned his neck, the metal door burst open. Three men in identical gold tunics entered the cell and carted away the tub of water. A fourth stood at the door with a weapon pointed unwaveringly at Arika's chest. One of the men reentered the cell and gave Slate an injection which he accepted only because Arika nodded for him to allow it. The same man returned a minute later with a tray carrying three cups of water and a brick of bread. No one spoke until the men had gone and the door was again shut.

"I feel better." Slate sat up slowly on the cot. "Stronger." The dizziness passed in a few seconds. Arika sat next to him while Leonora retrieved the tray and sat with it between herself and Arika.

Leonora broke apart the loaf of black bread and passed each of them a piece. "You'll forgive me if I don't wait for you. This is the first food I've had in three days." The crust cracked as she bit into it. She put the cup to her lips and drained it in one fast gulp. Leonora regretted the impulsive act immediately. "That was stupid," she said, blushing. "I know better."

Slate examined his own bread and then stared at Leonora. At a nod from Arika he offered Leonora his cup, which was still nearly full.

Leonora shook her head and swallowed with obvious difficulty. "Thank you, but no. The bread will last longer this way. Besides," she said firmly, "I wasted my water. I won't waste yours as well."

Slate and Arika exchanged a glance and began eating. The dry, powdery bread was nearly impossible to chew, but Slate found that he was ravenous. As he ate he walked, examining the cell. The floor, ceiling, and windowless walls were constructed of the same uniformly gray metal as the door. Dim light came from a translucent panel in the ceiling, three yards from the floor. The cell was four yards by six, with two cots arranged end-to-end against one of the longer walls. A wash basin and toilet were built into the opposite wall. He tried the plumbing; there was no water to either.

He turned to see Arika and Leonora watching him, sipping from their cups. He could understand why he and Arika were here. Ransom, information, perhaps an exchange of prisoners, depending on how the battle went; clearly, it had not been decisive, or he wouldn't be alive. The thought gave him hope.

But why Leonora? She seemed to be a captive, as they were. But he'd seen long ago that Leonora was not what she appeared to be. Obviously his captors were also of the New Army. Leonora's presence here could mean that a rift had developed within its ranks. Mutiny? That could be good news; a divided enemy was always easier to defeat. What might have caused the division? And which side had the support of the GeeBees—Alti F'ir?

His legs were mildly tired from the brief movement. But he felt in fair condition, considering. It helped, waking up to ebony Venus. He asked, "Sweetie, how long have we been here?"

"You were taken nine days ago," Arika said. "You have been in this cell for the past four."

"And you?"

"I was abducted from ProLab while making that call to you at Barrow." She smiled at him. "I knew you would come for me. But frankly, I expected a more gallant arrival."

"How did the battle end? And where, exactly . . ." An agonizing thought struck him. She'd been in their hands for eighteen days. "Sweetie, did they do anything . . . Did they torture you?"

"Leonora has told me about the process of transmutation. I assume you mean that."

"That's what I mean."

"No. I haven't been changed in any way. But they told me at first that you were dead. Later they told me that you'd been captured alive, but that you were dying. I didn't know which statement was a lie until I was allowed to see you. So yes, I was tortured."

"I'm sorry, Sweetie." He crossed the cell and bent down to take her face in his hands. "I'm all right," he said, kissing her. "We're both all right."

He straightened and turned to Leonora. "I know how to kill what you are."

Leonora gasped and stepped backward as if physically struck. She blushed red and swung a hand at him. Slate caught it easily, ten inches from his face, and pushed her roughly away. She retreated halfway across the compartment. "After what you did to Arika, and to Briones and his crews—" He strode after her, fists clenched.

"Stop, Ben." Arika placed herself between them.

"Sweetie, she's one of them. Because of her—"

"Stop. Don't hurt her."

"Why? She's a murderer. A hundred billion—"

"Ben!"

He felt her hands pushing back against his shoulders, and saw through a red haze that Leonora was weeping. It was like the dream aboard *Troubador*. But there, he'd been called awake. This time was different.

Arika pushed with all her strength against him. He barely noticed her force; but her eyes slowed him. "Ben, I know about the dead. Leonora has told me everything. Please, listen to what she has to say."

Her eyes held him as he backed away to the opposite wall. "I'll listen. For you." He sat cross-legged on the metal floor and took a deep breath. He held it for a moment and pushed it out slowly. "Go ahead."

Arika took Leonora's hand in hers and led her back to the cot. When they were seated she said, "Tell him, dear. Tell him what you told me."

"All of it?"

"Yes. From the beginning."

Leonora nodded and turned to face Slate. "You knew about me, didn't you? You noticed something about me soon after we met."

"I knew you were different," Slate said. "Everything I've learned since has ..." He paused, watching Arika look from Leonora to him and back again. "... has confirmed it."

"Different," Leonora said. "Yes, that's the right word. I didn't know."

Slate nodded his head. He hadn't understood it then, but it made a little sense now. Brother John's memory didn't return for fifteen years; there were still many things he couldn't remember.

"I thought ... how do you say it? I *thought* I was like everyone else? I *assumed* that I was a human being?"

"That explains nothing, Leonora. Brother John went through the same process you did. It changed his body, but not the essential man."

She shook her head. "No! It was not the same. I was first taken by Alti F'ir at birth."

"At birth? You told me you were raised on Meersopol, in an orphanage you called Home."

"And I told you that I have no memory of my parents, or anything at all before I was seven years old. Do you see? I was with Alti F'ir for seven years before I was taken to Meersopol. I didn't know that, until recently."

"They killed your parents to get you?"

"No. Alti F'ir could never do a thing like that."

He laughed bitterly. "Either you're a fool, or you think I am."

Arika said quietly, "Ben."

"You mentioned Brother John," Leonora continued. "Alti F'ir changed his body to save his life. In my case, it was the mind, for another purpose. The changes in me were deep and elemental. There was some surgery, but most of it came from being exposed to Alti F'ir since birth. I became . . ." She hesitated, looking for the precise word. "Acclimated, to Alti F'ir."

"Imprinted," Arika said.

"What?"

"You were imprinted at birth by Alti F'ir. The phenomenon is experienced by all individuals, of every sapient species. It is the process by which an infant feline, for example, becomes aware that it *is* a cat, and belongs with others of the same species."

"Yes, that's it, then." Leonora turned to Slate again. "When I was returned to human company I remembered none of it, on a conscious level. I grew up to be fundamentally, but nearly invisibly, different from everyone else."

Arika said, "Returning to Alti F'ir has nurtured in Leonora's mind seeds that were planted in her early childhood."

Slate smiled at her. "Sweetie, I thought you were a spectranalyst."

"I am. But I was born in a library." She laughed at his blank expression. "A joke, Ben. Imprinting. It's a joke. Do you see?"

He loved her. "Yes. Go ahead."

"Alti F'ir taught her to live by the way it perceives reality. I confess that I don't understand everything that Leonora has told me about it. But in essence the differences she speaks of are alien only in that they are ideally, rather than commonly, human. One of the things you saw in Leonora on that mining colony was her open honesty. Normal human interaction is nearly impossible without some form of deceit. This is commonly human. So much so, in fact, that its absence is disturbing, at a level too subtle to recognize or name. Leonora was always uncomfortable with such things as manipulative behavior, or true but misleading statements. Now she is totally incapable of deceit."

"If I understand you, you're saying that Leonora was made better. Or an alien concept of 'better.' Those changes you're describing are subtle. But they experimented on Brother John's brain also. In his case there was nothing subtle about what they did. They put him through agony, and they made him love them for it."

Leonora objected. "No. Brother John came to love Alti F'ir naturally. He stayed with Father for nearly a year after his transmutation. But when he saw Ravi again, everything changed for him. Ravi claimed Brother John as her lover, and her property, for eternity."

"Why did she butcher him?"

"He remembers that?"

"Yes. In detail." *And what did you intend for me?*

"I'm sorry, Ben. Ravi told me about it the first time we met. In detail. I'd seen her with a Duelist named Jerzeel . . . It's something she enjoys doing."

"Answer my question."

"Ravi is . . . I don't know how to explain Ravi. I know that in her mind it made perfect sense. She believed that by doing what she did and then bringing Brother John to Alti F'ir for transmutation, she was both killing and giving life. She expected him to realize this, and to acknowledge her as his master. Forever. As others have."

"He saw things differently."

"He hated her for what she had done. But his time with Father had had an effect on him. Instead of taking revenge, he went to Alti F'ir and asked for justice. Ravi was banished with those who wanted to follow her. She was to be in exile for ten years. But she came back and abducted him." She lowered her head again and was quiet.

Arika squeezed her hand. "Go on, dear. He must hear this."

Leonora nodded and looked again at Slate. "Brother John was bound and given a pain-enhancing drug. He was starved and tortured for weeks. Ravi offered to 'forgive' him, but he cursed her." She looked up at him. "I don't want to tell you this."

"Go on," Slate said through clenched teeth.

"She put him in a coffin, Ben. It's a special device she keeps above her bed. I was in it twice. I nearly went mad."

"He escaped?"

"No. The drug kept him in pain, and awake. After a few days she shut off his air. When she thought he was dead, she had him taken back to Father as a gesture of contrition. She knew Alti F'ir could restore his body, but she believed his mind was irretrievably gone. Alti F'ir managed to repair most of the damage—but Brother John was never the same again."

Slate said disgustedly, "I see. So then Ravi was welcomed back, and made the leader of the New Army."

"No! She was made a permanent outcast. Ravi built the New Army from exile. She told me she used the oldest principle of politics, that the way to gain power is by promising it to those who will follow. During the next fifteen years, most of those who were transmuted went to follow her. Those who refused, she killed. That's how Ravi built her Army of God. The ships already given by Alti F'ir became her Legion."

"Wait. Are you asking me to believe that Ravi and this New Army are totally separate from the GeeBees? From Alti F'ir?"

"That's right."

"And that it's been that way since *before* the killing began."

"Yes!" she said emphatically. "That's exactly what I'm telling you."

Arika said, "There is much here to absorb, Ben. Please be patient."

"I'm sorry," Leonora said. "I got ahead of myself." She took a sip of water and offered Arika the cup. When it was refused she placed it on the tray between them.

"But—" Slate's mind raced while he tried to put all of this into some logical order. Only then could he accept, or reject, what she was saying. "Why was Brother John left the way he was? If Alti F'ir is so skilled at healing—" He answered his own question. "Brother John didn't wait until his mind was completely healed. He escaped."

"That's the wrong word, Ben. You're still thinking of Father as Brother John's captor. That was never the case. Alti F'ir pleaded with him to stay and complete the process. But he was free to go at any time." She looked at Arika and then back to Slate. "I wish he'd been forced to stay. He went through so many years of confusion and pain because of the damage. But that's not . . . Alti F'ir will not compel a human to do anything against his will."

It was difficult to believe. And it was just as difficult to understand why he refused to accept it as true. Brother John had said as much, now that he recalled his friend's words: *Maybe it's something they made me feel, and maybe it isn't.* And something about transmutation giving Kiner the confidence to be more of what he'd already been. Why hadn't he listened? Why did he *want* to believe that the GeeBees were responsible for all the deaths? Because it was reasonable, he told himself. Humankind had never before met another spacefaring species; and never before had a hundred billion human beings been massacred. It was a reasonable assumption.

Or, he thought, it's because I don't want to believe that a human being could murder one hundred billion fellow human beings. And because the GeeBees aren't human. They're *different*.

Leonora misread the indecision on his face. "Let me give you an illustration. I never accepted transmutation."

His eyebrows crept upward.

"It's true, Ben. Cut me, I mend very slowly." She smiled and continued. "Father disagreed with me, believing that I was supremely foolish to reject such an offer. But my decision was respected. Do you understand the point?"

Full circle, he thought. "That brings us back to what you said before, about Alti F'ir not forcing anyone to do anything. If that's true, then the New Army was never compelled to kill for them."

Leonora said, "The New Army kills for itself, not for Alti F'ir. The attacks on those three Academy worlds were Ravi's acts of rebellion. Since then, Alti F'ir has waged war on her and the New Army."

It all fell together. "That's why those GeeBee ships we first met never fired at us. Those weren't New Army, they were true Alti F'ir ships." Then it fell apart again. He sat up rigidly. "Commodore Briones made a holo, Leonora. I saw what was done, and I saw you on *Kin'Te*."

"That was the ship we boarded?"

"That's right. I saw one of those things kill a man named Morales, then I saw your face at the hatchway." He turned to Arika. "Did she tell you about *that*?"

Arika said, "Yes, she did. Alti F'ir and Leonora arrived after

Ravi's ships had done their work. One of your vessels was left whole. That would be *Kin'Te*, then. When Leonora and Alti F'ir boarded, most of the crew was dead. Ravi's people had been there first."

Slate shook his head. "No. She lied to you, Sweetie. That holo showed Briones calmly describing the Alti F'ir ship. Nothing had happened yet. It went right on until Morales was killed. The ones he said were boarding were the ones who killed that crew." He turned to Leonora. "That was you."

Leonora looked at him, wide-eyed. "No! When we went aboard they were dead, Ben. All but one crew member. Alti F'ir killed him, because he was one of Ravi's people. That's the truth, Ben! I swear it, in Father's name."

"Then explain the holo. There were no gaps in it."

"Are you certain of that, Ben?" Arika asked. She turned to Leonora. "How long were you and Alti F'ir aboard *Kin'Te*?"

"Over an hour, Arika. We loaded the dead onto Father's ship. We were able to restore a few of them."

"Another lie," Slate said. "The tape was less than thirty minutes."

"Could someone have altered it?"

"Who? And why?"

Arika said, "It could only have been Mr. Morales. Perhaps he was to survive the encounter and present the tape to you. It would have given you many incorrect ideas. As it has."

Leonora said quietly, "You believe I'm lying to you, Ben?"

"I don't know. I just don't know."

"Why? Why would I lie? If I were what you believe I am—" She fell silent and lowered her head.

The story was plausible. She couldn't have known about the holo, and couldn't have had an answer prepared. But it was Sweetie who'd answered, not Leonora. Perhaps he'd said something about it in his delirium . . . No. Arika would never betray him. But if the cell were monitored . . . He'd nearly forgotten that he was a prisoner of the New Army.

Arika said, "There is no way to establish proof at this moment, Ben. It comes down to a matter of character. And faith. But I am willing to stake my life on the certainty that Leonora cannot lie. She had told the truth." Arika raised her voice and said emphatically, "Leonora is telling the truth. About everything."

Slate looked from one woman to the other, then said to Leonora, "You said Alti F'ir is waging war on Ravi and her New Army."

"Yes. Father was long in making that decision. But Ravi has to be stopped. She's given herself the title of Queen of Heaven, and claimed all humans as her personal property. Alti F'ir could never allow that. The ships, the immortal bodies, everything Alti F'ir gave was intended as a gift. But those who first received them demanded obedience from all others who wanted them. That's the basis of the New Army's strength. Ravi's first priority was to destroy the Duelists. That's how her first targets were selected. The second attack was to frighten the entire Great Domain into submission. *She* is the enemy, Ben. Along with her New Army. Alti F'ir created her, and is responsible. But Father never intended harm to humankind."

He said, sorting it out, "In that battle then, Alti F'ir and the New Army were fighting each other. But only the New Army ships were shooting at *us*. And we were killing both sides."

"No," Leonora said. "You were killing no one."

"No one? That's ridiculous. We lost nearly five hundred ships that I know about. But we destroyed a lot of theirs, too."

Arika said, "Ben, I would spare you this if I could. But listen to me. That data we transferred from ProLab to your fleet was flawed. Ravi's agents are responsible for that. Your weapons were totally useless against Alti F'ir shields. And of course, New Army shields are identical."

Leonora said angrily, "To be blunt, your ships merely got in the way. The New Army was delighted to kill you. But Alti F'ir was forced both to protect you as much as possible, and to fight the New Army. Your interference gave Ravi the help she needed, even while she was killing you. Father could have won that battle handily. True Alti F'ir ships are now superior to those used by the New Army. That was my doing."

"You?"

"Leonora is a brilliant engineer," Arika said. "You surely remember that about her, among other things. And recall also what I told you before about imprinting. Alti F'ir are her *parents*."

Leonora's eyes bored into his. "Alti F'ir pilots have millennia of experience to draw on. They are one mind, with coordination no human can begin to imagine. And with the improvements I made on the ships, there should have been no fight. Just a killing. But you and your ships made the task impossible." The anger she'd held in check came out in her next words. "Do you see what you did? You *rescued* the New Army!"

After several moments of stunned silence he said, "Sweetie, you believe her?"

"Yes, Ben. She's telling us the truth. We were together for several days before you were brought here. There is no deceit in Leonora."

And there never was, he thought, believing Arika. He had never known a more sure judge of people. "Then—" he didn't want to make it a question, for fear of hearing the answer, "then the New Army isn't holding us because they want something. The UDF is no threat to them at all. And Alti F'ir—" he said bitterly, "we prevented Alti F'ir from beating them."

"I'm sorry, Ben," Arika said. "But yes, that is true."

He sighed. "So. The war is over. The New Army won."

Both women looked at him, startled. Arika said to Leonora, "You didn't tell him? Why?"

Leonora flushed. "I couldn't, Arika. He was unconscious until you arrived. But it never occurred to me that he would assume ... I'm sorry."

Slate said, "I wasn't unconscious the entire time, Sweetie. I knew you were here when I was brought in. I heard you, and saw your face."

Arika shook her head. "No. That wasn't me."

Leonora said, "This is my cell, Ben. They brought you here because they wanted information from me. They knew that I ... They injected you with a bacterium that kept you in constant fever and pain. The price for the antidote was information." She lowered her eyes. "I held out for three days. You were dying of dehydration."

"She saved your life," Arika said. "And she made it a condition that I be brought here. I did not know until now that you were never fully awake." She put an arm around the younger woman.

Leonora returned the embrace and looked at Slate. "The war isn't over. Father prevented The New Army from escaping into a quantanomaly, a wormhole. But Ravi did escape into hyperdrive shortly after you were taken aboard. Alti F'ir followed. Forty-six of your ships survived, that I know of."

Slate exhaled slowly. Ninety-two percent of the UDF was lost.

But without Alti F'ir's protection, no human being would have survived the battle.

"Good. Thank you for telling me." Manner Longley, if *Miyoshi* survived, would have taken the remnants of the fleet home. They city-ships were too fast to catch in hyperdrive. That was lucky; the UDF forces had no idea how helpless they were. "And thank you for saving my life. But what information did they want? And why did they think you'd give it to them because of me?"

"Father distorted that quantanomaly," Leonora explained. "Ravi can't escape now. It will be unusable for millennia. There are others, but only Father knows where they are."

"Alti F'ir is still pursuing, then."

"Not yet. Father prepared for the possibility that help would be needed, before Ravi began that last assault on the Great Domain. I was there when Alti F'ir called in its other two minds, and all of its ships, from every part of the Universe. That's why I was taken. The New Army wanted to know how many of Father's ships were coming, and when and where they would assemble."

"You didn't tell them!"

Leonora sighed. "I didn't expect to. But yes, I told them."

"You lied?" he asked hopefully.

Leonora shook her head sadly. "I couldn't."

Arika nodded. "As I have said."

Leonora said, "Alti F'ir has been dying for thousands of years. There were only forty ships left to answer the call. The rest were already here, and most of them were recently destroyed." She turned away, not wanting him to see the anger again.

Arika said, "In total there are seventy ships left. All of them are on Barnabus. Ravi hopes to destroy them before repairs can be completed."

Leonora nodded. "That's where we're headed now."

Slate looked at her, surprised. "We? We're on a ship? I assumed this was a prison somewhere. A base."

"No," Leonora said. Her face broke into a grin, and she laughed. "This is Ravi's ship. It's the one you rammed."

"I didn't ram . . . Lucky me." He burst out laughing. The war was not over. Arika was alive, and they were together. There *was* hope.

"There is one more point to mention," Arika said. "Leonora

was kept in Ravi's coffin for four days. She nearly died, but she did not give her the information she wanted. She was then revived and brought to my cell. We spoke for several days. Ben, I have come to love Leonora. And she in turn has told me everything of herself. Apparently the New Army listened in on our conversations, as I assume they are doing now. That is how they learned that Leonora would give them information in exchange for your life."

"I don't understand."

"Then you are more dense than I have ever imagined. Think about it, Ben."

He thought about it. And he remembered a voice, half-heard through the fever. It had not been a dream. It had not been Arika. *Stay with me. Stay with me, my love.*

⇥22⇤

There was no reliable way to measure time. The meager rations arrived at intervals they called days. The dry bread was breakfast, and the cups of water were made to last until it was nearly time for the bread again. On the fifth such day the cycle was broken.

The same three men brought in the tub, this time filled with frothy, scented warm water. The fourth stayed at the doorway, as before, holding a weapon leveled at Arika's chest.

"Wash yourselves," the man at the doorway ordered. "And be quick. We'll be back with clean clothes in five minutes. Be ready."

"For what?" Slate asked, stepping toward him. The man kept his eyes on Arika, the gun held steady. Slate stopped. "Be ready for what?" he asked again.

The men left the cell and the door slammed shut.

Leonora undressed quickly and wadded the filthy tunic, using it to sponge water over herself. "This is a familiar routine," she said, scrubbing with vigor and obvious relief. "Come on, you two. We're about to meet the Queen of Heaven."

"You lied to me!" Ravi slapped Leonora again, this time knocking her to the floor. She stepped forward and kicked her in the stomach. Leonora moaned and bent double, clutching her knees to her chest.

Slate jerked his arms free of the men holding him. Batai Watanaba spun to face him. "Yes, Benjamin Slate. Master Duelist! Come! Come and stop her, before she kills the witch!"

Slate glared. Watanaba stood seven feet from him. It was as if he'd never seen her before. Her small face was contorted with hatred and blood-lust.

"You'll need your sword, Batty," he said. "Doesn't Ravi trust you with it?"

The man holding Arika laughed, pushing the blade closer against her throat. Slate put his hands by his sides and allowed the two men to grip him again.

"Well?" Ravi said, grinning at her ship's Captain.

"I don't need anything," Watanaba said. "Let him go. He has no courage. He is impotent. Is that not so, Master Duelist?"

"Under the circumstances—" Slate began.

Ravi sneered. "Circumstances? That is a coward's word for fear. You are all going to die, coward. You know it, and I know it. Why not die as a Duelist?"

It was tempting. He had seen Brother John with Kiner; he knew how to kill these immortals. Even as weak as he was, finishing Watanaba would be the work of seconds. He felt it in his bones. But Arika would be dead the moment he moved. While they were alive, there was hope. He remained still, saying nothing.

"Very well, then," Ravi said, turning back to Leonora. "Get up, whore."

Leonora climbed unsteadily to her feet. "I never lied to you, Ravi. You know I can't lie."

"Like Father?" Ravi mocked, slapping her again. "Like those hideous creatures that made you a freak?"

"You are more of a—"

"Quiet!" She knocked Leonora to the floor again. Ravi took a step back, breathing heavily, then said in a quieter tone, "Your lives are forfeit, because you lied to me. The sooner you tell me the truth, the less you will suffer. If you do not—" She let the words hang in the air.

Leonora stood up slowly. "I told you that Father was on Barnabus, with the last seventy ships. I told you the truth."

"My reconnaissance ship has arrived there three hours ahead of us. Barnabus is deserted!"

Leonora's eyes narrowed. She smiled after a moment. "Of course it's deserted. Did you expect me to keep your plans from Father?"

Ravi stared at her and then shook her head, amused. "Do not attempt another lie, Leonora. I understand now. It was obvious

that I would come, was it not? Father has run from me." She repeated the words in awe. "Father has *run*. From me!" She
clapped her hands in delight, hugging Watanaba and laughing
hysterically.

"Father did not run," Leonora said evenly. "You'll see the
proof of that on your screens very soon."

"Leonora, you are clever," Ravi said, flushed and beaming
with joy. "I truly wish you had joined me when you were given
the chance. But I know that you have not communicated. You
were never told of any plans. You have no idea where Father has
run." She touched her fingers lightly to Leonora's bodice. "And
so, you have no further value to me. Except"—she pushed her
face close, and traced a finger across Leonora's breast—"that
you will give me pleasure. For many days. I will save you for
the last."

Leonora answered calmly. "Ravi, I'm in contact with Father at
all times. All seventy ships are closing on your formation now.
You have seventy-two, which includes all your reserves. And
you will lose. Your only chance was to catch Father unprepared."
She lowered her voice to a whisper. "You know that I can't lie.
You've cursed me for it. Look at me," she challenged. "Am I lying?"

"Of course you are. Father cannot know where my ships are.
My instruments are as powerful—"

"Father knows where I am. Why do you think your ship was
untouched during the battle? Father knew I was aboard, and
knows where I am now."

Ravi hesitated. "How? Tell me how, liar."

"You know I was taken at birth. I received the surgery necessary to understand the sounds that Father makes. But the effect
was different for me because I was an infant. Now I don't need
to be close, as you do. I communicate with Father as the individuals communicate among themselves."

"Impossible! I would have known."

"Why? How would you have known? Why would I ever give
you such information?"

"You are lying to save your life."

Leonora laughed. "Oh? And how will this save my life? When
Father arrives, I'll die with you. I'm glad, Ravi. I'm glad to die."

Arika said, "No! She is lying, Ravi! She told me the truth. *All*
of it. You heard her!"

Slate coughed and cleared his throat. "Sweetie!" He'd just begun to understand Leonora's plan, and Arika was about to ruin
it.

Arika stepped away from the man who'd restrained her. He
lowered the knife. And then, incredibly, he handed it respectfully
to her. She took it and crossed to Leonora, holding the point of
the weapon two inches from her face. "Tell her! Tell Ravi you
are lying! You told *me* the truth!"

Slate pulled free of his guard and stepped toward them. "What
are you doing?"

Arika spun on her heel. "Be still!" she snapped. "If it is necessary I will cut her throat." She turned back to Leonora. "Tell
her. Now."

Ravi said to Slate, "It surprises me that you have not understood before. But since you are irreconcilably stupid, I will explain." She smiled warmly at Arika. "She has agreed to accept
immortality. In return, she has merely told us a few things we
wished to know, and sent you information which was not quite
so . . . accurate."

Slate's heart was breaking. "Sweetie—" he began.

"Never call me that again," Arika said angrily. "I have always
despised that common epithet." Her eyes softened. "Your value
to us was that this child loves you. You were revived only because Ravi wanted to hear Leonora's story repeated once more,
in your presence. I did not enjoy manipulating you as I did. I do
care for you, Ben. But our minds could never meet. You are
merely . . . a Duelist."

Slate was stunned. "*You* gave us the wrong setting for the
guns? A hundred billion people died, Swee . . . Arika."

"That was a small price to pay for what Ravi is offering the
Great Domain," she said. "Are you so dim that you cannot see
it? Immortality, Ben! Wisdom! The knowledge of the Universe
itself! I will walk that path of eternity, and I will never end! I
will know—"

"Enough!" Watanaba said. "You are pathetic, Arika. You are
nearly as stupid as he is! Ravi does not know the secret of transmutation. I was the last to be changed by Alti F'ir. But she does
know that you are a fool. And so does Leonora. She has used
you, also."

Arika flushed. "No, that's not possible. She told me everything. She *can't* lie."

Ravi's eyes hardened. "Then she is speaking the truth *now*?"

"No! I don't understand, but she couldn't deceive me. I know she couldn't."

Watanaba leered at her and said to Ravi, "Commander?"

Ravi laughed. "Yes, yes. Now."

Watanaba took a step toward Arika. The petite woman paled, moving the knife between them.

Slate said, "Batty, don't—"

The right foot of the Oriental woman flashed in a blurred arc that ended at Arika's throat. Her eyes bulged as she stumbled backward. Before Slate could reach them, it was over. Watanaba's hands closed over Arika's face and twisted. Her neck snapped as she screamed. Watanaba stepped backward, smiling into her dying eyes. Arika took a half-step forward and toppled. The knife clattered uselessly away. She twisted on the deck, as death came slowly.

Watanaba spit on her and turned to Slate. "You may end her suffering, if you like." When he hesitated she kicked Arika's chest, using the flat of her foot to inflict maximum pain. "Shall I continue?"

"No," Slate said.

Batai Watanaba stood aside and leered at him as he approached.

Arika was moving her hands together as her mouth worked, producing no sound. Slate saw what she was doing. He knelt beside her and gently took the ring she was holding out to him. Her eyes were wide with agony, and pleading. "Goodbye, Arika," he said. And then in a whisper he knew she would not hear, he added, "I can never forgive you." His hand went to her chin and touched it lightly. Arika closed her eyes and Slate jerked his hand upward. She gasped as her spinal cord was cleanly severed, and died.

"Now," Watanaba said. "What about this one?" She stepped toward Leonora.

Slate stood up slowly. "Me first, Batty." He slipped the ring in a pocket and held out his empty hands. "Let's do it the right way." He felt again the odd fear she'd once evoked in him. He welcomed it. He was going to kill that, also.

Watanaba bowed formally. "Since it must be so, Master Slate."

"Both of you stay where you are," Ravi said. She wanted

them alive, for the time being. And if Watanaba were to be in-jured, she'd learn that she too had been deceived. At a hand-signal from their commander, eleven New Army troops entered through three low hatchways and stood with Barrows aimed at Slate and Leonora. Ravi said, "We have business to dispose of first."

Slate and Watanaba regarded one another. "Soon," he said.

"Soon," she agreed.

Leonora's face had regained its color. Tears streamed down her face as she watched Slate.

He said to her, "You knew?"

"No," she said. "I'm sorry, Ben. I loved her. I didn't know."

"Then why did you lie to her?" Ravi said. "You caused her death, whore."

Leonora spun on her. "I did *not* lie to her! Don't you under-stand, you monster? I can't lie! I wanted to, so many times with you. But Father's training is too strong. I *can't*!"

"Then why did you not tell her of this ability you claim?"

"With you monitoring every word?" She shook her head as if losing patience with a particularly dull child. "Poor Ravi. You still don't understand, do you? I'll explain, very slowly. I resisted you only long enough to give Father time to prepare. When I gave you the information you wanted, it was to lure you here." Triumph shone bright in her eyes. "Do you understand now? I *wanted* you to go to Barnabus. I told you the truth, and it's going to cost you your life. You're going to die, Ravi. If you want to kill us first, you'd better do it quickly."

"Is that your plan? To obtain a quick death?"

"Stupid! You are astoundingly stupid!"

Ravi raised a hand to strike, then lowered it when Leonora refused to flinch. "Then why? Why are you telling me this? What do you hope to gain?"

"Satisfaction, Ravi. I want you to know that you're going to die. I want to watch your face while Father comes closer and—"

"Stop!" Ravi shrieked. Her violet eyes shone with rage. "How dare you. I am the Queen of Heaven. You will address me with respect!"

"You'll be dead, Ravi. Very soon. There's nothing you can do to save yourself. Father's ships are faster than yours. You'll see them on your screens within the hour."

"An hour." Ravi looked at Leonora for long moments, then at

Slate. She brought her breathing under control. "I will not die. And I will allow you to live, for one hour. We will see."

"Leaving me alive won't help you," Leonora said, taunting her. "Kill me now, if you dare."

Ravi flushed. "Under the circumstances, I will—"

Slate said, "Circumstances? A coward's word, Ravi. Remember?"

Ravi jerked her head around to glare at him. "We will see, Master Duelist. In one hour I will begin your death. You will beg me to let you end your own pain." She smiled. "But while we wait, please, sit and be comfortable. Would you like something to drink?"

"Ice water," Slate said. If he was right, it was what Leonora had flowing in her veins.

"Of course you remember me from Barrow Academy," Ravi said later.

"Vaguely," Slate replied truthfully. Her monologue had droned on for nearly an hour. He feigned interest, hoping she would lose track of time in the nonstop tribute to herself. But even if it would prolong their lives, his tolerance was near the breaking point. "You were three years behind Brother John and me. I remember you only enough to be amazed that Brother John chose you as his lover."

"I chose him. Among others." She laughed. "I am delighted that you continue to insult me. It will add to my pleasure when Leonora is proven a liar."

Slate said, "If you doubted her, we'd already be dead."

Ravi ignored him and resumed her life's story. "Four years after I graduated I returned to my home on Atlantis. My father had died by then, which was no loss to the Great Domain. My mother was remarried to a long-haul spacer who was away when I arrived. When he returned, he thought it quite inviting to find a beautiful young woman in his home. During the night he left my mother and came to my bed." She paused, smiling. "Apparently he had no understanding of what a Duelist could do. Unfortunately, he retaliated against my mother. She never forgave me for killing him." She glanced over her shoulder. "Ten minutes remain. Would you care for more water?"

"No," Slate said.

"A pity. I would enjoy watching it flow from your stomach as

I begin my enjoyment." Ravi shrugged. "To continue, my mother refused ever to see me again. A year later I returned to Atlantis once more, to see if she had regained her sanity. As I stepped through her door she shot me in the stomach. I believe it was a Barrow, although I never was certain. Her newest husband flew me to the hospital. When I woke up again, I was with Alti F'ir." A bright smile spread across her face.

"That was the true beginning of my life. I was immortal! Months after my awakening I left Alti F'ir and returned to fighting. It was glorious, knowing that I could not die. I encountered Brother John again just prior to the battle on Lancaster, and determined to give him eternal life. In return, he had only to enjoy my company. That was surely the greatest bargain anyone was ever offered, do you not agree?"

"No."

"Ah yes, I heard Leonora telling you precisely how I made the offer. And of course she told you the truth. Alti F'ir cannot refuse to restore the ones I kill, and Leonora cannot lie. Can she?"

"No." His body was set; he was ready for the lunge that would remove her head.

"We will know differently in eight minutes." Ravi glanced over her shoulder again. "Seven minutes and . . ." Her face went pale. She jumped to her feet and called across the compartment. "What? What are you all staring at?"

Watanaba called, "Commander, they're here!"

Ravi ran to the screens. Slate watched, and from the corner of his eye saw Leonora slouch forward.

She was ghostly white, trembling. He stood to reach her. "No!" she whispered urgently. "Sit down! I'm all right." She pinched her cheeks, hard. The color returned, and she straightened. "I'm all right," she repeated. "Please, sit down."

Slate took his seat. "What is it?"

"Don't say anything," Leonora pleaded, barely audible.

He turned round to watch the commotion at the battle console. The screens were tilted away from his viewing angle. But the faces of the New Army told him all he wanted to know. The GeeBees—no, he would never use that word again—Alti F'ir had come. It wasn't a bluff! he thought, amazed. Leonora really couldn't lie.

Ravi returned to them, still pale. Leonora sat composed, looking calmly up at her. "Goodbye, Ravi. Father will catch you within four hours, assuming that you turn and run at top speed."

"Contact them!" Ravi snapped. "I want to send a message!"

"I am always in contact, as I told you. When you speak to me, you are speaking to Father." She smiled. "But don't beg for mercy. Father is coming to kill you."

"I offer to release you. Your life, for mine."

"No. I will not make the offer."

"Because Father would accept! You will make the offer, or I will kill this man."

"Try," Slate said low in his throat, standing. "Please. Try."

"Wait," Ravi said. She turned back to Leonora. "You said just now that Father can hear me when I speak to you. Then the offer has already been heard! You cannot lie! Has Father heard the offer?"

Leonora sighed. "Yes. Your offer has been heard."

"Ah! And what is the answer?"

"The answer is n—" Leonora lowered her face into her hands. "The answer is yes."

Ravi exulted. "Yes!" She glared in triumph at the top of Leonora's head. "Then it is done. I am pleased for once at how Father has shaped you, Leonora. You may go. I will order a scouter prepared for you immediately."

Leonora looked up. "Prepare the scouter for three passengers. Ben is coming with me. And so are you."

"What? That is preposterous. I will not leave my Army, and I certainly will not surrender to a pathetic . . . child."

"Good," Leonora said. "I'm relieved to hear you say that. You heard Father's offer, and it is not negotiable. You've refused. Father has heard you."

"I have *not* refused! I am considering my options, only. I have not reached a decision."

"Decide, Ravi," Leonora said. "You have no time to consider."

"But my Army—" She bent forward and said quietly, "Watanaba is filth! She would attack even her Queen, if I sought to leave her to Father."

"Tell her you're surrendering to save them," Slate said. "You have no trouble lying, Ravi."

"But . . . if I . . . I will be a prisoner. Forever. Is that so, Leonora?"

Leonora wept into her hands. "No," she said miserably. "I prayed that you wouldn't ask. But no. You are to be released. That is Father's bargain."

"And are there other conditions you have not told me about?"

Leonora looked up, tears streaming down her face. "Only one. We are to leave this ship immediately."

"Then I accept!"

⇒23⇐

Brother John stood at the barracks window, peering out at the autumn-browned expanse of Hernandez Field. Damp leaves caught by drizzling gusts of wind scuttled by and tumbled in herds, here and there sweeping upward at the heavy gray sky in tiny whirlwinds. A circle of students he was watching huddled closely around three stones, showing no other reaction to the soaking cold.

"You should be down there with them," said a voice from behind him.

"I'll go when they're finished, Myra. They did the work. They're entitled to these few minutes every morning."

"But you could speak to them. It would be good for you, and you know they want you there. The Pritchers were your closest family. And Ben was—" She let her voice trail off to silence.

He turned and smiled at her. "It's been two weeks since they died, Myra. I've accepted it." He kissed her forehead. "Having you here has helped."

"I was surprised to get your message. I tried . . . Well, I thought of you often."

"I guess we were thinking the same thing." He turned back to the window and watched the students for several minutes. "You're right, I should speak to them. It would be good practice. When the war is over I'll have a permanent position here at Barrow." He laughed. "I'll be the immortal freak who stands next to the memorials and talks about Maggie and Colonel Pritcher, and Benjamin Slate. People will come from all over the Great Domain to see my tribute to the brave sacrifices—"

Myra slid her arms around his waist. "Brother John, please. Don't."

"And who knows how long I'll last? I could go on doing it, for thousands of years!"

"Brother John."

He pulled her arms away and turned to face her. "That's how long it'll take, Myra, before I can forget what I did. That's how long!"

"You made the right decision," she said, taking him in her arms again. "It's over. Don't go back to it."

"I left him there, don't you understand? He was still alive, and I *left* him there!"

"He ordered you to go. He knew he was dying, Brother John. You couldn't have helped him."

"He helped me when I . . . Myra, taking me along when he left that mining colony was a risk, the way I was. It could have cost him everything. He *knew* that, and never even mentioned it. The one time he really *needed* me, I left him to die." His voice rose. "Now tell me how I can live with that!" Her eyes stopped him. He brushed the tears from her cheeks and held her gently.

"I'm sorry, Myra. I am so very—" She hugged him violently, pulling him against her with all her strength. The anguish poured out of him in great wracking sobs.

The New Army ships were an hour gone and Slate thought he would go mad. Leonora squeezed his shoulder from the rear seat, and he turned to look at her. She put a finger to her lips. And then from beside her it started again.

"The Bordelons were not as bad as the Gaasmund Zealots painted them, Ben," Ravi said, having paused for several seconds. "I signed on to fight against them strictly for financial reasons. The Bordelons had a government to run, and could not afford the best help. But the Zealots were able to pay very well, if one insisted. Still, I knew of many Duelists, including our mutual friend, who fought for nothing but food and glory."

He was near jumping out of his seat at the words "our mutual friend." Leonora's hands grasped his shoulders again as she pulled her face close to his left ear. "Let her go on," she whispered. "It's important." She kissed his cheek quickly and resumed her seat.

Ravi never missed a beat. ". . . that the passion for justice never survives beyond victory. Colonel Pritcher said that, I remember. But for me, those days are over. I have seen glory, more closely than anyone who has ever lived. Now I shall seek knowledge. You know, Ben, Brother John spoke of you often at Barrow. He admired your affinity for books, particularly the ancient ones. Perhaps you will advise me on which are the best—"

Bricks and walls, bricks and walls, he thought, trying to block out the drone of her voice. Could she possibly believe that all was forgiven, now that the final end to the war was only hours away? Incredibly, Alti F'ir had agreed to release her; Slate would not interfere with any bargain that led to the destruction of the New Army. He'd let her live, for now. But she'd corrupted Arika, and killed Maggie and Colonel Pritcher, along with billions—billions!—of innocents. There was nowhere this monster could hide. If she were lucky, the Peacekeepers on some world would find her before he or Brother John, or any Duelist, did. Ravi's immortality was due to run out very shortly.

At last Slate felt sleep coming on him, and said a silent thank-you to Morpheus. The hours passed while the scouter moved at dead-slow, heading in no particular direction. When he woke, nothing had changed.

"... long will we be out here? Leonora, did you hear me?"

"What do you want, Ravi? I was sleeping."

"I asked how long it will be until we are picked up."

Leonora narrowed her eyes for an instant. "Father destroyed the last of your ships just moments ago."

Ravi shrugged. "That does not answer my question. I am cramped. When are we to be picked up?"

"Let me check the time." She pulled herself up and leaned forward, over Slate. "Shhh," she whispered in his ear. With one hand she reached forward to a bank of switches and activated the emergency beacon. A tiny light at Slate's knee went on and began pulsing. She said aloud, "Move your arm, Ben. I can't see the clock."

"I do not care what time it is," Ravi said testily. "How long must we wait?"

"Five hours," Leonora said. Again she whispered in Slate's ear, so softly he barely heard the words: "I've been lying. Be ready to subdue her."

"What?" Ravi asked. "What did you say to him?"

Leonora took her seat. "I said your incessant whining is boorish."

"How dare you ..." She checked herself. "You should have

mentioned it earlier, Leonora. I was merely trying to help all of us endure the waiting. Have I disturbed you, Ben?"

"No." Slate was close to shock, gripping the controls with both hands. *Lying?* Alti F'ir was *not* on the way? He'd seen the screens before they left Ravi's ship. They were THERE. Seventy of them, five groups of fourteen.

The beacon light pulsed steadily, one beat every two seconds. This scouter was a new model, built by one of Dianymede's companies. Weren't the new beacons warpsignals? If so, and the New Army were still alive, this was suicide. But Leonora must know what she's doing, he reasoned. What an incredible job of acting. She had won their freedom with a bluff! But he'd seen the screens. *How* did she do it? And how long could they remain free?

Ravi stood to stretch. "I should be accustomed to this," she said. "Those ridiculously cramped compartments on Father's—" Her eyes strayed to the instrument panel. "Beacon. Flashing . . . ?" She lurched for Leonora and slid a forearm beneath her chin.

"Stay where you are, Slate," Ravi grated out, hissing. She yanked Leonora back against her. "The beacon. The beacon is on! You two are signaling for help! Father has *no* idea where we are. Leonora, you lied! It was all a lie!"

"What are you doing?" Slate said, trying to remain calm. "That light? Is it a beacon? I'm not familiar with this type of control panel." That was partially true. He'd been unable to find a MusicLase or a warpsignal, both standard equipment in most newer scouters. "I must have hit it with my knee."

"Quiet!" Ravi snapped, then demanded of Leonora, "The truth, whore! Tell the truth, or I will kill you instantly!" Leonora clawed at Ravi's arm, strangling. "Be still!" Leonora sagged and dropped her arm.

"Please," Slate said. Ravi was a Duelist. There was no chance for him to reach her before she could snap Leonora's neck. "Please let her go."

"Leonora?"

"I'll tell you," she said hoarsely. "Let me breathe."

Ravi released some of the pressure. Leonora gulped air, her throat rasping. Ravi warned, "If I suspect you are lying to me again, you are dead." She looked at Slate. "And turn off that beacon!"

Slate hit the switch instantly. The light stopped.

"Good. You have confirmed for me that you knew what the beacon was. And what of you, Leonora? You are not as slow-witted as he is, but you are caught just the same."

"I have no remote communication with Father."

"Obviously. How did you know to expect the ships?"

"You told me that we were three hours from Barnabus. I assumed that we were traveling at top speed, so I knew what the distance to Barnabus was. And that meant that thirty minutes later, Father would have you on screen."

"Stop." Ravi tightened her grip. "You have lied twice. First, our reconnaissance ship arrived at Barnabus to find it deserted. Second, I would have seen the ships coming at the same moment they saw my Legion. Father's instruments are no more powerful than mine."

"They are now. You heard me tell Ben that I'd improved the true Alti F'ir ships. That included speed, detection, and weapons range. And your reconnaissance was wrong. Father's ships were based underground. But the moment your fleet was detected, Father would have destroyed your forward ship and left Barnabus to come after you. By knowing when that would occur, I also knew when Father's ships would arrive on your screens."

Ravi stared at her for a full minute. Finally she nodded and said, "I believe you, only because I saw the ships myself, as did others. You cannot have lied about what was on the screens of every ship of my Legion. And you were correct that my only chance of victory was to catch Father unprepared for battle. That was not the case, I see now."

"You didn't know how quickly Father could repair any damage. And you didn't know about the enhanced weapons range. You were careless."

"Yes. My Legion would have been annihilated. As I am sure it was." She smiled suddenly. "And Father never knew that you were aboard. I survived the battle because of my skill." She paused, a question in her eyes. "You saved yourself, quite brilliantly. But why did you insist on my coming with you? If you had not, I would be dead by now."

Leonora cleared her throat and tried to pull away. Ravi tightened her arm. "Answer me."

Leonora rasped, "I didn't want you to die, Ravi. I want you to live forever. I want you chained and locked away, and aware of every moment, for all eternity."

Ravi bristled. Then she laughed. "As I told you long ago, we are much alike."

Leonora flushed crimson and opened her mouth to speak, producing no sound.

Slate said, "Let her go. You know I'll kill you if you hurt her. You have nothing to gain by holding her."

"I will gain your promise. Give me your word as a Duelist that you will not attempt to harm me after I release her."

"You have it, Ravi. My word as a Duelist. Let her go."

Ravi relaxed her arm. Slate caught Leonora as she slumped across the back of his seat. Her breathing was still ragged, but there was no indication of serious damage.

"Now," Ravi said, taking her seat. "You may engage the beacon again, Ben. We will wait, and see who answers us first. Alti F'ir, or humans."

"Either way," Slate said, "you lose."

Ravi smiled. "Perhaps. Perhaps not."

That warm evening on the North continent the celebration ended with a final toast from Brother John.

"And Adrienne, before you depart for what is sure to be a night of unparalleled boredom"—he paused, waiting for the raucous laughter to die down—"allow me to say a final word to Admiral of the Fleet His Lordship and Exalted In His Own Mind Emperor, Manner Longley."

The Long Man rose, blushing and grinning, to stand next to his bride.

"Manner," Brother John said. "There are two things I want to say. But I know that after her journey here from Paulus, Adrienne is impatient to get this nightmare over with. So I'll be brief." His expression became serious. "During the past several months you have faced our enemy with courage and distinction. You have taken a great fleet into battle, and brought many of us safely home again. In every way, you have proven yourself to be a fine commander, and an exceptional Duelist. I honor you, my friend. And I salute you." He raised his goblet in the sudden silence and drank deeply.

One by one, realizing that the expected joke was not coming, those in attendance stood and raised their cups to a stunned Manner Longley. Adrienne Longley nee Kingman took her goblet from the table and joined the salute. Longley bowed formally amid thunderous cheering.

"But ... But!" Brother John called over the applause. "But, since I can see your interest, I will say the other thing I had in mind." The room quieted in mixed expectations. "Manner, the struggle is not over. Very soon you will need all of your courage, all of your skills, and all of your judgment, to—" He stopped and said gravely, "Of course I could be wrong. Marriage isn't always that bad."

Myra pounded the table. "I knew it! I *knew* it!"

She kicked at his leg under the table, evoking a surprised yelp. "*That* is marriage. Is this a proposal?"

The newlywed couple made a hasty exit through the backslapping, well-wishing crowd. When they were alone in the scouter, Adrienne shot the craft skyward and made a looping pass over the waving crowd below.

"Your quarters or mine, husband?"

He looked at the flaxen-haired woman beside him. They'd known each other since early childhood. And he'd always loved her, for as long as he could remember. He'd begged her to come to Barrow, afraid for her safety. To his immense relief, she had. And she'd brought his father.

"Neither, wife. You owe me a dinner. Where you buy it is up to you."

"I expected you to say that. I've made arrangements for you to have your favorite meal. Smorst."

"Smorst! Good Lord, Adrienne, that swill ... aboard *Miyoshi*." He looked at her, shocked, and laughed. He was the luckiest man in the Great Domain. "You know me too well already."

She squeezed his hand. "We'll see, after dinner."

"Sshh!" Myra whispered, giggling. "You'll wake them!"

Brother John stopped singing. "I can't believe Longley brought her here aboard *Miyoshi* tonight. And I can't believe they're asleep. I've got to talk to my little friend about life, and the enjoyment thereof." Seven hours had passed since the wedding reception.

"Which is your stateroom? Steady there!" The past three days had brought a remarkable change. It seemed that the worst of the grief was behind him. He had not yet told her the thoughts which allowed him such peace. But she rejoiced for him, and basked in his newfound happiness. For the past seven hours they had been together in a borrowed scouter above the dark clouds, him sipping bourbon while she piloted and listened to stories—exaggerated, she hoped—of the early days with Ben Slate.

"I'm not drunk, Myra. I'm happy. This was just my way to lure you aboard *Miyoshi*." He slid an arm around her waist and pulled her close.

She laughed. "All you had to do was ask. But I don't think I should be here, Brother John."

"Hey, I'm a Vice-Admiral! I can invite—"

"There you are!" Longley's cabin door swung open. "Brother John, I've been trying to reach you for an hour."

"Then you really are crazy, if it's me you've been trying to reach." He turned to Myra. "Look at him. He's in uniform! Didn't I tell you?"

"Myra," Longley said, "you'll have to leave *Miyoshi* immediately."

"Wait just a minute, Manner. You've got Adrienne in there. Fair is fair."

"My wife returned to Barrow more than an hour ago, Brother John. Are you sober?"

His expression froze. "Completely. What's happened?"

"Contact me as soon as you can," Myra said. She kissed Brother John quickly and walked away, looking back once as she left the corridor. The two Duelists were already entering the wardroom, pushing the door shut behind them.

"Listen to this," Longley said.

The city-ship winked into normal-space and hovered two miles from the drifting scouter.

Slate jumped from his seat. "Blessed Saint Barrow!" Without the lights of battle to illuminate it, the ship was only a vague presence against the darkness; insubstantial, as though only part of it had emerged from hyperspace.

The eerie craft hung motionless in space, dim and ominous against the blackness.

"Are you a gambler?" Ravi said to Slate, visibly shaken.

"No," Slate said. He faced Leonora. "Can you see whose it is?"

She shook her head. "Father's ships were modified at the shield arrays and sensor towers. I can't see enough detail from here."

"It must be mine," Ravi said firmly. "Destiny is my servant."

Slate stared at her, red-faced with anger. "Ravi, that is the most pompous, ridiculous—" He couldn't go on. Leonora looked at him and smiled, then giggled. Within seconds the two were convulsed, laughing uproariously until it was excruciatingly, delightfully painful.

"You may laugh," Ravi said evenly. "But you will not be forgiven. I may have been deceived, Leonora, but I have never surrendered my dignity."

"Please!" Slate said, holding his aching stomach. "Please, be merciful. Don't say any more!"

Leonora squeezed his arm. "Shall we address her as . . . Look!"

The city-ship was approaching. They were silent, not breathing, as its form grew larger. Leonora released her breath in a long sigh. "I don't believe it. It's neither Father's nor New Army."

"Whose, then?"

"I hope I'm right," she said excitedly. "We'll see."

"Can we contact them?" Slate asked.

"How?" Ravi said testily. "Those things don't *use* radios."

The golden craft veered at half a mile from them and flew a wide circle around the scouter. When the maneuver was complete, it moved slowly away in a straight line and halted three miles distant.

"Let's go, Ben," Leonora said breathlessly. "We've been invited aboard."

"That's the third series, monitored ten minutes ago," Longley said. "The first came in an hour before that one."

Brother John listened to the steady pulses. "I don't recognize it. It's an emergency beacon, I'm sure of that. But whose?"

"It's coming from near Paulus," Longley said. "The Peacekeepers there have a ship on screen, but can't determine the type. All they can tell us is that it's alone out there."

"So you think it's a trap?"

"It could be. The GeeBees can come out of hyperdrive with incredible precision. There could be dozens of their ships waiting for us. Unfortunately, Paulus doesn't have the new equipment to scan hyperdrive."

"I think we should go. If it's not an ambush, they could be getting ready to launch another attack."

Longley glared at him, offended. "Of course we're going. But it could also be a diversion, and we've only got forty-six warships left. I'm sending ten of them out in echelons of two, staggered at half-hour intervals. The first two left nearly an hour ago."

"When do *we* leave?"

"If we hadn't seen your scouter coming, *Miyoshi* would've gone out in the second echelon. You took your time about getting here."

"Maybe I forgot to monitor the . . . Aren't we wasting time? Let's go!"

"We're leaving with *Troubador* in six minutes. Those were my orders, whether you decided finally to come aboard or not."

"No one at the hangar-deck said anything about this."

"Only the ship commanders involved know. I'll make a general announcement once we're underway." Longley turned for the door. "I'm going to the Control Center. Get yourself in uniform and join me."

"Manner, you seem . . . I don't know how to say it. This could be the chance to get this over with, one way or the other. We all need this."

Longley turned to face him. "Nothing is sure until we get there."

"Nothing is ever sure, Manner. That's not what's bothering you."

Longley spun away, then stopped at the doorway. "All right, I'll say it. My wife will be on Barrow, without me. If this is a diversion, I may not be able to help her."

"Manner," Brother John said to his back, "Adrienne loves you. She knew what she was doing when she tied her life to yours. She'd never forgive you if you let personal feelings interfere with professional judgment." He clapped the smaller man on the shoulder. "Believe me, my friend. I know what I'm talking about."

Longley touched his hand. "I know you do, Brother John."

⇀24⇀

She told him they wouldn't need suits; the invitation would not have been extended unless everything had been prepared.

The air was rich with oxygen. They pulled themselves along a narrow corridor that wound in a gradual spiral upward from where they'd entered, at the base of the craft. This was one of the towers, he was sure.

Leonora led the way with Slate at the rear, watching Ravi carefully. From the fine weld-marks his fingers found on the bulkheads he knew that the overheads and hatchways had once been no more than three feet from the decking. The work appeared to be new; the interior of the city-ship had only recently been enlarged, to allow human passage.

Leonora confirmed his thought. "This is one of the ships Father called in," she said. The light was starkly bright, seeming to come from all directions at once. "We're the first guests," she added, turning her head to smile excitedly at him.

"They work fast," Slate said.

"I doubt if all of this took more than an hour," she said with obvious pride.

For the first time, Slate saw free-fall as natural. Alti F'ir had lived for billions of years in the ships, and had no need for gravity. But, as Leonora explained during their passage, the individuals were incredibly strong and dense-bodied—by Alti F'ir design. Quintillions of planets in the Universe were hospitable to them.

"What do they breathe?"

Ravi said irritably, "Poison. They trap molecules in their appendages. They can go for years without resupply."

"Father manufactures air and food right here. On these ships," Leonora said. "Nearly any raw element can be transmuted."

"But how?" He thought for a second and added quickly, "Never mind." If Alti F'ir could transmute human beings into virtually immortal beings, then putting together a little air and food should be no problem at all.

"Let's go!" Leonora quickened her pace, pulling ahead of them and rushing on like a happy child.

They passed through several open spaces, pushing off from entrances that were set midway up the bulkheads, and floating across the chambers to the far doorways. Slate insisted that they execute the maneuver together, reluctant to allow Ravi a moment's freedom with Leonora. Most of the open spaces held a number of enormous metal blocks, machinery of some sort, all of it unrecognizable to Slate. The objects were cubic, varying in size, and all indented in one or more places. The indentations appeared to be the shape and size of the Alti F'ir individuals. The appendages, then, would operate interior controls.

The upward angle of the corridor sharpened. At last they came to a chamber with an entrance more narrow than the ones they'd passed through. A translucent panel blocked the way. Leonora was visibly excited. Her mood was infectious.

"Shouldn't we knock first?" Slate asked.

"Never," she said.

The panel slid upward as they approached within two feet. Several minutes elapsed before Slate's eyes adjusted to the intense light. He gripped Ravi's ankle while waiting, as a precaution.

The chamber was gigantic, thirty feet high and sixty or more on each side. The bulkheads were covered in what looked like sheets of gold. This area showed no marks of recent change. This was the way Alti F'ir had lived for billions of years. He could picture them, weightless in their natural state, floating in open and perfect precision throughout the cavernous space. The walls—he'd stopped thinking of this room as part of a ship, with bulkheads and decks—were inlaid with designs. Some were simple and open, some were ornate and self-contained. The designs were pleasant to the eye, but he could see no particular pattern in them. Rather, they seemed to work together as a total design, one conveying harmony and purpose.

He was startled by sudden movements. There were seven of them.

Leonora had seen them immediately upon entering. She said, "You're not accustomed to looking at the floor to find your hosts."

They were fifteen feet below and another twenty feet away, floating slowly toward them, a few inches from the floor. There was no visible motion on their bodies. And these were not the same as the creature he'd seen.

There were none of the "spindly little crab-legs" he'd thought of. These wore golden manes: the glory of the lion, or the beards of ancient kings. The seven rose up as they approached and stopped four feet from Slate, at chest height.

"They're beautiful," he said, stunned.

Leonora reached for his hand. "Yes."

"Can they understand me if I speak to them?"

"No," she said. "These individuals are part of a mind which has never encountered humans before. I've seen them described by Father—this is confusing."

"I think I understand," Slate said. "Brother John told me there are three minds. They're in contact with one another, so they know who you are. But this mind hasn't developed the capacity to understand our speech and communicate back to you with mental images. But the other mind sees and hears us through *this* mind. So we're communicating one-way, in effect." He shook his head. "Is that even close?"

"Exactly!" She beamed happily and hugged him. The embrace tumbled them together in the null gravity and ended in a kiss which both were reluctant to end. She eased back from him, her face flushed with happiness.

The room seemed to spin, and it took a moment for him to realize that he wasn't seeing a romantic metaphor in action; *they* were spinning, with precisely matched velocities.

Blessed Saint Barrow! he thought. For the first time, he realized that he loved Leonora. And that he had loved her, since they'd met. Suddenly, to his astonishment, he found himself blushing like a young boy. Leonora had embraced him intimately—embarrassing because it was in view of her parents. The two held hands while they floated across the chamber, moving together as if caught in their own orbit. Slate's back touched a wall and he used it to stop their tumbling.

Ravi snorted. "I have now suffered adequate punishment. Shall we proceed with my execution?"

The two glided back to the entrance. Leonora faced her. The happiness had left her voice. "This isn't about you, Ravi. You've become irrelevant."

"What, then?" Some of the color returned to her face.

"If you understood Alti F'ir at all, you'd know. Father . . . *my* father—" She turned to Slate. "You know what I mean, Ben."

"Yes. I think I do."

"Father wants to be assured that I'm well. This mind is in contact, and has satisfied that desire."

Ravi sighed with relief. "I see." But then her anger returned. "You are lying. Again! A simple overflight would have served the same purpose. All of this has been to take you aboard, and to take me as prisoner!"

"It was done this way because I prefer it this way! Father knows my mind, and—" Leonora went ghost-white. She choked and brought trembling hands to her face with enough force to start her spinning again. "No!" she screamed. "My God! Oh my God! nnNNOOO—! *nnnNNOOO!*"

Slate was in momentary shock. What came from Leonora's throat was anguish, hellish-pure and terrifying. It sounded as if thick cloth—or flesh—were being ripped from her body. She was spinning away, shrieking and kicking in empty air. This was the same grotesque free-fall "dance" he'd seen when Brother John had gone berserk aboard the transport to Barrow Academy.

Slate's reflexes took over. Grasping the edge of the hatchway with one hand and reaching for Leonora with the other, he caught her arm and pulled her back. He stabilized her against him, then slid a protective arm around her waist. She pulled back with violent strength, staring wide-eyed at him. He knew it wasn't him she was seeing. Her eyes were wild, unfocused. And full of pain. He held her as gently as he could, but her physical power was astounding. Finally she stopped struggling and went limp.

"Leonora. Leonora! What is it? Can you hear me?"

Father knows my mind. She heard her own voice saying it over and over, like an echo, growing shrill, then fading, and she hated that voice, because that voice could not lie and could not stop and what it was saying was worse than death.

How could I have forgotten? Father knows my mind! The full impact of the recent past hammered like a blow against her battered soul. *What have I done*? She felt as if her mind and body were being torn apart. There had never been so much pain. Not even when her mother and father were killed. In delirium she saw that scene again, through unknowing infant's eyes. Warm bodies that touched her, one soft and smooth, the other hard and scratchy. Their faces looked strange and then they were gone, and she was lying on dry warmth that tickled her when she moved. That made sounds in her head, and moving colors. That filled her with love and laughing delight when she thought, saw the Universe, as she was instructed. *Father. Parents*.

Leonora heard Slate calling her name. She forced herself to follow the sound, until she saw him beside her. The way it should be. She understood now. *This is the way it should be*. She believed that, hard. As she did, the terror ebbed away. In its place was a sweet regret, and a deep fatigue. It was clear now. Something new had come to her, and she had been forced to choose. Was it right? It only mattered that it was real.

There had been something she didn't—couldn't—say to Arika, or Slate. Alti F'ir had taken her again, because of her early exposure, to convince Ravi to disband the New Army. She had failed, because the task was simply impossible to accomplish. Ravi would never obey. It was not a question of persuasion and patience. Ravi was evil. Beyond changing. Father understood that, finally. And so it was determined that Ravi be killed or made powerless. At this, Leonora would not fail.

But she had now driven a permanent wedge between herself and Alti F'ir.

In saving Ben Slate's life, she had lied. And she'd been open, as the seven individuals communicated her image to Father, about her hatred for Ravi.

Lies and hatred, or boundaries of any kind, were impossible—alien—to a mind that was perfectly open to itself, as was Father's. Alti F'ir would forgive her, yes. Welcome and love her, yes. But only as Father would accept any human; never again as that *special* child. She was separated, again and permanently, from her parents. The separation hurt worse than anything she had ever known. She was no longer of Alti F'ir; and since birth she had not been human. But there had been no other way to save him.

"Leonora!" Slate was holding her tightly, looking into her eyes.

She found her voice. "I'm all right." She hugged him again, pulling him as close as her strength would allow. "I am." He would never understand what price she had paid for him. How could he? And so she could ask nothing in return. What she'd given him—his life—must be a free gift. She had chosen her course freely, and so must he. "I'm all right, Ben," she repeated.

He held her, while the seven individuals floated back and forward, moving less than a foot in either direction. "I think you'd better tell *them* that," he said.

She pushed herself back, feeling stronger. "They understand," she said. "Look."

The seven individuals moved in synchrony. Three of them formed a side-by-side line of three. Just above them a line of two formed, and above it, one individual moved into place. Like a mountain, Slate thought, holding his breath. No. A pyramid.

The seventh individual floated over the peak of the formation and stopped nine feet directly above it.

"Blessed Saint Barrow!" he whispered. As he watched, slender appendages appeared from within each of the individuals. Within a minute they were intertwined, forming a network that linked all six with thousands of threadlike cords.

The seventh individual moved slowly in place, rotating flat on its axis in the free-fall air. From the peak of the pyramid hundreds of appendages rose toward it and stopped, halfway. The seventh sank gradually down until it met them, then stopped, immobile as the others.

Leonora pulled herself gently free of Slate and faced the formation. She laced her fingers together in front of her and bowed her head until her chin met her chest. When she raised it again, she was weeping. "They know," she said quietly.

"What is next?" Ravi said sharply. Her shrill tone pierced the air like a dagger.

"I don't know," Leonora answered. She didn't know. Whatever it was, it would be different from anything she had come to expect of life.

The formation unlinked itself and approached, as before. One of the individuals began moving around them. It completed one and a half circles, and then floated toward the entrance. After a few yards it stopped and moved aside.

"That's clear enough," Slate said. "We're being asked to leave."

"We are to be stranded?" Ravi said, alarmed.

Leonora glared at her, happy to feel the hatred that welled from her depths. "You really are stupid, Ravi. If we're leaving, it means two things. Help is on the way, and your New Army is dead." She smiled. "Very, very dead."

As the three of them proceeded back down the winding corridor Slate was unable to shake the picture of that formation from his mind. It was magnificent, solemn, and beyond anything he could translate into meaning. As they boarded the scouter again and he sealed the craft for space it struck him.

Brain cells. Great, golden, brain cells.

When the scouter door popped open, the cheers, whistles, and shouts from the Duelists and crew of *Miyoshi* were earsplitting. Slate's first thought was that he would go deaf. His second was that he didn't give a damn.

Brother John yanked him out of the pilot's seat and nearly crushed his spine in the embrace. "Get rid of the beard, Sapper. It looks like your eyebrows have—" His face froze. "She's here. She's with you."

"She's in the cargo hold," Slate shouted above the noise. "It's over, Brother John. Do you hear me? Over!"

The giant looked at him darkly. "Longley told me you reached us by radio as soon as we were in normal-space." Then, deep in his throat, he said, "He didn't mention her."

Leonora came around from the far side of the scouter and wrapped Slate's arms around herself. She smiled and tried to be heard. "Hello, Brother John!"

He looked at her blankly. Recognition dawned, and he nodded in greeting. He turned and called to a young woman Duelist standing nearby, raising his voice to be heard above the noise. "Fontaine, there's something in the cargo hold. Bring it to me."

Twenty seconds later the noise level edged off sharply. Slowly, as heads turned, it dropped to absolute silence. Brother John cursed and disappeared into the crowd.

"Listen to me!" Ravi stood behind Fontaine, one arm around the Duelist's neck. In the other hand she held a dagger jammed against the woman's throat.

"Who is your commander?" Ravi demanded.

"I am." Manner Longley stepped forward.

"I'm sorry, Admiral," the Duelist said calmly. "She said she needed help getting out of the hold. She had my knife before I knew what she was doing."

"My mistake, Fontaine. I should have had her in chains by now. It's an error I'll correct immediately."

"I must have your promise, Admiral," Ravi said, "that I will be released unharmed on a world of my choosing. Otherwise I will—"

"Go ahead," said a voice from behind her.

Ravi turned, keeping Fontaine ahead of her. "Brother John. How pleasant to see you again. You are as handsome as ever."

His face reddened, but his voice remained level. "Go ahead and kill her. She won't mind, will you, Fontaine?"

"Not at all, Brother John. But I'll be sorry to miss what you do to her afterward."

"Then I'll tell you now. Do you see what she did to my face fifteen years ago? Picture hers the same, but without the winning smile."

The silence was shattered by waves of laughter.

Slate chuckled and nudged a Duelist beside him. "What Grade is Fontaine?"

"She's a Novice, sir. Why?"

"A Novice. Perfect." He clapped the young man on the shoulder and watched Ravi and her captive. "I was remembering something the Queen of Heaven said not long ago about dignity."

Ravi's face was deep red. She stared around her at the grinning faces and then sighed, beaten. "I have not been among Duelists for many years. You will understand if I have forgotten."

The wrist of her knife-hand shattered and her eyes widened in shock as an elbow drove hard into her stomach. Fontaine whirled in a lightning arc and speared four fingers into the same spot. The breath exploded out of her as Ravi was driven backward, teetering. Fontaine stepped forward almost casually and delivered a kick that smashed Ravi's nose and sent her sprawling on the deck.

"You've forgotten more than you thought," Fontaine said, picking up her dagger and wiping it symbolically on Ravi's tunic. She grinned down at her while the laughter and applause crested and died out. "You should never borrow a Duelist's weapon without permission. And never relax your grip, until you're sure the match has ended." She pushed the point of the dagger under Ravi's chin. "Well?"

Ravi moaned. "It is ended!"

"Not quite," Brother John said. "Let her up, Fontaine."

"Yes, sir."

She moved aside and Ravi leaped to her feet, backing away from the approaching giant.

"Brother John, no!" Leonora called.

"Leave him alone," Slate said. "He needs to end it himself."

Leonora said quietly, "Don't let him, Ben."

He looked at her. "I don't understand, Leonora. After what she did to him—"

"She deserves to die. But not quickly. And not in a way that he'll regret."

"It's his choice," he said firmly.

Leonora ran to the giant and pulled at his arm until he turned to look down at her. His scalp was red and twitching. She fought back the impulse to turn and run. "Brother John. Please, listen to me." She gestured for him to come close.

Slate was astounded to see his friend bend almost double and put his ear down next to her face. She whispered for several seconds, and smiled up at him.

He straightened and considered what she'd said. Then he laughed out loud. His face was calm when he turned to Longley. "We're taking that scouter out."

"Go ahead. But why?"

"It's personal, Manner."

Leonora turned to Slate. "I'll be back, Ben. Pick us up here in five days."

"But—"

"It's personal." She turned and walked to the scouter they'd brought from Ravi's ship.

Ravi was being held by two Duelists. They'd moved in to stop her from running, but found themselves helping her to stand. She'd gone white.

Brother John smiled at her. "You," he said pleasantly, pointing. "Come with me." As he turned he said under his breath, "I will teach you what we are, now."

From the Control Center, Benjamin Slate and Manner Longley

watched the scouter's image move out from *Miyoshi*. Its beacon was on again.

The city-ship appeared on their screens one hour later. Two hours after that it was out of range again.

Miyoshi waited for nine days. When the beacon came on again, the flagship of the disbanding UDF raced at maximum hyperdrive for three hours before reaching the scouter.

Brother John strode directly to the ship's Control Center, where he ignored everyone except Slate. The warrior said, "Don't ever make her mad, Sapper." He shivered slightly and added, "Not ever." Then he was silent as a stone. He turned and went directly to his quarters. It was clear to everyone who saw the eyes of Brother John that the giant would remain undisturbed during the return trip to Barrow.

Leonora apologized for the delay, but would not explain it. She would only say to Slate when they shared the evening meal privately, "The individuals you saw were too weak to live. Only one mind remains."

He stood to embrace her. "I'm sorry, Leonora. I'm very sorry."

A single tear ran down her cheek. She said, "Alti F'ir knows now that it was not the Creator. It has gone to find Father."

EPILOGUE

A.D. 2331

The moon of Earth gave its final light to a wooded horizon as the stars blazed into being, imparting a gentler glow to the night. The silence was open and comfortable, the air fresh with the waning scent of new flowers.

Benjamin Slate heard her creeping up behind him and kept his eyes skyward as slender arms encircled his waist. "Got you!"

He gasped in mock surprise and turned, lifting her under the arms and holding her high above him. "Nora! You frightened me!"

"I'm sorry, Daddy. Mommy told me to do it!" The little girl squealed in delight as he tossed her high in the air. He caught her and brought her against him in a warm hug.

"I told her to come out and say good night before going to bed," Leonora said. She held out her arms. "Come here, you!"

"But I'm the oldest!" Her father set her on the ground and she stood, hands on hips, pleading defiantly in the age-old way of children. "I'm ten now!"

"Your birthday isn't until tomorrow, child. Now say good night to everyone."

"All right. But tomorrow night when I'm a year older—"

"We'll see, Nora. Say good night." The girl bounded into her mother's embrace and kissed her cheek. Then she ran to Myra, jumping into her arms and whispering in her ear, "Mommy is getting me a red scouter. Don't tell!"

Next was the giant, whose forearm she hugged while he raised her high enough to climb to his neck. She giggled. "It sounds so funny! Uncle Brother John!"

"Hmmm," he said, nodding thoughtfully. "That is a serious

242

problem." He brightened. "I have it! You can call me Commandant."

The little girl returned his thoughtful expression. "Yes," she said gravely. "That will do."

Brother John kissed her lightly on the cheek and set her down. "Did Daddy tell you I'm his boss now?"

"Yes, Commandant Uncle Brother John. Mommy said you asked him to help you learn to be a good administrat—"

"Nora!" Slate said quickly. "Didn't you want to hear about those plants on Eusebeus again? You'd better hurry, before the boys pick out another story."

"The magic plants!" She ran for the house, calling "Uncle Wilmer! Uncle Wilmer! Wait!"

"Uncle Wilmer?" Myra asked.

Brother John sat next to her on the log. "It's her rule," he explained. "No bird-names for people. And she's the only one who's allowed to call Crow by his birth name." He smiled ironically. "You'd know that, if you'd been here last year."

"You know I couldn't," Myra said. "Some of us have real jobs."

"Had, you mean. Had."

"That's right, had. And now that we've got my retirement income, you can afford to play head Duelist—"

"Commandant," he corrected. "Commandant and Lord Supreme of Barrow Academy. Doris Mannheimer was a good replacement for Colonel Pritcher, but she retired after only ten years. I plan to keep the job for at least a century. Or two."

"Maybe," Myra said. "But if enrollment doesn't pick up, there won't be a Duel School left open." She instantly regretted her statement. It was true, of course. Duelists were not popular nowadays, since it had become known throughout the Great Domain that the warrior class had nearly prevented Leonora and Alti F'ir from defeating Ravi and her New Army. The profession had lost its allure, and Myra was delighted. But it was a source of deep pain for her husband, and for most of their friends.

"But," she said quickly, "that's why you accepted the appointment, isn't it? To turn things around again."

"Exactly," Brother John said. "And remember, Barrow Academy has always been the best. Even if the other schools go under, we'll survive. Within five years we'll have a hundred applicants for every one we can accept. You'll see that I'm right.

We'll have to expand!" He grunted in satisfaction. "I may even rescue the Longleys from that godforsaken farm on Paulus, and let them wash dishes or something."

"How kind of you. And what do you have in mind for your wife?"

"You will bear me thirty children and become hideously old, while I remain the envy of—"

"This is a lovely spot, Leonora," Myra said, turning away from the familiar badinage. It was the best way to win, she had learned. And she had learned to hold him quietly in the dark hours of morning when he shook awake from the dreams. Those times were rare, now. "Ben tells me it was in his family for centuries."

"Yes," said Leonora. "His uncle Cardelius sold it to pay for his education at Barrow and to set up a trust fund for him. In fact, his mother was born right there." She pointed down the hill at a small clearing that formed a narrow border between dense woods and water. Beneath brilliant starlight the trees swayed in a warm breeze. The water glistened like sheets of silver. "That's the Piscataquis River. An ancestor of hers bought this property and built a house there, more than three hundred years ago. We have a still-shot of him standing in front of it. I only wish we'd had this place back before they tore the old house down. But" —she shrugged—"this is a good place for Ben to work. The government made it a gift to us."

"Not exactly," Slate said, sliding an arm around her waist. "The gift was to Leonora. I've read the deed."

Myra said, "The serenity here is priceless. I can see why your ancestor chose it, Ben. Was he happy here?"

"I believe so. He and his wife raised a remarkable family, and he wrote books."

Leonora said proudly, "Much like his descendant, my scholarly husband."

"Speaking of which," Slate said, "I received another manuscript this morning. This one isn't bad."

"Then you'll endorse it?" Brother John asked. "More importantly, did they get my name right?"

"It's fairly accurate, which is a refreshing change. I'm beginning to think that most of recorded history is fiction. But the author ruins it at the end. He claims to know positively that Ravi is ... It doesn't matter what he claims."

"That's true," Brother John said. "It doesn't matter." He said to Leonora, "Is he still bothering you about that?"

"No," she said honestly. "He's finally conceded defeat."

"You've changed, Sapper."

"That's what age does, old friend. But you wouldn't know about that."

"Aging is a mystery that only we mortals share," Leonora said, leaning closer to Slate and sliding her own arm around his thickening middle. There was one other thing she'd never told him—Alti F'ir's final gift to her. Perhaps she never would. But when they were old, and mortality was more than a distant promise, she might tell him about what she'd learned. And let him decide, then, if he'd like to live forever.

She looked around at her friends, happier than she'd ever been. "It's a lovely evening, isn't it? I feel like a roaring fire. Shall we?"

When the flames had warmed all of them, Slate clapped his friend on the shoulder. "Brother John. Do the dance."

"Sapper!"

Leonora breathed deeply and raised her face toward the sky. "The air truly is wonderful tonight. The fire is warm. And the stars are so beautiful. So deep, and beautiful. They go on forever, you know."

She looked far into the night and thought contentedly, *Almost forever.*

• • •

Twenty billion light-years from Earth a golden city-ship fell toward an abyss that could not be measured, having neither matter nor space. The journey would take, almost, forever. Alone aboard the craft a wretched, barely human figure chewed her hair and mumbled a name in the burning darkness, raking yard-long fingernails across a dead power console.